TOGETHER FOREVER ?

by

SIMON POTTER

T-O-P

2020

"Together Forever?" was first published in Great Britain by *Trans-Oceanic-Press* 2020

Mike's story of his life in L A and return to London appeared first as the framing narrative of the multi-part novel "Shooting Europe" (2019)

www.simonpotterauthor.com

ISBN No: 978-1-9164295-5-0

A catalogue record for this book is available from the British Library.
Cover design by Nick England

Printed and bound by Witley Press, Hunstanton, Norfolk, PE36 6AD

Chapter One: **She just gets worse**.

I was in L A in my sterile, expensive apartment up the hill towards Bel Air on the 17th July 1999 at 11.50 pm when that bitch Mopsa Greene slammed the door, whacked up the dimmers and slouched towards the sofa, where I lay blinking. She stank of the filthy offal piled up in her Perspex coffin where she'd been lying naked for many hours.

'Heavy night's work?' I said, switching off the glow in my brain made by memories of London.

'Oh, don' you start being nasty,' she snapped. She clawed at her tank top. Mopsa used to be able to undress anywhere with an amazing disregard for appropriateness, but what had once intrigued me now made me feel bored and upset.

'Must you do that in here?' I muttered.

'Not more of that rubbish on?' She jerked her head towards the loudspeakers.

I was playing Grieg's piano concerto. Along with other sad pieces like *The Pathetique* and Dvorak's *New World*, it was one of the classical things I used to put on when Bitch-face was out.

'Please don't drape your rags around this room and *don't* sit down,' I said.

'I'm tired. Why can't you ever support me?'

'You've got bits of chicken beak stuck in your waistband.'

'Where? Where's the beak? I don' see any beak.' She whirled round trying to examine her rear end, like a whisking kitten. 'Oh, I see. Funny sad old man – he thinks he sees beeeeak,' she crooned, stepping across the wide passage to her own bedroom.

After galactic quarrelling about it, she had acceded the previous June to my urgent desire to sleep alone. It had been a strangely big decision. Strange because we had given up most of our earlier intimacies since Mopsa had met Georgie, and I so often went to bed before she came in and went out to get breakfast before she came to. I am – was – a *fastidious* person, and I needed the sweet delicacy that close loving companionship brings. I thought I did have it with her, at the start, but it was she, not me, who had changed so dreadfully. And how long can one take cursing by day, and snoring with a hard, brassy drug-induced blare at night, and going on and on about 'Art' when I yearned to slip into unconsciousness like that poor diver in the poem which my brother Anthony quotes who "bares his breast to the pearly seas"?

I could hear her pulling off clothes next door. Her chain belt was jingling.

'Well?' she called. 'Don' you even want to KNOW how it went?'

Touching on that thing about intimacy again, I was faintly surprised that she was still with me in late-'99. Of course she needed the financial support I gave – you can't be as self-indulgent as Mopsa and make or retain money – but I had thought that trekking off to our separate beds would have begun the process of unloosening a grip which I was finding imprisoning. Apart from my personal inclinations, I hadn't known how otherwise to set about making a move into the light. I surprised myself then, and I'm still surprised now when I reflect on those months, that I hadn't simply walked away, sold up, moved, gone East or gone home…. It just goes to show that stasis, although it poisons bit by bit, is easier to sustain than action. I was not, perhaps, as unprincipled as I thought I was, either.

'Why don' you ask me how it WENT?' she suddenly screeched. There was a banging of drawers.

'How went it?'

'Oh,' she hooted, 'At least gimme some question to hang information on. At least TRY to show a little animation when you ask me about the most important evening of my LIFE!'

'Were there many – er – visitors?' I wasn't interested. Who cared how many disordered freaks took the trouble to go down to The Caplan Room to see Mopsa's and nut-case Georgie's "Organic Sculpture" Concept Art?

'Yeah, a lot, if you wanna know. And Mikey, you know something else? One guy asked if he could BUY me!'

'What do you mean: buy you? Buy the idea, or actually buy loveable you and the piles of rotting meat?'

'I guess the whole caboodle. He was real serious about it afterwards. Georgie's got the details. He's got a gallery in Fresno. It just shows.'

'It shows what? Yaw-aw-aw,' I yawned. 'That they've got stupid non-paintings and pretentious bits of scaffolding called "*Scream Of The Id*" in one-horse Fresno as well as here?'

'No, I don' mean: WHAT it shows. I mean it just shows WHAT…'

'Lucid, at any rate.'

'It just SHOWS that people are interested! That they get the point of what we're doing. Oh my, my, you're just being deliberately obtuse because you have no-oooo idea...'

'All right. All right, I get the point. Everyone was, is, and always will be, extraordinarily interested.'

There was a snort from Mopsa's room. I thought at first that the snort was a substitute for a suitable response to my comment. I could get the last word with her, if I bothered. But the snuffling went on. It didn't sound quite like her over-dramatic blubbing, but I couldn't be quite sure. I brought my feet to the floor, stood up with rather a reeling head – probably from sheer exhaustion – and went over the passage to the door of her room. Oh God, there she was, sniffing at herself. It was a procedure I had found repellent the first time she'd done it. There was, I gathered, a shower-room out back at The Caplan Room – there had to be for "artistes" like Mopsa and Georgie – but she often fancied that a miasma of offal still clung about her, as though fragments of putrifying meat were continuing to rot in the crevices of her body. It made me retch to watch her.

'Oh, Mikey.' She looked up, pleased, I imagine, because I'd taken the trouble to get off the sofa. 'I heard something else really interesting tonight.'

I gazed at her naked breasts. I made no reply. I couldn't generate the spark. She padded through to her bathroom, continuing to address me over her shoulder. 'Can you come to Van Leyden's Gallery on Thursday? Anytime through the day? Next Thursday, the 22nd?' She wrenched on the power-shower, drowning out her next sentence.

'What?'

'Van Leyden's. They've got a show all next week, starting Monday. Georgie and I finish this Wednesday, remember?'

The jet of water ceased to gush.

'What's the show then?'

'It's a guy called Pantan – that's how you say it – and he's living sculpture, but with a twist.'

Living Sculpture indeed! It was such rubbish. Mopsa claimed all sorts of artistry in it. But I think art should involve the manipulation of paint or stone. From base materials comes structure, forged by intellect and craftsmanship. Mopsa and Georgie believe that Art should arise out of the organic, out of that which already has co-existence with themselves, and decays as they do. That's why it was ART that that week in July '99 (until Wednesday) she and Georgie sat naked up to their necks in chicken giblets in coffin-shaped Perspex. *"The BEING (when the flesh is alive) is at one with the BECOMING (flesh dead)"* proclaimed the gallery notes. What pretentious bull.

I wonder if I will come over as a bitter, horrid person in these pages? By the Fall of 1999 I was close to the mental breakdown that has taken so long for me to recover from. I see that now. I was surrounded by horrid people, but that's not the same as being *like* them, is it?

'And you imagine I would *enjoy* this twist of Pantan's?' I asked, with just that distant top-spin of irony that she hated.

'Look, I jus' mentioned it.'

There was a sudden re-gushing of the shower. Sitting down again on the sofa, I called over it,

'Pan – tan? Have I got it correctly?'

'Pronounced Pantan; spelt Pintin.'

'P-I-N-T-I-N?'

'How many times have I gotta say it?'

'Funny name.'

'I guess I've known funnier. Saxe-Coburg-Gotha is funnier.'

'Don't you start on the Queen's family, you republican Yankee cow. What does this Pintin do?' I asked. I almost feared to hear the reply. The water stopped.

'Pantan is said in the French way, as you damn well know. Pantan stands in the gallery on a metal plate. You know how big Van Leyden's is, right? This huge room an' just him. Over his head there's this shiny ball on a stand. The plate and stand have got cables going from them over the window-sill to a generator. Actually, Georgie told me they're having to cut holes in the frame because of the air-conditioning. Well, this generator makes the ball live when a touch-switch in the gallery closes the circuit.'

Mopsa came in, sweeping the English Mason-Pearson brush I had given her in easier times through her dark hair. She had been, once, wonderfully attractive. There was a touch of Snow White about her – when she wasn't in cargo-pants and a vest. I found it all lovely, until she got mannish in those hateful Georgie days – aggressive, combative, and shrill in defence of her new obsession.

'Now,' she went on, 'Pantan doesn't get electrocuted

UNTIL that touch-switch is trodden on.'

I must have looked blank because she spelt out, very slowly, 'T-h-e s-w-i-t-c-h i-s u-n-d-e-r t-h-e f-l-o-o-r-b-o-a-r-d-s.'

'Yes, yes, I realise that. You don't need to make out you've got a degree in astro-physics and I'm Mister Minibrain from Minnesota.'

She gave me a look.

'It's radio-controlled, so there's no wires or nothing like that. Okay? So the evening starts; there are thirty, forty people milling around and WHAM! Someone's foot lands on the touch-switch, a big current goes through him an' he screams an' usually faints – an' that's the end of the show. Excuse me.'

Mopsa stepped over my out-stretched legs and went back to the bedroom.

'Doesn't it hurt?' I asked.

'The electric shock? Oh, sure. The voltage isn't so great, but the amperage is high, so Georgie says. He's got a fifty-fifty chance of a heart stoppage. He really goes through it. He's got burns on his feet and his head an' legs. You can see them because he's in the altogether.'

'What! Naked? And he often does this?'

'Often.'

'Is he famous then?'

'Oh, Jeez. Listen to him! Famous....! Where do you live nowadays, Mike? On Planet Zongo where the dead people go?'

'So he's as famous as – as *Michelangelo*, is he? A household word from Iceland to Tierra del Fuego...'

Bang! Went some object in the next room, then Mopsa was back standing over me, looking shiny. She used to wear make-up before Anno Georgie, but since then she'd favoured the flayed-buttock mode.

'DO you wanna come?' she yapped querulously.

'And the POINT of this living sculpture show? You haven't told me the sodding point of it yet.'

She whisked away from me down the long parquet passage to the kitchen. I lounged up and followed her to the door. The tiny spotlights spangled the top of her swaying head every few feet as she moved away from me.

'I suppose YOU can't see it,' she sniffed over her shoulder. I heard the clack of jar and mug – she was piling decaff into the percolator. Isn't arsenic used to make decaffeinated? Surely straightforward bean would do one less harm? I drifted along to the kitchen after her.

'No, Miss Greene, I can't see why a bloke stands starkers for some hours in a draughty gallery on the off-chance of being electrocuted. Not really SEE it.'

'Oh, you're hopeless,' sighed Mopsa, jamming the perc plug into the wall socket as if connecting one of Pintin's cables to his generator. 'A Bloak Stends Starkers,'she sneered, imitating my English accent and lapsing into her idea of an upper-class Brit toff – her final resource when peevish irritation at losing sets in, 'Eow, thet's a concept that hai faind too bally odd to swalleow. Look, you bastard,' she went on, cheesing the ersatz Bertie Wooster demotic, 'Pantan doesn't KNOW whether or not he's going to get the shock. He doesn't know where the touch-plate is, or whether or not he's gonna DIE that night. The gallery owner doesn't know where the touch-plate is, or whether he's gonna have a stiff on his hands. And the gallery crowd don't know whether they're going to see a naked man, or an electrocuted naked man, or a dead electrocuted naked man.'

'So?'

'SO, anything goes. Don't you see? ANYTHING can happen!'

'And that's the thrill?'

'That's the thrill.'

'And that's it?'

'That's it.'

'And the visitors KNOW there's a pad under the floor?' A sudden picture formed in my mind of Anthony and how if we brothers understood that a three-inch square would, when trodden on, cause an electric shock to shoot through a nude banana-case on the other side of the room, we would meticulously tread over every inch until we had hit the jackpot. 'I mean,' I went on, 'why don't they tread meticulously over every inch until they hit the jackpot? Anthony and I would.'

Mopsa disliked any reference to Anthony. She only met him once, but found his ironic schoolmaster-ish, Shakespeare-quoting patter just too camp and toffee-nosed for words. In her eyes he was the worst type of Brit.

'Oh, you!' she cried nasally, 'You take nothing seriously! You've got no feeling for *Art* at all.'

'Well, *don't* people stamp about to find the magic button?'

'I don' know. But that wouldn't spoil things, I guess. It

would bring comedy to the smell of fear. It would make the kinetic reality of the climax of pain even more subjugate to the corporate will.'

I poured out a little of the coffee she had made. "*She likes coffee, I like tea, a-cup, a-cup, a-cup, a-cup, a-cup*" as the song goes. I took a sip. Vile, and brim full of arsenic powder, I was sure. Mopsa was the only American I have known who drank cawfeee strong – most like hot, brown water. 'Actually,' I went on, 'the funniest thing would be to nip out to the generator and switch it off. You could call the show "The Anti-Climax of Anti-Pain".'

'You are SO annoying,' hooted Mopsa suddenly, banging down her mug. 'Jus' when I need some support. You're just a sick person.'

'ME sick?' I cried. 'You tell me about this freak of Georgie's and his generator, whose greatest pleasure in life seems to be to fry himself in public, and you and Georgie spend all evening – HOURS for Christ's sake – sitting in coffins up to your necks in putrifying chicken giblets, and you call ME sick!'

'But it's ART! 'she screamed. 'Can't you understand? ART!'

I cannot nowadays pin down the exact moment when I felt it was dangerous for me to go on living in America, but it must have been about this time – the summer of '99, during this sort of conversation with poor Mopsa, then West Hollywood's second most dedicated Excremental Kineticist after Georgie Koscynska – when everything had gone wrong.

I don't know how much the public really knows about *Schlock* Art, even now we're well into the 21st century. It gets in the papers over here now and then: that German loony who displays skeletons, and the harmless variants of it, like that pile of bricks some years ago in the Tate gallery, London. There is the organic art of Damien Hirst: his sectioned cow comes to mind, and that shark. But the furthest edges of Art without boundaries were and are obscene by any moral code and involvement seems to corrode and madden its practitioners until they become different people – or, perhaps, the people they actually were beneath, but who were kept hidden.

As Mopsa's voice screeched on I had a flitting memory-surge of a London street, a little boy crying with a torn elbow and a bobby saying, "Nah then, nah then. Jest a little scratch. 'Ere's a sixpence for a brave lad." The London street was round the corner from the Edgware Road in Maida Vale, the sixpence bought a few sherbert flying-saucers, the boy had been me.

'ARE you coming with us to the gall-ery, then?'

'Yes, yes, yes, I'll COME, I suppose,' said I, feeling utterly defeated.

Mopsa had known Georgie at that time for about six months. Georgie had gotten her involved in the furthest reaches of *Schlock* and had taken to coming round to our little stress-nest to discuss their plans for future exhibits. They hear that a sectioned human corpse with a dead dog inside it has been put on display and Wow! – how can you follow that? Mopsa's name was quite well-known then –

over on the West coast, at any rate, although most people would never have heard of her. In that Spring only the Gay Channel would give her and Georgie airtime, but by the summer they'd got respectable enough to appear at galleries like The Caplan Room, following what I see as an American passion for aggrandising novelty into 'culture'. It was as a species of defence against all this that I found my brain returning again and again to home. Once upon a time I had thought to have turned my back on Britain for ever, but after sixteen years I was wavering.

I first met the zongo Georgie when I had to go and bail her out of the Central precinct cop-shop.

Mopsa had been gassing for days about this wonder woman she had met after the New Year at a PSB art-freak forum for Bay TV in San Francisco.

'You have simply GOT to meet her, Mikey,' she had cried. 'She is stupendous!'

'How?' I had yawned. Mopsa had always thrust her latest fads at me, while remaining uninterested in enthusiasms of mine.

'She's so clever, so original, so daring, Mikey. She challenges every single concept of conventional thought. I mean she is IT, man. She is I-T.'

'Thinks the earth is square, does she?'

'Oh, Anagram of dog. You're just gonna be hateful, aren't you?'

This was round about the start of the de-sexualising of our relationship that I alluded to earlier and the growth of my sense of being trapped. When we spoke to each other at that time we had begun the retreat into role-based positions: she the eager, open-minded, free-spoken, young(ish), adventurous, exciting, media-sought-after American culture fiend, me the ironic, carping, censorious, debunking, philistine, snooty, older Brit businessman.

'Well, what do you mean: "she challenges every piece of conventional thought"? Is she the next Plato? The next Einstein? The next bleeding Darwin? And if she is, why haven't I heard of her already?'

'Huh, whadda YOU know?' had sneered Mopsa. 'You're just a moronic real estate agent. I don' know why I'm bothering to tell you about her at all.'

'You haven't told me anything concrete, actually.'

'Eow, eckcherlie hai hevn't, hev hai? But that's becawse hai carnt get a bally word in hedgeways.'

'Oh, piss off.'

Mopsa at that time had been working as a production assistant in Dan Bright's new movie unit and Georgie had been employed to do some sort of design work for a project. They had met again at a party at Dan's. Mopsa had gone over on her tasselled Wild-West looking Yamaha Virago motorcycle which she rode whenever there was an R in the month. I had not gone with her. I'd little to say to these Hollywood types. I think they respected me because I'd made money since I'd got there, but I didn't know the people they thought of as the right people and I didn't know the film biz. At parties like those of Dan Bright's I always got the feeling that my interlocutors broke off their conversation with me as soon as someone more important in their eyes hove into sight. This was not a congenial sensation and it put me off going. Mopsa, therefore, had met Georgie again on her own.

I gathered that Georgie had a brother called Witold who had emigrated from Poland to England with their family, but that he had stayed in London when she moved to the 'States. I wasn't to know then how closely Witold and I would be coming into contact – would that I *had* known. Georgie had one maxim, apparently: "Extreme Experience Frees The Artist". According to a besotted Mopsa there was nothing that Georgie hadn't thought, seen, smoked, drank, eaten, sat on, bathed in, injected, flown in, ridden on, lain under, opened, shut, made love to, written or painted. Superwoman wasn't in it.

'Georgie's in trouble!" Mopsa had screamed over the 'phone on that night I was destined to meet her. 'She's bin ARRESTED! Can you come and bail her out?'

'Why me?' I had asked grudgingly.

'Mike, darling, who else do I have to turn to?' said Mopsa, for once taking the right tack.

'Oh, all right. How much?'

'It's two thousand dollars.'

'Two THOUSAND!' I had cried. Had she tried to top the President? 'What's she done?'

'Oh, I'll tell you when I see you,' Mopsa had screeched. 'Just come!'

So I had gone downtown to the hearing at the Central precinct all-night sessions and paid up.

'You oughta take her to an institootion,' the cop who saw us off the premises said. 'She ain't normal in the head.'

I had bundled Georgie into the Jag with the hysterical Mopsa by her side.

'Oh, Mike, Mike. It was awful!' she had sobbed. 'Those pigs in there! They don't see that it's Art. They don' realise how Georgie has freed us all. She has discovered The Way Forward,' – her voice had risen on the capital letters – 'an' they go and arrest her, the filth!'

'What IS The Way Forward?' I had asked.

Georgie had uttered not a word. Mopsa was uttering enough for both of them, of course, but I was wondering if I was going to get any thanks from the Genius, or should rest content knowing that, in my small way, I had advanced the cause of great creativity and should regard that as thanks enough.

I had stolen a look at the famous Georgie in the rear-view mirror. It did not strike me until later that Mopsa had got into the back with the great artist. In the time before they met, she would have got into the front with me.

Georgie's silence was massive and her physique striking, large and hard-fleshed, like one of those womens' tennis finalists at Wimbledon. Her jaw was square, her spectacles steel-rimmed. She looked older than Mopsa, who was then thirty-four. I put her down as about my age – perhaps a little younger – but it wasn't easy to judge.

'So, what happened?' I had asked.

'Oh gosh, it was like this,' Mopsa had gushed before the silent genius had had time to open her mouth. 'Georgie had targeted that street downtown – er, you know, the one with Ponte Nuovo on it.'

'Latest Italian In-Spot. Yes?' I had turned into Benoit

and was heading towards the Southern freeway.

'Georgie is an Excremental Kineticist. Oh, Mike, I've TOLD you a dozen times.'

'You haven't told me what....' I had been about to say "bollocks" but stopped in time, '...what artistry she is involved in.' It had seemed by tacit consent that Mopsa was going to have to act as Georgie's mouthpiece, that we were going to have to refer to her continuously in the third person, and that I was never going to hear Wonder Woman speak.

Just then a deep voice had filled the auto.

'I make CONNECTIONS.'

It was as if Bela Lugosi or Darth Vader had been taking a ride in the Jag.

'Only CONNECT, says the English novelist Forster. Remember?'

I had peered at the big face in the mirror.

'Just so. Um, Mopsa tells me you're Polish.'

'Yes, I am – I was – Polish. Not now. I am an American, of course. My brother, he stayed in England. Have you ever been to London, England?'

'Has Mopsa not told you that *I'm* British – from London?'

Georgie, breathing in her noisy, stately Darth Vader-ish way, had then said, 'No.'

There was no reply to that. I mean to say, how unimportant can you get? 'Oh yes, I am an American woman. Since 1983 I am living in the 'States. It is where I shall die.'

And I had thought: how extraordinary! 1983 had been

my last year in England and first over here. I had been silenced, musing on coincidence, while the car thrummed over the tarmac.

'Tell him,' had come Mopsa's voice. 'Tell him what you did.'

'I connect. It's what I do.'

'Oh, you do! You do! I mean, it's awesome in its simplicity, in its shocking, but hey, *natural* directness.'

'It makes alarms ring. This is the purpose of creativity.'

'It is. It is!'

'Look,' I had interpolated, breaking into these Greek Drama-like strophes and antistrophes to try and reach the only point which interested me, 'what was serious enough to warrant bail of two thousand dollars? Which,' I added, with a touch of asperity, 'I paid for you.' But still no luck in getting thanks for services rendered.

'You know what the kinetics of my art involves, yes?' Georgie had asked.

'No,' I replied.

'What Georgie means,' Mopsa had twittered, 'is that in ONE SIMPLE ACT of living sculpture she connected the interior world of art's enemies: the philistine, the bourgeois, the money-grubbing Ponte Nuovo fat cats, with that world OUTSIDE the restaurant: our world of strife, pain, realism and nature. She connected the array of rich dishes with the waste that it will become when it has been eaten. And finally,' Mopsa had gasped, nodding in the back of the car like one of those plastic dogs, 'she made connections between the Ponte Nuovo – the corporate act – and herself, the individual – via the transparent membrane of division between them!'

'Uh, huh. And she was arrested for all this. So? What did she DO?'

I had addressed my remarks to bitch-machine who was gobbling and slobbering over the great Georgie, but the deep voice of the genius, interspersed with deliberate breathing, had rolled from the back of the auto.

'I pull down my pants, yes, and press my buttocks to the outside of the window and I shit down the glass.' She had turned to Mopsa. 'Is it right I should say "shit", or should I be saying "shitted" or "shat"?'

I had swerved violently, nearly connecting the *exterior* world of the Jaguar with the *interior* world of a passing liquor-store.

'What ART!' Mopsa had gasped. 'So pure.'

Thursday had arrived. The chicken offal crap had ended at The Caplan Room and Mopsa and Georgie were at leisure. That day we were due to see Pintin and his Boys' Own Electrical Kit at Van Leyden's in Beverly Hills and I was at the wheel of the Jag with Mopsa and Georgie, as usual, canoodling in the back. I was driving with a little difficulty because Mopsa had stabbed me in the groin with a paper-knife after an unpleasant tussle in my bedroom. She frowned in the back of the car with a dark shade under her eye where I'd punched her. Tensions were high.

'Yup. I noo we were gonna be late. Yup, I noo it. No good in bed, no good at the wheel.'

Just as I was about to crash the Jag deliberately and kill all three of us, Georgie began to give tongue.

'I am thinking that you are asleep. Van Leyden's is behind me.'

So I slowed to a crawl, counting to ten under my breath.

'Hey, hey, Mikey! You've driven past it, you dozy dick!'

Mopsa's finger drove into my shoulder. She and Georgie continued tut-tutting in the back. I pulled in at the curved driveway in front of that exotic, jungly Thai place near Hamburger Heaven. A uniformed Asiatic shot forward and whipped open the rear door.

'We're not stopping to eat,' called out Mopsa. 'We're jus' turning. Turn, Mikey.'

She dragged the door shut again. I reversed, blocking the awkward curve. There was a bump. The car-hop appeared round the front, mouthing at me.

'He's quite sweet, I suppose,' said Mopsa.

'You are smiting his limbs with your fender,' said Georgie.

It had turned into one of those evenings.

Fuming, I shot over to a vacant parking slot, the rear-view mirror showing a bent, uniformed youth caressing his shin.

'Right. That's it!' I hooted. 'I can't EVER go back to that place, but, as I'm starving I'm going to have a burger.'

Mopsa had been in such a state about getting to Pintin's show that we had dashed out to meet Georgie miles too early. I had not eaten since lunch and was now at Level 9 of grumpiness.

'Mikey!' shrieked Mopsa. 'We can't! We'll be late!'

'Late for bloody *what*, exactly?' I howled, exasperated.

'That maniac of yours stands all night on his plate, doesn't he? What are we going to be late FOR? Are you worried you might miss him shifting his weight from his left leg to his right?'

Before going into the Heaven, I thought I'd better make amends at the rival Thai establishment. I fumbled a note from my wallet. Mopsa tried to ruffle my hair from the back – attempting a placatory gesture, no doubt, but I pulled away. Graceless, perhaps, but it was extraordinary how every single thing she did maddened me in those days.

'Mopsa,' asked Georgie, 'is Mikey a little annoyed?'

We got out. Mopsa took Georgie's arm and turned towards me.

'Our Lord Michael wants to eat, so we eat.' She pulled Georgie up the steps. I darted into the Thai driveway and pressed $10 on the car-hop.

'Sorry about the – erm….' I muttered.

We sat on one of those round, red sofas which the Heaven used to feature. Perhaps it still does.

'Just *think*,' said Mopsa, 'we're sitting where Whitney Houston sat last time we was here.'

'Is that he is a friend?' asked Georgie.

'It's a SHE, not a HE,' I replied, 'and it's WERE, not WAS,' I added, turning to Mopsa.

'Frig you, mister. If we gotta eat I guess I'll have spicy wings an' fries an'….'

I cut across her.

'What would YOU like, Georgie?' I asked the apostle of E-K. I took a quick dekko at the windows. Fortunately they had deep plant tubs in front of them and would be hard to reach with bared buttocks, should Georgie have felt like repeating the Ponte Nuovo episode of eighteen months earlier.

'I want only salad and still water.'

Thank God.

Forty minutes later we strolled down to Van Leyden's. On the sidewalk outside was a huge moulded caterpillar cut in half by an aluminium razor blade. Beneath the cuts lay pools of red.

'Oooooh! Everyone's bin talking about THIS!' cried Mopsa. 'Isn't it wonderful? You can see how peoples' feet have smeared the blood.'

'What is that blood?' asked Georgie.

'Oh, it's only tomato ketchup. They put a new lot down every evening. Wow! That's such a great idea, isn't it?'

Inside the foyer, the low-voltage spots pierced down from the curved ceiling. Several people were shuffling forward in front of us. To my surprise, I noticed an accountant I knew in company with an odd youth in a lime-green jump suit. I was about to hail him when something whispered to me not to. That and the quartz-halogens decided me to put my shades on. Mopsa squeezed my arm – all matey again.

'Isn't this quite something?' she whispered with that eternal American enthusiasm for the latest sensation.

We came up to a trendy stainless steel counter. A middle-aged man with a Pancho Villa moustache nodded at us.

'A hundred and five dollars,' he muttered.

'I'm sorry,' I replied. 'Did you say: five dollars?'

The Mexican bandit smiled wearily.

'I guess I said a hundred and five dollars, sir,' said he. 'Hey, but that's for the three of you,' he added by way of comfort. Speechless, I paid up.

'This had better be worth it,' I hissed at Mopsa.

The corridor opened out into Van Leyden's famous art gallery. Usually (and I had been there before to day-time showings of ordinary, dull retro-art – you know, paintings) the place had that decorous babble of the aspirant-connoisseurs locked in private debate about which one was the cheapest they could get away with buying, and in public criticism of the drinks and nibbles. On Pintin night, however, it was like walking through the mourners preparatory to throwing one's bit of earth on the grave. Not a word from anyone. The fifty or so present gazed at Pintin's *tableau vivant* in total silence.

He, for his part, stared stonily ahead. His feet (with bad corns) were planted on his shiny disc. The chrome ball above just touched his head. Between corns and ball he was naked, apart from a thong, and relaxed into a long-term pose, arms a-kimbo, feet apart. A thick cable ran from the plate to the stand supporting the ball then out to where the generator hummed in some back yard, I supposed.

As I gazed at him, it darted into my mind that none of us had any proof that there WAS a generator out there. The best fakes are the audacious ones.

'So, I've paid thirty-five dollars each just to look at this…. git,' I murmured in Mopsa's ear.

'Gee whiz, isn't it worth it just to BE here?' she whispered back, hardly able to drag her eyes from the enthralling sight in the corner.

'The feet of mine may be one centimetre from the mechanism to shock him,' gasped Georgie.

'Why don't you both shuffle around a bit, then we can go home.'

'Go ahead, spoil it,' hissed Mopsa.

We moved a little and gazed at Pintin from another angle.

'So this is IT?'

'Jesus, Mikey, what more can you WANT?'

'You said His name just then. You know you never say His name.'

'So I did. Well, you're annoying me. Anyone would think you're a Pharisee, the way you go on.'

'Do you mean Philistine?'

'I mean what I mean.'

Our mutual hissing must have encouraged those around us to break out of their shells, for there was a little timid conversation at last.

'Hey, real interesting show.'

'Yeah, yeah. If artistic creation is, like, an admixture of anticipation and requitement, this little guy lets you explore the anticipation.'

'Oh, you're SO right,' beamed Mopsa, horning in.

I moved away. I'd had enough of Pintin. Besides I wanted to avoid the man I knew and his epicene lime-green companion. I wondered if the $35 included drinks and I meandered back to the bandit in the lobby to ask.

There was a shout.

'Hello! Whaddya know!'

I looked round with one of those guilty starts people make when they think they're being hailed in public. 'HEY! Excellent! It's Mike Greville! Mike, hi! Over here. I've bin trying to call you at the office. What a coincidence.'

I peered beyond the bandit into the lobby. There, his dome-like head catching the spotlights' gleam like a planet photographed by Voyager III, was Dan Bright.

'Wait there,' I cried, waving him back. 'Don't go in,' I whispered hoarsely as I reached him.

'What?' he grunted, fumbling for his note-case.

'I said don't go in. It's a load of horse-manure. There's a man in the corner in the altogether, and that's it.'

Dan Bright lifted his impressive eyebrows up the dome.

'In the altogether? One guy? So what are you saying? That I ignore the hysterical press notices and give the show a miss?'

'Give it a miss, Dan. Take it from me, it's just a more laborious method of chucking money away than leaving your note-case on the side-walk.'

'Are you here on your own, then?'

'Er – ah, no, I'm not, but in another sense I am. Let's go for a drink.'

'I don't drink.'

'Oh, nor you do. I'd forgotten. Well, let's have coffee or something. Isn't Il Fornaio still open? Come on. Let's catch up on news.'

'Mike, I DO have news for you, my friend.'

He slipped his wallet back into his jacket. I shepherded him out of the queue, amazed that anyone else would want to come in. I could sense the bandit's eyes following me disapprovingly as $35 walked out of his life.

As Dan and I reached the street doors, a blue light behind us seemed to flicker brightly and there was a single hoarse cry, then a silence, then a deafening babble.

'What the....?' began Dan, turning back. People surged in the lobby. From their comments I gathered that Pintin's show had provided the hoped-for thrill – and proven that he was no fake.

'What gives?' asked Dan. 'Why, there's Mopsa Greene,' he added. Georgie was leading a sobbing figure out towards us. When they drew close, Georgie steadied Mopsa in her brawny arms.

'She is excited right now,' explained Georgie, 'because of her foot....'

'Yes, yes. I guess I stepped on the wrong spot, and....'

'Mopsa did it. You should have seen Pintin get his juice! Everything stood on end.'

'Yeah,' gasped Mopsa, 'an' she does mean *everything*.'

'They are sending now for the ambulance. He is in a coma.'

'Lucky escape for you, Dan, I'd say. You'd have paid for only thirty seconds of the show – over a dollar a second.'

'Oh, I don't know. I feel like I've missed something now,' sighed Dan.

'Well *done*, Mopsa,' said I. 'You made jolly sure it was value for money.'

'Oh, yup. But that bang was such a shock. Gimme a tissue, Georgie.'

They tottered in each others' arms, one sniffing and gurgling, the other plying Kleenex. Dan took my elbow and led me a little apart.

'What I've been trying to contact you for, Mike,' said Dan, 'was to ask you up to *Danmar* on Sunday. I'd like you to come to a bar-b-que.'

'You're a kind guy. I guess I am a little overwrought,' Mopsa called over. 'We'd love it, wouldn't we, Mikey?'

'Well, to be honest, I meant just Mike here,' said Dan, giving Mopsa a grim stare. 'Mike, there's someone real special I want you to meet. Look, Mopsa, it's business, ya see?'

'I do NOT see,' snapped Mopsa, clutching at another tissue.

I composed my features to look regretful and was about to frame an excuse – partly so as not to provoke an outburst from bitch-face, and partly because my earlier connections with Dan on business matters had not been particularly pleasing – when the wail of a siren interrupted. Help for Pintin was at hand. The bandit shoved us back against the wall and a stretcher was galloped into the gallery.

'Mike, I won't take "no",' persisted Dan. 'You'll see why when you get to *Danmar*.'

'Well, it's very kind of you....'

'You're coming?'

I hesitated, and a still form under a bright blanket was hurried past us.

'Well, if you put it like....'

'That's settled. Sunday it is. Marsha will be thrilled. And, Mike, YOU will be thrilled.'

Chapter 2: **The Final Outrage.**

'I swear to God if you leave me out I'm gonna open my veins on you! I've done it before, an' I'll do it again. You KNOW I will, Mikey. DON'T you turn away when I'm speaking to you – jus' don' turn away.I mean what I say. I mean it! I mean, I MEAN it! God, You leave me behind today an' I'll slit my….'

So, after endless shrieking, Mopsa persuaded me to tote her along to Dan Bright's bar-b-que. She most definitely had not been asked, but I hoped he wouldn't mind too much; he had introduced us, after all. When she was acting as his assistant deputy executive stand-by art director on *Full Circle* back in 1990, I had thought her the most attractive woman in California. Originally from Roanoke, Virginia, she seemed to have preserved her sanity out west in her ridiculously worded non-job for a long time. Then, in the fifth year of our relationship, she had bought her Yamaha custom bike, a snake (which drowned in the john after a horrible month) and added mescalin, speed, E and crack to her usual bouts of coke. A year beyond that she tried to kill herself for the first time. Then she met Georgie and my love for her dried up like an old, old oyster in an open shell.

A heavy transistor radio had flashed across the room. It had cut my cheek bone before crashing to the floor.

'Well, AM I coming or not?'

'You're coming, Mopsa dear. And you used His name back then.'

'I did not! YOU say that! YOU would say anything!'

'Be ready in two hours. Not three, not four. If yew ain't in the auto as the clock tolls fahve, yew shore ain't-a-comin'.'

'Mm. I rather like your Dolly Parton voice,' she grinned.

'It was my Johnny Cash voice,' said I coldly.

It sounds ridiculous and melodramatic, but there was a particular moment when I felt that I had to return to Britain or lose myself. I think it was sometime between two TV shows. The first one was on PSB. It was all about the breakthrough at the Channel Tunnel – where the Brits and Frogs had hacked towards each other in the greatest engineering feat of the century and joined what He had put asunder since the Ice Age. The honest, embarrassed face of a British digger had emerged from a jagged hole and had mouthed a few words of excruciating French. "Wee, wee. C'est bon. Bon jewer," he had intoned. I loved him. No one I spoke to afterwards had seen the programme or had any opinion about the tunnel. But then it had been on PSB, so who could have been watching? I and a few Anglos back east. In Cali-forn-eye-ay not a soul cared for any news further east than Las Vegas.

The slipstream of humid air lifted Mopsa's dyed hair. We had the windows open. The Jag twisted up to Bel Air. It was only 5.30, yet the white-faced junkies were beginning to crowd on Santa Monica Boulevard.

'You're such a cow,' I said, fingering the plaster on my cheek. 'Why do you have to THROW things all the time? No wonder you weren't asked. It's two years since you threw Dan's mother's portable TV into the pool. I actually remember Dan's expression.'

'Oooo, you ECKCHERLIE wemember it, do you, you sarcastic eunuch.'

'Don't mock, bitch.'

'Who's mocking? Mikey, I *do* love your way of saying things. For Chris' sakes, you know that.'

'I know nothing of the sort, and you used five-sixth's of His name there,' I growled, as Dan's gates came into view. 'You blasphemer, you'll roast like a fatty, greasy pig in Hell.'

'Hey, hey, ho, ho. What's the five-sixths math joke? Yo' is better than Arsenio Hall.'

I snorted, adding a further vocal effect to the growl.

'Don't you mention Arse-has-been-hole in this *British* car, you scrubby, gate-crashing harlot, or I'll push you out.'

'Oh yeah, an' my guts'll split and spurt on Dan's purty hillside; and, Mister, you go to ALCATRAZ for murdering me.'

'Oh God, you're so ignorant! Alcat....'

'Aaaaah! YOU used His name then! After "Oh".'

'Don't interrupt when I'm trying to educate you, you bog-trotting, backwoods, Virginian hill-billy. Alcatraz isn't a prison. It's been a TOURIST attraction since Burt Lancaster was a kid, ackcherlie.'

'Think I didn't know? Oh, you're so literal and soooooo boringly British!'

'Shut up, scum. We're here.'

The second programme which tightened a little screw of endurance inside me was not a serious one, nor was it on Public Service TV. This was a mid-afternoon comedy which I watched after Mopsa had over-dosed and I stayed in to nurse her into consciousness. It was about a fictional sassy, wise-cracking family in a run-down part of a run-down city. Black pa, black maw, sassy black kids and their teenage friends – all were hateful, not because they were black or poor, but because we were invited to roar with laughter at the appalling catalogue of their misfortunes. The father drank, the mother was a refugee from another man who beat her (she had a real amusing bandage over one eye). The youngest boy had been offered drugs. The canned laughter was as its loudest when he and two others pulled the wool over a teacher's eyes to get out of class and meet a pusher in the school yard (although I admit I approved when a group of them beat the pusher up). The daughter was living with a boy and feared he might have got her pregnant. There was unrestrained mirth when her paw, angered by this information, chased her round their tatty sofa and tripped up over the junk in the room. Drugs, teenage pregnancy, separation, domestic misery and poverty were all presented as the richest possible recipe for comedy viewing. It led me to reflect that America, once so prim that Hollywood films were hedged about with regulations about twin beds in bedroom scenes and strict time limits to kissing, seemed to have lost direction so badly that even its laughter was no longer healing, but tinged with the madhouse. I recall that I sat revolted, with tense shoulders, mesmerised by the awfulness of the "fun" while keeping one ear cocked for the sound of vomiting that would herald Mopsa's return to the world.

Dan's gates were enormous, electronically-powered and

made of lilac-painted wrought iron with DANMAR in foot-high gold letters on them.

'Welcome! Hey, it's Mike!' cried Dan, catching sight of me as I climbed to the terrace between tumbling rock flowers and dwarf palms. The house was built on a steep slope and to reach the rear terrace you had to negotiate rocky steps after you'd left the auto at the car-port. Breathless, I stepped onto the flagstones from the shade of a flowery arch. Nat King Cole's voice honeyed out from Dan's playroom.

'Whaddya *know*!' cried Dan, just as if he hadn't been expecting me.

'Er, you don't mind, Dan, do you? I brought along Mopsa Gree….' I stopped and looked around. Mopsa was nowhere to be seen. Where WAS the wretched girl? Why had she not followed me up the path?

'Come an' see who is here!' Dan went on, unheeding my mutterings. 'C'mon, Mike, I think you know him.'

He took my arm and propelled me into the playroom. In the gloom a great mass of stomach lay in an armchair. As my eyes accustomed themselves to the shade after the violent sunshine, I recognised a shape I hadn't seen for a few years.

'Mike Greville, baby,' came a wheezing voice. There was a sound of grunting. Either Dan had acquired a warthog as a pet or Yuri Buczenko was commencing the long task of heaving his bulk to the perpendicular. 'I said to Daniel, it'll be real maximum to see Mike Greville again after so long,' gurgled Yuri. Dan had followed me in.

'Ah,' said I, 'so this is the Mystery Man you wanted me

to meet today?'

'Hell, no, Mike. This is only Yuri. You remember him? No, Yuri and I are in *partnership* with the Mystery Man. He'll be along any minute.'

I stared at them: Dan's gnome-like frame topped off with Sergeant Bilko glasses on one side of the armchair and the Russian rhino on the other. Geez, it was quite like old times working on *Full Circle* – and I wished I hadn't come, and not for the first time regretted that I had made the sort of money that interested the sort of people like Dan.

As soon as I had reached New York in 1983, I introduced myself, on my mother's instructions, to a man who had known my brother's and my grandfather on the London Stock Exchange. He invited me up to Newport. In his wood-panelled study in the mansion on Ocean Drive he had draped his arm round my shoulder, kissed my cheek, said, "I hope you'll always be a credit to dear Guy. Excuse me a moment, young man", left the study, crossed the marble lobby and closed a heavy door in the quiet house. I heard a muffled bang. He had put a shotgun to his double chin and blown his jaw off.

I went in my only suit to his funeral in Hackensack. He was buried in the same grave as his sister who had died of leukaemia in the 'sixties.

'Why did he kill himself?' I asked a friend of his.

'Oh, money, of course,' I was told. 'He bankrupted himself after re-location problems for Vitagraph's manufacturing base. He couldn't stand the strain of the lay-offs, the run-down of the firm, the delays of building the new plant.'

That set me thinking as I lay awake, disturbed and nerve-wracked by the shock of his death. Since leaving school in 1976, and after my student job at EMI, I had worked first for Gamage and Stringer and then for Porter's Properties in London. This meant I had become a real-estate man through and through. But not until that New York night had I realised that for every firm needing to re-locate to a new site or to premises delayed in the construction, there must be dozens of speculators with offices or plant standing empty. If there were someone who could bring the two parties together....

I formed *Royal Greville* within the month. The "Royal" was designed to make an impression out of town where most of my business would lie; there is no greater lover of the British crown than your middle-aged American suburban aspirant high-flier, and such a fleeting word-association could only help. I went to the NY Jesuit church and introduced myself on the grounds that I was new to the parish and that my mother was a Catholic and lived in Italy. I volunteered to work in the bookshop and was accepted. From that point I took a chance and directed all my mail to come to me there, giving me the downtown office address that would impress a guy out of town in, say, Peoria.

Within two weeks I found a stationery concern with offices and packing-plant in Buffalo which was poised to re-locate up-market to the Jersey corridor. Their green-field site was already a year late, owing to environmental protests, and they had a customer for the old plant. I found them a refurbished waterfront premises ideal for small scale packing and admin. In from Dobbs Ferry there was easy access across to Sawmill Parkway and west over the Tappan Zee to their old hunting grounds. There were no takers for this place so I secured a mortgaged temporary lease on the package – Lowenthal & Fox to let the main waterfront site until the stationery firm's new premises were completed – and presented it to my client. The deal involved $1,500,000. I asked for, and got, 2.5% or $30,000.

My next deal featured an insurance company employing four hundred workers going into temporary offices in Manhattan for two years during complete rebuilding of their original, historic headquarters. This time my share came to $270,000.

I now rented a tiny one-room office in a prestige block. I made sure from now on that I met clients over lunch at The Pierre, not from my base. This all this sounds as if I was a bullshitting con-man; that is, after all, what those early junketings of mine seem to add up to. And especially my name change. It never occurred to me tell my L A associates that the name "Greville" was a recent, though entirely legally contrived, acquisition too. Who was going to rent office space from a guy called Crepwright?

Before the end of the '80s I had moved over to the West Coast and Royal Greville California was born. I succumbed to local snobbery about living in the city and bought a frigid, white-arched Spanish-style house at Malibu. The drive over there was so tiresome that I also took an apartment near the Beverly Centre, then the vast nest I shared with Mopsa up near Bel Air. Royal Greville's office was two doors from what became Conran's shop.

I had been dragged into the filming of *Full Circle* by Yuri and Dan purely because they knew I had cash. They had heard from a contact in Lucas Films who had given me a land deal in Marin County that I was becoming interested in investing in movies. I had come down to the set as the shoot was nearing completion and had been ignored for a week until, on one very early morning, Mopsa Greene had taken notice of me. She was not yet unhinged, not yet involved with Concept Art, still caffeinated. She led me to a location van. She made me the mug of coffee I needed to pull me round. 'Have a taste of this', she had said – thrusting a really sugary, dark-crusted doughnut towards me. A few bites later and I was hers for life. From cawfeeee an' do'nut came dinner, theatre, a trip to Aspen, residence at Malibu, then at Bel Air, and, in the background, a vague understanding that wedding bells might chime.

Yuri pushed me into one of the squidgy armchairs.

Dan beamed at me from the bar.

'Drink?' he asked.

In the pause, while I was wondering what drink I'd like, a shadow fell across the window.

'Oh yes! You just went on in an' IGNORED me!' screamed a sudden voice from under what looked like a piece of semi-tropical shrubbery.

Mopsa had, at last, arrived. I had forgotten that she was with me.

'Look!' she screamed again.

Dan, Yuri and I looked, as bidden.

'What the great Sam....?' gasped Yuri.

'Is...is...is...is that...is that Mopsa Greene?' stuttered Dan.

'Who the HELL do you think it is? Hillary Clinton?'

'But what are you DOING here, in Christ's name?' cried Dan.

'I came with Mike, of course, you silly old dummy, an' DON'T use His name. I don' like it.'

'But what,' said I, breaking in at last, 'have you got a bush on your head for?'

Mopsa let out a shriek like a Saturn rocket heading for Pluto and stamped one foot, then the other (she was always rather a foot-stamper) then screeched again,

'I fell off the steps. While you were poncing up the...the path – that SHITE path of yours....' She suddenly yelled at Dan. 'I lost my footing and I fell backwards into a thorn-bush an' it's sticking to me now! And YOU, you thick Limey, you didn't even NOTICE! No, sireeee, you jes' moseyed in here an' asked for a drinkie while I'm nearly pricked to death!'

'My dear,' said Dan, smothering the smile which I felt was hovering about his sardonic lips, 'let me help you. Come in and Marsha can sort you out. What a horrible thing to happen.' The very picture of creaking gallantry, he led Mopsa in to the house from the playroom, shedding assorted strands of bush as he did so. When they had disappeared, Yuri turned to me,

'Jeez, man. You have got bad noos in that woman, Mike.

What you want to go bring her here today? Dan and I have got a surprise lined up for you. Mopsa's too big a junk-head these days. She's goin' ter spoil it.'

I felt, oddly, that I had to defend Mopsa – or, more accurately, my decision to bring her along.

'Yuri, she is my – um – partner.' (How mincing that word sounded in my ears – like "comfort station" – and how untrue by that time.) 'She was hopping mad when I suggested she didn't come today. I know how you and Dan feel about her, but what could I do?'

There was a silence. I knew what Yuri was thinking: only a soft Brit would let his girl walk all over him.

'Well, hell – I don't dislike the chick,' he said. 'It'll work out, I suppose.'

I grunted, fearing it wouldn't.

'Dan was saying something about a drink,' I suggested. I was too old to blush, but I was blushing within. I remembered the many things I didn't like about Yuri. It was so annoying that he had this new reason to feel contempt for me.

'Bourbon? Am I right, or am I right?'

'Well, no. I'm driving. I'd rather have….'

But he had elephantined to his feet and his fat hands were opening a bottle.

'Bourbon, right?'

'Right,' I replied wearily.

We drank.

Noiselessly, their movements unheard above the humming air-con, Dan's Filipinos were lighting the big Thermos Bar-B-Que outfits and setting out meat, fruit and sauces.

'So – who is coming?' I asked.

Yuri looked like a childish old Russian peasant and closed a fat eyelid.

'You jus' wait an'see.'

I almost hated him for a moment; for the stupid games he loved to play; for his liking to appear a shrewd savant.

'Fun surprise, eh?'

I got up and went across to the huge panes of glass. Beyond the terrace, far below, the boulevard twinkled with cars crawling in haze between the leaning telegraph poles. The sun was going down and the light was honey-orange, the shadows long.

In '98 Mopsa had said to me,

'You wanna see something really unique, Mikey? It'll be expensive – pretty expensive, but you'll never see anything like it again.'

'I don't know,' I had replied. I had been thinking sadly that she and I had grown so far apart that nothing could bring us together again. She had been sniffing, her lips were wet and her eyes glazed.

'It's a private art show, Mikey. Georgie knows the man. She can take us two. It's a bit secret – a bit, whaddayacallit, hush, hush.' She had gazed up at me, her eyes rotating in their wet sockets. 'Shush, shush, tweetie-pie. Chris', you gotta come, Mikey. You don' come an' I'll....you don' let me come....you don' pay for us....an' I'll cut...open...my...'

'We'll both go,' I had snapped.

We set off in a cab to meet Georgie at Bullock's. She turned up with a young man called Jonathan. He was slender and wore his hair like Pu-yi, the last emperor of China. It was decided that we should go in his car to our destination, towards Pasadena.

He clasped my hand with long, damp fingers.

'Hi. What's up?' said he.

'Where are we going exactly?' I asked.

'A very private place, man,' Jonathan had hissed.

Either our pig-tailed pilot had little sense of direction or this venue was even more hidden than he had supposed, for we had got lost in dreary Glendale. I sat with Georgie who was frowning in the back. I had to ask the way at the La Quinta outside which we pulled up. We headed towards Forest Lawns Cemetery. On the long cropped verges the tractors were spraying the dead grass green. The car swung wildly as Jonathan twisted off down a dirt road between a row of trees and an art-deco warehouse.

'This is it,' he exclaimed – but then he'd said the same about fifty times already. Having more confidence in him than I did, Mopsa, giggling, flung her left arm round his shoulders. The cloud from Georgie's smoke wafted across, mixing with the car seats' aroma of urine and bursting foam. Every few minutes the joint passed over to Jonathan. His pig-tail whisked from side to side as he tossed his head. I hoped we would make it to the end of the dirt road alive.

Scree-ch!

Jonathan had slewed the car round, sniggering.

'Here 'tis, man. No sign of pigs, man?'

'Why are you worried about the LAPD?

'This is a very PRIVATE show, man.'

'Wait a minute,' I rejoined. 'What the hell are we going to see? I'm not going to break the law.'

'Don' be a dinky-doo, Mikey,' said Mopsa and I relapsed into weak silence.

So we had gone into the back of a disused light industrial shed which was surrounded by inexplicably abandoned artefacts such as a mobile crane, a burnt-out black pick-up of 1940s vintage, a steel tank, a VW Beetle, a duo-tone Chevy coupe, rusty bedframes and a heap of tyres.

Georgie had started sneezing. My eyes adjusted to the scene inside the shed.

A dark, shiny-floored space with chairs round the wall and a black slab in the middle; a bank of intensely white spotlights, all focussed downwards; nothing else.

'What IS this?' I had whispered to Mopsa. Something in the atmosphere had made me feel sacrilegious about speaking aloud. The thirty or forty other people in the room had also been silent – apprehensively so, I realised later, How they had got there (the VW? the Chevy? the pickup?) and how long had they been waiting?

'This is a really *special* piece of living sculpture, Mike,' Mopsa had gone on. 'It has been banned from almost every state in the USA.'

Jonathan breathed over me with acrid dampness. 'Yeah. The pigs closed him down in San Fran and at Palm Beach. This guy Spiro Giro started in Montreal, but they banned him in Canada. Then he went to Seattle an' they banned him there. An' he's banned in England, Europe.'

'Don't tell me that Spiro Giro is the freak's real name.'

'He is negatorily NOT a freak, man.'

Georgie then whispered, her tongue touching my ear-lobe.

'It is a real name for because he am from Greece coming, nevertheless becoming Canadian, isn't it? For because Giro is some Greece name.'

'Hang on, hang on,' I said – in a voice louder than a respectful whisper – 'What is he banned FOR? If you think I'm going to sit through some disgusting pornogr....'

'Hush now there, Mikey darling,' had come Mopsa's whisper, cutting across my protests. 'How can you think that Art could be pornography?'

Obviously she wouldn't have seen eye-to-eye with my hero of those days: Mayor Guiliano (Mayor Fooliano to his critics, Mayor Guili-anus to the concept artists) of New York. He was going to stop the Brooklyn Museum's grant, and prevent the YBA (Young British Artists) invasion at the end of the '90s. According to him, all modern concept art was a disgusting outrage.

'What happens?' I insisted.

'Just cool it, Mike,' said Mopsa.

'You'll see, dude,' had growled Jonathan. 'The show's starting.' He whisked his pigtail in the direction of the door. From out of the shadows had come a man – yet not a man. Tall, with cavernous chest, naked from the waist up, moving in silence, Spiro Giro floated to his table. At first I had thought he was wearing a singlet or vest, but with a shock I perceived that the bright splodges of colour on his torso were made of metal or plastic and seemed to be riveted or stapled into his flesh. This flesh was puckered and red. In the shadows I had got an impression that he had very long fingers. When he had moved into the light, my heart almost stopped.

'See....' hissed Mopsa, 'see his hands? They based Edward Scissorhands on this guy.'

At the end of each of his stick arms an array of sundry domestic items was displayed. On the right hand, where the thumb should have been, was a fork. Apart from his digit finger, the rest of the hand had featured – in place of fingers – a yellow spatula, a picnic knife with a red handle and an apple-corer. On the other hand were stuck an old-fashioned gent's razor, a hard-to-identify tube and a bright picnic spoon.

'Is.... is that glue?' I gasped.

Jonathan leaned over. 'When the wounds heal, he fixes his stubs into sockets on the forks an' things with cyanoacrylate adhesive.'

I remember being faintly surprised that he knew long words and could pronounce them. He's a fake air-head, I remember thinking. Like all of them.

'What do you mean: wounds? What wounds?' I hissed back.

But Spiro Giro had lain upon his black altar. Expressionless and flat, he had remained for many minutes. A squat young man, as round and heavy as Giro was long and lean, had emerged from the darkness.

'That's Frank Bradney, his disciple,' Mopsa started gibbering in the gloom. 'He's already had his toes on one foot removed, like the Master.'

Georgie joined in, leaning wetly and hotly in to my ear again, 'It is he, Mr Bradney, who washes and helps the Master for to eat,' she mouthed, 'for with so much cut off he can do not so much for himself any longer.'

The disciple had limped round to the back of the altar, to the side hidden from us. From the back he had lifted a gantry of chrome tubes with a belt running over pulleys. He had positioned this above Giro's left arm. Springs built into it kept it level and balanced, like an Anglepoise lamp. From a drawer in the altar, the disciple had retrieved a stainless steel ramp and had fixed it to the side of the table so that it pointed down at the floor. Under the floor end of it he had placed a glass jar of about two quarts' capacity.

There was a whirr. Electric motors in the table had been started. Rhythmic gears sounded within the altar's depths.

No word had been spoken. The others in the room, like Mopsa & Co, who had come to witness this most extreme manifestation of conceptualised art, clearly knew what to expect. I glanced round at them. All eyes had been filled with a glistening, feverish excitement, a silent devouring of the thin limbs in the glare, a darting appreciation of the chrome rods above and the empty jar at the end of the ramp. I had an impulse to blunder from the building, opposed by an equally powerful one to stay and witness the abomination.

'Is not this so exciting?' came a gasp. Georgie was on the edge of her chair.

'The – um – probabilities are all in place,' whispered Jonathan's voice from the other side of me. 'Is he gonna do it? Which part has he chosen? Will he shriek? Will he be able to stand it when it starts? What will he substitute for it? Hey, this is, like, creation AND destruction, living AND putrescence, agony and joy, light and shadow, natural and man-made, master and servant, sadist and masochist....all held in one – uh – one glorious dichotomy an'... an' ambivalence in the same instant! Shee-eye-t, it's just genius, ya know?'

But it wasn't. It was just sick.

Mopsa's wet-lipped head jerked up and down like a crazy puppet's. So sad, so frightening, this intellectualising of nothing.

Electric humming had begun. At the end of the chrome rods a small rotary saw had been positioned over Giro's left hand and then lowered just above one of his two remaining fingers – the wedding-ring one. The disciple stepped back. The tiny saw dropped gradually and began to bite into the flesh. Blood spurted off the blade. A stream of water, directed down the chrome rod to the saw pivot in a thin transparent plastic sheath, was washing it clear, so that the white bone had been visible under the ripped tissue. Pinkish water ran down the ramp and began to fill the jar.

The saw blade sung a shrill note as it started on the finger bone. Its little, fine teeth took a long time to get through. Giro had lain unmoving, staring at the battery of lights above him. By no gesture did he betray the agony of those minutes.

With a final whistle the saw cut the tissue at the base of the finger. Its positioning had not been quite accurate and, small as the blade was, it slashed deeply into the base of the little finger. This too bled profusely. The detached finger followed its blood down the ramp, plopped into the jar and sank.

The disciple lifted the chrome gantry up and away, held up Giro's arm to exhibit the livid, bloody stump to the Art lovers, had shown us the bright orange picnic spoon with socketed handle which, Mopsa told me afterwards, had been selected to make the point about man-made and artificial and was to match the one on the other hand, and jammed it home on the stump. Adorned thus with a further piece of kitchen-ware, Giro had risen unsteadily to his feet, his face white and wet. He was led away by the disciple and the lights dimmed. After a corporate gasp, there were loud shouts and clapping and jabbering. The "Living Sculpture Exhibition" had come to an end.

In the car there had been more horse-manure: 'Hey, like, I loved that idea that the spoon, 'cos it's made of plastic which'll never degrade, replaces the finger which would have died anyway.' 'Yeah, yeah, it's like he's slowly making himself immortal.' 'The finger in the jar is going on tour with the "Body Parts Exhibition", y'know. They're gonna embed the parts in Perspex.' 'Jeez, that's so clever, 'cos the part of the body has parted!' 'I've heard it said that he's gonna remove his own head in Montreal where he used to live.' 'For he am saying that he do it when his hand and feet are all gone.' 'Boy, I wish I could be there!'

I was asked what I thought. Having recovered from the shock and having time to think, I had stiffened upright on Jonathan's uriney car seat and delivered my opinion.

'You Yanks are SO bloody naïve. It was a trick.'

There was a storm. Mopsa tried to slap me, missed, and caught Jonathan on his pigtail, nearly making body parts of us all as the car swerved.

'He never had a finger taken off!' I cried.

Screams and denunciations.

'Well, if he did – the mad bugger – he had an anaesthetic.'

Scratching nails and hysterics.

I thought then: yes, of *course* it had been a con, like a medium raising a spirit – and I'd paid $400 to be taken in. I never learned whether or not it was a trick – but I was to discover that such atrocities could be contemplated, 6000 miles away in London, over a year later.

It was that trip down Pasadena way which made me fall out of love with America forever.

As I stared through the heavy, floor-length window-pane, one of Dan's Filipinos came forward from the terrace and slid open the doors. The evening air brushed me with a warm breath.

'Mr Buczenko,' he said, ignoring me, 'the meal ees nearly ready. Mrs Bright asks eef you would bring your drinks out with you.'

Yuri put a podgy arm on my shoulders.

'Eats, Mike. Couldn't I jus' lam into a thick steak right now. Good, there's Marsha.'

'Mike dahling. Ah have been looking forward to this.'

Marsha Bright dug her red nails into my arm and favoured me with one of her ear-banging kisses. Her Southern drawl – the product of a million cigarettes and the baking of the desert sun – always used to bubble up from her lined neck as through a soufflé of phlegm. I was sorry, but not surprised, that she was carried away by cancer in 2012.

'Oh, it's been too long, honey. Ah was just thinking of you the other day when Dan told me you were coming. It's just made things for me, Mike.'

Don't overdo it, I thought to myself.

'Enrico!' she suddenly snapped. 'Watch what you're doing with that juice! You've got some right on my table-cloth!' The Filipino straightened the dish and smiled sheepishly. 'Now Michael, honey, try one of these little burritos while Ah get Dan to put the lobsters on. Where IS Dan, anyhow?'

'Marsha, I – um – I brought Mopsa Greene along with me, and she fell into a bush from the path. Dan took her off to show her where to clean up. I think he went to find you, so you could lend her a hair-brush or something. You know, girls together.' I tried a conspiratorial grin, but her smile had ebbed noticeably at the mention of the walking thorn-bush. Then she rallied – magnificently, I thought.

'Mopsa is most welcome. Whoever you bring to *Danmar* is welcome.'

'This mother has got my name on it,' gurgled Yuri, selecting a vast lobster, ready halved and basted, and flipping his fingers at the Filipino to place it on the nearest of the Thermos grills. The terrace was filled with the rich tang of spiced butter.

'Okay, okay,' came Dan's voice – on a querulous note – 'we're all sorted now. Ah, Marsha, Mopsa's turned up.

Unexpectedly,' he added, shooting a bit of a look at me. 'She fell off the path, but she's feeling better. And, Marsha sweetie, I've lent her one of your blouses. Hers was torn and sandy.'

'You're damned right it was', snarled Mopsa. 'I'm only not SUING you because you're an old friend and gave me a job back when. That path of yours should be bull-dozed, Marsha. Anyone could jus' drop their ass right off of it.'

I tried to catch Bitch-face's eye.

Marsha managed a tense, wrinkly-brown smile.

'You are welcome to my blouse, honey,' said she.

Mopsa stared at the viands. I wondered what she was glaring at.

'Oh, I HATE lobster,' she cried. 'They're like giant insects blown up by radiation poison.'

'Well, we're all together now. How nice,' said Dan. He looked at his watch. 'Any minute, Yuri, an' Mike's gonna see why we asked him here. Let's get more lobster and some steaks on so we're ready.'

'You are being tremendously mysterious,' said I. 'I've gathered someone else is coming.'

'Any minute, son of a gun.'

'And you aren't going to tell me who it is?'

'Wouldn't want to spoil the expression on your face, my boy.'

'Oh, I know who it is,' sneered Mopsa. 'It's Val Page, isn't it? Anagram of dog, he bobs up like a corpse in the water.'

'Is it?' I asked. This Valentine Page was a studio Art Director with whom I'd struck up a friendship on *Full*

Circle, but Mopsa's dislike of him had led to our drifting out of touch.

'No, it's not,' said Dan. 'An' stop trying to guess, Mopsa. You're only doing it to spoil things, young lady – and that is not a pleasant thing to do. In any case you wouldn't get it right in a million guesses. NOBODY knows this baby. Yuri and I have only met him once. But it's where he's come from that'll amuse Mike.'

Ticked off, as if by a disapproving and elderly uncle, Mopsa was silenced. I was about to ask another question when there was a sharp peal of Dan's bell from round the front of the house. Clearly a car had circled up from below, but we hadn't heard it over the crackling of the bar-b-que.

It was now almost dark and I didn't at first see the shadowy form, led by a Filipino, coming through the playroom. Then out onto the terrace into the light the figure stepped and I uttered a gasp of astonishment.

The years had flashed by, as they do, but I immediately knew that face.

I had last looked on it in 1982. Even before I had left London, I had lost contact.

The well-remembered features broke into a grin.

I was aware of Dan and Yuri exchanging blissful glances, tickled that their little surprise had been effective.

'Sherbert!' I cried, thrusting my glass into Mopsa's hand and bounding forward.

'Bop Crepwright! And just the same!'

'Sherbert Lemon!'

'In the flesh.'

'And YOU'RE just the same too!'

'It's been about seventeen years, dear old boy.'

'I can't get over it. Sherbert in L A!'

'Good old Bop. Dan told me he had a rich Brit on ice – but you!'

'You know Dan? But of course you know Dan or you wouldn't be here. But how on earth did you meet him? Surely you're not in Dan's game!'

'Bop Crepwright!'

'Come on, Sherbert. WHY are you here?'

'I'm working on a big project in London – and Dan and I think it needs you.'

'London!'

I stared at his unchanged face: good-natured, creative, unpredictable.

There was a shrill screech from Mopsa – part amused, part possessive and hostile at having to share me, part alarmed.

'Another Brit! Now Mike's goin' to be REAL unbearable. And whaddya mean about London? You mean *going* to London?' She turned towards me. 'And WHY is he calling you Crepwright?'

Sherbert, startled for a moment, said, 'It's Mike's name, of course.'

Dan gasped, 'What do you mean? This is Mike *Greville*.'

And I, realising that it was explanation time, looked round at five surprised faces. Sherbert and Marsha clustered close about me with Dan and Yuri, but, retreating to the background, Mopsa, having asked her question about my real name and now being ignored, was, I noticed with misgivings, twisting the splines of her fork into a lobster's eyes.

Now that so much time has gone by since my flight home and her revenge, I've been able to pull back from those L A days and have come to know that there was a form of love in the possessiveness she felt for me.

Chapter 3: **I See a Way Out**

I sometimes dreamed of a London street in my last strange days in L A. I was never sure which street it was – although I know now, of course. For a long time I thought it might have been Glebe Place, that tiny arm parallel to The King's Road where I dossed in my brother's flat for a few months in the late '70s and where Anthony stunned the locals in '77 by getting Peter Buchan to bring John Lennon to supper. His Roller had filled the roadway. Peter, our childhood pal, was working at EMI's Abbey Road studios then and had the entrée into all sorts of rock celebs' lives. Anthony had gone back up to grandpa's old house, Glenturret, to teach when it briefly became a school, but he kept the Chelsea flat on for a while. After he bought Glenturret back into the family with his inheritance in 1981, he and Peter turned it into a hip recording studio for a short and disastrous time. When the studios collapsed, and money grew tight, the little Glebe Place flat was let go.

I could never see over to the other side of my dream street, but I had an impression of unusual walls and Egyptian windows. What bugged me was the near certainty that there had never been an end wall in Glebe Place. My psychiatrist told me that if you dream of large rooms or broad streets, it is a sign of unfulfilled potential; and if you dream of tight, closed spaces and high walls you are full of deep-seated, unresolved neuroses…..

Sometimes I thought my dream was of Warwick Avenue, the Clifton Gardens end, facing down towards the church with the tube station on the right. But this picture comes from earlier. It belongs to Anthony and me unwrapping Christmas presents: Hornby-Dublo trains and Corgi toys in the circle of the gas fire's glow. Dad's real candles are on the tree, the even grey sky fills our high windows, and beyond is misty, friendly London. The silent avenue used to hover on my mental retina in the Californian night.

I never see people in these visions – odd, because my life in England had been so thickly populated with vanished faces I had left behind: Nigel and Amanda, Jem and Jo-Jo, Mark, Phil, Mr Chessman, Lily, Hector McAird, Melanie, Carrie, Choo and Richard, Lucille, Wanda and Eddie May. I never saw bright sunshine either – not that endless, burning afternoon of hot smog in L A. My dream is cool as Tuesday morning in mid-term at school: calm, realistic, unhurried, unthreatening, ordinary.

When I thirsted for sleep and the wailing of L A sirens out on the hot, despairing boulevards rang in my ears, I fought to bring my quiet, sane street picture to my aid.

My other dream – and I have it still – came only on waking. It was always the same: an indistinct landscape stretching from ear to ear behind the curve of my eyeballs which seemed to roll up from the right as I regained consciousness. In it were rounded hills, a sweep of conifers dark and tall and near them, again on the right and the first to vanish as the dream rolled up, a rising series of sloping lawns with a neo-Gothic Scottish house crowning the eminence. It was Glenturret. From just after my fourth birthday until Grandpa sold up, Anthony, Ma, Dad and I travelled up from Euston to dream away the long summer holidays amid those lawns and pines.

I thought of this as my "Scottish" vision and I clung thirstily to it, telling no one of it, especially Mopsa. It was sometimes, back in '99, the last happiness I could sense before awakening fully to the squalid hum of air-conditioning, cold but smelly, and having to face another day in America.

It was to those Scottish pine-tree days of childhood that Dan's mystery guest belonged.

I sat in a trance, gazing at him.

Dan and Marsha exchanged amused glances which seemed to say: how the Brit is being carried back to little olde England.

Sherbert! I had first met him thirty-four years ago in the summer of '65. Grandpa had encouraged Anthony and me to play with him. He was "the right sort" and Grandpa was a terrific snob about things like that. Sherbert's father, I seemed to recall, had been the land agent for the local Tory MP and was Grandpa's neighbour. Before we began to be inseparable friends, united by Anthony's older-brother tyranny in our gang, Sherbert had had to undergo revolting initiation ceremonies. This was because he had curly fair hair and popping blue eyes. His eyes no longer seemed to pop, and his hair, with just a trace of "silver threads among the gold", as Anthony always puts it, was no longer as curly. With a shock, I realised he was exactly my age, but he looked younger.

'Sherbert! My God! Do you remember The Cone?'

'Where your Bruv, Peter Buchan and Hector dangled me

head-down over a pyramid of cow dung? Oh yes,' he went on, turning to the others, 'you don't forget a thing like that.'

'Cow dung?' said Dan.

'A sort of gang bravery test, being dangled upside down on a rope from a tree above a cone of farm animal crap. I passed with flying colours: not a squeal, but you…!'

'The gardener, Barable, came roaring over and Anthony, Hector, Peter and YOU belted off and let go the rope.'

'Ha, ha!' roared Sherbert. 'Poor old Bop. Squelch! Head first, right in it!'

I was aware again of the blank stares around us under Dan's patio lighting.

'Sorry,' I grinned. 'This,' said I, 'is Sherbert-Lemon, my oldest and dearest pal from the far-off days in Scotland.'

'Why do you call Mike Bop?' asked Dan.

'Can I tell them, Mike? Bop is short for Bottom Of Pile. Youngest in our gang.'

'Only by a month, you hierarchical git,' I smiled.

'What – er – what kinda name is Sherbert-Lemon?' asked Mopsa. 'If you'll pardon my saying,' she added. Sherbert's calm presence seemed to have had an effect on her. Almost polite, I thought, and seemed to have forgotten about the bush.

'Aha,' said Sherbert, with a great deal of assurance and ease. 'My name is only a jolly jape from childhood.'

'Jape?'

'Or whacky Wheeze from infancy.'

'Wheeze?'

'Mopsa,' I murmured. 'Don't repeat every word.'

'Whaddya mean "jolly jape" an' "whacky wheeze"? I don' get it.'

'My name,' explained Sherbert, 'is a PUN on my surname...'

'Which is...?' prompted Mopsa.

'Oh yes, I'm sorry,' broke in Dan. 'Let me interdooce you, Dave. Marsha, Mopsa, this is David Sherwin-Lemond, known, I now gather, in his formative years as Sherbert Lemon.'

Sherbert shook hands with Mopsa, beaming at us all, and receiving double-strength beams from Marsha in return.

'Well, okay, okay, folks,' cried Mopsa, waving a fork in a devil-may-care manner, 'but jes' WHAT kinda name is Sherwin-Lemond?'

'Mopsa, it's a *British* name,' said Dan, as if that were explanation enough. 'What they call double-barrelled over there.'

'Oh yup – like Laurel and Hardy,' said Mopsa.

'But, Sherbert, dear friend of my "salad days", as Anthony calls them, what on EARTH are you doing in America? In L A? In Bel-Air? In Dan's house? And what's this project? Come on, Dan, Yuri – explain!'

Dan continued to smirk at Yuri, tickled no doubt by this display of Britishness, by double-barrelled nicknames, by "jolly" and "dear boy". I felt irritated for a moment that somehow Sherbert and I had dropped effortlessly into our assigned parts of Brit fruitcakes for the entertainment of the Yanks.

'All will be revealed,' said Dan.

'But first,' purred Marsha, 'let's eat. Enrico, give our

guest a drink. Sit, people, sit. Enrico! Open the wine! Oh, and Enrico, turn up the patio lights, and when you've done that, leave us. We can help ourselves, ah guess.'

The Californian night settled further on us. Up on the heights a thousand bar-b-ques burned and a generation of lobsters died. Big insects clattered round Dan's patio lights while Marsha drawled, Mopsa squealed, Yuri rumbled and Dan yapped. Sherbert, at ease, with elegant cream trousers crossed, balanced a well-filled plate on the arm of his chair. He seemed to accept the fact of a meeting which struck me as miraculous. That we, who had eaten jam sandwiches in that distant heather in the priceless past, should be brought together in Bel-Air in the stale present, was too momentous for speech.

'Yes, Dan's told me all about you, Mike,' said Sherbert, collaring the air-waves. There was something about his clear RP English tones which dominated the others, louder though they were. 'You've done jolly well out here, I gather. Abso-blooming-lutely rolling, Dan says. AND you look marvellous, old bean – well, not a day over forty at any rate! I saw Anthony at Christmas, you know, so I've had news about you at his end. He's a bit miffed that you haven't been in contact as often as you used to be. "When is he coming to see us" is the cry of the moment at Glenturret. And he says it's three years since you went over to see your Ma in Italy. I shouldn't be surprised if they all decide to do a Mohammed and come to the mountain – so watch out!'

He laughed and forked in some salad. I had last seen him at Dominic's restaurant in the King's Road in 1982.

'Is Dominic's still going?' I asked suddenly.

'Dominic's? Dominic who?'

'Dominic's restaurant – round the corner from Glebe Place in The King's Road. You remember.'

'Oh, yes. Yes, of course. No, it's gone. Went some time back. They pushed the rents up too high or something.'

'You weren't at my inheritance celebration night, were you? My dinner with Anthony and Lucille at the Savoy. I've thought once or twice that you were there, but ……..'

'Not me, Mike.'

'I am sorry Sherbert. I don't know what happened at that time, or why we'd lost touch. I was having trouble with several people then…' my voice trailed off.

'You were ratty with me because I was trying to stop you making a complete prat of yourself over Lucille. Never mind. My fault, I expect. But you're right about Dominic's. We did eat there quite a bit. And at Asterix and at The Stockpot. They're still going.'

'My God! the Stockpot! The pauper's Great White Hope. And as for Lucille….'

He had touched a dim, dim nerve; and I felt like someone hearing a bell ring in a far corner of a huge building. Lucille had been one of my reasons for going to America.

'I wonder what's happened to her.' said I, thinking of that brash London dolly-bird.

'Who's Lucille, exactly?' asked Mopsa, harshly joining in the two-sided conversation.

'An old, old friend in London, Mopsa. It didn't work out.'

'Obviously – as I ain't heard of her,' grunted Mopsa. I saw Sherbert fix her with a level gaze for a moment. I was sure he was thinking that I still lacked the knack of choosing women well.

'Mopsa is into Conceptual Art,' I said. She's an Excremental Kineticist.' Sherbert made a non-committal sound and took a swig from his glass.

'I DO like American beer,' he said.

'AND,' continued Mopsa, 'What is this about crep right?'

'I still can't think of you as anything other than Crepwright. How could I after thirty years?'

'Ha, ha! Ah, You mean Mike craps right? And how do you know? Joke, guys. Jokie,' smirked Mopsa – all roguey.

'Oh, blimey, Mopsa. It's nothing. Nothing. Give over on the jokie-pokies.' I looked round at Dan, Marsha and Yuri – still waiting, as was Sherbert, for that explanation about Crepwright. 'I changed my name, that's all.'

Mopsa gave a gasp.

'Oh, I see. Hey, what an evening of revelations THIS is. First you gotta London girlfriend, now you're Mr Mystery Man with half-a-dozen false names.'

I was aware of Dan's elevated eyebrows, of Marsha's surprised stare, of Yuri's plump derisive grin.

'It was just for biz purposes – when I was in New York for a while. It was all part of starting again, of being a new me. That's the long and short of it.'

'Don't blame you, Bop,' said Sherbert stoutly. 'Crepwright's even worse than Sherwin-Lemond.'

'There's a lot in a name in my line of work,' said I.

'Crikey, Mopsa, you going on about crapping right so *wittily* back then just convinces me I did the right thing.'

'Yeah, I guess I unnerstand. My pappy was called Breitolowski. Bright was easier,' agreed Dan. 'And as for B.O.P – well, time plays strange tricks. 'Mike's a rich big-shot now.'

I was feeling a strong urge to turn the conversation from myself.

'We've covered me,' I said strongly. 'So now it's someone else's turn to explain WHAT Sherbert is doing here.'

'Yeah, you're an even bigger mystery man than Mikey,' articulated Mopsa through a mouthful of cheesecake. 'Anyone gets an invite to Dan's place up here just has to be a guy Dan wants to get somethin' out of.'

Dan narrowed his eyes at her.

'You're here, and I guess I want nothin' from you,' he said, without a trace of humour.

'Naaah, but then I wasn't ackcherlie invited, from the expression on your face when I got outa your bush!'

'Girls, girls,' murmured Marsha. 'David, will you take the floor now and put poor Mike out of his misery?'

'No, I'LL tell him,' cried Dan, jerking his old frame out of its chair,' because I want to put it so Mike can't refuse what we are going to ask him. Right, Yuri?'

'Oooch, groogh, yup, ooogh,' gurgled Yuri, caught with half a pound of steak in his podgy neck.

'Mike,' resumed Dan. 'You clearly do not know what David has been doing for the last – what is it, Dave? – six, seven, eight years. If you visited England more often, or even just visited once, you would have seen something produced and directed on TV by Dave. You turn on some Brit intellectual radio station and you'll hear Dave talking about his latest with a panel of critics. Am I right, Dave?'

'Well,' smiled my old pal, 'Put on Beeb 2, Channel 4 or Radio 3 and I'm there strutting my stuff – but then eighty per cent of the good old Brit public wouldn't be listening or watching because they're looking at an Aussie import on ITV. Dan slightly over-estimates my influence, I fear. I'm an acquired taste – like scrofula – and a member of a tiny intellectual elite; but that's fine by me because I believe that elites should, by definition, be small.'

'Oh, jeez, I can never get used to you Brits being so modest,' went on Dan. 'Who won a prize at Cannes for that interpretation of *"Shirley"*. Who won awards with that series on India with Nawab Singh? Who scooped a BAFTA with *"The First Day of my Life"?*'

'Sounds high-brow,' frowned Marsha.

'What's *"Shirley"*?' asked Mopsa.

'Novel by Charlotte Bronte,' replied Sherbert.

'Who's Char - ?' began Mopsa.

'Highbrow, my ass,' interrupted Dan. 'We're talking class programming here. Which is why, Dave, we can go on to Part Two an' tell Mike what your latest project is, can't we?'

'I'll break it to him,' replied Sherbert. 'Top up our glasses to the very brim and "we'll sit upon the ground and tell stories of the death of kings"....'

'You sound like Anthony. He's always saying that sort of thing. In fact he often comes out with that very one.

Shakespeare, I suppose?'

'Right on the wicket. Ricky II.'

Below us, L A flamed in rushing red lights and smog-softened neon. The cicadas were insistent and the night air hot.

Marsha got up.

'I'll go get cawfee,' she said. 'I know what's coming next.'

'Right,' said Sherbert. 'Time for details. Yuri and Dan here are going in big-big on a joint project for BBC2, WGBH Boston and Radio Italiana, as well as PSB here. Guess who will be director in chief?'

'You?'

'Yup. Kubrik's dead, Scorsese lacks my touch and Spielberg turned it down.'

'Ho, ho. And its theme?'

'Political and cultural, and it's going to feature twelve self-contained docu-dramas examining Britain as the American cultural base in Europe, the decline and metamorphosis of America culture – the "drive-thru' museum" idea of the US and its distance from the rise of the new European and Chinese world identity.'

'G –O –D! Sorry, Mopsa – I mean, bloody hell – you'll need a hundred episodes to cover a theme like that.'

'My idea is that we take the strictly Victorian approach. That is to say, we use fictive and metaphorical material to get over the moral, artistic and political points.'

Yuri grinned delightedly.

'Will you jus' listen to him! WGBH love the whole fine idea!'

'Mike, when I tell you that Len Culdenbringer *and* Adrian Booker are leading the scriptwriting teams, you'll realise we mean biz.'

I had no idea who these guys were at the time, but I didn't admit it to Sherbert. I stuck to what I did know and asked,

'So it's going to be expensive?'

'Yup. Top presenters involved. Top scriptwriters and top fees going to the writers whose scripts are being adapted.'

'So you want money?'

'Yus.'

'And it really will make the fifteen per cent I expect out of investment?'

'Can't fail.'

'Would I be in if it didn't make dough?' rumbled Yuri.

'Where are you filming all this?'

'In Europe, starting in London, at Ealing and Leavesden, and then over to Rome, then Paris and, in late-2000, Poland. It will cost more than seven million dollars, but we three have a lot of backing already.'

'But you could do with a bit more?'

'That – in a nutshell, Bop – is why you're here,' smiled Sherbert.

Marsha ushered in a Filipino who wheeled a big trolley over to us with coffee, fruit and chocolates on it.

'Cawfee, Mr Sherwin-Lemond?' she purred. 'and won't you try a See's molasses Chip? Our local chocolate company, y'know? And Mike?'

I stood up and had the oddest sensation.

I seemed to be looking out of our high windows across Warwick Avenue in the morning and the snow was falling. Back in the winter of 1963, a man, they said, had driven a car across the frozen Thames at Richmond. Going to Christmas Mass with Ma up at Lisson Grove had been an arctic expedition, for the snow lay over a foot deep. Every year after '63 I prayed it would be like that again. Across London the peaked roofs and chimney stacks were plumped white. There was not a single sound, even from The Edgware Road. Near the window a starling ruffled its rainbow feathers on a black branch. Further up Clifton Gardens a humped vehicle – a sidecar outfit, I think - was buried in snow. My fingers nipped with chill, but a scent of sausages was coming up from below. The silence of Little Venice imprinted my soul. I was happy. I was in dear old London.

Sherbert's face floated back in the California night. Marsha's deep, gurgling laugh replaced the winter starling's squeak. Back came the roar from far-away Santa Monica Boulevard.

Did I really want to sink money in some arty political TV project of Sherbert's? Would I really make a decent return? For a second I saw Sherbert as he was in our youth: popping-eyed, curly-haired, unpredictable, and wondered at the backing he said he had received already.

Yet – London! They were going to film at Ealing. There had never been a satisfactory reason for not leaving for London at any time since 1996. A sense of responsibility for Mopsa, a stasis born of depression and increasing introspection, the habit of work – these had kept me in L A.

But now.......

I found myself saying, 'I will put up some money. But on one condition: I come to London to get involved.'

Dan broke in, 'Ah, Mike – that isn't necessary.'

'Sorry, Dan. I put up a lot of cash for *"Full Circle"* and was left in the cold.'

'But I never realised..... I mean, hell, Mike, you're not a movie man, so I jus' thought...'

'I want,' I insisted, 'more involvement than my name appearing in small letters in the Associate Producer list.'

A grating screech heralded the entry of Mopsa into the dialogue.

'What! – So you think you are gonna leave L A – leave *me* – and go back to *London*?'

Sherbert spoke, not exactly ignoring her, but looking beyond her.

'Okay with me. I think you'd enjoy coming home for a while.'

I spoke, not exactly ignoring her either, but speaking across her to Sherbert and Dan.

'Right. You have a deal.'

In the sudden incandescent blaze of happiness that irradiated me, I should have taken more note of how Mopsa was taking this, and been a little less dimly aware that she had, for about five seconds, rocked to and fro with her eyeballs turned up so that the whites seemed to dance, and had then said not a single word more until a screeching tirade began in the car on the way back to the condo. But you know what? I didn't listen to the tumbling words, or heed the flying spit.

Chapter Four: **The Glass Elevator**

It was midnight in L A, one week later.

Georgie had gone to New Orleans with Jonathan Pig-tail Weirdo. The "Living-Sculpture-Which-Consisted-Of-Sitting-Up-To-Your-Neck-In-Rotting-Giblets" exhibition had ended. Mopsa prowled and moped, muttering. She had taken to wrapping things in cling-film. She tried to interest me in the work of that guy Christo, who used to wrap cars and buses. She showed me an article about how he had wrapped an office block in paper and string. He wanted to wrap a river from its source to the sea, but couldn't find a short enough one in the USA, so he hoped to get better luck in England. Yesterday, in silence, Mopsa had thrust a picture of a Yorkshire beck under my nose. This did not fire me with an interest in Christo, but led me into a reverie about Britain and memories of cool, often damp days in the heather at Glenturret.

The mad bitch had wrapped a mouse in cling-film but, in spite of the hole she had left for its nose, it had died. She wrapped every pen, spoon, bottle, ashtray, glass and piece of soap in the apartment. She found a big box of drawing-pins and started on that, trying not to pierce the film with the points, so that every surface had tiny replicas of Explorer satellites on it.

Sherbert had flown back East for talks in Boston and rang to say he wanted to introduce me to the writing team in New York on the 20th.

I watched Mopsa with sidelong eyes after I told her this. Not one word had been spoken by either of us for five days

– not since she had specifically forbidden me even to THINK of leaving her and going with Sherbert to Europe.

'You are NOT going, you bastard!' she had screamed in the car on the way back from Dan's bar-b-que. She had been silent until we were crossing Langley Boulevard, then she had grabbed at my arm and screeched, nearly causing an accident.

'For God's sake!' I had cried. 'Will you watch what you're doing, you hysterical fool! And as for going to London, well, why not? Why on EARTH not?'

'I won't talk about it! I won't! I won't! I WON'T! What about your life here? Your life with me? Your life is here!'

'Let's be honest, shall we? Here is just where my life ISN'T at the moment. I haven't done any real work since that publishing offices let at Belmont. And why haven't I? Because I've lost interest in the whole damn thing. I've got money. I don't want any more. What's the point of going on and on and on? That's all people do in this damned country – work, work, work. And what FOR? I'm not DOING it for anyone. In the past I did it for myself, then, I suppose, for us; now there's no point in any of it. So I might as well take up an interesting offer.'

'Don't give me that offer-schmoffer crap! You wanna get away from me, doncha? DONCHA? That's what it is! From ME – after all I've done for you!'

'"Done for me", she says! WHAT have you done for me in the last two-three years? You've got high on my money, you'll filled our place with your sick rubbish. Your friends are a pack of fake, mentally-disturbed animals. CHRIST knows what you get up to with Georgie! Oh yes, you think

I don't know about you and Georgie! You – you go on and on about ART, ART day and night. Ye Gods, you thick cow, you wouldn't know real art if you studied it for a century!'

'Just because you meet that smoothie British prick....'

'That prick and I were friends more than twenty years before I had the misfortune to meet you. Don't spout loyalties at me.'

Then she had started crying, in a halting, snivelling way that I always found self-dramatising and affected.

'Sniff!....But....wha.....what.....about....US?'

I hardened my heart, like Pharoah of old. I should have remembered that her long bouts of substance abuse had unbalanced her, but I just felt again that moment when Sherbert's eyes had rested on her and then on me – and the embarrassment of feeling judged.

'US! What is LEFT of US? I'LL tell you what "US" is. it's pain, sneers, violence, watchfulness....it's no....no room to be happy....' To my amazement, I had found my voice shaking with a genuine emotion – although part of me was enjoying the easy flow of words. After all, Mopsa and I *had* once been happy.

Tears had started to pour down her face.

'But....but....Mike, Mike....how has....it....been all my fault?'

'Well, Mopsa dear, you haven't been quite yourself recently.'

At the absurd respectability of that doctorish sentence, its ludicrous understatement, Mopsa appeared to de-shrivel in her seat. Mentally I gave her a full card of brownie points as she rallied.

'Ooooo! Not MAISELF recently? Not mai-self? And what's "myself" when it's at home? Let me tell you, dog-face, that I AM MORE MYSELF than I have been for years. You just don' want me to fulfil myself. Well, let me say this, because this is what's at the bottom of all this crap: I'M fulfilled an' you're NOT. THAT'S what's wrong with you, Mister Envious Loser.'

A shrewd hit.

She was right. In a bizarre way, she did have a direction, a reason to get up in the morning, whereas I....

I moved on to another tack.

'That's another thing I hate about you these days. Your language is often vulgar and your voice always shrill.' With the unerring accuracy of the practised hurter I thrust home with that sharp spear which only I possessed and against which she raged impotently – my British snobbery. 'You seem,' I drawled, with flared nostrils, 'to have forgotten completely how to behave like a lady.'

She gasped.

'Like a lady! LAIKE A BLOOMIN' LAIDEEE? Listen, God! God, GOD, listen to him! You...you British little bastard! And IF you was a gentleman, baby, you'd know what gentlemen are supposed to do now and then, except that your aristocratic little prick can never seem to get up and DO it! Never!'

This was very true. But I had my answer and shouted,

'Oh, and you're SO appealing, covered in dead meat, or or drugged up to your eyeballs, and so – so obsessed with that depraved, revolting, mentally-retarded, perverted, lesbian freak, Georgie!'

Mopsa had grabbed the wheel of the auto.

'I'm gonna kill us both. You deserve to die for what you've gone and said – AN' YOU ARE GOING TO DIE!'

I had been compelled to punch her full in the mouth to regain control of the steering-wheel. Blood had spurted over my knuckles from her lips.

So.

So now she wrapped increasingly tiny objects, her face still bruised.

Two days after that, on the eve of my departure for New York, she started howling. I had decided – God knows why – that she could have the apartment. I knew I would never be coming back and she probably knew it too, though I had said nothing of my plans.

She howled all evening – an appalling test of my reason – with the long-drawn howl of a whipped and solitary dog. I tried to ignore it. I put the TV on over it, but the dual cacophony was more than I could bear. She howled all night and all morning, rocking to and fro, her voice husky, on the living-room floor. I had slipped out to put the Jag up for sale and to tell the agency over in the Rondo district that I did not need their cleaners anymore; I knew Mopsa would never pay them. She seemed not to have noticed that I had popped out, even though I had been busy for three hours. When I got back she was still at it, lying on the carpet, saliva dripping down her chin, her heels drumming. The timbre of the howls had changed as her voice roughened – she sounded now like a cow with bursting udders. Thank God I no longer had to face the neighbours.

'Are you STILL making that absurd noise?' I said coldly.

She dashed spit away and jerked up.

'Oh, Mikey, please, please, if you gotta go, take me with you. You NEED me over there. Remember how it used to be? Remember what I used to do in the past? I'll do it again. Hey, I'll be your slave. Whatever you want I'll do it! Christ! I mean Anagram of dog, Mike! You can't just LEAVE like this – I mean leave all this frigging stuff. You can't jus' frigging leave. What about ME? What's gonna happen to me? Okay, okay, you bastard, so you gotta go. Mister Big-Shot Producer is too important nowadays to bother about little bits of nothing like me. Yeah, ye-aaah, is that it? Yaaah! That's IT! You're jus' too good for poor Mopsa now. Oh, Mikey, no. Mikey, I din' mean that. Hey, oh Chri -, Oh, look, I din' mean…. I dunno what got into me. Okay, you gotta go. I see that. It's – It's business. An' you wanna go back for a visit. That's natural. You're not an American, after all. I think you SHOULD go….but….but….take me with you. Let me come. Jesus God! I swear if you don' let me come, I'll….I'll….'

'You are not coming, Mopsa. You don't belong there. Get up and act your age. You look ridiculous squatting on the carpet.'

She bounded to her feet like a squeegee ball. She drew a deep breath – presumably to start all over again.

I went to my bedroom, opened the wardrobe and drew out the small travel cases I had previously packed. I hadn't let the bitch see them being filled. She would have known they had the stamp of farewell on them. There was the album of photographs, my copy of *"Londoners"*, the Mont Blanc pen which had been given me at the conclusion of my first property deal back East, my old school tie, a brochure from the Morgan Car Company, my old albums of *"Dark Side of the Moon"*, *"Tubular Bells"* and *"Music for the Queen's 1977 Jubilee"*, a guide book to New York – a present from Dan Bright who came from the Lower East Side and was as fond of the *idea* of New York as I was of London, and a few shirts and toiletries. Everything else I could buy on arrival.

I put the cases in the vestibule and came into the living-room.

'Well, I'm going, Mopsa. I'll ring you from New York.' (Like hell, I thought.)

She had a heavy crystal vase in her hand.

'Whaddaya mean?' she cried. 'Your plane doesn't go 'til tomorrow morning. Where are you going tonight?'

That was a point I hadn't quite decided upon. An airport hotel was better than another night in the nut-house.

There was a peal on the bell. The cab I had surreptitiously ordered had arrived, bang on cue.

'Ooooooooooh!' screamed Mopsa. 'First Georgie, then you! Everyone's leaving me! Everyone!'

She hurled the large vase in my direction through a free-standing bookcase which divided the room. Rather remarkably, it went right between the shelves without hitting anything and plumped unbroken onto a deep sofa behind me. I was glad it would live to see another day; it had cost me $400.

'You're risking it all being an anti-climax,' said I. 'I'd leave the discus throwing there, if I were you. Goodbye.'

And I was gone.

I seemed to have done it at last.

In the cab I felt those evanescent shackles which had bound me to Los Angeles dropping away. The curse of being self-employed is that you never stop networking and hunting new opportunities because you imagine that each deal will be your last. However much dough you pile up, when you sit down to calculate how long it would last if you lived, pension-less but in luxury, until ninety, it never seems enough. That's why, rich though everyone thought me, I hadn't taken a vacation for years, had seldom seen Ma in Italy or Anthony at Glenturret, but had ploughed on. During the United flight to Kennedy I thought over and over how strange and wonderful it had been to see Sherbert again, and, through him, to be free. I had, in the end, spent my last night in California on a couch at the airport. There was no discernible reason why I should have done this, but I guess I felt it too was part of that process of letting go. Successful guys of forty, I realised, have lost the knack of coping with discomfort, but on my new journey of going forward into the past, I was twenty again – even though stiff, unshaven and headachy. In the muzziness was the thought that I wouldn't have met Sherbert if it hadn't been for Dan, and that was all down to "*Full Circle*", (appropriate title), and that if I hadn't visited the set during the filming for it I wouldn't have met Mopsa, and if I hadn't met Mopsa I wouldn't be leaving....

It all went round and round, mingling with the muffled

roar of the jet engines (invented by Frank Whittle: British) until I slept.

'This is Adrian.'

Sherbert met me, all smiles, at the airport. With him was a plumpish, dipping-and-ducking type with dusty spectacles and eager, wet lips. I could feel him appraising me; pity I looked like a hobo.

'Adrian Booker,' simpered this individual, holding my hand limply and beaming.

'Adrian,' said Sherbert, 'is lynch-pin of the writing-team. I believe we're really lucky to have you on the project, Adrian. He's with me, Mike, because we've been in conference all day with the screen-writers and we're giving him a lift.'

He ushered us out to the high-ramped roadway which the United terminal building shared with other airlines into the muggy afternoon air where an enormous white limo pumped a haze of exhaust.

'Good Lord!' I gasped. 'We're not getting into that, are we?' I had managed to avoid riding in a "stretch" during all my time in L A.

'We are,' laughed Sherbert. 'All those times you wondered who the pretentious plonkers were who went round in thirty-foot long gas guzzlers – well, it's people like you: rich, executive associate producers.' He turned to Adrian. 'He's r-o-l-l-i-n-g,' he spelt out silently, mouthing each letter.

'Fancy,' said Adrian. He evidently didn't think I looked filthy rich.

'You're English too,' I said to the famous script-writer (well, not famous to me, of course, as I'd never heard of him; but clearly well-regarded by those who were in the know). My comment must have come out like an accusation, for he gave a series of nervous titters and his long fingers fluttered around the thick spectacle frames.

'Oh, we're most of us Brits on the editing and commissioning team, Mike,' said Sherbert, before Adrian could make a response. 'Except, that is, for Len Culdenbringer, of course, and Renzo, oh and Holly Miall – she's from California – and Lee-Ann Gagliano. Pongo Vine is British.'

That was the first time I heard Holly's name uttered, and, naturally, what came to mean so much to me meant nothing at all in that long car in New York.

'How many writers have you roped in, Sherbert?'

'Seven. Why, does that seem a lot? Believe me, you should regard it as positively manageable. I had over twenty contributors on my series about Serbia and Kosovo.'

'So this Pongo Vine, and Adrian here, and you and I, are British, and the other five – sorry, seven, counting Dan and Yuri – aren't?' said I. 'Oh well, four out of eleven isn't too bad.'

'Oh, it seemed more,' said Sherbert. 'Anyway, you and I are Brits, Mike, so we can apply the right tone and standards to the enterprise.'

'Tee, hee, hee!'

Adrian giggled frantically at this piece of whimsy. 'Yes', he gibbered. 'Bringing what you call "clAss" over here:

with the "a" to rhyme with "ankle". Tee, hee, hee, hee.' He looked unduly pleased with this mildest of not very original quips. I hoped his scripts were better.

'Where are we going?' I asked.

Bump – bump went the car. The hot suburban streets flickered past. Weighty, soft-sprung Lincolns floated with us over the pot-holes. Hairy men with round bellies thrust under their chrome and plastic steering-wheels stared ahead with jutting under-lips or picked their noses. Californians drive more Jap and European cars than back East, and are more careful about The Body Beautiful. Personally, I was quite pleased to see a bit of honest ugliness for a change. Neurotic beauty isn't restful. Our own driver was invisible behind a fake mahogany coloured panel.

'How does he see out behind?' I asked.

'He doesn't bother,' replied Sherbert. 'Drink? He flicked open the lid of a lit cabinet and fished out three glasses, ice and a bottle.

'Beer, perhaps,' I said. 'Just a Bud, or something.'

Adrian poured himself a brandy. This seemed to be in character, but I had no idea why I should have thought this, as I didn't know what his character was.

'"Never mix, never worry",' he said, sipping coyly.

'Ah, "*Who's Afraid of Virginia Woolf*",' smiled Sherbert – a comment I found very cryptic.

'Well, Sherbert, where ARE we going?'

'Adrian's getting out at Grand Central and I'm taking you to the Waldorf Astoria. Lucky old you – you've got one of the top suites. Richard Burton once stayed there.'

'Yes, and look what happened to him. So, VIP

treatment, eh?' I smiled. 'Fancy you doing a series about Serbia, Sherbert. I never saw that. I mean, it never appeared in L A, I don't think.'

'Well, it wouldn't, would it? It was for Auntie.'

'Auntie? Oh yes – the BBC.'

'Auntie Beeb – the old frump,' giggled Adrian.

'Yes,' I found myself saying austerely, for I didn't like hearing Adrian knock her, 'I'd forgotten we used to call her Auntie. It's been so long. I do hope I qualify for this British part of your team, Sherbert, old boy.'

'Of course you do. There – you called me "old boy". What Yank would have said that?'

Breakfast at the Waldorf was varied and excessive. I can hardly put into words the strange turmoil that churned in me as I let the air and spores of the Eastern seaboard soak into my skin. Around me were the snappy Italo-American accents of Brooklyn and the Bronx, the cool clip of New England. My ear ceased to be muddied by Californian baby-talk. You aren't aware of being on the ocean in the centre of New York, but knowing that the Statue of Liberty was barely a mile or two away, I felt I was already as good as in Europe. Until you escape the centrifugal pull of L A, you don't realise that it's as shattering to fly out of as a black hole. So much myth keeps you there: the myth that the cancer-inducing sunshine is good for you, that the choked freeways are letting you speed to your dreams, that the cruel desert and the merciless earthquake faults can be magicked out of worry by the sustenance of illusion.

It had been all so tiring, living in that children's nursery for fractious grown-ups where the economic miracle, even then, was fading into a third world with swimming pools. Somewhere in Toytown on the Pacific rim, Mopsa was probably wrapping things in cling-film and hoping to put her kinetic art show on again, climbing into a zinc bath slimy with putrescent chicken guts. Somewhere in West Hollywood devotees of the street art movement were thumbing through "L A Weekly" in search of tonight's outrageous sensation, or gazing with naïve sincerity at the Gay Video channel for its news and views. Somewhere, under the smoggy glare of neon, those terrified people – whose fear of death is as ignoble as ungoverned glands – were partying with lost, desperate, raucous cries of enjoyment. Unhappiness (like obesity, poverty and not knowing someone who knows Tom Cruise) was, in 1999, one of the Hollywood Seven Sins.

An intelligent-looking bell-hop came hurrying through the salon crying, 'Mr Michael Greville! A message for Mr Greville!'

'Here!' I called.

'Sir,' said he, pushing into my hand a message from the desk. It was from Sherbert. A car was coming to pick me up at ten-thirty to waft me to the script-writers' meeting.

When you work free-lance for big money, you can never fail to answer a letter or email, a fax or call. If you do, you offend – and/or you lose out. My mobile, then, in '99, rang all weekend, in bed and in the john. I developed a hearty, bluff, fake-interested phone voice – full of roguery and mild *double-entendre* for a woman, full of *bonhomie* and name-dropping for a man. I was vulnerable but inviolable, visible and available, but lonely. I was in that glass elevator – always going up, always on view, fearful of stepping off.   As I waited for the auto, I felt myself going hot and cold when I reflected that I had not responded to calls for forty-eight hours, that I had notified some contacts that I would not be available for six months. I felt like puking when I stopped to think that I had let the Royal Greville office to an importer of CD players. I had given EVERYTHING up!

And for what?

You know the stereotypical picture of a man back East on the verge of a breakdown, who wants only to stop and discover himself in Cali-forn-eye-ay in a noo future in the sun? Here was perverse me, whizzing in the other direction, giving up a life under the palms to return to the cloudy Britain I had left sixteen years ago; a sort of Ellis Islander in reverse, tearing back in the direction of the dawn to rediscover myself.

Well, I had wanted to halt the glass elevator and peer over the rail at the little floors serried beneath. And having got the taste for looking down, I wanted to reverse the elevator and get off at those fascinating floors, past which I had flitted so blithely in my greedy trajectory towards riches, and discover what lay on them. I would be going, not forwards into an unknown, but backwards into my partially-understood yesterdays to make sense of all that had happened up to the present. 'Never job backwards', Grandpa used to say, and no one had agreed more heartily with him than I. Anthony, at Glenturret, had, since I left for the USA, made a life's work (until it all went pffft) of jobbing back: preserving the past in lacquer. Every object – every box, jar, cigarette packet, toy, tin, lampshade, vehicle, can-opener, pen, radio, tool, penknife, pamphlet, catalogue, photograph and instruction sheet – acted as a tape-recorder of the lost past of the 20th century. Anthony had his being in a universe where cars wore fins, locomotives ran on steam, hi-fi on valves and packs were made of cardboard. And watching him become like this in the late '80s and early '90s, I thought he seemed a sad case, bottled up in the image of a lost cosmos, like one of his faded specimens.

Now I wondered if he had always been right. When first in New York, in 1983, I felt I'd left an imprisoning era behind me and was free of it. By that late summer of '99 I longed to re-knit the severed strands to the past.

We were three hundred feet up on Fifth Avenue. We sat in capacious chairs round a massy light-wood table. In front of each of us was a tray of Diet Coke, English Buxton Spring water, fresh juice, Graham crackers and Planter's peanuts. A bright, yellowy glare streamed in through sun-filter blinds. I had looked down at the street when I had first come into the room. The Guggenheim Museum on the corner of 88th squatted far below, like a fat white toad. It had rained, violently with thunder, at ten o'clock and Fifth Avenue glittered away into the steamy distance. Thirty-seven floors above the tarmac the air-con whirred and it was cool.

I peered round the table at the assembled mob.

There seemed to be dozens of people in the room. Each was fiddling with a mound of papers. The air smelt of copper and sunlight-through-glass.

I felt nervy and redundant – that old *"Full Circle"* sensation.

No one had spoken to me; some had nodded. Adrian, who sidled in just after me, giggled and let his hands flutter round his mouth.

The door opened with a sudden gush of voices. Sherbert whisked in, followed by Dan Bright and a lovely, purposeful young woman in a sleek, light-grey suit.

'Morning! Morning!' chirruped Sherbert. 'Remain seated. "No ceremony, no courtship" – feel free to relax, even though your primary instinct is to leap to your feet, go through debasement and then remain standing as in the presence of a god. It's all quite understandable. MIKE! Tip-top! You're here! Well DONE! And who's missing? Adrian? No, you're there behind the astronomical telescopes. Len? Pongo? Yup, all present and correct. Mike, a thousand times welcome and all that jazz. Let me introduce you.'

He bounded round to my side of the table.

'Hi-ya, Mike,' smiled Dan, dropping into a chair. I beamed at him. With Sherbert's arrival, the atmosphere had suddenly become easy and informal. Even though I was reminded of two of his characteristics which I had forgotten – namely, a desire to show off and a fear of silences – I thought he displayed a masterly talent for injecting warmth into a clump of unpromising-looking people. The vast mob which had seemed to fill the room when I had first arrived resolved itself into a group of eight.

'THIS is Mike Greville,' cried Sherbert, banging the table with a Diet Coke. 'Mike is a property dealer from Los Angeles, but he has wide interests in the film and TV industries and an inexhaustible knowledge of cultural affairs, thanks to his connections in the modern art movement. We have been friends for over thirty years AND, most important of all, he is a multi – (it is multi, isn't it, Mike?) millionaire!'

At this hearty endorsement I remember them all beaming at me in turn.

'Hi.'

'Hiya!'

'Yo!'

'Hello again.' (Titter, titter, flutter, flutter.)

'The Man with the Money, eh?'

'Greetings!'

'You don't have to be as mad as Dave, but it helps.'

'Oh,' said Sherbert. 'And this is Holly Miall.' He put his arm across sleek grey shoulders and propelled the lovely girl toward me. 'She is our script administrator. Very bright girl, Holly. Not a locations expert like Renzo or Lee-Ann, but she has a wonderful eye for detail.'

She grinned frankly at me. I liked that grin.

'Not THAT bright or I wouldn't be working for David. But in the recession, you know...'

She shook my hand. I noticed that her hair was a honey brown, her face open and delicately tanned a shade below that of walnut coffee cake, the front teeth were large and white in a handsome boy's sort of way and the eyes had slight dark smudges under them, but were direct and clear.

Living with Mopsa and failing to avoid her friends had accustomed me to the zombie look – so this Holly made a vivid impact.

'Mike, take a chair,' boomed Dan.

I slipped into a seat between Holly and Len Culdenbringer, whom I immediately thought of as a J. Edgar Hoover lookalike. He held out his hand for me to shake it.

'I've done some scenarios set in Eastern Europe. Used to be Washington Post correspondent in Berlin before I took up script-writing. Call me Len, right?'

'Ladies an' Shentlemen!' bawled Sherbert over a melee of voices, once again banging on the table with a bottle. 'I think we must resolve this now. I'm sorry, Holly, but I have to agree with Adrian that Pongo's idea is the best one. Mike,' he said, turning to me, 'there's some difference of opinion about what should kick off the series. I might as well tell you that, apart from being at one with Adrian and Pongo about its aptness, I've decided to have the lead episode filmed in England, partly for logistical reasons. Renzo's script about neo-Nazis in Paris won't now be kicking off.'

I remember stealing a glance down the table. From the frowning expression on an intense, dark young man's face down there next to Dan, I could make out who Renzo was.

'I guess I thought….,' began he.

'I know, I know,' said Sherbert soothingly. 'But when you wrote the script the situation was different. That's precisely why I don't want to run the risk of tying the series to political situations which change overnight.'

'What,' I asked. 'Is Renzo's script about?'

Sherbert and Renzo, eye to eye in disagreement, looked rather startled. All faces turned to me and there was an expectant, surprised silence.'Well, sorry,' said I, 'but I don't know the ins and outs, as I've just joined the team, so I thought you'd like to fill me in a little.'

'Of course, Mike. I do apologise,' smiled Sherbert. I could see that little had changed since about 1969. In Sherbert's mind I was still B O P – useful nowadays for cash; not so useful for interruptions or objections. I needed to bang that idea on the head right at the beginning. I'd had enough of being the cypher on "*Full Circle"*, making no single contribution except working capital.

'Hell, Dave, I'll tell the man,' said Renzo. He stood up, walked round the table and took my hand. 'Renzo Bartolini,' said he, introducing himself. 'I wrote the political screenplay for "*Crossing the Bridge*". I'm from right here in Noo York, but I've been on two, three long assignments in Paris, France when I was a journo with NBC, so I know it, right? And I know something of the French cultural *zeitgeist*.'

He spoke about his ideas for several minutes. I realised that I hardly understood what he was talking about. Sherbert turned to me.

'What do YOU think, Mike?'

Put on the spot like this, I replied as best I could; the goldfish in the shark's pool, but clinging to the plan to begin filming in England.

'Politics and art aren't my natural interests,' I twittered, oddly anxious not to seem moronic in Holly's estimation, 'but I don't think either are as important as the media makes out. High culture and government leave most people cold. Take great Britain. Parties are in power, then out of it, ideologies hold sway, then die – but cricket, or strawberry jam, Cotswold villages, flower shows, Shakespeare at Stratford, Henley, The Edinburgh festival, the Proms, er, the Boat Race, preserved steam railways, Dundee cake, hot cross buns.... These go on forever. You should ask my brother; he's one of the people who make sure they do. Starting to film in Britain sort of establishes a norm. Doesn't it?'

There was a silence. I drew a breath.

Holly smiled at me and murmured, 'Hear, hear.'

'Now you are agreeing with Pongo and me just because Mike's spoken,' said Sherbert. 'Really, Holly. "Oh woman! In our hours of ease, uncertain, coy and hard to please".'

'So, listen to Greville,' said Dan, clearly amused. 'I guess I'm happy we start in Britain, not France. Renzo, looks like you're dead in this act.'

'Okay, cool. A guy's gotta fight his corner, is all.'

Sherbert gestured down the table.

'Pongo. Let our co-producer have a look at your script.'

A very fair, pinkish man of indeterminate age stood up. He wore his hair long, like Paul McCartney used to in '99 and, as with McCartney back then, he was a little too old for it to suit him.

'I'm Francis Vine, Mr Greville,' he said to me. 'Everyone calls me Pongo.' He had the unmistakeable accent of a British public school. 'I've got two scripts here, that's all. We'll need more copies, Dave.'

'Right. Holly, would you go and make enough copies of the script to give us one each?'

When Holly had gone I looked over at Francis.

'Everyone calls me Mike,' I said, 'even though this American habit of first-time intimacy isn't quite the thing!'

'Poozle! Don't you believe it, Mike,' laughed Sherbert. 'Everyone's on first-name terms in Britain now, although there is a funny quirk about TV and the lower classes. I mean a top interviewer will call a cabinet minister John or Richard, but if one of the *yobocenti* is on the show, it's *Mister* Funge or *Mrs* Scroddy.'

'Funge and Scroddy! What a snob you still are, Sherbert! Well, I haven't been in the UK for sixteen years, Pongo,' said I, 'so probably I'm not such a good judge.'

'See if you like this,' said Sherbert, 'while Holly's making photocopies. I want it to kick-start the series and I've already got Tom Shepherd looking at UK locations.'

Pongo shoved a folder over the table for me to look through. As I flicked over the pages, with Dan and Sherbert gazing at me intently, Mopsa, Georgie, *Schlock Art* and all their works seemed as distant as Aldebaran.

When Holly came back into that high, light-filled room with an armful of copied scripts and we all settled down to discuss the filming of the first episode of Sherbert's TV series, I thought three or four hours had not passed so pleasantly for years. What I didn't know was that it was the calm before the tornado.

Chapter 5: **The Tornado.**

Brrrrrrrrrrring! Brrrrrrrrrrrrrrrring!

My eyes flickered open.

Brrrrrrrrrrrrrrrrrrrrrrrrrrrrrrrrrrrrrrrrrring!

My bedroom at the Waldorf-Astoria was dark as a hat –
as American bedrooms always were, I recall. The air smelt
cool, but stuffy and metallic. My pillows had travelled to
one side of my bed, causing my neck to crick agonisingly. I
seemed to be on a stage which sloped away from me
towards a restless and hostile audience. My legs were
leaden as I walked on down the slope to a drum kit. They
were waiting for me to play, but what was this? Someone
with his or her back to me was already sitting on the high
stool clawing at a cymbal. I feared to reach the humped,
long-armed figure which perched with its spine facing me,
jiggling.

I had now been in New York for a week, and each day
had featured quite lengthy idea/scripting/location meetings
with various members of Sherbert's team. Not surprisingly,
my dreams were strange.

BRRRRRRRRRRRRRING!

My telephone was insistently shrilling beside the king-
size bed.

I grabbed at the receiver.

'Uh, oh, urgh, yes?'

'Mr Greville?'

'Yes.'

'The lobby desk here, Mr Greville. My name is Donny.'

'Yes?'

'Er, I guess there's a person downstairs wants to be shown up to your room.'

'A person?'

'Yessir.'

'Wants to be shown?'

'Yessir. She says you are expecting her.'

'She?'

'Sir.'

'Uh, well, I don't know … You are Donny, eh?'

'Yessirree.'

'What time is it, Donny?'

'Just a quarter of six, Sir.'

'Oh, ah.'

To be honest, I had thought that it must have been at least one in the morning, but 5.45 was still pretty early. Who could want to have my company at such an ungodly hour? You know, I thought suddenly that it must be Holly. I had surprised myself by catapulting her straight to the top of the likely list. I hardly knew her: the efficient Miss Miall, organiser to the haphazard Sherbert Lemon. No, no – I realised it could hardly be Holly; not before at least nine o'clock. Someone had got the wrong room number.

'Donny?'

'Yessir, Mr Greville?'

'Did this person give a name?'

'No, Sir. She says you are expecting her.'

'Donny?'

'Sir?'

'Can you find out her name?'

'Wait a min…. Hey, I guess I'm sorry, Mr Greville, but

she she's not in the lobby anymore.'

'Donny?'

'Yes, Mr Greville?'

'You are a moron.'

'Yessir. I guess I'm sorry, Sir. Have a.....'

'And DON'T say "Have a nice day" – it's still the middle of the night. Goodnight, Donny.'

I plonked down the phone.

Sherbert in drag, being silly? Or that Booker? He was extremely effeminate and I had already suspected that he was rather strange and probably unpredictable. I should have asked Donny if the 'person' had worn thick, dusty spectacles.

I drifted slowly back to sleep, plumping the pillow under my stiff neck. Quarter of six, eh? Well, that meant another two hours of slumber at least. Holly Miall. The name formed itself in my mind. Suppose it HAD been her? Suppose it *was* her, coming up now? Suppose I let her in? What then? She had lovely – and smudgy – eyes. Mind you, she was at least ten years younger…. Perhaps more? Twenty-seven, say. A good age. Experienced….only thirteen years younger…. Would she, I mused, sail in and on to the king-size bed? Donny didn't say what… she…..was… wearing… Pyjamas? Just a top… with…naked…legs….

'WAKE UP, FILTH!'

BANG, BANG, BANG, BANG, BANG, BANG, BANG, BANG, BANG, BANG, BANG, BANG, BANG, BANG, BANG, BANG, BANG, BANG, BANG, BANG,

BANG, BANG, BANG, BANG, BANG, BANG, BANG, BANG, BANG, BANG, BANG, BANG!

I shot towards the ceiling, scattering bedclothes like confetti. My God! What's happening? Wassappening?

'LET ME IN, YOU DISEASE! YOU TRAITOR!'

BANG, BANG, BANG, BANG, BANG, BANG, BANG, BANG, BANG, BANG, BANG, BANG, BANG, BANG, BANG, BANG!

I leapt across the room and clawed at the door and its many security fitments ("installed for your safety and peace of mind"). I tore the door open and glimpsed several astonished, scared faces lining the corridor before a heavy-handed smack caught me full in the face, spinning me off my feet and landing me half-way back into the dark room again.

Framed in the doorway – back-lit from the corridor – was a wild and dishevelled figure. I lay on my back, staring at it, too paralysed to speak.

'Well, traitor?' said the avenging shape.

That voice! Of course I knew that bloody voice!

'WELL?' shouted the shape.

So, this mad figure, hair bursting from the scalp in electric curls, flecks of foam giving an edging to the lips, was Mopsa, the inescapable.

I struggled to a kneeling position. Mopsa's foot shot out and slammed into my neck. I caught the boot she wore and held on to it. She flung out her arms and began to shriek. At last, as I stood up, holding her foot and lifting it ever higher, she overbalanced in her turn and crashed backwards into the corridor, her head tapping on the carpet. She gave vent to peal after peal of screams – her face like a demon.

'Well, my dear, you've found me,' said I, throwing her foot down. The moment I finished speaking, I heard the querulous, high male voice of one of my fellow guests exclaim,

'I guess that about does it. I'm gonna call the cops.'

I yanked the sprawling Mopsa to her feet.

'Get in here, you revolting cow,'I hissed. Loudly I said, for the benefit of the guests, some of whom were backing away after I had appeared in the corridor. 'I'm an analyst. There's no danger. No alarm. This is one of my more disturbed patients. I will soon have her under restraint.'

I smiled – a sickly smile, no doubt – and bustled Mopsa into the room, banging the door behind me.

Bitch-face ran through the suite – once occupied, as Sherbert had mentioned, by Richard Burton, a man used to such drama as this – waving her arms like a threshing-machine.

'Where is she?' she cried. 'Where is the whore? Out with you, whore! WHORE!'

'Mopsa, for God's sake will you shut UP! You'll have the police up here soon.'

'Don't speak to me, you scum! Georgie was right, the bitch!'

'Right about what?'

'Right about MEN! Oooh, an' what does she do? she jus' goes an' abandons me for that disgusting Jonathan, an' you abandon me for the whore. Where? Where have you stuffed the harlot? Hey, that's wharrimean – she's a HARLOT!'

She wrenched open cupboards. 'Come on out, Harlot! You scarlet Babylon! Come out!'

'Mopsa, there is no one here. I give you my word.'

'Word? The word of a vicious, hateful dungheap of a man? You think I'm gonna take your WORD, you dungheap?'

'Look,' I said wearily, 'what woman do you think is likely to be up here?' I sat on the edge of the bed, for we had now reached the bedroom, propelled there by Mopsa's wild searchings. I was relieved that she could be got talking. As each minute passed and there was no sound of the NYPD in the corridor, the more I felt I could cope. 'What woman am I LIKELY to have here? I've been in New York barely a week on business. Why should you assume that I've launched on a whirlwind love-affair at the Waldorf?'

I pulled her down next to me on the Hyper-Gigantico king-size bed. 'Things have gone spectacularly wrong between us, haven't they?' I went on. 'But it's not because there's someone else.'

The moment these words were in the air, I remembered my dozing thoughts – and I compared Holly's cool intelligence with my poor Mopsa's destructive viciousness and I felt hypocritical. There WAS someone else – even if, then, I hadn't quite realised it. I didn't stop to wonder how on earth Mopsa had heard of Holly's existence.

'There is no one else,' I repeated. I hoped it rang true.

Mopsa's fingers were twisting and flexing. Suddenly she gave a sharp howl.

'How did you find me?' I asked. I realised, without at

first thinking it odd but now surprised by them, that she was wearing yellow fabric gloves. Very peculiar. She never wore gloves. 'Tell me. I really want to know.'

She gave me a look.

'I guess I don' get a Nobel prize for that,' she muttered. 'I rang Dan's office to speak to that faggot British friend of yours with the silly name, and his secretary tells me that's he's going to be in New York for a while. I didn't know if you'd gone straight over to Europe, or were in Boston, or – or what. So I took a chance that you'd be where he was.' Something whispered to me that she was lying.

'How did you track me to this hotel?'

Mopsa's eyes screwed up tight and tears spurted between her lashes. It was an old trick – a fountain of lachrymose self-dramatisation – and I steeled myself against it.

'I've bin walking, an' taking cabs all night,' she sniffed. 'I – I didn't know what hotel you'd be stayin' at, so I got this list of the top places, and began to work through them, looking for your name on the guest-lists. I've bin to The Regency and The Pierre an' – an', an' The Plaza, an' ....'
At the thought of her self-imposed odyssey, and overcome by the piteous spectacle of it all: the abandoned, wronged woman pathetically seeking in every hotel in New York for her errant man, she began to cry in earnest, rocking to and fro and lifting her voice in a wail of lamentation that seemed, to my ears, deafening in the early morning.

'Hush, hush, Mopsa, please. Hush!' I twittered. 'Mopsa, PLEASE! There, there. Oh, for Christ's sake, Mopsa, pull yourself together!' The twitter ended in a snap.

'Uh, ahuh, aaahuh, you, you used His name, you friggin' sacrilegious…... Uh, uh, uuuh, huhuuuuuuuh, you used….'

'SHUT UP, will you!' I hooted. Oh, these idiotic dramatics. 'Mopsa! Mopsa, how many hotels did you have to try?'

'I – I – I – bin' to The Pierre, an' – an' – '

'Yes, I know, and to The Plaza and The Regency. But how many altogether have you had to go to, to find me?'

'Well, I guess this is the fourth.'

'Fourth!'

'Yes, yes, you bastard,' she snarled, pulling away from the arm which I had placed round her shoulders. 'The FOURTH! How many you want me to go schlepping round all night? I only got in at twelve.'

'And it's taken you five, no, nearly SIX hours to get from the airport and drop in at four hotels?'

'I guess I had to have somethin' to eat, an' I wasn't in a cab, Mikey. I started out walking….. I – I wasn't thinking. Oh, oh, you're such a cold-hearted person. S-o-o-o-o cold an' s-o-o-o-o superior! Aeow, honley four 'otels, ackcherlie, old fruit. There aren't many in a city the size of New York, doncha know, ol' boy, ackherlie.' Mopsa had slipped into her not-very-good-mimicry of an English toff. Her eyes rolled up and her voice shot up the scale. 'Oooooh, YAAS, old turnip, the silly moo only had to geow round four 'otels, ackcherlie.'

I made a move to grasp her collar. I think I was going to slap her, but my hand fell. I stood up and looked down at her.

'I'm tired of this,' I said. 'Get out.'

She too stood up.

'I'm not going.'

'Yes, you are.'

'I'm not, so.'

'Mopsa….'

'I can't go. I've no money. What I had I've gone an' spent on the air-fare. I've got no one to go to. Mikey, please. I'm not just *anybody*. Remember me? I'm Mopsa. I've looked after you for more'n five years. You need me. An', Mikey, Mikey sweetheart, I really need you. I can't tell you what I felt like when you walked out; or what an effort I've had to make to come after you like this, because I – I felt so dejected.'

'You complain that Georgie rejects you, that I reject you. You never stop to think why people eventually just get tired of being with you. You're so manipulative, so self-obsessed, so tied up with this ghastly, depraved ART crap of yours, so full of self-pity. No one can stand it for long. At any rate, I can't. And just bear in mind that of all the people who've had to put up with you, I've hung around the longest. I'm being honest with you, Mopsa. I'm not having an affair with anyone. I'm just so tired. I want to go home – and stay there.'

'Going home? What d'you mean – home?'

'Home.'

'What? You mean back to L A?'

'No, of course I don't – and you know I don't.'

'You mean ENGLAND! Home? You haven't been near the place for years. You haven't lived there since Reagan was President. How can it be home?'

I was silent. I wouldn't explain further. Really, just then I couldn't be bothered.

Mopsa went on, 'You said you was going…'

' …were going,' I put in.

' …*were* going over there for a visit. I – I didn't want you to go, but – but I thought you'd be BACK. You mean you're not coming back – ever?'

'Yes, I do. The scripting sessions have been done; they were largely sorted out before I joined up. Discussions are going on about the order of shooting and some location arrangements have still to be finalised. The production team leaves for London soon where filming will begin, and when it goes I'll be going with it – one way.'

Until I'd put it into words, just then, in that big hotel suite at the Waldorf at six o'clock in the morning, I hadn't realised how far I had abandoned all thought of a return to the West Coast. Whatever London was like since I last knew it, it was where I wanted to be.

'But you don't know anything *about* modern Britain!'

Silence from me.

'You're nuts!'

Silence.

'An' you're not taking me with you?'

Silence.

'Jeez! When *exactly* do you leave?'

I said no more. I had said far too much already. I felt free and yet trapped, exhilarated, yet guilty. But I was adamant. The uncontrolled Mopsa belonged to the recent, uncomfortable, lonely past; my future lay in the London streets (or so I romanticised internally). There was no slot for the loony in that cosmos over the ocean. And…. then there was Holly….. no place for bitch-face near *her*…

I stepped to the phone.

'You hungry?' I asked – breaking the chilly chasm of the unuttered.

'I guess a little.'

'I'm going to order breakfast up here. We'll eat it together. Then I have to go to a meeting – alone. I will give you a cheque to cash. I think you should fly back to L A and press on with your kinetic art.'

Mopsa sighed. She lifted her tasselled, hippy bag from her shoulder. She withdrew from it her little blue book – a book I had come to dislike in L A.

'I – I might stay in New York, Mike – jus' for a while,' she mumbled. 'I wanna look up some friends. I might even go home for a few days now I'm back east.'

She flipped her gloved fingers (about which I had still made no comment, and the mystery of which I felt I ought to have solved before we parted forever) awkwardly through the book. It contained the names and addresses of her friends arranged in three sections: those who had died of AIDS, those who were HIV positive with full-blown AIDS, and those who were just HIV positive. She was always updating the Dead section.

We said very little more. Breakfast came. I expected to have coffee, eggs and rolls thrown at me, but nothing happened. Mopsa made a couple of calls. I wrote out her cheque – a large one, God knows why. I dressed to go to Sherbert's meeting. At the door of the suite I said,

'I don't want to find you here when I get back.'

Her eyes widened in hurt, and I stepped quickly out into the corridor before she could reply. If I weaken, I'm done for, I told myself. The surgeon's knife…

Mopsa's sudden irruption seemed to start the day off badly. I felt grumpy and critical at Sherbert's meeting because the ideas flew past without opportunity for me to comment. Had Sherbert dragged me over to New York merely to be a yes-man observer? Surely at these pre-filming meetings, when there were chances to make changes if needed, the opinions of the Associate Producer (me) were of importance?

At one point I circumnavigated the table in a manner I knew was didactic and intimidating. Pongo Vine said nothing, but sat twiddling a shapely gold propelling-pencil. My eye was caught by a headline in somebody's paper on the table: "Homeless in New York could fill Shea Stadium (capacity 76,000) – New Shock Report."

'I'm not sure that future planning is best done in committee like this,' said Sherbert – probably regretting he had brought me in at all by then. 'Why don't you folks move on to chew over the script about the Parthenon and the Greek policy on overseas treasures while Mike and I go for a little walk to talk things over?'

'Do you need me, David?' Holly asked at that point. And I was delighted when Sherbert replied,

'Oh, yes, okay, if Mike has no objections. I suppose you could minute our little talk.'

So we three emerged onto 89th Street and walked across 5th Avenue. A little guy was flying a bright orange kite, and it flamed against the white of the Gugg.

'I've never seen the Guggenheim,' said I. 'Shall we stroll round it?'

'Sure. Let's,' said Sherbert.

We went into Lloyd Wright's chubby radio set and gazed up at the gentle spiral above us.

'The Vatican has a set of staircases like this,' I remarked. 'One goes up while another lot comes down.'

'These aren't stairs,' Holly said. 'They're ramps. One can take the elevator to the top and come down from the new show to the permanent exhibits at the bottom.'

'If that's what we're supposed to do, let's do the opposite,' I suggested rebelliously, probably because rebellion was now in my blood, and probably because Holly's presence was making me show off. We walked slowly, spiralling upward. Each of the oddities which the museum has made its own plopped out at us from its pool of light. God, if I thought I was James Dean, fascinating rebel, going up the down ramps, what would I have thought about the way I was to go up those same spirals in a few days' time?

'Marvellous,' breathed Sherbert.

'Not really my idea of art,' I replied.

'So,' said Sherbert,' you've become a hearts-and-flowers, Stag-at-Bay, Laughing Cavalier, Hay Wain, Glorious British Landscapes sort of art lover, have you? Not the Bop I remember.'

Sherbert was not as easy as earlier. I knew he thought I had over-stepped the mark in the meeting.

'You're cross,' I said quietly.

'No, I'm not.'

'Yes, you are.'

'I'm not, Mike.'

'You are, mate.'

'Okay. I'm a little peeved.'

'Thought so.'

'Do you blame me? It was awkward in there'

'No. Yes. No, perhaps not. But don't you WANT me to react to the ideas for the series?'

'Well...'

'You mean – NO. It's what I suspected in L A. Mike's just there to hand over large sums of cash and leave the mental processes to intellectual Sherbert-Lemon, the Beeb's Man of Thought. Well, why did you drag me to the meetings at all?' I gazed at a particularly odd drawing of an eye, a fried egg and a crown of thorns round a bottle with "Urine" blazoned on it. Shame, I thought. I'm going to have to pull out of the TV series after all.

Holly gave a little cough. I thought that she could make a splutter attractive.

'Er – hem. I think Mike is right, David,' you said.

'YOU agree with Mike?' said Sherbert.

'I think he should have a say if he's paying,'

'Well!' gasped Sherbert.

'Why not give Mike copies of the finished scripts?'

Sherbert nodded wordlessly.

So, after lunch – the sort of big snack that Noo Yark does well: eggs benedict with crisp leaf salad, blinis on the side and key lime pie with coffee – Sherbert went off to see a bloke from WGBH Boston, while I accompanied Holly back to the production offices to pick up a pile of paper.

'So you didn't like the Gugg?' she asked.

'I don't like conceptual art much, 'I replied. 'I can't see why it's ART when some twit like Serra props up a piece of rusty tin sheet against the wall and everyone goes on about how it defies gravity. There are plenty of tin sheets in builders' yards, but they're just junk. What definition can there be of "Art" when just being IN the gallery makes a pile of scaffolding priceless, when, in the parking lot, it's worthless?'

I was finding it so easy to talk to her. She listened without shouting me down, as Mopsa used to do, and at a pause she said,

'Did you know that a section of one of the episodes is going to be on that very topic? How galleries are replacing stuffy old trad art with The Shock of the New, as the famous art guy called it.'

'I hope we're not going to make out that the modern bollocks is better than the old, are we?'

'Have you heard of a man called Nicholas Serota?'

'No, never.'

'You'll be meeting him, I expect, in London. He's director of the Tate Gallery and David hopes to rope him in as an advisor on that episode.'

'The Tate. Yes, I remember it. It was full of British paintings. My uncle fell down the front steps when I was a boy.'

'It's controversial now, with a big, big "C". It exhibits a lot of what trads call hyped-up junk and Serota is one of the judges of the Turner Prize. That award causes more controversy in the English press than any other cultural event in London. Ever heard of Tracey Emin?'

'No,' I had to admit again. Rembrandt? Yes. Turner? Yes. Emin? No. But that was in '99. Now that I'm in England and read a paper now and then, I find she's become a Great British Institution.

'Her claim to fame is her exhibit for the Turner this year – a mattress with soiled sheets, surrounded by cigarette packs, a condom, her knickers and vodka bottles. She calls it "*My Bed*".'

'It's amazing. I've just left that sort of horse-shit behind in L A, and now you tell me it's in front of me again. I don't think I can stand it.'

'It's the new wave, Mike. What did you mean about seeing it all in L A?'

By this time, we had got back to the 37th floor office. There was a hum from behind the double doors. The production team was at its biz. I couldn't bear to see them again that day, so I hung back.

'I'll tell you about L A another time. I've seen a lot worse than a rumpled bed. Can I take the stuff I asked for and leave you? I'll get back to the Waldorf and start reading.'

In the ante-room she sorted out sheaves of paper from a dozen piles, arranged them neatly as I watched, then handed me a large wodge of photocopies in shiny covers.

'When you've ploughed through this,' she said, scribbling on the back of the pack, 'would you like to call me on this number? I'm staying with friends in the Village and I'll be back after seven. I guess I'd like to know what you think.'

Back at the Waldorf-Astoria, I gingerly opened the door of the suite. I half-expected Mopsa still to be crouching there.

Nothing.

Phew!

I called room service for a salmon sandwich and some tea. I lay in an armchair by the window and started reading. I gave up on the working script of the first episode after a while and turned to the second. The politics was, frankly, boring, and the detail about the cultural landscape unfamiliar. The scripts were interleaved with suggestions for stills and moving images. As a real estate guy who hadn't read a book since leaving school, I began to realise that Sherbert and Co were right. I shouldn't try to horn in. They had no idea what a difficult task they had set me.

Village Schoolmaster

'Hullo-eee? Eastside Home for Reformed Nuns.'

'Erm, is that….? May I speak to Holly Miall, please?'

'I guess so. It's a free country. That's what we vote Democrat for.'

'Thank you.'

'Thank-a-yooooo.'

There was a clashing of plastic as the receiver over in the Village was dropped on a hard surface. I waited. Then over the aether came Holly's voice, slightly husky, kind, engaging.

'Hello? Is that you, Mike?'

'Holly? Yes, it's Mike Greville here. You said I might ring about now after I had read some script details.'

'Oh, I hoped you would. Which episodes did you read?'

'"I – um – I couldn't get on with the first, so I read on. I – er – wonder if you happen to be free about now? Do say if it's a bad moment – going out, going to bed early, washing hair, having supper – whatever…'

'No, Mike, it's not a bad moment at all. As a matter of fact we're going to be eating in half-an-hour. Hang on.' There was a null at the other end. I strained to hear Holly's voice, but I think she probably clapped her hand over the mouthpiece. 'Hello? Mike? Have you eaten? I mean, if you haven't, why not grab a cab over here and eat with us? It's only pasta *vongole* and salad, and we can open another can of *vongole*.'

'Are you sure? Do your friends mind?'

'No, no. I just asked. Hey, they'd be tickled to meet you.

Blundell just loves new people. It's more a question of whether a humble supper with humble folk in the Village meets with what you millionaires would call a proper meal.'

I chuckled at that. I was beginning to appreciate Holly's sense of the ironic and the self-deprecating. It's not a common American trait, I used to think, except among Jews. Californians in general took themselves and other people pretty seriously, and I'm sure they still do.

'Hell, I can slum it down-market for one evening,' I replied. 'Open that other can. Be with you in the wink of an eye.'

In the event my journey took the full half-hour because the cab driver could not at first find the tiny alley-way off the street behind the avenue next to El Bodegon in Greenwich Village. At least I was lucky enough to find a driver who could find the Village itself, I suppose.

'I can no drive up here, man. Iss pee-destrian.'

I got out.

The stifling New York night – exhausting and raucous with sound – boomed around me. With a shock, I realised that, apart from my walking from the hotel to the door of a stretched limo, and that brief walk we took over to the Gugg, I had not left the whispering embrace of air-conditioning since I had arrived. The tiny streets – the only ones in the monstrous grid to dare to run at odd angles – and the low, cramped houses gave the area an aura of European glamour – a touch of Montmartre on the Hudson.

I peered down the short cul-de-sac ahead of me. Period lamps made pools of yellow on uneven, heavy flagstones. I went down to the furthest house on the left, as per phoned instructions. It was painted a dirty off-white. At right angles to it was a low wall with a gate set into it. The extraordinary thing was that I knew this little street. On the low wall were two bas-relief porcelain designs, rather in the mould of what my brother had educated me to appreciate as Della Robbia, of leaping horses rearing in the hands of angelic figures whose streaming robes poured out behind them like flames or ectoplasm. A short flight of steps flanked with black, wrought-iron handrails went up to the front door. In the gloom I could see that the upper storey was entirely covered in luxuriant creeper. The houses opposite were similarly covered.

I wrestled there in the roaring night with memory. Was it because it was so like Glebe Place, had so much of the feel of London's Chelsea, that it seemed familiar? My initial start of recognition had been right; this street had for some time been imprinted on my brain. I gave up the struggle and pulled on the round, discoloured knob on the door. Far-off a chime clanged. Then the door was opened by the fattest man I had ever seen. Holly's 'honorary' uncle must always have made an impact on other people. Size – sheer, vast avoirdupois, giant buttocks, pendulous dewlaps, triple chins, massive breasts, rolling layers of stomach, pear-shaped tracksuits in the brightest of colours – this is what I had got used to seeing in California, where half the population is dieting down to Size Zero while the other half gorges itself to death. But this – this apparition was almost on another species level – as a super-jumbo jet is barely of the genus: "aeroplane".

'Yeah?' said the huge man. He seemed to thrust out a bushy, greying beard and his stomach all at once.

'Have I the right address?' I asked. 'Number 18, Miss Miall?'

'Oh, sure, sure. Bin 'specting you. C'mon in, an' welcome.' He manoeuvred out of the way so that I could insert myself into the narrow hall-way. No chance. 'Pardon me,' rumbled the vast shape, 'Follow me, an' shut the door, if you would be so kind.'

I followed him down the narrow passage-way and round an L-shape into a brightly-lit kitchen. Holly was there, beaming with pleasure, and next to was her a tiny bird-like woman with sequinned glasses. I glimpsed them both for an instant before my host blocked the view into the room, as the sun is eclipsed momentarily by the ponderous moon.

'Mike!' Holly cried, darting forward, 'This is great! Hey, let me introduce you folks. Mike, this is my uncle Blundell – well, he's not really an uncle, you know; he is my Dad's oldest friend. Mike Greville, Blun. And this is Twinkle.'

'Blundell and Twinkle Capitanchik,' smiled Blundell, enfolding my hand in a soft, warm grip like a floury, newly-baked loaf.

'Holly's daddy an' us go back when….,' croaked Twinkle. Her voice, hoarse and beguiling, seemed to come from a much larger woman.

'Holly's real excited about this TV series you all got yourselves engaged in,' said Blundell as, unasked, he poured a very large glass of dark Californian Cabernet Sauvignon for me. 'Sit, sit. Come over here. Dinner's bang-on ready. Twink, the poor man hasn't got a fork. Not that you need a fork to start off with,' he added, ''cos you don't. Here, try this.' He cut a long slice from a crunchy submarine loaf and then, with slow, loving movements, scooped with a giant spoon a globe of rich, horse-manure coloured pate from a vast dish of the stuff and passed it over to me. I marvelled that Holly and Twink would be able to eat so much of it – and then I realised that they weren't going to – it was all Blundell's. 'We've got a real Eye-talian deli round the corner. He makes chicken liver pate with so much garlic in it that it scents the bowl for weeks to come. Try it. More wine? That's it. So enjoy. Enjoy. Holly, mmmmm, you gotta try a little of this. Grab a knife.'

'Now, Blun,' she remonstrated. 'You know I couldn't eat more than a thimble of something as rich as that. No one should eat *too* much of it.'

'Aaah, she's right,' croaked Twinkle. 'Me, I don' eat meat at all, but that's because I suffer *down here*.' With an extraordinary grimace and a flash of her sequinned specs, she stole a dramatic look at her lap, but I was unable to tell whether it was her stomach, groin, bowels or knees that suffered from the mastication of flesh.

'Whaddya think?' gasped Blundell, as he shovelled fist-sized wedges of bread and pate down the hatch. 'Whaddya…. urrrch, gurrrgh, urrrrchch…. Whaddya think?'

I hope I didn't come over as gluttonous that evening, but the pate was glorious, and I do remember attacking it with near-Blundell-esque fervour.

'Why,' said I, during a pause in the gurgling and slurping, 'should this street seem so familiar to me, even though I don't recall ever being here before during my days in New York?'

'"*Strange Days*",' said Blundell, wiping his mouth with a fresh piece of bread.

'Come again?'

'Oh, Blun thinks this alley was used on the cover of an album made in the 'sixties by a group called The Doors,' said Holly. 'A bit before my time. It's sort of famous, like that walk-zone on the front of the Beatles' record. You know – the black and white stripes'

'Ah, Abbey Road,' said I. 'And *"Strange Days"*! Of course! That's where I've seen that wall and those horse plaques! God, I think Anthony bought that record in, let me see, in 'sixty-eight. I was only a little kid, but he propped the cover on the bedside table between our beds. I liked the little dwarf on it.'

'Anthony is Mike's older brother,' Holly murmured. I was too interested to think of explaining.

'But can it *really* be the same wall?'

'That's what I tell him. I say: "Blun, it ain't the same *wall*." An' you know why not?' came Twinkle's rasping voice. ''Cos The Doors were a WEST coast group, an' this wall is back East.'

'Someone tol' me that that walk-zone across Abbey Road hasn't changed either,' gurgled Blundell, ignoring her.

'I wouldn't know, alas. I haven't been to that part of London in years.'

'My man, you're lucky to have seen it at all! I have never been in London, England. In fact,' admitted Blundell with a sudden burst of candour, 'I haven't been outside the good ole U S of A 'cept once, and that was to 'Nam.' A strange hardness passed across his broad whiskered face, like a shadow flitting on a wall. 'I guess 'Nam's not like the rest of the world – it's like it was a bit of the U S of A gone bad, y'know. I saw things over there…. I saw things….' His many chins wobbled.

'Blun teaches school now,' put in Twinkle. 'His subject is History.'

'And Languages', Holly said, admiringly, 'Blun can speak Russian, French, Yiddish and Portuguese.'

'Hey, shucks! If you've got it, get a PR team to flaunt it!' cried Blundell, clearly delighted by these unsolicited testimonials. He gazed round the table with a grin which went from ear to ear. I noticed that as he ate he seemed to grow more rotund, shiny and expansive. He drank little, so I guessed he was one of those rare people who actually become drunk on food.

We moved onto a mountainous bowl of pasta and seafood, a forest of salad, bakeries of garlic bread. Holly ate with a good appetite – and I liked that. I wouldn't have admired her so much if I had found out that she lacked gusto. Twinkle tore out the centres of the garlic bread and chewed lettuce leaves and tomato slices. I too did well, for the meal, though simple, was delicious. And Blundell ate as if provisioning an army. His fork and active, plump jaws seemed almost to be a blur. While he gobbled, he talked incessantly, often gasping and choking as the words coming out clashed with the comestibles going in. He had latched on to Sherbert's TV project and its aims.

'....Urrrrgh. Gug. So, I mean, Mike, history IS fiction, right? The past is what we make it in a future safely beyond that present which once comprised it. We have the primary source texts, of course, but we *interpret* these. We look at *"Shirley"* by Charlotte Bronte, for example, an' we say we don' like the cool, unromantic, matter-of-fact world she presents. That's not how WE see the nineteenth century – all bonnets and looking out into the rain with heaving bosoms, yearning for love. So we start finding reasons, retrospectively, why she wrote it like that. Hell, what she was doin' was writing about what her world *really was like*, but because we don't see it that way, we can't accept it. No, take it from me, the study of history is an act of fiction. It's just....urrrgh.... it's just like fiction or art: a means of *interpreting* the present.'

I was silent during much of his talk, trying to bring back to mind who had mentioned Charlotte Bronte and her novel *"Shirley"* to me recently – for surely someone had? What with unsuccessfully trying to remember that and the unfamiliarity of the topic, and the loveliness of Holly under the Tiffany light, a lot of that meal's conversation passed over my head. Holly impressed me, though. Beneath his mountainous flesh and slangy speech, Blundell was a clever, educated man, and she parried him swiftly and with force – and, evidently, with love. Twinkle contented herself with gazing wryly but fondly at her garrulous husband, rather as the proprietor of an aquarium might gaze at his star performing porpoise.

'So you teach?' said I, finding an opportunity to ask a question which would get him away from Charlotte B.

'Mmm. More salad? More bread? Hey, more pasta, man? C'mon, you guys! You'll make me feel guilty and quite greedy, y'know, if you don' have a little more. Yeah, yeah. I teach school. I'm getting through my seventh,' he added, gazing round proudly.

'What? Seventh school?'

'Nooo way! Seventh nervous breakdown. Jest recovering from a real bad go. I was shot.'

'Shot!'

'Yep, by a kid of thirteen. Peppered my ass. But, y'know, he'd been threatening for weeks. His gang had got it in for me. That's way back in the spring semester. I had most of the summer semester out. An' now I'm waiting for the fall semester with just a hint of disquiet.'

'Surely such an awful thing's not likely to happen again?'

'Sure is. The little craphead's still on roll.'

'Wasn't he expelled? I mean, shooting one of the masters seems quite a breach of discipline.'

'Where they gonna put him? The policy here in New York is "containment".'

'I would have thought he'd be in a detention centre or something,' I said.

'Aaaah, Jeez,' broke in Twinkle's cackle. 'Blun is a saint. They wanted to prosecute the little termite, but my Blun says no, give the kid another chance, he comes from this no-hope home, an' all that. I tell you, I gotta admire courage like that.'

I remember scanning her face closely for signs of irony, sarcasm or belittlement, but there was none. She meant what she said, and as I got to know her better, I realised that her life began with, centred in and derived its meaning from Blundell alone.

'I have made the best of my time away from school,' continued Blundell. 'I gotta a lot of poetry written, an' I've bin out a lot on my 'sickles, right upstate, right to the Catskills, down to the Blue Ridges.'

'Blun,' Holly interposed, 'writes great poetry. He has been published in "*The Village Voice*", in "*Labyrinth*" and in "*The American Review*".'

'Now we're gonna have some real fine chocolate pie an' a few mugs of coffee an' then we'll go out to the temple an' I'll read you a poem or two. Okay?'

I glanced at my watch under the edge of the table. Nine o'clock already, and I hadn't had a single word with Holly by herself, and the meal still not over.

'Er, fine, super.'

Twinkle put on the table a deep-dish pie filled with wave on wave, ruck on ruck of dense milky chocolate. Blundell wielded a spatula and was reprimanded for the enormous slice he apportioned Holly.

'This little girl of mine jest does not eat enough,' he gurgled, slapping his own huge wedge down and commencing operations. 'Lemme…Ggrrrh….gurggugggg. lemme tell you about number Six. That was a daddy of a breakdown. There was this black kid, Norbert Wilbeam – a great, gangling type, the real "blue-black-nigra" as they might say – an', man, he jest did about everything he damn could to upset me in my History lessons. An' one hot, hot day, when, y' know, I had jest about HAD it, an' all the kids were as high as albatrosses, an' the police had already broken up a fight in English with Miss Szuznik because of some gang problem about popping X-tablets an' Wilbeam had had this knife taken off him....you know, typical day teaching school, I guess.... Well, this Wilbeam gets up an' starts prancing round the classroom. He points his finger at me an' cries: "This fat man is crazy, man. This is Mister Crazy. Hey, Crazy, why yo' so fat, yo' white piece o' blubber?" Now,' said Blundell, gazing solemnly at us, 'I know I am not slim, right? But there's such a thing as manners. So I say to him, "Sit down, Norbert, now you've done your funny turn." Then he comes right up to me, an' starts jabbing me in the chest, tryin' to push me back up against the wall. "Yo' so FAAAAT, you white turd, that Ah'm wonderin' how yo' gets yore arm round that blubber to wipe yore shitty white ass." When he said that, an' he hadn't sat down like he'd been told, I guess I just saw red – bright red. So what do I do? I take him by the throat an' I hold onto his neck, an' I fall to the ground. That,' said Blundell, 'is the great advantage to being a weighty individual; you have gravity on your side. There's no one man, however quick he is on his feet, that you can't overpower by just dropping towards the centre of the earth and taking him with you. So Wilbeam is crushed under me, an' I turn to get up an' kneel plum on his stomach, jabbing down hard on my knee. The air goes outa him like a punctured tire. You shoulda heard the whoosh of air – amazing. Well, I suppose,' sighed Blundell ruminatively, 'I shoulda sort of stopped there, but I think that's when I knew I was in the grip of number Six, because I didn't stop. When he was down I started yellin' at him. I am told I sorta screeched, my voice right up high: "Bastard! Bastard! Bastard! Bastard!" over an' over. An' then I started kicking him – slamming in my 'sickle boots to his gut, his kidneys, into his face, his balls an' up his ass as he squealed an' rolled. Then…… and hey! Are you sure you won't have another peck of pie?..... Then I guess I started spittin' on him, an' I spat an' spat until my throat an' gums were dry, an' he was speckled like – like a rock covered with guano. Then I was led away, and Miss Szuznik said I was cryin' like a baby.'

Blundell let out his breath with a soft prolonged whoosh, like Wilbeam's puncture.

There was a silence.

'What happened to you afterwards?' I asked. 'Weren't there disciplinary hearings and things like that?'

'Heck, no,' said Blundell, combing some pie-crust from the incult tangles of his beard. 'Wilbeam went to his tutor and asked what he should do an' Jim Feathers, bless him, told him he should apologise to me very politely for annoying me so much. Apparently he jest stood an' gaped. The rest of his class later said to me how they thought he had it coming to him an' that it was time someone thrashed his ass. I had a whole term off, and when I came back Wilbeam was gone. He'd blown the head off a policeman in Queens with a bird-gun. So, fiddle-di-dee, that was *Numero Sei.*'

I stole a look at Holly, but couldn't catch her eye. I was

unable to tell whether Blundell was romancing or not. During his story, I had noticed that his eyes had once or twice rolled up – a sure sign of mental agitation, I gather. I never did work out how much to believe him, even in England when I got to know him better, at the time he came to my rescue when I had been emprisoned by lunatics.

'At least it all shows,' broke in Twinkle's cackle, 'that you *can* get back on the black scum AND get away with it, even in this nigger-lovin' town.'

'Now, now, Twink. That's racist talk,' tutted Blundell. 'They aren't all bad.'

'That's all you know,' muttered Twinkle, snatching at our coffee mugs, but she said no more. Her jerky, bird-like form darted out into the kitchen.

'What was Number One?' I asked humorously. Blundell, looking down, fumbled with his beard again.

'Number One was in Vietnam,' he mumbled.

I realised I had said the wrong thing.

'Er, Holly,' I said to. 'Don't you think you and I ought to discuss the material you gave me to read? It's getting late and I know you wanted to hear some of my ideas.'

'Late? It's not late!' cried our host, looking up again. 'Don't sneak off an' break up the party. Come out to the temple. Remember I was going to read you some of my poetry?'

'Oh, Blun! All right,' Holly laughed. I could see that she was used to giving in to him and treating him like a preposterous fat baby.

Wheezing with the effort of re-assuming the

perpendicular after his gastronomic exertions, Blundell heaved himself up. He spooned a last whorl of chocolate into his mouth.

'Follow,' said he.

Twinkle put her head round the door.

'Blun, come here. I want you to gimme a hand in the kitchen.' He protested, but it was no use. Holly and I went in behind him to help, but Twinkle shooed us out again. 'You two got things to talk about, so you talk. Blun'll be back soon.'

And so Holly and I had our discussion about the project under the glittering Tiffany light, while Blundell and Twinkle clattered next door. I gave my opinions about modern concept art and expressed doubts about the amount of time to be spent on it in the series. Holly listened patiently. I hoped I had disguised that I had not read all she had given me.

It was a good twenty minutes before Blundell reappeared and we went behind him – like pilot-fish in reverse – through the door at the end of the lobby and out into the hot booming night.

Anthony tells of years ago, sometime in the late 1950s, when independent television first appeared, how our grandfather presented the family with its first TV set. Anthony was allowed to watch just three programmes a week: "*The Lone Ranger*", "*The Adventures of Robin Hood*" and the cartoon of Popeye the Sailorman. In one of these Popeye episodes Olive Oyl is kidnapped by Sheik Bluto, imprisoned in an Arab tent in the desert and forced to become one of his harem. Popeye sets out to rescue her. From the outside, the tent is six feet square, but when the sailor rushes in it seems to stretch to infinity: blazing lamps hang from the distant ceiling, Persian carpets run on forever, hundreds of girls lie on bolsters and pouffes. Popeye's jaw crashes open and his pipe turns upside down in surprise. Anthony had found it extraordinarily impressive. He says it was the first time his unsophisticated brain had been exposed (until it happened again in *"Doctor Who"*) to that disparity between illusion and reality which the modern techno-mind accepts so readily. The term: "Like Popeye's tent" slipped from him into our family demotic.

This is why, in the heavy, noisy New York night, with the Village pulsing all around us, I gasped: "Like Popeye's tent!" as we stepped from the world of Blundell's modest home into shattering discovery of his place of dreams.

What might have been a small back yard behind any other house was filled from side to side by a towering oriental palace. One might have been in old Aleppo or Samarkand. A slim minaret rose up from twelve feet above head height. All around it were onion domes and machicolations picked out in gold, red and blue. Shiny dragons with long tongues leaned over the edge of the peaked roofs.

To complete the Middle-Eastern/Chinese/Medieval *melange*, lancet windows with edges of scalloped colour ran round the faceted walls. Opposite us was a gateway – a miniature version of the sort of thing one sees in Chinatown. Shafts of yellow, green and amber light flooded the towers as Blundell threw some switches. I screwed up my eyes against the gorgeous blaze.

'C'mon in,' said my host. The gateway's width just admitted his stupefying bulk.

Inside the towering structure were four low curved benches around a circular carpet. Each bench was upholstered in a different fabric and the carpet gleamed. I was interested to see that the interior walls were made of unpainted chipboard. Next to a heavy-looking workbench was a striking sight: a restored Harley-Davidson Electra Glide motorcycle leaning over on its chrome prop-stand. In a far corner a huge humped shape bulked under a black canvas.

'Welcome to my temple,' beamed Blundell. 'Twink hates it out here, but I call it my study an' workshop combined.'

I smiled. Now I had had time to take it in, my surprise was abating. I had worked out where Blundell had got his astonishing erection.

'"*Aladdin*"?' I asked.

'Good guess. "*Ali Baba*".'

'Clever Mike,' Holly grinned at me.

'Oh well,' said I, 'it was the unpainted chipboard that put me on track. No scene painter decorates the places the punters can't see.'

'From the Yonkers Operatic Society's open Air show of 1994. And it's pretty weather-proof. There was a lot of snow on it last winter, but it's been coated in yacht-varnish. Yup, I wrote the script for them.'

'And co-produced it,' Holly put in.

'And co-produced it. An' it was a hit,' said Blundell. 'They were gonna chop this up, so I said: no way, I'll take it off you – just gimme time to ring U-haul. It's bin here ever since.'

'It's just so Blundell, isn't it?' Holly said, with real affection and admiration.

'But Mike, you interested in theatre?' asked Blundell.

'No. Well, Just at school. In a play and in *"The Pirates of Penzance"*.'

'Whaddya say to this?' came Blundell's voice, cutting into my momentary reverie about my school days. He had plumped down on one of the benches. In his hands was a green folder. Without waiting for an answer, he took a deep breath and, in a hard, thrilling voice, quite unlike his normal, fat, careless wheeze, he suddenly cried, 'BITE! This happened to me on a shore-line in South Vietnam on troop trans-shipment. See what you think.

I can hardly say, for what I saw will not believe itself.
Singing in ocean-hush of the broad wind, swept with birds
on blue,
I bent to find the sand apart, just there - where the soft suck
licks the weed.
Volcanoes of grains in a magnifying universe parted
beneath my foot-soles,
imploding into depths, and a mouth was seen.
It bit once, and slender beams of silica streamed
over its minute abyss. It closed, and tide bubbles
pushed my rooted feet from its hole.
But I still say it was human-formed, that rows of bright

teeth
Snapped and smiled at me.'

'Does the poem express terror of the natural world – eat or be eaten?' said I – the instant poetry critic. 'I mean, if I've got it right? The terrors of the sea; and that mouth looked up and "snapped" at you. It's quite foodie, isn't it?'

Before Blundell could reply, Holly put in,

'You see, Blun's got "oral rage". Doctor Johnson had it.'

'Listen to her!' chuckled Blundell.

'It's true,' she went on, solemnly. 'Johnson ate and ate, snapping at his food. So do you, Blun, darling. And when people do this it's an expression of hatred for the world and for other people. You reduce your enemies to food and eat them before they eat you.'

I didn't honestly think Blundell's poetry much good, but then I expected poems to rhyme, like limericks, or be about love and suchlike. In my chosen path of real-estate millionaire, I admit that I never read poetry, and you could throw bricks by the dozen and not hit a poem-loving property-shark in downtown L A. And suddenly I thought of Mopsa and her crew of crazy, desperate fellow-artists. This talk about Oral Rage had brought back to mind Georgie and the restaurant window.

'What do you know about Excremental Kineticists?' I asked swiftly, before Blundell could select another poem.

'Mike! How on earth do you know about *them*,' Holly gasped, with unflattering astonishment – as if the educationally subnormal child had suddenly come up with E=MC squared.

'Oh, I – I knew some people in L A who sort of dabbled in it,' I replied. I had not told anyone in New York about Mopsa, and Sherbert had only met her once at Dan's.

'I've read about them,' Holly went on. 'The rage they suffer from must be all-consuming. It's totally destructive; there's no creativity there. It's so eighteenth century: Swift and Johnson and "The Excremental Vision". God, how we studied that at Berkeley! So, you know about E K. Well, Blun, what do you say?'

With a straight face and owl-like eyes staring abaft his beard above the rolls of fat, he replied solemnly,

'Um – I think the excremental vision is…. a load of crap.' There was a second's pause. He slapped a podgy knee with a plump hand and threw back his head for a bellow of laughter. '….a load of crap, see? Ha, ha, ha!'

'Oh, Blun, honestly,' Holly grinned; the pretty clever girl humouring the elderly iconoclastic eccentric.

I smiled at them both uncertainly. Georgie wouldn't have understood at all. I was just reflecting how different all this was from my money-making days a week or two previously – poetry and Eng Lit at Berkeley in the same conversation – when my eye was held once again by the enormous humped shape at the far end of the temple.

Blundell had seen my gaze transfer to it.

'That's my other 'sickle under there,' he breathed. 'You prepared for … *anything*?

'Why?' I asked.

'Oh, you'll see,' Holly said. 'Blundell's bigger motorcycle is pretty unusual. He and Twinkle love it, although she won't admit to it. It's not unique because there are another… how many, Blun?'

'Another two hundred or so. Perhaps fewer. It's not what you'd normally see. C'mon, I'll show you. You interested in 'sickles?' He clambered, gasping, to his feet, the poetry folder (I was glad to see) forgotten.

'Oh yes,' I cried. 'I had several bikes back in England. So did my brother. He and I went all the way from London to Sicily on our bikes in 'seventy-seven, and broke down over thirty times en route. I used to love motorbikes, but I never owned one as magnificent as your Electra Glide.'

'Yeah, that is my TRUE love,' gurgled Blundell. 'Fully ree-stored to 'sixty-eight spec, but the one under here is new.' We stood by the dust-sheeted shape. Behind it were doors. 'That's where I get them out,' continued Blundell. 'This temple is my garage too. That's what I mean about my workshop; I gotta lotta tools here for bike maintenance.'

'When you say ONE is under there, you mean several, don't you?' From its enormous outline, I'd thought there must have been three or four machines under the dust-cover. 'How many bikes do you own?'

'I've just got my hog over there an' this one. There's only the one here. Look.'

He whipped away the cover. I received my n^{th} surprise of the evening. Before us was THE largest motorcycle that could be imagined. It was as long as a car, as wide as a dining-room table; like its owner, magnificently obese, breathtakingly excessive. In the '70s and early '80s, when I knew about bikes, I was familiar with the bulk of machines like the Laverda 750, the Honda 4s, the V-twin Moto

Guzzis, and my brother's BSA "Lightning". I knew, of course, about the Yankee love of huge machines: on the West Coast you could still see old Indians, and everywhere were GoldWings and rumbling Harleys – each one a Winnebago on two wheels – but this…. This was from a graphic comic drawn by a thirteen year-old high on Ritalin.

'What on EARTH is it?' I cried.

'Ah. It's a Boss Hoss.'

'A what?' I'd never heard of it.

'A Boss Hoss.'

'….as in chief or most influential horse, I presume?' Holly yawned. Clearly, to her eye a motorcycle was a motorcycle.

'Chevy V8 5.7 litre engine. No gearbox – no need. From 0 – 160 mph in one gear – smooth as a baby. Twelve inch wide rear tire inflated to only 10 psi to help you corner – you take it up on the rim and then down again back on the straight. Look, Harley "Fat Boy" tank with a welded centre section – brings it up to three feet wide. The clutch is out of a GM truck, servo-operated, servo fuel lines, servo brakes, the lot. What else? Erm, Harley forks – widened – an' electrics, but a Hoss frame – real heavy gauge tube.' Blundell reeled off this info in a manner which suggested that he had said it many, many times before. 'One drawback is fuel consumption, though. Seven to ten miles per gallon is all you get – an' that's going easy. Sometimes the tank's gone in fifty miles. She's one thirsty cow.'

'Where did you get it? You didn't make it, did you?'

'Hell, no. It's a firm down in Tennessee. Like I say, they've built two hundred or so right up to now. It's the ultimate, man. I'd never have thoughta *makin'* something like this. That's not to say I can't customise. I've got acetylene cutting equipment, an' a lathe. I've bobbed an' chopped Harleys and Bonnevilles in my time. But it's a big job, an' when you can just buy a mother like this....well.'

'And how much did it....? If you don't mind my asking?' said I, gesturing at the huge machine.

'Cost? Well, it woulda been near on thirty thousand dollars. I got it two years ago. I'd been down in L A with Holly's paw, Nathan, an' we went over to the Griffith Park Sidecar Rally; but, hell, you know what I mean, being from Los.'

'Sorry, but I didn't know there was such a thing. Do you mean in that park before the zoo? Off Crystal Springs Drive?'

'Yeah, every Fall they hold it. Biggest sidecar rally in the world. Been goin' on and off since 'seventy-two. You come off Hollywood Boulevard up to Los Feliz just below the Observatory an' then scoot on round about two, three miles and there you are. Zoo's right on ahead.'

'Well, well, and I thought I knew what went on. But sorry, you were saying.... It would have been thirty grand....?'

'This one was on a big side-hack, only a few months old, but the owner was selling. One guy bought the sidecar, I bought the bike an' had it shipped back East. Saved myself five thousand dollars. An insurance policy'd come in. I tell you, I had a lot of breakin' down of the objection brigade; but now she loves it – clings on its ass like a flea on a charging hippo. It's got 345 bhp, an' I once got 0 – 60 in under three seconds with Twink on board screechin' in my ear. But never again – it's fifty-five miles per now,' said Blundell virtuously.

'But you can do fifty-five on a Jap 100cc two-stroke,' I said. 'What do you need six litres for to do the same job?'

Holly stepped in with a plea for the defence.

'Blundell is a lovely, cuddly eccentric,' she laughed and, with a lithe movement which surprised me, because somehow I had not thought of her as athletic, she vaulted onto the bike's obese three-foot wide back and sat up there in, I was aware, an alluring pose. And yet, as I stood and gazed, I had that disturbing sense that here again was a metaphor – a gross metallic representation of all that was wrong with consumerist America.

'I guess I haven't taken a ride on it since last Sunday. So it could do with a run,' said Blundell. 'As you're a bike-lovin' man, Mike, an' you haven't seen one of these before, why don' you take it out and warm it up? You can go out East to FDR drive – you got eight, nine miles open road there. Forget about the 40 mph posts – most everyone does sixty plus.'

I remembered going along FDR Drive years before. Between 23rd and 30th streets, the highway is built on rubble from bombed British cities used as ballast in WWII freighters. I took a look at the monster.

'Thanks, Blundell. You're a trusting type. But I haven't ridden for years and, really, I'd rather just take it round a few blocks. Just to say I'd ridden a Boss Hoss.'

'Okay. But it sure is a peach to ride. Look, I'll help you start it. The rest is easy-peasy. You jus' sit.'

It turned out that the truck clutch was too heavy to be pulled out by hand, so hydraulics have to do that. But the hydraulics don't work until the engine is turning, and the engine can't be turned until the clutch is disengaged. Catch 22. Blundell explained that the huge battery powered all the pumps first before ignition. He turned a key and the temple was filled with an organic sucking and sloshing and whirring as the auxiliary motors came to life. 'Shift the gates, honey.' Holly opened the wooden doors into the alleyway which ran up from El Bodegon. 'Ready?' asked Blundell. He pressed a button, pulling the clutch in as he did so, and the temple shook with the rolling thunder of a Chevrolet V8 firing through short pipes. Holly clapped her hands over her ears. I imagined the sound cascading in long waves down the alley into the street beyond, round into the avenues and across into Manhattan before dissipating itself in a thousand lesser noises. 'I'll get her out!' shouted Blundell.

The monstrous cycle was manoeuvred with difficulty out of the doors and halfway down the alleyway. I was later told it weighed 1100 lbs with fuel, and I could see the strenuous efforts Blundell was making to keep it upright. He filled its ample saddle to overflowing. I suppose it was the only motorcycle in the world not to have been dwarfed by his blubber. Man and machine looked made for each other. Next to the Hoss, the bulbous Electra Glide seemed about as imposing as a Vespa scooter.

'Take her round!' hooted Blundell, dismounting and holding the shuddering brute upright. 'You don' need a helmet if you're only going round the Village – not for a coupla blocks.'

Reluctantly I took the saddle. The floorboards came readily to my feet, but the levers were a stretch. The widened Fat Boy tank heaved up like a porpoise; the width of the V8 forced my knees apart. I gave the engine a tweak of throttle and gentled eased the clutch home. The bite was immediate. To my horror, I was out beyond the side-walk without knowing how I'd got there. Brakes screeched. Horns blared. I struggled to halt the Hoss and keep it upright.

'Jerk!'

'Ass-hole!'

'You wanna kill yo'self, man?'

I don't know why I went ahead and drove Blundell's giant toy through the busy streets of Greenwich Village. I suppose I didn't want to appear tame in Holly's eyes. I hadn't been on a bike since the early '80s, and that had been a comparatively tiny Triumph TR6 650 twin. But the old trick of balancing came back almost immediately. The Boss Hoss felt quite stable going in a straight line, thanks to the gyroscopic effect of a 12" wide Corvette rear tyre and half a ton of V8 slung way down. Cornering was another matter as the beast swung itself up onto the edge of its obscene rear wheel, teetered round on the squared-off rubber and then slammed down squidgily as the bike straightened up. The effect was a powerful self-centring device and made the hulk reluctant to take corners. I appreciated on that ride how much muscle Blundell packed under his lard. Thank Gawd I didn't prang it, stall it or drop it – but gingerly got it round a few blocks and home – with

Holly, I fancied, smiling at my prowess.

And so my first enjoyable evening for ages came to an end. At the door at the top of the little steps, after I had bade goodnight to Blundell and Twinkle, Holly came close to me and said,

'Mike, I hope Blundell hasn't been annoying. I'm so fond of him and Twink, and I do indulge him.'

'Good gracious, no!' I recall gasping. 'I've had a marvellous time.' And I added, meaning it, 'What a fascinating life you lead, Holly.' I reached out to take her hand. I think I was going to shake it; Californians sometimes do this on saying goodbye. But I ended up holding it and feeling for its make-up and form. And she didn't withdraw. Behind us, in the passage which served as a hallway to the house, were five or six light, transparent, plastic warehouseman overcoats of outsize aspect hanging up next to a mirror. 'What are those for?' I asked. 'They *are* Blundell's, aren't they?'

'Oh, yes,' she smiled. 'Blundell uses them for teaching. I asked him why when I first came to stay. Do you know what he said?' She deepened her voice, drew down the corners of her mouth and put on a low Blundell-ish gurgle. 'He said: "I wear them when I teach tenth-grade History, my dear. I find the boys' spit runs off them more easily".'

I could think of no reply to that.

The soft, warm pressure of her fingers – like little dry sausages – tingled and lingered in my hand as I found a late taxi back to Fifth Avenue, wondering if Ben Jonson was the same as Doctor Johnson and knowing I'd heard of one of them.

I lay back on the cab seat as the smoke from the driver's spliff wafted back to me. Kaleidoscope faces, mad and pale in the thrumming night, filled the side windows. The boys' spit runs off plastic more easily, does it? Johnson had oral rage? – Well, well. A Boss Hoss has a six-litre motor and no gears? – Fancy. The cab smelt of marijuana, stale spices and petrol fumes. The city roared around me. It was an insistent nightmare – garish and new. But in its still centre, with fingers like small, dry sausages, I felt that Holly – with her Walt Disney child's smile and those movingly searching eyes – waited calmly.

And in the midst of all the new impressions, I had not had time to figure out: who had told Mopsa about her? Who had helped Mopsa get to New York? And why?

Chapter 7: **Sunday Snatch**

I flipped page after page of commentary from the enormous folder I had been given. I couldn't get any form of grip on what I was reading, with its many references to artists and institutions I'd never heard of, and for all the guff about camera, setting and direction I couldn't really visualise any of it. I stepped across to the 'phone. Out of the window, across the trees, a heat-haze made indistinct shapes of the Manhattan skyline. The Waldorf's near-silent air-con purred. A buzz started at the other end of the line in the Village. Then the receiver was lifted.

'Hello?'

'Hello, Holly? Is that you? Oh, it's Mike Greville here. Is this a good time to ring?'

'Mike? Of course. No problem.'

'Well, I know it's Sunday. Sorry to commit the solecism of ringing about biz on the Sabbath, but…..'

'Any worries? Is it the scripts?'

'I'm finding it a bit hard reading.'

I paused. New York on a Sunday is a lonely place. In L A, when every day was devoted to business and to the socialising which oiled the wheels of that business – and, of course, trying to avoid Mopsa and her latest crap – I had never noticed the yawning nature of Sunday. There, then, back East, in that hotel, it yawned round me like an echoing canyon. Sherbert was out of town in Boston, finalising the deal with PSB TV. I knew no one else.

I had been glancing through the huge Sunday paper, and its thick bulk sprawled by the phone. "Increased Fears

About Racist Chemical Tests" read the headline article. "Claims have been made that the chemical which leads to wanton violence, alcohol and drug dependency, and other forms of anti-social behaviour, is present to an unusual extent in that part of the population affected by diabetes: African-Americans, Hispanics and Indigenous Americans. These findings have continued to fuel controversy."

'Um, Holly, shall I pop over to the Village to discuss it, then?'

'Today's not the best of days, Mike. We've been asked to a cousin of Blundell's in Yonkers and we're sort of on our way out right now. Is tomorrow at the office okay?'

'Of course. I mustn't delay you. Have a nice lunch. It is lunch, isn't it?'

'Yes, it's lunch. We're back again this afternoon, but I don't know when.'

'See you tomorrow then.'

'Of course. Goodbye, Mike.'

'Goodbye, Holly.'

And I thought: DAMN!

I picked up her efficient plastic wad again and riffled through it. I then dragged the armchair to the window and plumped down. How *annoying*, I thought, that I wasn't in a cab on the way to Blundell's house to spend Sunday with Holly. I put my legs on the coffee-table.   Twenty minutes passed. I turned the pages slowly; the air-con hummed. I got up and stretched. I felt imprisoned by the room. I thought I would try to digest the rest of the material out in the park. Anything was better than being confined to a hotel suite on a warm day. I slipped the sheaf of papers under my arm and went down in the elevator.

I had just nodded to the girl at the reception desk – a brunette with long hair with whom I'd struck up a twice daily nodding and grinning relationship – when there was a blurring rush by my side and my arms were pinioned from behind.

In my astonishment and alarm, I nearly dropped all Holly's papers. The grip on me was so strong that I simply could not turn to see who had grabbed me.

Around me, I was aware of puzzled stares, then frantic excitement and shouting.

The brunette was staring with eyes round in alarm and indecision. I heard a scream. It seemed to come from an elderly blue-rinser at the corner of my vision. Two porters rushed towards me, one of them carrying a rug. He was waving it in an odd manner like someone pretending to be a Spanish bull-fighter.

All the time this was happening, I was thinking: Careful. Don't drop the folder or you'll get the pages mixed up. The folder was, however, as sharply pinioned as my arms, tucked under my left bicep, its folded edge making an uncomfortable ridge between my arm and my thin cotton jacket.

The bull-fighter stopped in front of me. Then, as he dived to my right, I was quickly twisted round to face him. He held out the absurd rug, flapping it. He was fat and making grunting noises. Uproar increased around us.

Up to this point – and it can only have been a minute or two since I had stepped from the elevator – I can honestly say that I had not considered what was holding back my arms. Nor had I struggled or made efforts to see who lurked behind me. I was in suspended animation – a detached witness at my own violation. But now I started in earnest to twist round to see who or what was behind me.

I thrashed my way out of that ferocious, nipping grasp, ridiculously mindful of not letting Holly's folder drop underfoot.

I had some sort of – of band round my body, like – like a huge dog's collar.

I pulled my way towards one of the long mirrors in the panelled walls near the restaurant. Behind me came gasping breaths as my unseen assailant struggled to keep me close. I felt that I was being torn down towards the floor. The shrieks and roars from all around were deafening. A woman, entering from the street, dropped an oblong box with ribbons on it. Another woman, who had come into the lobby with two children, gasped and wrenched the kids back. I bull-dozed on towards the looking-glass and turned forcibly to see who or what was behind me reflected in it.

It was Mopsa.

And she was birthday naked.

Her teeth were bared in a snarl.

She had thrown a belt – no, a chain, encased in blue plastic - around us both. The ends were padlocked with a huge lock.

Even as I gaped at this astonishing reflection, she was dropping a small, shiny key into her mouth.

My arms viciously pinned, I was unable to clutch at those flecked lips to claw back that disappearing key.

Mopsa swallowed – her eyes pumping with triumphant gleams.

'GOTCHA! You devious bastaaaaaard,' she crooned.

The uproar in the lobby of the Waldorf-Astoria was stupendous. I spun round and round; blue-rinses, pot bellies, big curved noses, designer stubble and leather mini-skirts hemmed us in as with a wall. Yet all were equidistant – creating that careful circle which is interested in, but wary of being too close to, nutters who cause outrages in public places.

'I swallowed the key, Mikey. You are NEVER gonna get free!' howled Mopsa.

'For God's sake! For God's sake!' I kept repeating.

'Jeeesus whizz! She's not got *one* goddam thread on her ass.'

'I guess this is some sorta show.'

'Dorian! Dorian! Call the hall porter!'

'Get 'em outa here, Scobie!'

'Yessir!'

'....an if I now DELIBERATELY give myself constipation, you're gonna be tied up to me for a long, long time, lover of mine. Together forever, Mikey.'

'Over here, Mr Hepworth, sir. Scobie's called the cops!'

I was aware that a tall, dark figure seemed to have detached itself from the careful, gabbering circle.

'Mr Greville? Can I be of assistance?'

It was the hotel manager. I had seen him once before and he had greeted me with the easy equality which those who are used to dealing with the famous can summon up. Even now, faced with one of his guests (the one who occupied the suite once graced by Richard Burton) in a state of bondage with a naked female lunatic in the public forum of his lobby, he lost none of his effortless assurance. 'Perhaps you would both like to step across to my office, Mr Greville? Scobie, Landon, please assist Mr Greville and this young lady into my office. Thank you, Ladies and gentlemen, the Starlight Bar is now open and the restaurant will soon be serving brunch.' It was smoothly done. My head in a whirl, my arms pinioned (the scripts trapped under the left one), Mopsa snapping and snarling behind me, I was led into a dark panelled room. He did not bid me sit down, and I appreciated his sense in not doing so. Upon whatever piece of furniture I reposed, Mopsa would have had to act as my cushion. With a wave of a hand, he dismissed Landon to the porter's desk; with the other he positioned Scobie with his back to the door. He then sat down and regarded us calmly from behind his desk.

'I am in possession of the facts,' said he.

'Brave words!'sneered Mopsa, speaking for the first time since she had been hustled from the lobby. 'You wanna have more facts? The fact is that this – this sputoid to which I have gotten myself chained has cast me off for another.'

'Another what?' gasped Mr Hepworth, his composure rattled by Mopsa's sudden volubility and by the impossibility of his knowing where to look. He seemed only then to be aware that she was unclothed.

'Fact Two. I am remaining chained to the sputum until he renounces another entirely. Fact Three. You cannot free him – or me. My chains are without, but the key is within.'

'Scobie, you called the police?'

'Yessirree-bob.'

'Emergency or precinct?'

'Precinct, sir.'

'Ring them again and call them off. We can't afford a scandal. Tell them it was a joke on a guest, and it's been cleared up.'

Scobie slipped from the room.

'Mopsa....' I gurgled, trying to see behind me.

Mr Hepworth stepped into a closet at the back of the office and took out a light grey overcoat. He came forward with it.

'Madam,' he said, ' I'm going to slip this over your shoulders.'

'You do, an' I'll start screaming,' cried Mopsa, whisking round so that I was face-to-face with the coat. He advanced, making encouraging sounds. Mopsa kept me between herself and the coat. Scobie popped back into the room.

'They ain't comin', sir. Matter of fact, they hadn't started yet. They's used to fruitcakes in hotels.'

At the combination of the flapping coat and the word "fruitcake", Mopsa began to scream. With her nails digging into my back and sides, she let out peal after peal of shrieks. I stood, helpless and deafened.

'Eeeeeeeeeeeeeee!'

'Scobie!'

'Yessir?'

'Eeeeeeee!'

'Fetch the chain-cutter from the underground garage.'

'Yessir.'

'Eeeeeeeeeeee!'

'We'll soon have you free, Mr Greville.'

'Eeeeeeooooooooooow!'

We swayed to and fro in front of Mr Hepworth's tidy desk. After what seemed about four hours, but was probably only five minutes, Scobie returned wielding a pincer-like device.

'You gotta hold the young lady still, boss,' said he, 'case I get a finger off in error.'

Resisting wildly, trampling the coat on the floor, Mopsa's damp, naked flesh gyrated in Hepworth's grip, while Scobie took one of the bands which coupled us in the jaws of his pincers.

'You won't cut through these!' cried Mopsa. 'You think I've got no brains? You think I'd buy cable you can cut like it was bubble-gum? You insult women's intelligence through me!'

She gargled up saliva and began spitting it out over the persistent Scobie. He dodged, but grew spattered as he strained the bring the blades of his cutter through the armoured wires.

The globules of spit irresistibly brought Blundell to mind. I suddenly seemed to see his array of rubber warehousemens' coats. Surely, had he not told me that he possessed an oxy-acetylene cutter for motorcycle restorations in his Aladdin's cave?

'Ring this number!' I cried. 'Here, in my folder. Under my arm. First page. Ring the number under "Holly"!'

Mr Hepworth whisked the folded pages from under the

cable and my elbow. He stepped to his desk and started punching buttons. Scobie, having captured a circle of cable in the cutter's jaws, was putting his beef into severing it, growing pink with the effort. Mopsa spat and spat while he clucked, 'Nearly there! Nearly there!' But he wasn't.

'Phone's ringing, Mr Greville. Hold your head still and I'll place the receiver to your ear.'

'Holly!' I yelled – thinking I was speaking to her.

'Hey?' came a sharp squark from the other end. 'Who is it?'

'That's not you, Holly, is it?' I babbled. 'Can I speak to Mr Capitanchik, or – or to Miss Miall?'

'No, you cain't, mister, 'cos they ain't here. That's for why. Who's this speakin'?'

'Oh, Twinkle!' I gasped. 'I mean, Mrs Capitanchik. It's me, Mike Greville. We met the other evening.'

'Oh yeah, I thought I recognised the voice – kinda British. Holly's out, you know.'

I drew a deep breath. Mopsa was trying to pull me away from the desk. Scobie had lost grip on the cable. It was now or never.

'Can I.....?' I shouted, while Mr Hepworth continued to press the receiver manfully to my ear. 'That is to say....I'm in trouble. Can I come over straightaway? I'll – I'll have to bring someone with me......'

There was a pause.

'I guess I didn't go over to Yonkers, 'cos I wanted a quiet day. So now I don't get no quiet day anyway. Okay, so come over. What I can do I dunno – Holly's out, as I say – but come.' With a shriek, Mopsa jerked us both from the desk. 'Thank y....' I spluttered, but the phone had crashed to the floor and Twinkle and I were cut off. We stumbled into Scobie. Mr Hepworth retrieved the instrument with a pained expression.

'You can't help me,' I said to him. 'neither of you can. I can help myself if I am able just to get over to the Village. Will you call me a cab?'

Mopsa shouted,

'WHAT are you planning?' She pressed her mouth into my neck. I could feel her wet tongue and sharp teeth. 'I'll bite my way through your spinal cord, you traitor. I am the toothy-machine...!' She started gnashing loudly, snapping too close to my ear-lobes for comfort.

'I don't think a yellow cab driver will take you both, Mr Greville,' said Mr Hepworth solemnly. And then I started laughing, and he looked pained. 'But,' he went on, 'I should be happy to take you over to the Village in my car.' He picked up the script folder and slipped it back under my arm. We bundled out of the rear of the Waldorf-Astoria – a very different zone from the awning and art-deco of the street frontage – and, with Scobie and me doing our best to hold Mr Hepworth's coat over the squirming Mopsa, drove in the manager's shiny Buick to the Village. I gave directions and we drew up outside El Bodegon. 'I guess it doesn't look like I can drive you up to the house, Mr Greville.'

'No, I know. It's a pedestrian precinct. Can you back up round the side of this block?' We edged to the end of the wall behind which was Blundell's fantastic oriental "temple". 'Scobie,' said I, 'would you run round to the front and tell the lady who opens the door that we're out back?'

Mopsa, who had not spoken directly to me during the car ride, but had contented herself with struggling and hissing obscenities, now gave tongue.

'You know what this? This is kidnapping! I'll get a subpoena! I'll have you in court. This is what Georgie warned me about! MEN! Ooooh, Georgie!'

Twinkle Capitanchik appeared at the side of the car and peered in. I had not seen her in daylight and I realised with a shock that she was years older than Blundell. Her spangled glasses seemed to take in everything with a swift, gleaming glance.

'Chained together, huh?' she grunted.

'Er, hello again,' said I, 'and thank you for coming to my rescue. I remember that Mr Capitanchik said he had cutting equipment here and I rather hoped…..'

'Rescue! I'm being kidnapped!' screeched Mopsa.

The mad bitch and I were levered out of the Buick. Scobie and Mr Hepworth, after depositing us inside the "temple", discreetly made their farewells and drove off. People who claim that real olde-worlde service is no longer given in New York hotels are wrong.

'Wha' happened to her finger?' asked Twinkle.

'Her finger?'

I peered down at Mopsa's hands. It was difficult to look behind me, of course, but now that Twinkle had drawn my attention to it, I realised that the little finger on Mopsa's left hand was missing. In its place was a raw, red stump with puckered skin.

'My God!' I gasped. 'That fool Scobie! He didn't…? He couldn't have……when he was trying to cut the cable…..'

'Who IS this old whore?' snarled Mopsa.

'Mopsa! What happened to your finger?'

'The stump looks healed, but it ain't healed well,' said Twinkle.

'If you MUST know, you prying perverts, a friend of mine, yes, a DEAR friend of MINE, bit it off recently,' said Mopsa with dignity.

'Mopsa!'

'You,' went on Mopsa, wearily, 'whoever you are, you old corpse, would not know of whom I speak, but sputoid here knows her. Georgie tried to stop me coming to New York. All men are evil, she said. And yet she was going to go off with someone whose name I will not utter, an' I told her that we would never meet again in this world or the next. I said I was gonna grow my hair and dye it an' wear glasses an' go to England with Mike here and that she'd never find me. "Oh," she said, laughing and taking me by the hand, "I'll recognise you, my little egg," an' she put my hand to her jaws an' bit off my little finger.'

I twisted round to search her face, but it was expressionless. So THAT was why she had been wearing yellow gloves when she barged into my hotel room! 'She ate it too. She crunched it up,' added Mopsa.

I was speechless.

'Nice friends you got,' drawled Twinkle. 'I'm gonna get some tea, an' it's not fancy, just Lipton's, so you can both wait here; although how you gonna sit down, I dunno.'

We stood until Twinkle returned with the tea and we

drank it standing up, Mopsa trying to get her cup between her face and my back, and sticking her stump out genteelly, Mr Hepworth's coat still over her naked shoulders. The situation was so absurd that I began to have the strongest conviction that I was going to break into convulsive hysteria which might never stop.

'Yeah,' said Twinkle, collecting cups, 'I can't stay in here all afternoon. I got things to do. My husband won't be back for a while, so I guess you better just lie here. And you, young lady,' she said to Mopsa, ' you oughta go to college an' do something useful.'

'Why don't you drown in your phlegm, corpse?'

'An',' continued Twinkle, 'Learn to talk more lady-like. I don't know what you see in her, Mr Greville, I really don't.'

She whisked out with the cups.

'Oh, but......I say – she and I aren't.....' I began, but with a flash of spectacles she was gone.

'CORPSE! COW!' screamed Mopsa.

'Oh, for Christ's sake!' I cried, wrenching hopelessly round to look her in the face. 'You are sick, hopelessly ill. You need treatment. You can't say.....can't do things like.....' But it was no use. Mopsa was laughing in a gurgling way and I could feel her saliva on my neck.

'You turn your head again, lover-boy; you say another word, an' I'm gonna bite off your ear-lobe,' she crooned.

So we lay on the springy sofa-like bench, Mopsa against my back, me facing the great shape of the Boss Hoss. Ironically, coupled as we were, the only object on which we might have been comfortable was its huge, capacious saddle. As the springs of the settee ground into my leg, I wondered if I might suggest moving to it. But Mopsa had lapsed into silence. Soon she began to snore. I realised she was high on something – God knew what.

I pulled Holly's TV scripts from under my arm and managed to prop a bit I hadn't read in front of my eyes. It was what my book-worm brother would have done, no doubt. Until that afternoon, chained to a drugged-up maniac, with hours to go before release, I had not appreciated how important it is to have something handy to read.

Chapter 8: **The battle of the Hog and the Hoss**

I laid the bulky sheets of Holly's file down on Blundell's oriental palace's floor. My right fore-arm was cold with the effort of holding the pages up before my eyes against the pull of the cable. The blood had slipped away from my fingers and had left them white and without feeling. My hip dug into the settee and was beginning to have that atrophied sensation which comes before bed-sores. I had not moved for nearly an hour. Behind me, her back pressed into soft cushions, Mopsa continued to doze. No wonder – she was comfortable and drugged up and I was neither. I don't know why Blundell's back alley should have felt cool – a July day in New York is a July day – but I imagined that the sloping canvasses of Shangri-La permitted no ray of sun to penetrate.

I made a stiff movement. Mopsa gurgled, but did not awake.

And what was I thinking about? The high bullshit quotient of the scripts, and my strong feeling that much of what was due to be filmed would not bring light or entertainment, or find an appreciative audience, and, more important to me, a return for my investment. Once again, I made a mental note to tax Sherbert on the drift of these episode ideas which, I kept grimly reminding myself, were under-pinned by my dough.

Then it became a case of move or get gangrene of elbow and hip. So I wriggled, dragging the supine bitch up with me into a semi-seated position. Disturbed into wakefulness, she immediately began to give tongue.

'What are you MOVING for? Think you can get away? You an' me, together forever, Mikey – an' that's what you want deep-down if you just examine your rotten little leather-purse of a soul. This is the reality you try to escape from – this is the sort of Art you say you hate – well, the reality and the Art are one. One! Jeez, will you STOP draggin' me! We represent what we really are, Mikey. We are together because we ARE together, an' that's what I want. The key to release is IN me. In ME, you unnerstan'? IN me!'

Her hard voice dinned on in my ear, but I was listening to other sounds: a deep voice, a door closing. Blundell? But what time was it? Had I slept? I must have done….

'Mopsa….Shut up, can't you?'

'….an' what's IN me can't EVER get out. That key is in my black hole, boy, an' you try an' reach into me, an'….'

'Mopsa, you cow! What is the time? Look at my watch! You can see it more easily than I can. What's the bloody time?'

The door into the "temple" opened. Blundell's huge form blotted out a sudden shaft of sunlight – a one-man solar eclipse. He lumbered forward, his circumference shaking. He looked, I thought, a little peeved, but also faintly amused; a tight line seemed to lie between his eyes, but a grin simultaneously writhed under that bushy beard. I knew what he was thinking; his beloved Holly had gotten herself interested in the sort of guy who is intimate with weirdo druggie bimbos from L A. Should he help me or not? Keep his previous good opinion of me, or not?

'You came, Blundell!' I gasped, too het up to think of a

more suitable formality to address one whom I had met but once and who was so much senior to me. I tried to twist Mopsa and myself round so that I could see him properly, for the sofa faced the long wall and the motorcycles.

'Sure. Twinkle rang me out at Yonkers. I set out as soon as I could, but hell, I finished lunch first, Mike. Knew you'd understand that.'

'Blundell, what's the time?'

'A lil' before four, I guess.'

Good God, I had only been yoked to Bitch-machine since mid-day! It already seemed several centuries since I had, as it were, walked alone.

'Did you bring...? Er, that is... is Holly here too?'

'She's comin' later, Mike.' Again I detected disapproval. 'I thought it best. Twink says you two have got tangled in some shit an' need an oxy-acetylene cutter.'

Blundell stepped up and peered round the settee at us both. As he took in that Mopsa was naked, his saucer-like eyes widened into protruding globes. Then he grinned – a big, big tolerant grin that spread across his moon of a face. 'Saw this one other time in Saigon – hell, it was at Loopy Lu's whore-house when Kam Ling was running things for the soldiers. Shit, an' I was highern' the Empire State that one time, and I hadn't seen bondage like it...'

'Blundell,' I snapped, cutting off the 'Nam reminiscences, 'I'm sorry to interrupt your trip down memory-lane, but do I take it that you think this is some sort of freaky Sunday afternoon sex-game?'

'Twink does. Ain't it?'

'No, it jolly well isn't! Mopsa, will you PLEASE

explain. I'm sorry, I should have introduced you before now: Blundell, this is Mopsa Greene – Mopsa, Blundell Capitanchik.'

'May I *interduice* you! So British!' chuckled Blundell. 'So this isn't a love-game gone awry?'

'Of course not,' I snapped again.

Up to now, Mopsa had not spoken. I couldn't see what she was doing, of course, but I imagined that like most people confronted with Blundell's enormity for the first time, she had been stunned into silence. Now she cried,

'Of course it IS!'

'Mopsa!'

'Mikey likes his fun real freaky. You should see his chains, his TONGS, his SPIKES at home in L A. He doesn't really want you to try an' release him. It's part of his game.'

Blundell gazed down at us. I sought his bulging, glassy eyes.

'Blundell, I hardly know this woman. What she has done is beyond my comprehension. The last time I saw this poor, wretched girl was in a mental home in L A.'

Mopsa began shrieking wildly. 'Yes,' I went on, 'in a home for the terminally deranged – in Glendale.'

'Liar! Scum!'

'I –er – I used to visit the inmates as my contribution to charity, you know, to bring some happiness and normality into their twisted lives. This patient developed a sad and violent attachment to me....'

'You lying BASTARD!' Mopsa's fists pounded my shoulders.

'....in her deranged sort of way. She pulled this absurd stunt in the hotel – I mean actually in the foyer – this morning when I was on my way out to the park. If you don't believe me, ring Mr – Mr – (at this juncture I nearly forgot the Efficient Manager's name) – Mr Hepworth in his office. He'll confirm what I say. He and Scobie, a bell-hop, brought us here. Look, that's his coat! They couldn't release me at The Waldorf – they hadn't the equipment. Then I thought of you and all your tools and suchlike.'

I'm ashamed to think of how I reeled off the fibs to Blundell, but I had visions at the time of his banning me from seeing Holly, of his writing to his old comrade, her father, of his distaste for me. I was angry with Mopsa for dragging me into such a compromising and embarrassing farce so close to Holly's life. I had a dreadful image of her dropping into the "temple" to find us doing our double-act if Blundell delayed much longer. I wanted to establish in Blundell's mind how very, very sketchily I was acquainted with this naked girl attached to my back.

Now Mopsa made a mistake. So typical of her. If she had quietly explained to Blundell her prior claims over me as she saw them, and her need to take this step as a metaphor of her belonging to me, and begged him to mind his own business, the eccentric gentleman in him might have agreed. But, observing how he took my information about Mr Hepworth and seeing his eyes rest on the efficient manager's coat – that circumstantial detail in the midst of lies, so necessary to secure belief – she turned her spate of invective on him instead.

'You fat tub of offal! You think I'm from a nut-house?

You moron! You *believe* this slimy piece of shit, you cretinous fat pig? Well, where are you from then? A freak circus? Roll up, see the lardiest freak in the world! Sink your arms in his blubber! Lose your best friend in his folds of greasy, stinking meat! Hey, Fatso!'

His expression suddenly grim – as I imagine it might have been on the day he began spitting on his disruptive pupil – Blundell lumbered to a large wooden chest between the two motorcycles.

'Jus' wait a moment, Mike,' he grunted. 'I'll have you outa this in no time. What an awful thing to have happened.' And to Mopsa he said,' I know you can't help everything you say, missy, but you need to learn to keep a more po-lite tongue in your head...'

'Freak! Fat bag of pus!'

'....or you'll get a *spanking.*' His threat was so like that of an Edwardian father, so unlike that of an ex 'Nam Hells Angel free-thinker that I had to smile.

'Mind Holly's script!' I cried, as he pulled a gas-cylinder and cutting-torch towards the sofa. He fielded the folder and shoved it onto a table.

'Keep very still, Mike, an' don't either of you look at the flame. I'm gonna slip a piece of asbestos and leather between the cable and you.' There was a sudden smack. 'An stop wriggling, young lady, or you're gonna burn your ass.'

'You – hit – me – again – an' – I'm – g-g-gonna – SUE YOU, FATSO!' roared Mopsa.

Slap!

Shriek!

Slap! Slap! Smack!

Silence.

'That's better,' said Blundell grimly. 'Now hold on.'

There was a snick of a match and a hissing. 'Don' look at the flame,' he warned us again.

A stench of burning plastic filled the "temple" as the covering of the cable was seared off. Then we kept very still. Even Cow-face had enough sense, I reckoned, not to invite that extremely fierce blue flame – hot, even through the thick asbestos padding – to make contact with her.

'There,' said Blundell. 'Don' move yet.' He reached into his tool chest and fished out a heavy pair of metal cutters. 'Jus' cut through the last bit,' he grunted. With a snap we were free of each other at last. I jumped up, slapping Blundell on his fat shoulder. My *"decree nisi"* had come. Never had a divorced man felt at such liberty. Resisting the opportunity to taunt Mopsa, I took Blundell to one side and whispered,

'Blundell, I can't thank you enough. But look, I want to get her away before….' I was going to say: before Holly arrived, and I saw that Blundell knew I was going to say it, so I changed it to: '….before she gets troublesome again. And I can't take her out of here dressed only in Mr Hepworth's coat, even in Greenwich Village.'

'Twink's got nothing that would fit her. And if you take something of Holly's, you're gonna have to tell Holly…'

Mopsa had slumped down on the sofa again and was crying noisily, her head in her hands. I wondered if the key she had so unnecessarily swallowed was cutting into some vital organ. 'I guess I know where I can get us a pair of jeans an' a T-shirt,' said Blundell. 'It's a little place down West Houston Street, somewhere between here an' Lafayette. It's open Sundays – I've seen it.'

'So what do I do? Out of here, take a right, left at Avenue of the Americas, down to West Houston...?'

'No, hang on. Hang on. I'm sorry, Mike,' hissed Blundell, 'but I'm not stopping here alone with your lady-friend. I got Twinkle to think of. *I* go for the clothes for the little lady. *You* wait here.'

He restored the cutting equipment to its chest, carefully re-packing it and checking the taps on the gas-cylinder. Then he fumbled with the choke on his Harley and started it. 'Pull back the doors, Mike,' he shouted. Mopsa started up at the roar and at the daylight pouring in from up the alleyway. Blundell swung a vast leg over his hog and, letting in the clutch, paddled the machine to the doors. He slipped into neutral again. 'Tell Twink where I've gone, if she comes out here. Won't be long – less than quarter of an hour.'

I nodded.

Just as I did so, I felt a violent blow over my kidneys. Mopsa had kicked me and sent me toppling forward on hands and knees as if about to offer libations to Blundell's hog. Vaulting over me, she ran full tilt at Blundell, pushing at him. His left leg was holding up the bike as he straddled it. His right was on the footboard and he just put it down in time. With a roar he wobbled off on the right and the Harley leaned over onto him. He yelped as he took its weight. Mopsa seized the bars and, with the astonishing strength that she sometimes displayed, heaved the cycle fully upright. It was ticking over with its steady thudding beat – that famous, patented "potato-potato" Harley-Davidson sound. Hair streaming, eyes wild, Mopsa vaulted aboard and hauled the twist-grip round. With a clamour of valves, a blast of exhaust and an agonised wail from Blundell, she was gone!

'My hog!' roared Blundell. 'C'mon! C'mon!' He told me many times later how pole-axed he felt at the outrage – his hog ridden off under his nose – yet how his old training had honed him for action.

I scrambled to my knees. 'Come? Come where? She's gone. Gone,' I kept repeating.

'We'll get her. Help me!'

He was tearing at the grand-piano-sized dust cover beneath which was his obscenely enormous second sickle: the six litre V8 Boss Hoss. 'Help me round with her,' he gasped. We wheeled the giant vehicle in a wide circle, round the sofa, past the table, past the chest to a position in front of the double doors. The dust from Mopsa's passing still hung in the air. Blundell jammed the electrics on. The subsidiary hydraulics pumped juice, whirring. A second later there was power to get the clutch withdrawn. Blundell started the V8. It turned over once and a rolling, easy bellow filled the "temple". 'Get on. Get on!'

I hesitated.

'What about Twink…?'

'Get ON, frig you!' shouted Blundell. So commanding was his tone that I found myself behind him on the bare few inches of saddle left unoccupied by his immense buttocks. 'I need you to ride the hog back when we get it!' he yelled. As Mopsa had done before him, he hauled twist-grip and, a bare minute after the fleeing Harley, we too were barrelling up the alley to the street. 'She turned left!' cried Blundell back at me. 'I heard her!' So left we went, up to Seventh Avenue. We careered out on it. Blundell took a quick glance down the curve towards West Houston, then slewed right and roared up, crossing West 14th Street at, I thought, 80 mph. I had no time for any reflection other than that I was on the world's biggest sickle with the world's fattest man, in deadly pursuit of the world's maddest woman, on the tiniest portion of seat imaginable and without a crash helmet. 'We gotta catch up before Times Square!' raved Blundell. 'Why! There she is!'

Mopsa was pulling away from the traffic lights at West 23rd Street, making a middle-finger gesture at the pedestrians gaping after her. Why she had stopped for a red light, I couldn't imagine, but the fact that she had done so had given us a chance. Over Blundell's rounded hump of a shoulder, I saw her look back for an instant, peer into one of her mirrors and then suddenly accelerate. I understood that it was only *then* that she knew she was pursued by us. She had not known, of course, about the second bike. To match her speed, we accelerated too, and I was nearly thrown off. I dug my fingers desperately into Blundell's fat. 'Aaah! Ha, haaa, no, no, don't!' shrieked my pilot. 'Gee whiz, don't do that!' The Hoss slewed wildly on the road.

'What?' I screamed, as the wind buffeted my face.

'Don' grab me, Mike. I'm ticklish!' howled Blundell.

Speechless, I pressed myself to him – but without clinging on – as the old Statler Hilton flew past on our right, then West 34th Street; then we boomed into the tired precincts of Times Square.

'She's going round again,' I shouted.

'Where'd she learn to ride like that?'

'She had a bike in L A,'

'What bike?' roared Blundell.

'Yamaha Virago, I think it was called,' I screeched into his ear.

'Pile of Jap crap, eh?'

'Eh? What did you say?' I screamed.

'Pile of…. Hell, never mind.'

Blundell flung the Hoss into a sharp left turn. The heavy machine rose up on the edge of its twelve-inch wide rear tire, squealing squidgily as Blundell kept the gas on. The strong tendency of such a tire to self-centre kept my pilot yanking on the bars. I felt that the rear would squirm from under us at any moment. The Hoss, with a clattering shout, whisked up level with Mopsa.

I made slowing-down movements. 'Mopsa! Mopsa! Stop!'

Mopsa's mouth moved in an obscenity – I couldn't make out what – then, after looking momentarily ahead, she screamed. Her hog had nearly gone into the back of a yellow cab. A plume of rubber smoke came from her back wheel as she stood on the brake pedal. Deftly, she swept round the taxi, on round the square, bumping up onto the pedestrian area and sending howling onlookers fleeing. I saw a young Japanese man rush out to stand for an instant posing, with Mopsa's naked form rocking away behind him. Before his friend's Canon could take the video, Blundell had bumped him over. I had a confused impression of glasses and T-shirt going down under our rumbling wheels. Mopsa blasted round once more and then went off out of the square down 42nd Street.

'She's maybe headin' for the airports!' cried Blundell.

'Queens Tunnel?' I shouted.

'Yeah, perhaps. God! My poor hog! But that bitch can ride! Who'da thought it?'

Past Grand Central, Mopsa took a look behind through her flying hair and suddenly hurtled up Lexington Avenue.

'Hold on!' gasped Blundell, forcing the Hoss into a turn and finding that the bike wouldn't be coaxed round quickly enough. We had to jump onto the sidewalk and, because the traffic was thickening, and Mopsa gaining, and the Hoss too wide to slip through the spaces she could get through, we stuck on that sidewalk for six blocks, horn blaring continuously and Blundell barely pausing to cross the intersecting streets. People came out of buildings and leapt back into them. I thought I heard a police siren behind us. The pressure waves kept the note constant, so I assumed that at last we had been spotted and that someone was on our trail. Unable to grip Blundell's wobbling rounds of flesh, I hooked my feet under the pegs and tightened my stomach muscles. It was like doing lengthy isometric exercise and I began to pour with sweat. An insect – a big one – hit me in the eye. But for the fact that it was a summer Sunday and New York traffic habitually runs slowly, we should have killed or been killed. Useless to appeal to my pilot; his blood was up, his precious hog ahead, and, no doubt, a thousand memories of his platoon pursuing defeated 'Cong filled his fat brain.

At 50th Street, Mopsa was once more in sight. Blundell gunned the Hoss up to, I should have said, about 90 mph, dived off the sidewalk and thundered up behind her. He tried to swerve in and trap the hog. She wrenched the grip open and tore off left. We followed, keeping level.

'Get off my HOG!' Blundell shouted, turning the Hoss's wheel in towards the Harley. Mopsa was forced to wobble to a halt by St Patrick's. She looked amazingly like a picture of Lady Godiva I had once liked in a *"Ladybird"* book of British history – except for the horse. Her hair streamed down her shoulders. Her legs bulged shapely against the Harley's fat tank. I suppose one can admire what a person looks like without in the least liking them – and any residual liking I had for the mad bitch had long evaporated. Then I saw blood on her foot. Steadying that heavy bike without boots! Poor idiot.

'Mopsa, please. What's the point? Just turn the motor off and we'll talk,' I pleaded. We were practically abreast of the Waldorf: full circle. 'Look, if you want to come up to my suite to talk things over, you're welcome – and I'll get you some clothes.' For a fantastic second a vision of Hepworth's and Scobie's faces as Mopsa sailed back naked into their foyer for the second time that day came into my brain.

'Yeah,' added Blundell.' Just switch off like a good girl. We can come to some agreeance. There's no need to go on like this.'

Blundell had rested his boot on the ground. I had begun to dismount. The Hog and the Hoss ticked over together, one with emphatic thuds, the other with a rolling, complex baritone – a conversation of machines paused in chivalric combat. Already the police siren was getting distinct again. A crowd, jeering and jabbering, gazing with wonder, had appeared from nowhere off Fifth Avenue. As if making up her mind to continue the impossible in preference to the insupportable, Mopsa shook her head violently from side to side, jammed the Harley back into gear, rammed the Hoss's front wheel, so that the handle-bars shoved Blundell back into me and, hanging a sudden right, roared the hog away up Fifth Avenue.

'Now I am getting SERIOUSLY annoyed,' articulated Blundell, and, deaf to any protest I might have made, he righted the Hoss under his great buttocks, nodded for me to re-mount which, as if in a trance, I did, and, with a bellow from the exhausts that must have been heard all over Manhattan, rotated his grip to the stop. In less than five seconds the Hoss was doing, it seemed, 100 mph, running dead centre up the wide avenue between the slow, wallowing cars, and gaining almost instantly on Mopsa. I slid right back under the fierce forces, off the seat onto the rear fender, and was only prevented from shooting onto the tarmac by the rear licence plate which jammed into my crutch agonisingly. I clutched desperately at Blundell's flapping shirt. Up the side of the Park we boomed and, at the Metropolitan Museum, had to decelerate violently, throwing me back up against my pilot again. A crocodile of students was strung out between the "Walk" signs. Burning rubber came up to my nose as it rammed into Blundell's podgy neck.

'C'mon! C'mon!' roared Blundell. The last of the party scampered onto the sidewalk and, without waiting for the lights to change, we rocketed forth once more. This time I very nearly did come off. Only a clutch at Blundell's collar saved me. 'Wurrrh!' gasped he, fighting to control the swerving Hoss. 'Wharrer you tryin' to do?' A second later he cried, 'Look! Look!' A well-known shape, aboard a cream Electra-Glide, was glimpsed whisking right into 88th Street. We shot round after it.

Then the surprise.

The road ahead was empty!

The usual desultory cabs and sedans were gliding up and down, of course, but of the familiar flying hair, bare butt and cream and blue machine there was no sign. Blundell screeched to a halt, the V8 shuddering under us, the exhaust banging. 'We can't have lost her!' he shouted. 'She came up this way!' He turned his head round and round on its plump neck until I fancied for a moment that his bulging eyes and bristling beard would go right round 360 degrees.

Well, well. Home, sweet home again. There, over the street was the frontage of the Guggenheim Museum. Round the corner was Sherbert's borrowed office. I could hardly believe that I had been in New York only a few short days – several months seemed to have lain between the chase on which Blundell and I were engaged and my stroll with Sherbert and Holly round the Gugg.

Blundell, blipping the throttle, continued to stare around

him.

Then, as I gazed over the road at Frank Lloyd Wright's bizarre edifice, as I stared at its soft white layers and the entrance set back from the sidewalk, I knew! Confused noises, screams, audible even over the traffic and the Hoss's tickover, were coming from the public entryway. People were running out and then running in again.

'Blundell! Blundell! She's gone into the museum!'

'Eh? Gone in there! Hey, yeah, I guess it's open a while longer. Yeah, but what's she done with the hog?'

'No! NO! She's gone in ON THE BIKE!'

Blundell's head again oscillated 180 degrees so that his eyes met mine.

'On my *hog*?' he whispered.

He gunned the mighty V8 and dragged the Hoss round in a semi-circle so that it faced the doorway of the Gugg. 'Steady the sickle.' A foot clumped into my stomach as he dismounted. I kept the bike upright. There was a snap behind me. Blundell clambered back onto the saddle, stuffing the Hoss's licence plate into his shirt. 'Shoulda done that earlier,' he said. 'Y'know – in case the pigs spot us.' Then, in a strange, sacerdotal voice, he intoned, 'SO – BE – IT!'

I closed my eyes.

The Boss Hoss bounded across the street towards the museum entrance. The dark aperture awaited us like the gateway of Destiny. I breathed deeply. With pipes bellowing, we cannoned up and over the steps and, on the track of the irrepressible Mopsa, plunged after her into the unknown.

Chapter 9: **How I came to love Holly**

'So – where do you come from?' I had asked Holly in the only slot we had had together at the Capitanchik's, back on the occasion of my first visit there. Twinkle had put her bird-like head round the living-room door after Blundell, standing, and filling the space between table and wall, had spooned the last whirls of chocolate tart into his capacious insides. She had cried,

'Blun! C'mon here. I want you.'

'Hey – ahey. I guess I was gonna take Mike and Holly out back to the "temple", Twink.'

'That can wait. Washing-up 'n' tidying comes first.'

I had jumped to my feet at the appearance of the pointy head. Not many men of my age do things like that anymore; feminism probably killed off the chivalric urge. Anthony told me he had offered his seat to a girl with shopping on the London underground in the late '80s and she had called him a patronising prick. But I sensed that Twinkle would see it as gentlemanly.

'Let me help,' I had cried. 'I'm very domesticated.'

'No, not at all. You jus' sit an' talk to Holly. Blun' can earn his supper.'

Blundell had steadied himself on his substantial feet, placing giant fingers on the table to counterbalance his weight.

'I guess I'll be out in a few minutes. Holly, offer our guest a lee-cure and a little more coffee. Excuse me, Mike.'

Thanks to Twink's tact, he had lumbered off and the room immediately seemed to double in size. Above our heads, the very bright Tiffany-style lamp made the table a bowl of light. Clearly the Capitanchiks liked to see what they were eating. Holly and I regarded each other in silence, and she looked away first. Then she rose and went out of the glare to the escritoire.

'I don't know what Blundell has got in,' she said. 'I don't really drink spirits. But there's a bottle of Southern Comfort and what looks like apricot brandy.' She fished out a tall bottle of colourless liquid. The writing on the label was unfamiliar. Polish? Czech? Yugoslavian? She was no doubt right in ascribing its contents to apricot, for a large yellow fruit was blazoned below the script. 'Mind you, it could be radio-active plum,' she laughed. 'So which is it to be?'

'Oh, I think it's a bit tame to swig Southern Comfort,' I replied. 'So I'll try a slosh or two of the Chernobyl plum.'

She poured a big measure of the mysterious drink into a glass on a stem and returned to the table. I took a sip.

'Brave you,' she smiled.

I sensed about then that she and I had something – some quirky and kindly love of the absurd, perhaps – which was drawing us together; and I also sensed that I was falling in love with her. Nothing in my long years in L A had prepared me for the impact she had made. I guess that many families just don't have members that set to, marry at the expected times, produce grandchildren, live near each other, and come together at the great Christian feasts in close – if not necessarily loving – conglomeration. Anthony is just not the marrying type; I don't recall his ever having had a girlfriend, unless one counts his affectionate relationship with Peter Buchan's sister Meriel in the summer holidays of our shared childhood in Scotland. He seemed happy as a bachelor in that rambling house of our grandfather's. He was, and is, as little travelled as I was restless. In his entire adult life I shouldn't think he has been close to more than three women, and that includes Ma.

I was so different from him. Up in Glenturret's time-capsule, he stoked his narrow-gauge engines. At school I had a difficult love-affair – painful at the time. In London I had disasters with Susie, that hippy Helen, Melanie, the other Melanie and Lucille. They were all dolly-birds with silly names, scented with cannabis, with lime flares and white lipstick, clumping on platform soles. Some I knew for barely a month. I liked none of them very much.

Anthony may not have fallen in love, but he does *like* women. I had assumed for years that his sense of the ridiculous (which I think I share), his capacity for irony, his boarding-school ethos, his schoolmaster's display of arcane knowledge, his clergymanish enthusiasm for trains and old toys and that once-upon-a-time queer sense of his destiny as a national preserver of such things, left him no time for people and relationships. He seemed to me, when I thought I knew him best – if I have ever known him – to be more at ease with machines, with objects; more interested in past than present (and women, if I've got it right, live for the present – nostalgia is a male disease) and inorganic rather than organic. I believed, when we were younger, that Anthony saw women as grotesques, as objects of schoolboy ironies.

PC, as practised in Cali-forn-eye-ay, would have had a field day with his many opinions and infelicities. He doesn't mind things a little battered, things that have to be fixed. He is tolerant, and has low expectations. For years, as a child, he would dread going to parties, and then would come home having had a wonderful time and been the hit of the occasion. I would look forward to them with feverish hope, and return with the acid of disappointment in my mucus.By the end of the century, however, I perceived him to have been on the emotional high ground. He would never need a shrink. He would never contract AIDS, commit a murder, destroy the happiness of a woman. He was, I now saw, happy, with a happiness born of a species of lay chastity, a refusal to act out a part assigned by society, a refusal to be enslaved by the world's demands on personal identity. He was free. I was the prisoner.

Few of the females I knew were what our grandmother would have termed "nice girls". She'd have thought Holly a nice girl, but not my old unfixed, self-obsessed, insecure, manipulative, fantasising organisms, as unsettled as I was. Helen left me in Tangiers, on a trajectory to dissolution. Melanie II ("Son of Melanie", as my brother called her, because she came after Melanie I, and her name was thus easy to remember) was the best of them. Yet my only memory of her is one wet eyelash hanging off as she curled up in a wet foetus of misery at the Gare du Nord. As for Lucille - how sordid were my attempts to buy her once I had come into grandpa's money. And at the end of the line: the appalling Mopsa.

I compared them all to Holly as I sipped Blundell's

strange booze.

And she sat across the table in a halo of silence. She had no idea, I'm sure, that thoughts of my failures were whistling through me.

'So, where do you come from?' I had asked, feeling it time that I found out something about her.

'From Ventura, California.'

'Really? How extraordinary. Well, it's not in the least extraordinary, I mean. But I actually know it fairly well.'

'Do you?'

'Didn't Sherbert tell you? I've been living in L A for twelve years – no, thirteen years coming up.'

She smiled. Her smile's attraction lay, I thought in its commingled wisdom and innocence.

'I *did* ask David about you,' she grinned, not entirely coyly at this admission of interest in me, but not escaping the delicate blooming of a blush, 'but he mainly confined himself to your boyhood, to that place in Scotland where you both met.'

'Glenturret – my grandfather's house.'

'….Glenturret, that's it. And about how bloated a plutocrat you had become and how he needed your backing for the series.'

'Hm. Ventura. It's got a nice pier. I thought that was rather a British touch when I first saw it, but then Santa Monica reminded me straightaway of Torquay.'

'….which is?'

'A seaside town in Devon, England.'

'I guess Ventura's a very ordinary place, Mike.'

'It's got a hideous freeway.'

'Oh yes – but that's always been there. Must have been built before I was born.'

'Fancy putting it right slap-bang-wallop on the front.'

'Front?'

'Oh, that's what we call it in England. The bit where town and beach meet. In fact, in the UK, it might be called Marine Parade.'

'Over here it's Ocean Boulevard, as I guess you know – much the same.'

'Won't you have some of this Three Mile Island juice? It's quite pleasantly anaesthetic once the lips have gone numb.'

'David also told me all about your grandfather – the haughty old gent who left you a lot of dough, and all that.'

'He left my brother Anthony a lot more. We think he did it to ensure his old house would be kept in the family and preserved. Anthony went to school there, you know, after Grandpa was forced to move back to London and the place became a Boys' Academy. He taught English there after university too, so he practically IS Glenturret. But tell me, what are *your* parents?'

'Dad's an attorney. He deals mainly with local property transactions. Mom teaches school. That's how she and Blundell met years ago. They were students together. And then, to make it almost seem like the hand of Fate, Blun got friendly with my Dad over in Vietnam. I suppose you could say Blun was a sort of fairy godmother because he brought them both together. Without him I wouldn't be here.'

'A toast to Blundell then,' said I, raising my glass and

taking a swig of the DDT, 'but your parents are elderly then – comparatively, I mean?'

'I guess not. Dad's fifty-seven and Mom's fifty-five.'

'Did you live in Ventura throughout childhood?'

'I went to High School there, but I was at UCLA. I majored in English Literature.'

'In English! Why did you pick that particular subject? I mean, I didn't go to university myself – although Anthony did – and he read English too, with History, I think.' (That was the second time that I had mentioned that my brother had gone to university, as if to prove that we were not all uneducated money-grubbers in our family.)

'I guess I could never cope with numbers,' Holly smiled,' so that ruled out Math, and I had no feel for chemistry or electricity or things like that thing….what do you call that thing….?' And she cupped her hands in the air while the Tiffany light picked out the few tiny etchings of lines round the corners of her eyes and mouth and I calculated that she must have been about twenty-six or twenty-seven. '….oh gee, what *did* they call it? Yes, a Van Der Graaf generator.'

'There used to be a rock band at home with that name. My brother knew their lead singer.'

'Fancy that. Before my time, I guess. Anyway, my lack of feel for Van Der Graaf generators ruled out Physics. I nearly fell for Geography because I thought it would be about studying Europe, but someone told me it was all about Malaysian population censuses and earthquakes in Mexico at university level, so I thought: "Presume not the works of God to scan; the proper study of mankind is Man" and I did Eng lit.'

'That's very well put,' I replied. 'Who said that?'

'Pope.'

'The Pope? Which one?'

'No, not THE Pope. Your Pope. Alexander Pope. Your English poet.'

'I'm sorry, Holly. Forgive me. My ignorance is too shaming.' I recall scanning her face closely for signs of intellectual arrogance and scorn, but found none. Her lovely mouth, with its quizzical smile, did curve amusedly as she asked,

'You have never come across Pope – the Rolls Royce of poets?'

'No, I don't think so. No, I'm afraid not.'

'And you from London too!'

Actually, I think I leant back grinning. I was then already a little too old to feel really abashed by my failure to have registered Alexander Pope's existence. That's one of the pleasures of not being twenty anymore; one cares less about being shown not to know things, especially if one has been fairly successful in one's field.

'Did you study a great deal about Britain? During your work for the English degree, I mean?'

'I did indeed. But then I've always been fascinated by it. It's why I chose to major in English in the first place. My favourites are Pope, Keats, the early Tennyson, Owen, Lawrence and Betjeman among the poets.'

'You'll be chuffed to know that I've heard of ALL of them – even admitting that Pope is a late acquisition,' I laughed. 'And as for Betjeman, isn't he still alive?'

'No.'

'Oh, I thought he was. Plump, old-fashioned, posh, toothy, wears a hat? I'm sure I saw him on TV once before I left England. Don't tell me I'm thinking of someone else?'

'No, you're not. But he's dead now.'

'Ah.'

'And Dickens, Eliot, Conrad – everyone does Conrad in California since *"Apocalypse Now"* – Galsworthy, Trollope, Buchan, Scott, Hardy, Lawrence and Waugh among the novelists. I have masculine tastes. I'm named after a character in Galsworthy, you know; my Mom loves him.'

I must say, I had wondered why she was named Holly, but presumed it was either after Buddy, or the girl in *"Breakfast at Tiffany's"*.

'I *must* do some reading,' said I, not meaning it with quite the emphasis that I said it.

'And Marlowe, Jonson, Webster, Pinter, Priestley, Bolt and Arden among the playwrights,' she continued, warming to the Cook's Tour of Great Brits for Ignorant Real Estate Guys.

'Aha,' I said. 'And what about the one you've missed?'

'Whom have I missed?'

'Shakespeare,' I smiled.

'Oh, of *course* Shakespeare. He "bestrides the narrow world like a Colossus", doesn't he?'

'Y-e-s. Although I found him a little tiresome at school. All those *"thees"* and *"thous"*.'

'No credit to your school, Mike.'

'Holly, what are your long-term plans? You're not going to be Sherbert's Girl Friday for life, I imagine?'

'No, I imagine not,' she replied, looking up from the glass, the rim of which she had been stroking.

'I'm sorry I seem to be putting you through third degree. I don't know why I'm being the Spanish Inquisition.'

I did know why, though. I wanted her to be how I saw her – unsullied, good, fresh. I wanted to hear that she was free. I wanted to look down the hall of mirrors and see her reflection next to mine. I had not felt quite like I felt then, under Blundell's Tiffany lamp, for over fifteen years. I blurted out, 'And are you....? That is, is there anyone with whom you are....?' With a feeling of absurdity I realised that I had just stopped short of asking if there was a "young man" in her life, like some maiden great-aunt. She cocked her calm, ironical eye at me.

'No, there isn't,' she said quietly.

Before I could think of what to say next, there had been a lumbering at the door, and Blundell had elephantined back into the room.

'I gotta fetch out the glasses,' he said. 'You finished your lee-cures?'

I swigged away the last gooey drop of Isotope B plum and handed my glass over to him. When he had squeezed his way out again, I resumed the inquisition with greater urbanity.

'Well, what DID make you take on old Sherbert? Not an easy guy to keep in order, I can tell you.'

'If there was one thing I wanted to do after majoring, it was to get over to England – and I haven't done so yet, what with one thing and another.'

'Surely….? With a jet every few hours from L A?'

'Yes, but I didn't want to don the mantle of female Yank tourist doing Europe on twenty dollars a day. I know they serve Big Macs on the Champs Elysee in Paris, France – and that upsets me. It's the one side of Europe, especially in Britain, that I didn't want to see. So I intended to wait until I could select-a-dial the right kind of experience.'

'So that meant some kind of job?'

'Yup. Teaching school on an exchange, a scholarship bursary, transfer to a London office from an American firm….but, like everything else, much easier said than done. So seven years skipped past and then David – Sherbert to you – comes along with his idea for a series filmed in Europe. The White Knight. I'd been working for Apogee Films for five years by then.'

'Ah, so you never worked with PSBTV? Somehow I thought you did.'

'No. Gee, no way. Independent TV for me. I've got ambition and like to eat.'

'So this trip over to London will be your first?'

Something simple and exultant gave a lurch inside me as I said this; rather like remembering as a child that you are going to the pantomime tomorrow night. Holly was flying to London. Any doubts that lingered about how far and how deep I was going to get, and there were many doubts about the whole project, vanished. By her side in London would, I determined, be me. 'I hope,' I continued, 'that you will let me show you around a little?'

'Why thank you, Mike. I'd like that very much – if

there's time. I hope we get some slack before shooting in Europe. David wants to do work in Rome at Cinecitta fairly near the beginning. But I think he's budgeting about four weeks in the UK. We've got interviews and situation filming at a place called Ealing.'

'Not Ealing Studios! My God, I thought they'd closed years ago!'

'Oh, no. apparently they're new. David said something about their being famous years ago and being refurbished.'

'Huh. "Years ago"! You're talking about my childhood; well, infanthood. I suppose you're going to sit there and say you've never seen "*The Lavender Hill Mob*"?'

'I am.'

'Nor "*The Ladykillers*"?'

'Nor them.'

'Ignoramus.'

'Dinosaur.'

'Barbarian.'

'Those black 'n' white days, eh?'

'What's wrong with black and white? Look at "*Schindler's List*".'

'Never said there was. Nothing wrong with silent pictures either – except you can't hear anything. But we've got what I hope is plenty of time in the UK. And you know where I'd quite like to go? Where you and David talk about. Scotland.'

'Well, I can help you there, Sherbert's schedule permitting. I'll take you up to Glenturret to stay with Anthony. No Holiday Inn for you, Holly.'

'I was looking at the map. Why, London to Edinburgh is

only the distance between L A and San Fran. From novels I sort of got the impression that it was a long way away.'

'It IS a long way by European standards, Holly. I hope you won't be disappointed.'

Those intelligent eyes of hers took on a film. She seemed, I thought, to be seeing way beyond Blundell's cramped dining-room. I gazed at her, thinking that she wasn't like an American at all. Then she spoiled it a tiny bit by sighing,

'Disappointed? Gee – no way, buster.'

As soon as she had brought Scotland back to the forefront of my mind once more, the lens of my interior camera re-focussed away from the persistent image of a London street in mid-winter. The internal cassette tape playing my songs of home selected another track. Surely Glenturret had been nearly as much home as London? I saw, as if it were on a screen at the end of Blundell's room, the first-class compartment on the express from Euston to the North, paid for by Grandpa's money: that warm, speeding, magic room, with the family all around me. I had been too young to have appreciated those clanging couplings and cold sooty air at the very end of steam haulage which had always enraptured Anthony, but nevertheless I found the big diesels and, later, the electric locos on the West Coast main line, impressive.

'We really ought to go and see Anthony by *train*,' I said. 'There is no other way to go. We always went to Glenturret by train for the summer vacation.'

I was surprised that her eyes were slowly losing their

shine. They became cloudy and troubled and a frown appeared on her intelligent forehead.

'I guess I'm putting a lot on you, Mike. You won't want to be saddled with me when you're back home. Things look different when you're on the spot.'

I could understand that she was preparing herself for me to back away from the promises I had been making to be her guide to Britain. I could also see that she was steadying herself against the disappointment of that eventuality. After all, what did she know of me? She, with the greater reticence of femininity and youth had not asked me if I were unattached, whether or not I were free of entanglements. She knew nothing of Mopsa then – and I was determined to keep it that way. I hardly knew how I would have answered her if she *had* asked. If being locked in a miserable box of guilt, responsibility and lost affection was an attachment, then I was indeed attached elsewhere. The long shadow of the bitch threw a chill into the pool of light under which we sat. Surely the fact that Mopsa and I had not shown each other anything more than the twisted face of the torturer for over a year….that we were bound by no vows, custom or family expectation….were united only by sloth, habit and a typically Californian/Mexican laziness masquerading as tolerance…..meant that I would not be playing the traitor if……

At the reflection that Holly *wanted* me to accompany her on her voyage of discovery, that I would complement, not rend, the fabric of her dreams, a bubble of real happiness rose in me, round and twinkling, like laughing gas from the bottom of a deep cylinder of glycerine. The bubble rose and rose from the cold, sluggish depths, undeterred even by the noisy re-entry of Blundell, freed from his domestic chores, into the bright room on that fascinating evening.

Chapter 10: **Auto-Destruct America**

Round and round, up and up, we roared. A raging hubbub of screams rose above the bellow of exhausts – like the squeal of seabirds heard over the grinding ocean. Ahead of us, always just in sight, but never nearer, Mopsa's bare back leant the Harley towards the spaces of the atrium as she cannoned upwards. I peered through the fluffy tangle of Blundell's hair and over the swelling fat of his shoulder. From my perch on the rear of the Boss Hoss I saw the same view: Mopsa's buttocks, the chrome pipes of the hog and the gradually ascending balustrade of Frank Lloyd Wright's great gallery. The only thing that changed, every micro-second it must have been, for we were only on the ramp for seconds, were the faces that we passed, and the paintings they had been studying on the walls – a blur of modern art, better for being indistinct.

Mopsa, flat-footedly humping the hog over and through the entry gates, had chosen, with that sure and fallacious instinct of the pursued, to go upwards. As if designed for the purpose of providing a gentle spiralling climb for two heavy-weight American cruiser motorcycles, the Guggenheim's main gallery turned upon itself towards the roof.

'We damn well got her, Mike!' yelled Blundell, his words causing a shower of excited spittle to spatter my eyes. 'Why do they always go *up*? See James Cagney? Remember how he went up? A gas-holder, wasn't it? "*Top o' the world!*" Yeah, we got the goddam bitch!'

There are few, if any, museums which actively welcome

games of pursuit by powerful road vehicles on their premises, but from what I had seen of what the Gugg had to offer on my stay in New York, it was probably one of them. It was not so much an unusually enlightened attitude on the part of the authorities – although I gathered that the recent curators have been so regarded in museum circles, according to "*The New York Times*" – as a willingness to accept the avant-garde by the museum's clientele. The shrieks of horror, which had greeted the Hog's and the Hoss's thunderous arrival, had come from foreigners: serious South Koreans, earnest Japanese, introverted Swedes and Danes, hysterical Latins, all with pre-conceived ideas about art galleries. These tourists had not taken Mopsa's and Blundell's great pursuit in the correct spirit. The right sort of Gugg connoisseur, the American modernist with a child's thirst for novelty, had. Very soon I was aware that we were chugging past appreciatively clapping couples. On several faces I glimpsed that wise nod of understanding which only those who are masters of the mystery feel entitled to give; the sort of nod which implies: I see what you're up to – most interesting. Those very same seekers after True Art who would have carefully trodden through Pintin's Living-sculpture Show, wondering if they should hope that he would be electrocuted, who would have instinctively understood Excremental Kinetics and the chopping off of fingers without anaesthetic – these realised at once that here was a piece of the Real Thing. Two men, one extraordinarily fat, the other clearly deranged, chasing a naked girl on 'sickles from the bottom to the top just on closing-time? Why, this was the latest in a long line of thought-provoking ideas from that smart new director! Hadn't he brought in that scaffolding sculpture? The rusting sheets of corrugated iron called "The Transfiguration of Capital"? Those photos of dead men with light bulbs twinkling in their mouths? Hey, it's ART, man!

Suddenly I was aware that I could no longer see Mopsa's back. She had accelerated beyond us while Blundell had slowed the Hoss through our smiling admirers.

'She's gone!' I cried, digging my finger into his podgy ribs.

'Huh?' he grunted, in the act of giving the peace grip to a man as bearded and as dishevelled as himself – another 'Nam vet, no doubt.

'Can she go down?' I shouted. 'Down! Down! Can she get down from up here?'

Blundell took in what I was saying in a second and wrenched the throttle open. The Hoss jumped forward, roaring. The low-roofed spiral became choked with exhaust fumes. With a swish of twelve-inch wide tyres, we rounded the curve to the top of the spiral under the atrium.

Then occurred one of those things which afterwards one can only claim to have seen, but for which there is no proof. To our right was a smallish passage opening out of the spiral near the elevators into a rear part of the complex. From this, with bewildering velocity, shot a cream and blue Electra-Glide. It hit the curved balustrade wall, smashed through the concrete and plaster and, back wheel spinning, tipped over into empty space. Blundell spun the Hoss to the hole and kicked it onto the prop-stand, leaving the V8 ticking over majestically. He and I raced to the gap and peered out. With monumental purpose, Blundell's hog held its vertical posture in mid-air, plummeting downward with engine still running, rear wheel spinning. Some petrol was spurting from the carburettor, crystalline and seeming to fall more slowly than the machine in the still air of the gallery. To my horrified glance, its fall seemed to last far longer than it can have done. Face after face, shock of hair after shock of hair, poked out from the spiral below at different levels and followed its earthbound rush – falling like a comet in the elegant space between roof and floor of Lloyd Wright's masterwork.

When it hit the ground, the camera of my perception speeded up. Pointing down, as it still was, the machine crumpled its front forks, front wheel, head-lamp and fender. Chromed metal shot outwards from the impact. The flooring cracked, the headstock drove in to the surface and the Harley came to a rending, crashing, shocking halt. It stuck there, engine silent at last, mufflers pointing straight up – as remarkably still as so recently it had been remarkably speeding. Like slow-motion leaf-fall, the trim-ring from the shattered lamp, switch-gear torn loose, bolts and plates and gauges bounced down around it; the dust settled and there was a great quiet in the gallery. In that quiet, the Hoss's motor still turned over with a lazy, throaty rumble.

Suddenly, someone started to clap.

Then *everyone* began to clap.

I was shocked and unable to move from the smashed balustrade because I had thought that Mopsa had gone down with her machine. I was *absolutely positive* that I had seen her plummet over, still clinging to the Harley. Yet, as I jerked my head downwards, there was no sign of a bloody, dislocated naked body on the museum floor.

Where had she gone?

Blundell grabbed my arm.

'Oh God!' he howled. 'My hog! My Christ! My sickle!'

Leaving the Boss Hoss turning over, he began to run, lumbering, back down the gentle slopes to ground level, shoving gaping people out of the way as he did so. I followed, stupidly, for I would have been wiser to have remained up above and hunted for Mopsa. Clearly, I had been mistaken in fancying that she had gone down with the hog. When I retraced my steps, leaving Blundell to pant on down, and went back to the little passage from which the hog had been propelled, there was no sign of her.

A grudging admiration crept over me that she had had the presence of mind at the end of a long chase to find some means of jamming the bike's twist-grip open against the carb springs, for only at full bellow could it have had enough momentum and equilibrium to have gone straight through the wall. Later, I found out how. Blundell had had a *Throttle Meister* cruise-control fitted for hands-off freeway cruising. Easy.

Slowly, I went on down again after Blundell. I caught up with him standing, shaking his head next to the shattered heap.

'Oh, jeez, jeez,' he kept muttering.

The majestic ruin of the big machine stuck up out of the floor, the height of a man. Around its headstock and twisted forks lay a pile of bright metallic debris. Above the headstock nothing was damaged at all – paint gleamed, oil glistened, chrome sparkled, leather shone. I saw a tear steal into Blundell's beard. 'Oh jeez. Friggin' jeez.'

High above us, near the roof, the Hoss's big pistons continued to pump out sound. It reached us here below like some far-off thunder in cloud-canyons.

'Come on, Blundell,' I said. 'Presumably it's insured?'

He nodded.

'Yeah. It is. But…..'

Sadly, he tramped through the wondering crowd back up the spiral. At the top we mounted the Hoss - I had gone up with him, for it had not occurred to me to wait at the bottom – and Blundell carefully steered it round the spirals to the exit.

As we reached the desk, there was a twin commotion. From the street, came in two patrolmen in peaked caps and shades. From further back in the building strode a tall, light-haired man in tortoise-shell spectacles with three jabbering, grey-suited acolytes at his side. Remorselessly the forces of Law and Curatordom closed upon us. Blundell clutched his handle-bars, and I clutched Blundell. I could tell he was thinking of making a run for it. A second hectic chase in one day was unendurable, but if he was going to blast through the cordon I wanted to blast with him. Staying in the Guggenheim on my own and trying to explain everything in a British accent was, I knew, beyond what I could face.

The posse of curators came up to us. The tall, light-haired man held up his hand. The gesture was more what I would have expected from the policemen, but they, I could see, were still trying to assimilate what had been going on. Their round, bulging eyes moved from Hog to Hoss, from atrium to floor, from Blundell to the crowd. Perhaps they had too great a choice of felonies to charge us with to know quite where to begin. While they thus gazed, they were paralysed, it seemed.

Around the edges of our little group the press of the public grew. There was animated talk. Forbidden photographs were taken in a stuttering of blue light. A Japanese student was making notes, standing in front of the wrecked Harley. Already, cultured voices were being upraised: 'My dear, it's the new form of kinetic sculpture…', '…Art as *motional* statement, not *static* statement, is how I would define it….', '…a clear metaphor for the fall of industrialisation….'

The Curator stared round at the seekers after culture. Then, hand still upheld, he strode forward. I ducked, absurdly feeling that he was going to box my ears, or Blundell's. The policemen awoke from their trance at the same instant and closed in, loosening their pistols.

Blundell's right hand blipped the Hoss's throttle. Cops and Curator sought each other's eyes over the rumbling Hoss – then glared at us.

'Jes what the frig is goin' on?'

'Are you responsible for…?'

'Oh, I guess I'm sorry, sir, but I wanted to caution these guys…'

'Not at all. I just wanted to ask them….'

'Hey, you! Is this your shit here?'

'…..how much they would be prepared to *take* for this sculpture?'

The Curator's words won by a short head; the resonance of his high, academic, New England tones seemed to linger longer in the air than growled Brooklyn. Blundell turned off the Hoss's engine. He and the Curator smiled at each other. The policemen looked baffled.

'Ain't you gonna register a complaint?' one of them asked.

'A *complaint*?' said the Curator freezingly, arching his eyebrows way up above his tortoise-shell glasses. 'What on *earth* about?' The cops' eyes bulged at each other, at the shattered floor, at the wrecked bike, at the Hoss, with its missing registration plate, at the tyre marks all over the terrazzo, at the evident signs of a high-speed motorcycle chase inside New York's premier shrine of modern art. 'Nonsense,' snapped the Curator. 'This,' he went on loudly, for the benefit of the crowd, 'is the first of several new exhibitions of – of Mechano/energistic Sculpture. The title of this piece is – is….'

Blundell smoothed his beard with a podgy hand and his loud gurgle was heard, '…. It is called "Auto-Destruct America",' he said clearly. 'And I am empowered to sell it to the Guggenheim for fift…' I dug him in the ribs. It was a time for moderation. '….for twenty thousand dollars.'

One of the cops let out a sound like a stifled wail.

'I would be obliged,' said the Curator to Blundell and me, 'if you gentlemen would step into the office so that we might formalise this purchase for the gallery.'

We dismounted. The cops were already on their way out.

I almost felt sorry for them.

"The Art of the Motorcycle", the display of 114 bikes and the Gugg's biggest success, had just closed in '98. The press speculated that this latest acquisition might be the beginning of further expansion of the theme – this time featuring movement and crashes. It says a lot for Blundell's nerve and luck that "Auto-Destruct America" (sculptor: B. Capitanchik) was still drawing crowds and rave notices when, eighteen days later, I left the USA forever.

'It seems to me,' said Sherbert, 'that you've got to leave the Waldorf, and you can't really stay with Holly's friends in the Village for more than two weeks. Mopsa knows where it is, in any case, and she may be watching it. The only alternative, dear boy, is to stay at my place.'

Those who had my interests in mind were united in the belief that Manhattan was not big enough for Mopsa and me. Sherbert was nearly ready to fly to London, thence to Cinecitta, Rome, for some shooting, but he was not ready for his entourage to accompany him. 'Early September,' he said. 'There's no point in going earlier. I want Holly to make sure the final scripts are finished first. To be honest, we can't afford to fly Pongo, Len and Co over to London and put them up for weeks. We're not MGM, you know. Besides, I don't want tons of last-minute fiddling by the writers – it's not fair on everyone else. And as you've shown such bad taste, old mate, as actually to want to have a say on how your bloated money is to be spent, and as you clearly have no idea what the phrase "Associate Co-Producer" really means, the best thing for you is to stay here with Holly and get any final scripting issues sorted out.'

This decision couldn't have pleased me better.

Sherbert's place, which I had not had time to visit in the fierce rush of my first few days, turned out to be a splendid modern apartment over the Park. It was way up, and from it stretched an astonishing panorama.

'Mein Gott! Is this what I'm paying for?' I asked.

'No, you arse, it belongs to WGB. The Boston guys rent it to visiting directors. I've got it 'til the 15th, so you can stay here after I've gone. You just need to drop the keys in downtown at the office on Fifth Avenue. But look,' added Sherbert, kneeling on the long, soft window-seat, 'do you think it is significant that we are in an absolutely direct line with the Washington Bridge, Brooklyn Bridge, Empire State, Hayden Planetarium and the Jewish Theological College?'

'Significant of what?'

'What a question! But come round to the other side and I'll prove it.' I gazed south from the huge windows of that major bedroom which I came to know well. New York has its breath-taking beauty – but it is significant that it is only discernible from way up high where the squalor is negated by distance, and it is only permanently accessible by the rich. Somewhere between the doomed twin Trade Center towers and me was Blundell's eccentric nest, and in that nest was Holly. It was a thought which led to a tiny pricking behind my eyes. In all that vast cityscape, one precious life – fragile, new – was increasingly central to my thinking.

'She'll never get at you again, not up here,' said Sherbert, wrongly interpreting my thoughts. 'Mopsa, I mean,' he grinned, noting my change of countenance. 'Ah, so *who* were you thinking about? Don't tell me,' he continued, his satyr-like grin widening, 'I'm not blind – unlike Cupid.'

'She is a fascinating girl, Sherbert – she really is.'

'Holly, Mopsa: "weigh them, they are as heavy, sound them and they become the tongue as well; what is there in that Holly that she hath grown so great?"'

'That sounds horribly like the Bard.'

'It is. "*Julius Caesar*". Well, well. Wouldn't Anthony be interested?'

I could see that he was thrilled to have tumbled. I had not wanted comment on my feelings for Holly – yet I was pleased by his approval. It was extraordinarily vivifying being back in the company of one whom I had known for nearly thirty-five years and who could say what he liked. It struck me that I had made no solid friends like him in L A. I would have said, earlier in '99, that I was the centre of a large circle, but to each member of it I was the English guy, the contact, the useful Brit. I had forgotten the bliss of unthinking intercourse, of shared assumption and memory lying too deep for words. Poor Mopsa seemed now to be an implacable enemy, and that I had never been at ease with her – except at the very beginning, perhaps. You cannot be a friend if you are merely a prop, if you are medicine, not nourishment. As I smiled at Sherbert, before turning my eyes back over the enormous city-scape, I felt that my life was destined to go into a hazy, rosy future, with Holly, hand-in-hand, on the adventure. If only I had known! "More frightening than his pessimism is Man's baseless optimism", as Anthony is still fond of saying.

So I left the Waldorf-Astoria, walking, rather regretfully, out beneath that assertive canopy for the last time; stealing a glance up at the winged nude, tipping the red-coated Scobie lavishly as he piled my cases into Sherbert's stretched limo; giving a restrained wave to Mr Hepworth as he stood respectfully by the revolving door, his back to an advert for the Bull and Bear. I felt I had lived there many weeks. Perhaps this was a tribute to the hotel's courtesy, for I had no pleasant memories to associate with it.

The next day, Adrian Booker, hands fluttering in front of mouth and spectacles, came to collect me from Sherbert's apartment in the car. The last meeting before the team broke up and he and the director headed for London was scheduled to last half the night, annoyingly. I had made strong resolutions to stick to my guns about the content and drift of the scripts I had been given. Not much of a reader, I had digested more prose in that last fortnight than at any time in my life.

'Did you like the general direction of the series?' asked Adrian. His thick glasses magnified his restless eyes as they flicked to and fro from sidewalk to sidewalk. The limo was jammed solid in traffic on 59th St. I wished I had walked.

'I found a lot of it disturbing,' I replied. 'Why does virtually all human culture boil down to depravity in your scripts? There's no comfort or charm in the vision.'

'I notice you use the term "virtually" a lot, Mike. I find that interesting.'

'What?'

'...interesting, that your conversation is sprinkled with the word "virtue".'

'What ARE you talking about?'

'You're not exactly a *prude*, are you?'

'Where is this conversation going?' I asked.

'I've heard what I've heard,' he said.

There was a pregnant silence in the car.

'Do you sometimes pay for....well, you know what I mean?' said Adrian suddenly, his hands fluttering wildly.

I felt myself going red under his pale eyes.

'I know what you mean. No, I don't,' I replied shortly.

'But you have?' persisted Adrian.

'Yes. Once. Many years ago.'

'In Los Angeles?'

I stared at him. He raised his eyebrows, as if to say: "You can kid me, duckie, but I know what I know".

'What on earth are you talking about?'

The car rolled on for a block and then stopped. The air-con was cold, but I felt drops of sweat on my upper lip and wiped them away furtively. He opened his mouth as if to say something. Then he closed it again and looked, to my eyes, evasive. I can hardly express how peculiar I felt.

'You have paid for it in New York, then?'

I breathed hard.

'Yes. I told you. It was years ago.'

'Boy – or girl?'

The silence grew sticky.

'Why do you ask?'

'I really can't say. It just p-p-p-popped out,' he twittered.

'But why ask if it was a *boy*?'

Again that knowing look.

The silence grew sticky as he gazed at me.

'Well, there we are,' he said briefly.

'Such things seem to interest you deeply. The so-called "art" and the ideas for cultural motives in the scripts you have written all boil down to the same thing.'

He gave a frenetic giggle, and changed the subject.

'I – I like the variety you get here in New York City. Do you read "*Screw*"? Two hundred and fifty on Lexington'll get you some kinky stuff. But, but, what I *really* don't mind paying for, he, he, he, he, what I really am HAPPY paying for, he, he, he, is what's on 14th Street. Um? Know what I mean? The Upper East Side is ALL male hustlers and, you know, fair's fair. If you want the REAL thing, the best trannies are on 14th Street. Ask anyone. ANYONE!' cried Adrian accusingly, as if I'd ventured to contradict him. 'They have a private club there. Spanking! I've got lesions all over! He, he, he, he! Yes, I don't recommend anywhere but 14th Street for that sort of thing. I've never been to Harlem or the South Bronx – they're desperate there and not clean. They only make a hundred and twenty a WEEK and a hundred and nineteen of it goes bang on crack! And you can really get something *nasty,* you know. Don't think I'm being picky. I just think, Mike…' and here he laid a fluttering hand on my leg, 'that, that …. you ought to know who's WHO before you get to grips with them.'

His hand remained on my leg and I didn't know how I could remove it.

'Er, Adrian…,' I began.

'Mike,' he whispered, the hand that wasn't exploring my thigh fluttering madly in front of his spectacles, 'we could explore quite a lot *together*, couldn't we? You and me? At least we know we are both CLEAN, don't we?'

It was a horrifying moment.

With a gasp he lurched closer to me, pressing into my hand a folded sheet.

'What makes you think…?' I began, but the limo drew up at the offices. It swayed as the driver got out and the passenger door was flung open. Adrian sprang away from me. I caught the driver's eye. Adrian fished for mine.

'Business before pleasure, eh?' he smiled. But the smile was not, I felt, a pleasant one. My composure had all but gone and I roughly pushed against him to get out of the limo. You would have thought his peculiar confession and litany would have shocked me more than the doubts I had about Sherbert's judgement in making such a man responsible for the tone and direction of the TV series. But, as I barged into the building, leaving him fluttering behind me, it was outrage that the project would be filtered through Booker's obviously warped mind that filled me.

And that folded sheet of paper? It was a list of places and clubs that had featured in his gushing talk. From that time on, I knew that he was waiting for a response from me – biding his time on the assumption that, because of something he thought he had perceived, or been told, there would eventually be liaison between us. So that was why I was to destroy everyone's hopes and how, in that early part of September '99, I understood nothing.

'Holly,' I said. 'I want to go with you.' I lay back, shoes off, in one of the leather armchairs in Sherbert's borrowed apartment. I faced the great panorama north over the city towards the Jewish Theological College, if I'd known where to look for it. There was a haze over Englewood.

We had had supper, ordered up from Walden's restaurant. Talk had poured easily from us. Holly seemed in love with that time thirty years before in a London that she had never known, but I could pander a little to that phantom nostalgia in her, having actually lived off The King's Road, and by name-dropping those '70s and '80s figures that Anthony and Peter Buchan knew when they had set up a rock studio at Glenturret.

'Oh, Mike, I just can't WAIT till I get over there!' she cried. 'Only ten more days!' For a second we had mused, me on memories, she on the joys of discovery, I imagined. Then she went on, 'I'm flying back to L A, Mike. I've got to say goodbye to Mom and Daddy before we leave for Europe.' And that's when, without having planned to say it, I murmured: 'Holly, I want to go with you.'

I recall that she looked up at me from the rug where she reclined, her long legs stretched out to within an inch of mine.

'But, Mike… David… I mean, hasn't he got things….?'

'For me to do here? Nothing as important as meeting your folks – *particularly* your Dad.'

She looked startled. I think I knew then that she was falling in love with me; that future possibilities had occurred to her too. I thought she looked about eighteen for a moment. I was pleased that I seemed capable of doing something both impulsive and surprising; for a long time I had donned the leaden mantle of predictable caution. This idea smacked of the old me that I thought I had left behind forever, buried beneath an Everest of disappointments, hard work and survival of basic sanity. 'Holly,' I went on, getting off the chair and kneeling on the floor, 'if love is looking forward to seeing you every day, is dreaming of you in sleep, is finding more humour and kindness in you than anyone I've met for years, is being attracted to the grace of your figure and the honesty of your eyes, is enjoying a completeness with you that I feel with no one else… then I love you.' I don't expect it came out as smoothly as the above at the time, but I do recall a feeling of uplift at my own eloquence – at the exact *rightness* of it.

She said, 'Mike, I….,'and stopped.

'I am just on forty and I have never settled. I have been a workaholic. I'm difficult to live with, I'm sure. But I'm not in bad shape, and I don't think it ridiculous that….'

'No, no. I am not thinking… I mean I am attracted to you, Mike. Age has nothing to do with it….'

She reached out. Those little squidgy sausage fingers! She then drew my hands up to her chin and, as we gathered ourselves into a kneeling position, looked at me with eyes unclouded by doubt. Never had I loved their clarity and generous innocence more.

'Holly,' I said, very quietly. 'Have you seen the Jewish

Theological College?'

'What?' She gasped.

'From this height, I mean?'

Her look was worth a million.

'N-o-o, Mike,' she whispered, humouring the maniac.

'Come with me,' I said. We stood up, hands locked together and passed into Sherbert's vast bedroom. Below us, the city flamed. 'There it is – I think,' I whispered, guiding her face to the horizon. I stood behind her and kissed her neck as she gazed down at the cityscape. Then I started laughing when she asked solemnly,

'Which direction do I look?'

I was nearly breathless. 'Darling girl! God knows where it is! Ha, ha, ha – oh – oh – gosh!' And she started laughing too. Miraculous! We screamed, swaying by the window.

'The Jewish… Haaaa, ha, ha ha!'

'…Theo…. Ha, ha, ha, ha …. Theological…..oh! Oh!'

And I cupped her breasts from behind, she turned, and, both of us shrieking insanely, we kissed and kissed, falling backwards on Sherbert's bed.

'Jewish Theological College!' she screamed.

'A fine building, already!' I screeched.

'Ha, ha, ha, ha, ha, ha, oh, oh, ah…. Oooh! Oh! Oh! Oh! Oh, God! Ha, ha, ha, ha, ha, ha!'

When the hysteria was ebbing, we had most of our clothes off. The light had died, but the room glimmered with upward-thrown gleams. She seemed rather long on the deep bed – long and curvy. We were both circumspect. I was particularly careful, as I had no protection. Although we were rapidly aroused, the wonderful thing for me was our mutual feel for the ridiculous and how it passed easily into our separate moments of pleasure and final shudders of laughter – then peace in the dark.

'I want to be WITH you in London, I don't think you're the sort of woman to have a half-committed affair, and I'm not that kind of man.' (I had not been in any way honest about my past with Mopsa at that stage; yet so complete was my sense of break with that bitch that I hardly considered myself dishonest or duplicitous.) 'That is why I need to meet your parents. I need their approval if I'm going to ask if you'll have me – eventually,' I added, still conscious of the disparity in our ages. Still later that night, after I found out that her dad was called Nathan, she said, 'I'm older than you are, Mike, in spite of the years,' and I thought she was right.

'There are quite a few years between you,' said her father, after he had been told of our purposes and I was alone with him. He had given me a cigar in time-honoured American fashion. 'I was born during World War Two,' he had gone on. 'And I guess I was one of the first out to 'Nam. What we saw there makes a guy tolerant, you know. My pop wouldn'ta let some rich British guy from back East set tail after his little girl – not after they'd only met a week or two. But then he was of his age. I am of mine. Happiness isn't so darned plentiful you can afford to pick and choose when to go after it. We have no objections, Mike. I think you will look after her, I can see that. Know how I know? You've got vulnerable eyes. You're going to make this one work.' He stared at me while I wondered if

I ought actually to smoke his cigar.

I will never forget that long talk Holly and I then had about whether her dad expected us to have a formal engagement and when we might marry. After it, we went out into a brilliantly sunny day, and near the Mission Church in Ventura we saw a humming-bird in the cloister. In the evening we played my ridiculous family "telepathy game" when the Miall cousins came over to meet me, and Holly's dad got mad, trying for hours to guess how it was done – although she tumbled after a few goes.

Because that game was to save my life six thousand miles away later in the Fall, I'm going to explain how it works.

A person is picked to be "in-the-know". He leaves the room while the others pick a word. On return he is fake hypnotised by a "medium", who utters a sentence or two (while waving hands in "passes") As he has been prepared, he merely has to piece together the first letter of each sentence to get at the object chosen by the rest of the mob. He utters it in a strange, bemused voice, as if under the "influence". It drives those who can't see how it is done wild with frustration.

It has the weakness that the company can't choose words longer than "clock" or "vase" or "table"; it's harder to piece together the first letters of a sentence such as: "Sure, this entirely relaxes every ounce, gorgeously, relatively and meaningfully" in order to guess "stereogram"!

But it passes time amusingly at little parties.

Thank God Holly wasn't baffled when she had to piece together a mass of random remarks to rescue me from the clutches of a lunatic a few weeks later. I'm so grateful we played it.

I was happy on those last few days in Dan Bright's friend's colonial house in Massachusetts, near the Alcott mansion, while we waited for our flight out of New York on Concorde. In this piece of *ersatz* England, I poured into Holly's ears all that that I could find in my mind to give life and colour to her imaginings about Europe. As I spun the tapestry of someone else's memories for her, I could hardly believe that the Chelsea streets would lie beneath our footsoles in a day, in a few hours....

And so, in an Indian summer, we sailed down from polar skies, circling a long time above those miles of fields and then the bright gardens at the back of London's houses, Concorde barely a silver-fish in the empyrean to those idly watching from below, before dropping with the sun out of the west into the haze of unfamiliar air.

Chapter 11: **London**

Holly had told me that London Heathrow had been a magic name to her, but that it was much bigger than she had expected it to be, and, ridiculous when she come to analyse it, much *newer* that she felt it should have been too. She admitted that she was expecting Big Ben type architecture or colonnades. And the freeway into London, the M4 – she hadn't thought it would be there either. The horizon was flat too, which surprised her. She told me she had had a picture in her mind of a backdrop of mountains and those rooflines you see in *"Mary Poppins"*.

But then I had spent my first week or two in the US ditching the pre-conceived images I had suckled at the cinema in the '60s and '70s. And I think it's more difficult for a Yank than vice-versa. In the classic adaptations and costume dramas which scoop Oscars or are serialised on public TV: all those *"Emmas"* and *"Pride and Prejudices"*, Britain (or, rather, England) always has: 1) narrow lanes, 2) crooked houses, 3) soaring medieval churches, 4) (if you base your preconceptions on*"Sherlock Holmes,"*) the lonely sweeps of Dartmoor or the Highlands within a coach drive of Baker St and 5) innumerable pubs with laughing "characters" singing old songs round a piano. Judging from episodes of *"The Avengers"* or *"The Saint"* which used to crop up regularly on US nostalgia TV (and still do), no roads in England are wider than a single auto, everyone lives in Queen Anne mansions or mews houses, there is no traffic, no miles of utility 1930s villas (or "semis" as I explained they were called), no '60s

198

high-rise, no KFC drive-ins, no miles of neon-lights, so the Yank tourist is left to discover that he's been conned as soon as the airplane touches down.

Concorde had landed with the lightest of bumps. Holly told me later that my eyes were bright with tears and that she was astonished to see them. I would not have spoken of my nostalgia and my patriotism, hotter than the Rolls-Royce *Olympus* jet engines under us. But I used to sit in my (British) car, parked up off some hot and dusty Bel-Air avenue and bring back to mind London in the late '60s and early '70s: The King's Road, Maida Vale, that Christmas of '63 in the snow when I was a little boy, red buses, "The Bunch of Grapes" pub, daffodils, the Stockpot, EMG Handmade Gramophones in Soho Square, Veeraswamy's, Marble Arch, Daquis, Glebe Place, Sullivan and Powell's in Burlington Arcade where I got Turkish cigarettes when I came into Grandpa's money, Lewin's in Jermyn Street, the Coronet Cinema in Notting Hill, the Seashell fish-and-chip shop in Lisson Grove….. Anything and everything a balm to my brain, wounded by America.

'Got here in one piece,' I remember saying, letting go Holly's damp little fingers. Soothing, liquid music came on through those speakers which had earlier informed us, in faintly incredulous tones, that the sun was shining at Heathrow and that the temperature was 18 degrees centigrade. Holly translated this to 65F, and muttered, 'Wow! Cold!', but the voice went on, 'A nice warm end to a hot day.'

'Now, Sherbert is supposed to be sending a car,' I said,

but God knows if he has, where we're to meet it and where it's going to take us. I'd have booked us into the Hyde Park or the Berkeley.'

'Or the Savoy,' said Holly – having been reading the British Airways publication for passengers and learnt all about Arnold Bennett, D'Oyly Carte and the Grill Room.

'No,' I said firmly. 'NOT the Savoy. Some day I'll tell you why not. I still feel a slight crawling of the skin on my spine when I think of a dinner I gave in the Grill Room there.'

'Gee-whiz! Not food-poisoning?'

'No, of course not. Not at the *Savoy*.'

A Daimler *Van den Plas Princess* had been sent for us. One of those limos with long black wings hiding the rear wheels. I remembered earlier versions from back in '83. Inside were tables, little cupboards and very light tan leather and velvet. Up front the driver sat behind glass in a smart grey uniform and peaked cap. There was a bottle on ice too.

'Well, well,' I grinned. 'We've got Sherbert to thank for this. Yet he might have come to meet us himself.'

'I think it's rare tact NOT to meet us. It's so we can do our first exploring, or in your case, re-exploring, together. If he were here he'd be getting all sentimental about 1979, or whatever, with you – and I'd be the gooseberry.'

We drove out of a tunnel, past a big model of the plane we had flown in, onto the M4 and headed for the city. Holly got all excited at a sign for Hampton Court, just like a tourist Yank, in fact. It was a little time before she realised we were driving on what was for her the wrong side of the road.

'My God!' I found myself exclaiming every few minutes. 'It's still there! The Chiswick flyover! You'd have thought that would have fallen down years ago! Hey! Look! The Hammersmith Odeon! I saw some big Motown groups there, and, I think, 10cc! Talgarth Road! See those tall windows? They're old artists' studios. I dossed in one of those for six months in '77!'

At last, after a few twists and turns down unfamiliar streets, the Daimler drew up smoothly in front of a white building like an ocean liner. The driver up front jumped out and handed the door open.

'Mr Sherwin-Lemond thought you would like early supper with him, Sir. I'm to wait and take you home after.'

'What is this place?'

For the last mile I'd been thinking, I don't know this. Where the hell are we going? There's nothing down here except Wandsworth Bridge and some old wharves.

Our driver replied, 'Chelsea 'Arbour. Conrad 'Otel. Mr Sherwin-Lemond is in the bar, Madam. Sir.'

'My sainted aunt! All built since I was here last.'

'I will take the luggage on 'ome, Sir,' said our driver and, touching his peak, got back into the majestic Daimler and, reversing with a purr, disappeared down the narrow street up which we had come.

'Well, I don't know. How awful. I never gave him a tip.'

'We never asked his name.'

'I expect we'll hear it from Sherbert.'

In we went through a cool, plush lobby, up a few steps and into a bar with a low ceiling and Egyptian pillars.

Sherbert came bounding forward, beaming and holding out both hands.

'Bop! And Miall! The smouldering love-birds in person!'

'Put a sock in it, you git,' I smiled. 'But what a welcoming hearse. Couldn't you find a bigger car?'

'Holly, you are looking fairly ravishing, flight notwithstanding,' cried Sherbert, kissing her on both cheeks and then on the tip of the nose for good measure. Very roguey. 'In, in, in! Now what will you have to drink?'

'Seeing that we've been swigging all afternoon over the pond, I'll just have a mineral,' I said.

'Hey, yep. Um, a Coke for me,' said Holly.

Sherbert looked at her gravely.

'What makes you think you can get a drink like Coca-Cola in the UK?' said he. 'I don't think I've ever seen it for sale here.'

'Oh,' Holly gasped. 'Oh, all right. Well, whatever they've got. Tea, I suppose?'

Sherbert stared at her owlishly then spluttered, like a pert kid, and poked her in the ribs.

'Ever bin had, sister?' he grinned. 'Did you actually think you had hit on a square mile of the globe that wasn't part of Uncle Sam's empire?'

'Oh, you!' she cried, poking him back. It looked like being one of those pokey evenings.

'How long has this place been here?'

'Come through to where we're going to eat,' said Sherbert. 'There's a good view of the boats.'

'Boats?'

'Didn't Lane tell you that we were meeting at Chelsea Harbour?'

'Oh, *that's* his name, is it? Lane. He was murmuring to Holly when we arrived. But he mainly sat feudally behind his glass panel. Is he one of your minions?'

'Sort of. He's from the company. He meets visiting toffs like you. The old type who knows his place.'

'Let's see these boats.'

We passed into a large, nicely laid-out restaurant and out onto a balcony. In the slowly darkening evening, the white cruisers sat on their black sheet of mirrored lacquer.

'That gold ball up there tells you what the tide is doing,' Sherbert informed us.

'Are we on the sea?' asked Holly. 'Surely not. I thought you had to go out onto marshes. I remember reading about it in "*Great Expectations*".'

'When was all this built?'

'Oh, late 'eighties sometime. After you'd left. There's a lot of riverside development up and down between here and Canary Wharf – and *that* you'll be seeing, my boy, because the company has its offices there. I thought you'd rather stick to this side of town though – you being an old Sloane Ranger.'

'I *thought* we'd come along the King's Road for a bit, but it's been so long.'

After dinner – a very pleasant one, although Holly and I only had one course in honour of the occasion, having crammed down several on Concorde only three hours earlier – we took a stroll out of the little marina on to the embankment of the Thames.

'Where's big Ben?' Holly asked, peering about.

'Ah. A few miles from here.'

'Miles! Funny how I've got this idea that London is all real close together. And Tower Bridge – the one that opens up?'

'Further on again.'

There was a rumble across the water. A long streamlined train went slowly along over a brick bridge.

'That's a Eurostar train,' explained Sherbert. 'You go to Paris in one of those from Waterloo through the tunnel. I don't know what it's doing here coming north over the river.'

I was able to answer that. 'I do. I've been reading all about it – not to mention getting an immersion course from Anthony. He wrote to tell me about the latest Chunnel workings, and he says that the Eurostar sets get serviced at North Pole near Paddington. So I presumed they must cross the river somewhere in West London.'

'Well, well, aren't we informed,' said Sherbert.

Outside, the dusk came down, and the Thames looked more sinister.

'Aren't you tired?' asked Sherbert as the meal came to an end. 'Because if you aren't, I am. And I thought I might dump you both where you're staying and then get home.'

'Lane isn't returning at midnight with the black pumpkin?'

'No. I'm your driver now. My pleasure, and all that.'

'Where are we staying, anyway? The Dorchester? Hilton?'

'Ah, ask no questions and you'll get no, etc, etc. But you'll feel pretty tickled, Bop, old son. Of *that* I can assure you.'

We went down into an underground garage beneath the hotel and were led by Sherbert to a green Rover car and then drove out into the dark the way Lane had come. We slowed at a junction.

'The dear old King's Road,' I said.

'Yeah, it hasn't changed much,' Sherbert said absently, keeping his eye on a red bus.

'This is home, Holly. Oh, the times in L A I've dreamed about this stretch of road. The fire station down there, Dominic's....'

'....gone,' interrupted Sherbert.

'Oh, yes. So you said, back at Dan's in L A.'

And on I gazed, wrapt in the wonder of recognition as the street unfolded through the windows of the car, aware of an affectionate amusement in Holly as she studied my face.

'O yes! That really old place on the corner and....why, Sherbert, what are you doing?' Sherbert had turned suddenly down a street to the right. 'Good memory! He's going to take me to have a look at a place where I was living before I left. I must point it out to you, Holly, darling.' I caught sight of Sherbert's knowing smile in the rear-view mirror at that last word – the first time I had used it since we had landed. Out of the window I had caught the name of the road on the wall. 'Great!' I went on, as the car drew up, 'let's get out and inhale the past. My holy aunt, it hasn't changed *at all*.'

While I gazed up and down the street and Holly clambered out of the Rover, Sherbert was swinging open the boot and hauling out the light bags which we had taken in to the Conrad Hotel. Lane had gone off with our vast amount of valises (expensively way over the limit) in that Daimler and I'd just assumed they'd now be at some hotel where we'd be staying.

'Hey, I guess I don't need that little bag right now,' Holly said.

'I'm sure you do,' replied Sherbert, still with his mystery-man smile on, and setting off down the pavement ahead of us.

'Sherbert, where are you going? That's the way to....'

'I know. It's where you're kipping tonight.'

I grabbed his arm.

'What do you mean....?'

'Memory Lane, old boy. You supply the memory, I supply Lane and hey presto! A neat little nest in which to lay your weary heads.'

'I can't believe it! I just can't *believe* it! Holly, Hol – come on! It's where I was.... I mean, it's my..... How on *earth* did you manage it? It's incredible. You *bugger*!'

I put my arm across Sherbert's shoulders and hugged him with impulsive warmth.

'Steady the buffs, old bean,' he grinned. He was clearly thrilled at the success of his plan.

'What is all this?' said Holly.'Will someone please tell your American visitor why this place is so important?'

'Holly – that place I've told you about, the bit of London that's really home, the flat of Anthony's I lived in until I left in 'eighty-three? Well, *this* is it. Glebe place, Chelsea and the house on the corner. I can't take it in. Sixteen years! I think I'm going to have a stroke. What's having a stroke like?'

'What?' You mean your *actual* home?'

'Yes, yes, yes! Come ON, Sherbert, you torturer, get the door open. Oh fishcakes – I can't believe this is happening!'

Sherbert opened the front door. Lemon light poured out onto the sidewalk. I glimpsed our baggage inside.

'Ah, Lane's done his stuff,' said Sherbert. 'There you go.' He ushered us past him. As if in a somnambulistic state, I glided through the hall, laid a hand upon the balustrade and mounted the staircase.

'His flat used to be on the first floor,' I heard Sherbert say, 'so he's sort of conditioned to go up.'

They came up after me, and I heard Holly, the Eng Lit Anglophile, explaining her joy at being in London to Sherbert.

'When I saw Mike going up, I thought he "rose like a missioned spirit" – you know, as Keats says.'

'In *"The Eve of St Agnes"*, if I remember rightly,'

'Come up!' I cried.

I stood in a lovely, open room with big windows, low-sashed and with curtains back. A marble fireplace with a glowing bed of fire (gas, I discovered later), a gilt mirror with heavy bunches of fruit moulded at the corners, tyrian-veined side-lamps with gold-lined shades on dark, glossy tables, a big oriental carpet, a Chinese cabinet, two gilt chandeliers, two sofas and three deep apple-green armchairs completed the effect of intimate, homely, yet opulent good taste.

'How on *earth* did you get it, Sherbert?' .

'It was for rent. This house and the one next door are on the market for monthly let. I found out absolutely by accident when I was in Clutton's one day last week. I did vaguely think you'd like to stay in this part of the world while you're in London. Much better than hotel rooms, I thought; and then Bonk! There it was! Glebe Place – the very same old dosshouse up for grabs. I've been hugging it to myself for ages – soon as I knew you'd be over. And hasn't it changed? Talk about toffy. They wouldn't have you as your old long-haired self in the street now!'

'It's a hell of a lot more up-market than it was in the early '80s. Look at the chandeliers! And they've bashed my three little rooms into this socking great salon. Very open-plan and chic. Still it is wonderful just being in the place; like having one's life back all over again. Holly, see this end of the room? It was my bedsit, filled with furniture you only see now in repeats of *"Randall and Hopkirk Deceased"*. But, you know, the view, the feel.....they haven't changed somehow.'

'Not much of your flower-power or punk clashing colour about The King's Road these days. But it's still trendy,' Sherbert assured me. 'If that doesn't sound too *period* a word.' He slipped an arm through Holly's. 'Decision time, Holly. I have a room booked for you back at the Conrad for tonight if you want it. I know that you and Mike have become very chummy, and there is everything you might need here if you prefer to stay in this house; but I wanted you to be able to have a choice.'

'You'd like me stay here – while we're in London – wouldn't you, Mike?' said Holly, blushing.

'Oh, well, of course. I thought you *would* be with me. I assumed so,' I replied, suddenly feeling vulnerable.

'Everything you need is in the kitchen,' said Sherbert, stressing the Little Woman Cooking aspect. 'In fact Lane has helped to arrange a serf or skivvy to help with things over the next few days, so…..'

'Hey, no,' Holly said firmly. 'This servant bit's all right for you Bel-Air stinkos, but I don't want some old thing going on about "Up-the-apples-and-pears-and-isn't-the-Queen-Mum-a-luvvie?" all day long. If I stay, I do the domestic bit.'

'Gawd! Listen to her!' hooted Sherbert. 'You've got a bit to learn about England 1999. Queen-Mum-a-luvvie! More likely the undergrad daughter of a barrister slumming it between doing directors' dinners, or a Filipino who once worked for Mick Jagger and expects twenty-five grand a year.'

I said I liked Holly's idea because one woman in the place was enough.

'Oh, you!' Holly cried archly, like Vivien Leigh. Sherbert tripped off down the apples-and-pears.

'Where we meet tomorrow is on a card on the hall table. I'll send the car at eleven.'

'Bye, old bugger.'

'Sweet dreams, Mister Memory-Lane.'

'…..and thanks.'

The front door closed and we were alone – in London!

Lane was driving. Next morning we were going in slow traffic through what I explained to Holly was "The City".

'This has, and yet hasn't, changed much. I was just thinking of how I used to feel uncomfortable in The City in the old days. All those livery companies and identikit people. Did you ever get to see Tony Hancock's film "*The Rebel*" on PSB – about being a City clone?'

'Mike, I don't know who Tony Hancock *is*,' Holly murmured..

'Never *heard* of him? Well, I must admit his best days were over – in that he was dead – when I was still a kid, but not to know who he *was*…. This is what I get for getting fond of an embryo. You'll be saying you don't know what an Austin Allegro is next.'

'Dead right, mister. I don't,' she grinned.

'Well, when you're poor you distrust the City.'

'I can't think of you as being *poor*,' she grinned.

'*Poor*? We all were. Anthony was teaching at Glenturret when it was briefly a school, I made tea at EMI studios, was estate-agent skivvy and did some part-time dabbling in pine furniture at a shop in the Wandsworth Bridge Road. We lived in scruffy flats in twos and threes, drank *Le Piat d'Or* or "Bull's Blood" on special occasions, ate a lot of spag bol, thought that dinner at Maggie Jones was a treat – a "biss-tro" we called it, pronouncing "bis" to rhyme with "piss" - or at Dominic's. Veeraswamy's off Regent Street was where toffs went for a curry lunch, like when your uncle took you out. Most of the time we had our shot of dysentery at all those "Light of India" and "Star of India" places that were springing up all over London. I went everywhere on an old motorbike, cadging fags, kipping for the night on sofa cushions on the floor: out in Ealing, down in Tooting, over at Peter Buchan's place in Balcombe Street. They were wonderful days, Holly. Who wants to be a millionaire?''

'So you don't like being rich?'

'Oh well, it has its points. But it makes one so darned fussy. Why, I bet I wouldn't actually *like* kipping on sofa cushions on a floor in Tooting nowadays.'

'Perhaps that's age talking, rather than cash.'

'There you are!' I cried. 'I'm so bloody old!'

'No you're not.'

'Yes, yes. I am. I am. Just talking about things and realising they are more than twenty years ago and utterly lost…..'

'Mike,' said Holly, taking my hand, 'You've come back, and in doing so have *gone* back. I know the past is a foreign country and they speak a different language there, but you speak the same language. By returning to London, you *have* time-travelled.'

'Hm. That's good. "The past is a foreign country", eh? Who said that? That apt geezer Shakespeare?'

'The Bard didn't say *everything* worth repeating. That was L P Hartley in "*The Go-Between*".'

'Never….'

'Yeah, yeah. Never heard of him. The past isn't a foreign country to you, Mike, because you've never really left it.'

The car went down through a tunnel as this conversation finished, and emerged into a new, un-Londonish landscape. The London I knew vanished and was replaced by the all too familiar cityscape of the Americas.

I tapped on Lane's glass. It slid open.

'Where on earth are we?' I asked.

'Docklands, Sir,' said Lane.

'The docks? I heard they'd all been developed. Thatcher's government started it.'

'The production offices are at Canary Wharf, Sir.'

'I thought Sherbert was jabbering something about the East End last night, but I wasn't listening.'

Lane gestured at a block with a pyramidal roof. 'Tallest building in Western Europe,' he intoned with a melancholy pride. In London fashion he clearly both disapproved of and admired this symbol of modernity.

There were thirty-two elevators to choose from in the dark mahogany and marbled foyer, but reception had already telephoned upstairs and an exuberant Sherbert was stepping out from one of them to greet us.

'Mohammed comes to mountain. Penniless producer comes down to rich backer. Just as it should be!' he cried, embracing Holly and grabbing me on the shoulder.

'You could crawl a bit more, as we're in public,' I grinned. 'This is a fantastic slice of real estate.'

'Not bad. We felt we had to move in here. There's media all around us – as well as bloody bankers.'

'What happened to Wardour Street?'

'Still there, but not top flight. Too difficult to park.'

He led the way out of the elevator (which had shot violently upward; quicker than the Empire State's, I thought) into a corridor shiny with more marble and twinkling with halogen lighting. At the end of it were three dark doors. A discreet row of capital letters proclaimed that we were on the threshold of GOLIATH PRODUCTIONS.

'So, this is your outfit. Why Goliath?' I asked.

'Because of my name.'

'What? Sherbert? A bit cryptic.'

'No, nutter. David. David and Goliath. See?'

'Clear as pea soup. Very biblical. But you should have called it SHERBERT PRODUCTIONS as in fizzy and bubbly, *not* about a giant bloke who got defeated by a dwarf, AND you'd have kept what is, after all, your name.'

'Sherbert hadn't been my name until about three weeks ago when you started using it,' Sherbert reminded me. 'The last time it had a regular outing was back in the early 'eighties.'

'GOLIATH is okay, I suppose. But it still doesn't answer my point about his being defeated in the end.'

'We're not AT the end. We're at the beginning,' said Sherbert, throwing open the left-hand door.

A huge room with vast, panoramic windows seemed to hurl light and space back at us. Say what you like about rooms in 18^{th}c and Victorian buildings, they can never have this effect of spacious enormity, for their impact is bounded by their decorations and their many interior walls; the skyscraper apartment takes its personality from the vast spaces below and beyond it. I suppose it is corporate America's gift to the world. London sprawled below us, immense and imposing in its scale, carpeting the valley along the glassy river and losing itself in misty hills on the horizon. The lack of other really tall buldings gave greater emphasis to this one immense view.

There was a scuffling of chair and a familiar dipping, ducking, bowing figure came tacking from side to side over the prairie-like carpet.

'Here's Adrian,' said Sherbert. I shook a limp hand.

'Nice to see you again.' I lied, ingrained politeness on auto-pilot.

'"New York! New York!" twittered Adrian tunelessly, '"It's a wunnerful town".'

'Shouldn't that be "Maybe it's becorse I'm a Londoner"?'

'Just reminding Mike here of where we last met,' snickered Adrian, beaming at Sherbert.

'Do sit, Mike. Holly. Coffee?' asked Sherbert. 'Or is it not too early for a proper drink?'

'Don't you find that poor old London has gorn down dreadfully?' asked Adrian, baring yellow teeth in what I felt was a meaningless smile.

'Not at all.'

'Oh, it's not what it was – but then you get the feeling, the sense that Europe isn't where it's happening anymore.'

'Where *is* IT happening, then? America? The Islamic world? China? And what is IT anyway?'

'I don't get the feeling that it's in America,' Holly put in, 'I mean….since Bush and Clinton….'

'Oh, of course our sweet young production assistant *would* have all the answers,' sneered Adrian waspishly, baring his teeth. This dislike of Holly seemed new; rather puzzling. What on earth had she done to him?

'The material on which your finished scripts are based don't seem to be helpful or positive; typical examples of trite negativism….,' I began.

'I can't think you have read them with much depth of understanding. And, David, what is our backer going to make of the other six?'

'What six? Do you mean six more episodes?'

'Mike,' interjected Sherbert. 'I was going to tell you, old pal. Adrian wants to go much further into the cultural plateau of modern concept art and what it says about our society. He thinks it needs a lot more air time.'

'Oh, he does, does he? And what do the others think? The ones left behind in New York?'

Sherbert looked uncomfortable.

'Ah, well, Len Culdenbringer was not in favour, nor was Renzo. Um, actually, they've both resigned.'

'Resigned! What the hell is happening, Sherbert? I thought everything was sorted out.'

'Well, you see, Adrian has this remarkable idea….'

'Won't six more episodes mean a lot more investment?'

'I was going to leave that until later,' said Sherbert. 'Really, I hadn't expected all this to blow up on Day One. It's most annoying.'

'More of MY money? For what, exactly?'

'I – I have special advisers coming over from the 'States,' put in Adrian. ' People who really know about the cultural landscape, especially as expressed in concept art.'

'I know all about that bollocks too, you know!' I hooted. 'Sherbert, I told you about my L A connections with the fruitcakes there.'

'Fruitcakes! You naturally miss the point, Mr Greville.'

'Let's drop the formalities, Adrian, shall we?' said

Sherbert, staring at us. 'Christian names on the team, eh?'

'All right, b-b-b-but I resent the instant, uncalled-for, unk-k-kind hostility which I am g-g-getting now and got from the b-b-b-beginning....'

Adrian stuttered to a halt. His fingers fluttered wildly before his face. His insincere, toothy smile had been replaced by a bitter snarl. I sort of saw just then that he was actually more than just needled by me, but – if it didn't seem so ridiculous to suppose it – *hurt*. Sherbert looked most put out.

'You want my money,' I said 'And that's ALL you're getting, if that.'

Sherbert stared at me, wonderingly.

'Mike – what do you mean by "if that"?'

'I want to examine every line of anything else written by Adrian before I release a single dollar, Sherbert. Nothing personal, old friend, but I can tell you I already have a low opinion of much of the series – and it's going lower.'

It was a very uncomfortable meeting and did not last long. Even Sherbert's ebullience seemed dented by the electric sparking – and Holly, of course, had no idea why things had gone phut! on the team and seemed quite distressed. Sherbert said he hoped that I would attend some showing of the near-finished episodes for the first series (due to start transmission on BBC2 in Britain in the March of the new millennial year), but I declined.

'Not until I've seen all the new stuff.'

'You'll come over to Cinecitta for the European shooting, won't you?' Sherbert anxiously enquired.

'I might,' you said. 'But you two don't care to have my

opinions, so what's the point?'

'Oh, now Mike, you know that's not true – we *want* you to read the ideas, don't we, Adrian? You are such an important financial backer. Your *imprimatur*, as it were, is essential.' And, as Adrian remained silent, he added, 'Isn't it, Adrian?'

Back at Glebe Place, with me brooding and facing the reading of another large wodge of paper, and Holly rather silent and thoughtful, a perturbing incident occurred. A strange-looking person seemed to be interested in the house. I had noticed a thin, stoop-shouldered young man with long moustaches, like those of Fu Man Chu, standing outside the building with the creeper on it, that morning. I didn't expect to see him again – but there he was. The day following, having forgotten him, I spotted him once more. From that time on, I felt that I took him in through the pores of the skin. When deep in the house, I would just know when he was there, come to the front, look out and discover my instinct right. I swear it wasn't until day three or four that it occurred to me he was watching us. Now I was on the look-out. He wasn't stationary, but not moving either, He gave a peculiar impression of someone walking on the spot, as though a fantastic inner energy bore him up, but, as he was rooted to the earth, caused his outlines to shimmer with a barely-suppressed frantic activity, a neurasthenic action most disturbing to the viewer.

At first, I didn't draw Holly's attention to him. I didn't want to introduce a further bum note into the idyll of her first perfect days in London.

'How's the new script ideas?' she asked.

'I hate them. God, I can't tell you how I wish that Booker wasn't involved in this project. I'm sure Sherbert's making a bad mistake,' said I.

Before coming up to bed, I looked once more into the street. For a second I thought there was no one under the creepers.

I was wrong. The young man with Chinese moustaches, shimmering with neurotic motion, was still there.

Chapter 12: **The first attack**

'Mike! Mike! He's out there again!'

I jerked my head up from the manuscript I had started to read. I had told Holly about the figure in the road, and she wanted to bring in the police.

We were both getting increasingly disturbed by the terrible persistence of the strange young man whose odd, droopy, moustachioed face and peculiar figure I had now seen a dozen times, staring motionless at the frontage of the house in Glebe Place.

'God. There's only one thing for it. I'm going out to bloody well ask him what he's up to.'

'No. No. I – I don't think either of us should meet him,' said Holly. 'Don't you remember how Clint Eastwood makes contact in *"Play Misty for me"* and how it sort of establishes a bond which wasn't there before? We really, really ought to let the police know.'

'Oh, bollocks. I'm going to confront him. He's probably just some poor creamer who ought to be in a loony bin, but wanders the streets because the nut-houses have probably been closed by the government. Care in the Community, they call it. Well, I'm off to tell the freak how much we care.'

As soon as I emerged, the watcher took alarm and began to back away towards The King's Road. A brief chase began. I went about fifty yards after the fleeing figure and then stopped, holding my side.

'Did you see what he was like close-up?' asked Holly when I got back..

'Little bastard,' I gasped, red in the face. 'Oh, I've got a stitch. He's some banana-case, he must be. Did you see how he was running? Knock-kneed, like a schoolgirl.'

'Well, he ran faster than you,' Holly grinned, poking me in the tummy.

'True. Mad or sane, knock-kneed or not, he's quicker than I am.' We cast a glance down the street; the crowds at the end had swallowed him up.

'Mike, *please* let's tell the police. Perhaps he's a member of an East End gang who know you're rich.'

'Oh, foozle,' I scoffed. 'That's about two thousand on the hundred point Unlikely Happenings scale.'

'Maybe, but can we ring the cops?'

'Holly, this is London, not L A. There's nothing to this business. He's just some pathetic "care-by-letting-them-gibber-freely" type. He's had a fright. He won't appear again. No cops, okay?'

There was no further sign of our watcher on the following day, and we made the understandable assumption that he had, after all, been scared off.

Meanwhile, I was fast losing interest in what had largely passed out of my hands as shooting at Ealing commenced. The atmosphere of politicking and quarrelsomeness was spoiling what had seemed a great idea in L A. The key to the problems was, of course, the awkwardness between me and Booker.

'Little sod!' I exclaimed, as Holly and I sat in the kitchen while supper cooked. She had been to Madame Tussaud's and I had sat, bored and incredulous, trying to absorb a ridiculous story about some gallery in Dortmund which exhibited sawn in half animals embedded in acrylic.

Holly sighed. 'What's he done now?'

'Fake, pretentious little pansy. I can't think why Sherbert has kept him on the project,' I snarled. 'I doubt Sherbert's judgement more and more.'

'He's a real top guy in script writing, Mike. Don't forget what a success he had with "Flesh for the Angels". And he's supposed to be very good at supervising contributory authors. What about the "Doctors' Dilemmas" series? David and he were involved in that in '97 when I first joined the company….'

'I know, I know, I know,' I yapped. 'He's a prodigy, a genius, a Great Man, a Panjandrum, a little tin god, man of the moment, but….'

'What is today's argument about.'

'Oh, I'm sorry, Holly. The usual crap. How wonderful modern art is – unlike the old trad stuff. It's rubbish. Look, I've decided not to fly down to Rome for the filming of the next bits. Can you bear it if we don't go?'

'I guess I can bear it, Mike, but I can't like it….. I mean, seeing Rome, you know….'

And then Holly took a deep breath and told me I should pull out of the final filming arrangements now that it had gone sour. She couldn't see why I had to carry on fussing over the project, and why it seemed to matter so much that the episodes were slanted away from what I would have liked.

That evening a dreadful thing happened.

Holly had come back from a visit to Keats' house in

Hampstead, had snicked the keys one after the other into the locks, thrown her bag on the little dark table and run upstairs.

We'd planned to go for supper at Porter's in Covent Garden, meeting up there at 8.00-ish. I had spent the afternoon at Goliath Productions.

Holly came out of the house, pulled the front door shut and began to fasten the mortice locks. She turned from the door, looked down for an instant as she started to descend the steps and.... Zip! A sound like tearing tissue paper thrust into her left ear. Then there was a thud. She had spun round in astonishment to find a coloured, fluttery thing on the left-hand door panel. She hadn't time, she said, to decide what it could be (for a ludicrous second she thought it was a humming-bird) before she was hurled off balance by a terrible pain in her neck. She fell down the steps onto the pavement. Her hand had grabbed at her neckline and found a feathery, hard shape. An agonising shock clattered through her. She realised that she had to get the thing, whatever it was, out of her neck, so she wrenched it away.

It was a dart.

Three more brightly-coloured darts banged around her as she hunkered close to the ground. She realised straight away, she said, that they came from an airgun. And she knew who had fired it, of course. The bizarre young man had got tired of merely watching.

Holly decided to take a cab to Porter's, and pour her heart out to me. But that evening Sherbert had a girl from the production company sitting between next to me, and poor

Holly didn't feel it was appropriate to launch into the saga of the hole in her neck. It seemed, she said later, too odd among the steak and oyster pies of the noisy diner. So we spoke of other things: the exhausting long weekend last Sunday through Tuesday when we'd gone all the way up to Scotland by train to Glenturret, and Holly's amazement at the house up there, its model railroads inside and real railway outside, and her first impression of my brother with his droopy moustache, fluffy greying hair and plump, olde-worlde look – just what a Yank thinks an eccentric Brit aristo in a country house should look like, Sherbert and I agreed.

At last Sherbert and the girl dropped us home.

'Mike,' Holly began, 'See that little chip on the door? Well, just as I was coming out to meet you, I....' She stopped. A scooter was whirring up the street far too fast, lights blazing. No, it was on the pavement.

I gasped, 'Holly!' and grabbed her shoulders and pulled her towards me. Accelerating, the scooter screamed between the parking metres and the railings. It had rained while we had been over at Porter's so the pavement was wet. The lights on the machine – there were three, one large and two low smaller ones – jerked in jagged reflection along the smooth paving stones.

I felt a pinprick on my wrist, then several pinpricks. I heard Holly scream. I saw a hand with an empty bottle in it. The bottle was frosty and the hand had a finger missing, so it was gripping the glass between three talons and a thumb. The light bouncing up and down from the stones gave an upside down photo-print, just for an instant, of a moustache and a smooth, high-boned face.

I smelt the tang of two-stroke gasoline and something else, like a salty harbour or a swimming-bath, then, with a clatter, the scooter was off, tramping from the sidewalk to the road and away into the roaring canyon of traffic at the top of Glebe Place.

Holly was still yelling something.

Mystified, I saw the royal-blue of the front door dissolve and bubble, like that Bugs Bunny cartoon where the film catches light and melts. A fine drizzle began to fall again.

Why, I thought, is Holly taking her clothes off in the rain? Hadn't we better wait until we are inside the house?

Only slowly, in my stupefaction, did her shouting begin to make sense.

'It's acid! Oh God! I'm burning! It's acid!'

I kicked the door open, bundled her in, clawed off her jumper and wrenched her frock down. Amazed, I saw her dress disappearing before my eyes, eaten away at the edges like a child's attempt at making an "olde" manuscript over a candle.

By the time we had run through to the kitchen and I was throwing jugs of water and milk (for that is the most effective, I learnt that night) over Holly's arms and legs, and into her face, so that we paddled in a growing lake, I had grasped what had happened.

Twice in one evening Holly had been attacked.

'Oh! Oh! Mike! Mike!' she sobbed. 'Look at my hand! My face, Mike! What's happening to my face?'

'Christ! There's a hole in your neck!' I gasped, seeing it for the first time.

'Yes, yes, that was earlier! It was made by a dart, and my leg's covered in rashes! My face is burning! Oh, oh, I can't understand it, Mike!'

I clasped her to myself – soaking, red welts rising under the damp; a naked, sagging, shrieking figure dipped in diluted hydrochloric acid. Holly cried,

'And that man; he had only three fingers! That's a clue, isn't it? We can tell the police he had a finger missing. That'll be a clue, won't it?'

I felt my arms go slack about her. I too had seen the three-fingered hand, and only now realised, with a reeling lightning-bolt of shock, what that meant.

'What's wrong?' she cried. 'What's *wrong*, Mike?'

I gazed through her; a man facing the awful fact that his buried past has caught up with him and grievously hurt someone he loves.

'Three fingers, yes.' I gave a sob.

Georgie had bitten off Mopsa's finger, hadn't she?

As we stood unclothed in the soaking kitchen of the cute little Chelsea pad, it seemed that a great extinguisher had come down on the flame of our London adventure.

Chapter 13: **Obvious conclusions**

As we stood in the kitchen in Glebe Place, I felt something had wriggled up from the depths and come between us.

I had not told Holly in London any more about Mopsa and me than she had divined back in New York at the time of Blundell's Harley's destruction in the Gugg, and it just hadn't seemed relevant. Sherbert, who had met Mopsa at Dan Bright's, could see that she and I were at the fag-end of whatever life we had lived together. He hid nothing from Holly either; he just assumed it was all over.

When we clung to each other, wet, shaking and stinging with acid, my only savage emotion was regret that I had got Holly mixed up in the wretched bitch's insanities, my one over-riding desire now to see her dead.

Mopsa in London!

In quiet Glebe place, in friendly London with the seamless garment of my far past and my present coming together like two edges of a wound healing, I had believed myself made whole again. Then, that night, as the absolute certainty racketed through me that our attacker, our stalker, had been the bitch, I had to face the fact that the healing was no more than the skinning over of a well of pus, infected and virulent.

Very late, as Holly slept at last, her skin bandaged by A & E at the Charing Cross Hospital and with cold cream slathered on legs and arms, I had my old dream again: a London street, with chimney pots stretching away and a high wall at the end. I seemed, as usual, to be looking down from a height. As always, the only vehicle in the roadway was a dark, humped device, and the sky was grey.

I remember awakening with a jump. Holly was breathing regularly, with a tiny woofling sound.

The soft autumn darkness was still, but cars rustled along The King's Road. I went downstairs, feeling a wild hunger. I knew there was a wedge of soft brie, some salty St Ivel butter and slices of honey-roast ham in the fridge. I sat in the upholstered semi-circular bench at the table munching crusty bread with the butter spread thick. I felt that my nerves needed coating with fat. Hunger satisfied, I boiled the kettle and drank coffee with Nestle's condensed milk in it, gooey and sweet. Finally I lit a thick, untipped cigarette. I hadn't puffed for years – it was punishable by death in California, of course – but seeing Anthony up at Glenturret wreathed in rich Senior Service smoke, I just had to buy a pack to remind myself how much I used to love it.

After this trio of midnight indulgences, I began to think.

WHY was Mopsa in London?

That filthy, vengeful woman! Why should we have to put up with the misery inflicted on us by awful people whom we hate?

Why was she in London! Why had a loathsome bacillus, a fungal growth, a blind, parasitic spore borne on the wind from the alien jungle come to infect a verdant paradise? These were my thoughts as the cigarette smoke curled up into the kitchen spotlights.

Then I realised I was asking the wrong questions.

The correct question was: HOW was she in London? And the ancillary parts of it went through my mind in the following order:

How did she know where I was living?

How had she got over here?

Where had she got the money?

Where was she staying?

I had not told her where I was going, so *who* had?

Obviously she had known I was coming back to the UK, and she knew roughly when. I'm sure she had tried to find me in New York after the Guggenheim chase. Whatever else you could say about Mopsa, she was a sticker.

I hadn't left a forwarding address with Keyser and Di Gregorio, who were going to sell the old Royal Greville offices, because I didn't know where I'd be staying in London. And if I didn't, how did she?

The only address anyone had in the USA was the film company's. Even Dan Bright had only Goliath Productions as the point of contact. Mopsa must, therefore, have got the Glebe Place address from someone in Goliath.

I couldn't believe that it would have been Sherbert. No, of course not. And where was she living when not skulking on street corners, firing darts and throwing acid? And who was paying for it?

Someone at Goliath, but not Sherbert….. A kind of iron certainty began to form in my head, like the hardening arteries of one who eats too much salty butter and brie.

While Holly slept in the snoring sleep of shock, I ran the only candidate over in my brain. A bastard, a shit, a malignity, a misfit, an embarrassment, a traitor, a mischief-maker, a pervert, a thwarted lover, a hypocrite, a dissembler, a champion of modern crap sensationalism, a disappointed colleague: A. Booker.

Who else could it have been? I brought back to mind Booker's expression and searching directness in that New York limo, and did indeed believe that so far from being annoyed by my endless objections to the series, he was actually hurt by them. Perhaps, extraordinarily, he had conceived some sort of perverse love for me.

Just before he left for Rome I asked Sherbert if Booker had said anything about me.

'Hm. His attitude is rather ambivalent,' Sherbert had replied. 'He talks obsessively about you and your criticisms of the project, but in an odd way – a bit like a complaining wife, if you know what I mean. But you know he's pretty temperamental, I suppose.'

'It's being gay, I expect,' I said.

'Of course,' Sherbert had yawned. 'I expect that to him you're a rich hunk and he thinks you should be fawning over him, not Holly. Hell hath no fury like a bender scorned, and all that.' Nothing much from Sherbert then.

'Mike! Mike!'

Holly's hand was shaking me. I had fallen inelegantly asleep in the kitchen, face upwards, my neck sharply cricked. An empty plate told its tale. Light came grey and sad from the railed area. Holly stood next to me, hair all mussed up.

'Oh God! Damn! I can't straighten my neck!' I gasped, forcing my head forwards again.

'I wondered where you'd gone,' she said. She fumbled

for the back of a chair, the bandages on her hands looking like ski gloves.

'I – I didn't want to wake you, but I couldn't sleep. I was starving, see?' I flipped a hand towards the plate. 'Look, I've been putting two and two together and made a hundred and sixty squared at last. I *know* who is behind all this, behind the acid, the attacks, the darts. Not difficult to guess. And I *do* agree the police should be brought in.'

She just shook her head, hanging it down limply as she slumped onto the chair.

'Oh, Mike....' she murmured.

'Okay. Don't guess.' I heaved myself to my feet. 'I'll tell you. *Booker*. The bastard Booker.'

She gazed up at me with mournful eyes.

'Are you *mad*?'

'What? Mad? No – I've worked it out.'

'I am beginning to think this project has unhinged you, Mike,' she said slowly. 'What else are you going to blame Adrian for? The Turkish earthquake? The invasion of Kosovo? My God, can't you talk sense, especially now? Booker hasn't got a missing finger. He is plump, not skinny. HOW can you sit there and tell me that he did this to me?' She clawed at the red dart wounds and shoved her poor, bandaged hands into my face. 'HOW can you sit there and blame THIS on him?'

'No, no. Of *course* I don't mean that he shot the airgun or threw the acid himself. I mean he's BEHIND it. He's behind it all.'

She sighed. Sorrow had replaced anger.

'Make me some coffee. I can't use my hands.'

'Holly, Booker has his reasons…. I'm sure about that.'

And, of course, I got nowhere with her because I hadn't the guts to tell her about Mopsa being in London. How was I going to explain everything without doing that? It was plain stupid of me not to have come clean there and then, but – but I didn't.

I gave credit for what she did next: sitting quietly, with hands gripping the coffee mug as a panda holds bamboo, and asking gently,

'All right, Mike. What is your theory?'

'One: he doesn't like my criticism. Two: he thinks a real-estate man who is putting up the cash should just sign cheques. Three: he regards my opinions as conservative, small-town, anti-liberal and low-brow. Four: he tried, in New York, to – well – to make a proposition to me…. And I turned him down.'

'He …. *What!* What proposition? A business deal, do you mean?'

'No, no, of course not….'

'….What? … Trying to undermine Sherbert?'

'No, Holly, the other sort of proposition….'

'You can't mean….?'

'I can and do. And why sound so surprised? Am I a leper?'

The events of that night had that one further phantasmagoric absurdity to unleash: that I should be faintly piqued to hear that Holly might have thought me physically unappealing to Booker!

'Oh don't be so silly, Mike. I understand now, of course. But I'm just so – so staggered.'

'Couldn't you see that he's gay?'

'Yes. Yes, I suppose I did sort of subliminally realise it.'

'Well then.'

'And,' she went on, 'you think that's the reason for these attacks? He hires a psychotic killer to fire darts and acid at ME – not *you*, notice – because he thinks you aren't intellectual enough and you refused to play games with him in the back of the auto in New York?'

'Yes.'

'To borrow your fine old English word: BOLLOCKS!'

When I was sure that they would both be up and around, I made two calls: one to Anthony in Scotland at Glenturret and one to Sherbert. I didn't consult Holly about these at the time. The first of these calls was a success, the second a failure.

'Anthony? Are you properly awake?'

'Ah – is my "drenched nature lying in swinish sleep"? No, it isn't.'

'What's that from?'

'From whence comes it, you mean. Dangling prepositions are a bit American, old top. It's from *"Macbeth"*, of course.

'Yes, yes. Look, do you mind putting Holly up for a few days?'

'Holly Miall? Yes, of course. But you've only just been up here. Wouldn't it have been easier to have simply stayed on?'

'It's just Holly, OK? Do you mind?'

'No. Peter and I thought she was charming – but …. but has anything happened?'

'A rather melodramatic thing has – and I wanted Holly out of the way while the police are sorting things out.'

'Police!' gasped Anthony. 'Why on earth are police needed?'

I told him about the attacks. He was gratifyingly quiet as I did so. For a chronic gasbag, Anthony knows when to be attentive and serious. When I finished he replied robustly, 'She can stay as long as she likes. Actually Peter and I need perking up. We had some bad news about Glenturret last weekend. Just tell us what train to meet at Stirling.'

Reassured as to Holly's immediate safety and too wrapped-up in my own tunnel-vision to ask my brother what the recent "bad news" was (and it was *very* bad), I rang off and made the second call – to Canary Wharf.

'Sherbert!' I cried, as a thin voice came on at the other end.

'No. Who is this?'

'May I speak to Mr Sherwin-Lemond?'

'He's not here yet. Is that you – Mike?'

It was Booker. The last person I wanted to talk to.

'When will Sherbert – that is, David – be in?' I asked. 'It's nearly ten. I wanted to tell Sherbert that I was leaving London. I'm not sure the team needs me – anymore.'

There was a pause.

'So, you're leaving?' he said – his voice seeming falsely casual to my ears. 'Orf to Rome for the filming, then?'

'No. Not to Rome.'

Again a silence – as though Booker was collecting his wits at the other end.

'David is at home, you know,' he twittered. 'He told me

to inform anyone who rang here that he would be there all morning.'

'Thanks,' I said, about to put the 'phone down.

'Wait!' came Booker's squeal.

'What?'

'I've found a message for you here on the desk. He wants you to call in about one-thirty. There's someone he wants you to meet. He wants you to have lunch with him.'

I glanced at my watch. After ten o'clock. I wanted to find out train times for Holly.

'What do you mean: "someone"?' I asked Booker. 'Someone from the company? From America?'

Booker seemed not to know what to say next.

'Er – someone important, apparently. He asked if you could meet him at home – at one-thirty.'

'Yep. You've told me that already. But how did he know I was going to ring?'

'Oh. I expect he thought you would.'

'Why didn't HE ring to ask me over?'

'God! I don't *know*,' came an exasperated howl. Then, 'Why should I know?' in a flat and distant tone.

It was my turn to pause. It didn't seem the right time to tackle the freak about Mopsa and whether he knew her. I felt I'd need to see his eyes as I questioned him. But it just shows how much I underestimated him that I didn't connect his odd telephone manner to what was soon to happen. As I wanted to see Sherbert to tell him of my suspicions, I thought I might as well do as his message asked and go up to where he lived. So I muttered,

'All right.'

'Wait,' cried Booker, sensing correctly that I was at last about to hang up.

'What?'

'So you really are leaving London, are you?'

'Yes.'

'You and Holly Miall?'

'Yes. Goodbye.'

What I was going to do while Holly was in Scotland, I didn't know. I had the idea of finding Mopsa via Booker and sorting her out for good – buying her off with thousands of dollars, or bringing a court injunction against her for harassment and securing her deportation, or taking her back to L A myself – I really had no fixed plan, but I believed I'd have a freer hand with Holly out of the way; out of danger – if there was likely to be more danger.

Holly, of course, didn't play ball.

'It doesn't HELP that you're here!' I cried.

Tears stood out in her eyes.

'But I don't really *know* your brother, Mike. Anyway, I should be worried the whole time, and I'd have to keep up appearances and....'

'Not with Anthony and Peter....'

'Yes, with Anthony and Peter. I'm not in love with those two guys, Mike. I'm in love with you.'

'But think! Darts in the neck, acid being chucked. What next?'

'God, Mike, it's so ridiculously old-fashioned sending me away. "We must protect the little woman at all costs! Send her down to the marquis' seat at Courtleigh!" No, Mike, I refuse to play the part of a drooping Victorian heroine just to satisfy your sense of melodrama.'

'But Holly,' I hooted, 'I've told Anthony you're coming. I've found out the train times.'

'Well, you can un-tell and un-find. I AIN'T going.'

So – she got her way and was still in London, as the last minutes ticked away before my journey to Sherbert's.

'If you won't go to Glenturret, you're to stick with me. I want to keep an eye on you.'

'You'll have to keep an eye on my photo then. I told you what I'm doing today.'

'Did you?'

'The National Theatre. *Henry the Fifth?* Matinee? Remember?'

'Oh, surely....'

'Tough. It doesn't sound like I've been invited, and I need something to cheer me up after last night.'

So I left for Sherbert's place in the hired car alone and with the whole Anthony/Euston/Scotland/Holly biz unfinished. All that remained of my plans was an absolute determination to get her out of London the following day.

Sherbert lived in Little Venice – a part of London I knew well from childhood; Anthony and I had been brought up in Maida Vale. I had been obscurely delighted to think that Sherbert, whom I had first met in Scotland at Glenturret, should now, by chance, be living near my boyhood home. It had seemed a happy omen. I was also pleased to see that the streets hadn't changed much since 1983, and that I remembered them

My mind was 99.99% occupied with the problem of how

to persuade Holly to go up to Anthony and the poser of what to do about Booker and Bitch-machine when she was there, so I suppose I was driving "without due care and attention" as I zoomed round into Blomfield Road, turning left at a new (to me) little café on top of the Regent's Canal, otherwise I would have noticed the boy earlier as he darted out between the trees lining the towpath. But I didn't.

My foot crashed on the brake pedal.

The rear end slewed and I felt it crunch against metal.

Something bounced off the hood and slid off out of sight.

The view ahead was reddened by a thick smear of blood.

I juddered to a stop, stalling.

In very slow motion I saw a woman run forward and bend, screaming, over a shape lying in the road. I noticed, equally slowly, a blue-jawed man step out of a white sedan parked down on the right. He made his way over to me. I sat immobilised by shock, hands clenched on the wheel.

The blue-jawed man opened my door.

'Step outside, please, sir,' he said.

Automatically I obeyed.

The weeping woman was being helped upright by a fair-haired man in glasses. I watched – and, as I did so, something seemed to be missing.

'Sit in here, sir,' said the blue-jawed man, pulling open the rear door of the white car. 'I'll take your statement in a moment.' He went back to the front of my vehicle. A coat was being pulled over the still child's figure. An enormous quantity of blood glistened on the sloping roadway, pulsing from the shattered head.

I thought of Holly, safely going off to the National Theatre, and wished that I could have reversed the clock one hour and have been with her. I cursed Sherbert and his wretched message. My mind raced with excuses: the boy had run out, the woman should have been supervising him, it was a blind corner. I clung to the impossible belief that the child wasn't, after all, dead; impossible indeed, as the river of blood continued to creep from beneath the coat.

I had been in the white sedan some minutes before the first of several ideas cracked across my brain so violently that I could feel the impact in my spinal cord.

How *could* Blue-jaw be a policeman?

Conditioned, I suppose, by what I'd expected a car accident to be like, I'd assumed he was – but there hadn't been time to call the police, and it wasn't likely that he would have been sitting on the spot all along, waiting for this precise collision to happen.

And what about an ambulance?

No one had rung for one – not the distraught woman, policeman or fair-haired man, not for me, horribly shocked, nor for the dead boy.

I think the overmastering emotion that shook was a surging rage. God! How thick they must think I am! So – this is all a sham, is it?

I grabbed the handle, wrenched the door open and staggered back out into Blomfield Road. Two or three spectators were being shooed away by the fair man. Blue-jaw jumped forward in alarm, dropping his silly notebook.

'Mr Greville, get back in!' he shouted. I hadn't told him

my name – but he knew it.

I made for the dead boy.

'Bruno!' roared Blue-jaw. The fair-haired guy in glasses ran up to me. I dodged him, bent down, and whisked the coat off the still body. My eyes drank in the football bladder, the jammy theatrical gore and twisted dummy limbs. The two men closed on me. The woman was pulling the coat back over the fake corpse. The three gaped at each other in alarm.

I began to shout hoarsely for help. My arms were seized.

'Let go!' I yelled, swinging round at Blue-jaw.

Often and often in L A, I used to imagine myself flooring muggers, robbers, burglars, drug pushers. I knew that if attacked I would thrust my right knee into their balls. As they crumpled up I would plug them with iron fist between the eyes, or, indeed, shove either my finger, or a convenient biro or key into the eyes themselves.

As spectacled Bruno and Blue-jaw began operations, I started to put into practice my mentally well-rehearsed routine. I got no further than clutching the iron fist. There was a heavy, crunching sound, a bright glare, a void.

The next thing I knew I was looking at two searing suns in a metal sky. I was aware of the hardness beneath me and of the agonising fact that my legs were as wide apart as they could be, and would not respond to my attempts to move them.

Chapter 14: **The Rubber floor**

A voice like the screeching of birds of prey came from just out of my line of vision. There was a wrenching at my hip joints. Above, like blazing stars anchored to the aether by immense hawsers, orbited two lights.

'How do you like it now, you snotty traitor?'

I struggled to sit upright. It was a hopeless attempt. The back of my head felt as if a crack, ever-widening, had appeared in it. Groaning, I fell back. Immediately there was a blow to my ribs.

'You DARED, did you?' came a familiar snarl.

How right I had been in my instinctive guess-work. Mopsa's Virginny twang came from behind me, shaky with the rage that possessed her.

I wanted to speak, but I had no idea how to put what I wanted to say. From her point of view I had done the unforgiveable: had abandoned her for another woman. Yet I thought I ought to explain how unfair she was being, how I had no formal contract with her, that her attacks on Holly had had no moral justification.

As the first words were forming on my tongue, my mouth was stopped by a stream of slithery stuff. For a frightful second I thought that undiluted acid was crawling over my face, but then I tasted the sweet squidge.

Honey!

What was the bitch doing now?

I gurgled as a thick wave of golden liquid coated my face from above. I still hadn't seen Mopsa. So – the daft cow was outside my range of vision sloshing honey, was she? It went into my nose, then ears as I turned my head.

'Like it sweet, do you, bastard?' she cried, dribbling it onto hair, neck, chest and upper arms. 'Reminds you of HER honey-sweet caresses, does it?'

'Grrruuurgh. Mopsa...... urrrgh – Mopsa, please. Gug – gug – uuurgh,' I spluttered, as about a pint of honey went down between my teeth.

At last the jar was empty. I heard a smash as Mopsa hurled it from her behind me. I was grateful she hadn't broken it over my skull.

I was beginning to pull myself together.

We were back where we'd left off in the lobby of the Waldorf-Astoria in New York – just as if the intervening weeks had been cancelled. Mopsa had tried to snatch me then and had failed. Here was another attempt, and this time she had succeeded. I gave an experimental tug at the leg irons which forced my feet apart. They were fixed into staples in the floor. The floor, although hard and cool, seemed, oddly, to be covered in rubber.

'Okay, Mopsa,' I said, my throat at last clear of honey, 'let's talk, and for God's sake come where I can see you.'

'Don't use His name in VAIN, you blasphemer!' came a screech. I sighed. Here we go again. And yet something of the absurdity of it all helped lift my spirits a little – almost as if part of me relished once again the tussle of words and actions with a familiar opponent at once resourceful and ridiculous. Like the villains in James Bond movies, Mopsa was always ready to stop and talk – and when we talked I usually got the better of her.

'Mopsa, dear. Let's at least speak face-to-face. Come

into my line of vision.'

There was a pause.

A scuttling came from the other end of what, I realised, must be quite a big room. She appeared in front of me. I gave a jolt which tore painfully at my hips. I gaped at her. What had happened? Mopsa had never been a beauty in the conventional sense, but she had strength of jaw-line, a tall carriage, snapping eyes and a dignified bearing (when not stoned); the whole effect was a bit like the young Angelica Houston. The creature which stood before me was twisted, old-looking.

'Mopsa! What have you *done* to yourself?'

She stonily regarded me. Her eyes were moist, but her mouth cruel.

'Have you forgotten just how you left me? Has it passed, like right oughta your mind, that you left me without a stitch on me in that shit of a museum? Didn't you even bother to find out that when that fat freak's sickle went over the edge and buried itself in the floor, I was on the roof with a million windows lookin' down at me?'

'On the roof? Is that where you got to? Mopsa, believe me,' I gasped, 'I did care where you had gone. It's just that I couldn't find out.'

'Oh yeah? Like the earth swallowed me up? You treacherous piece of filth, you didn't TRY for more than five minutes to find me, did you?'

Saliva dribbled from the corner of her mouth. Knowing her as I did, I could see that she was coming off a high and that soon I could expect violence. She had chucked acid at Holly while on the wings of a trip; I'm positive about that.

It was amazing she hadn't killed herself on the scooter.

Now I was still lying on my back with my legs stuck out apart, like that cartoon of Leonardo da Vinci's. The bash on my head throbbed. I feared that it might occur to bitch-face to put the boot into my testicles if she came round in front of me. I had to get released.

'Mopsa. Mopsa, please let me sit up. Then we can talk. I can't see you like this, and besides, what's the point? You'll have to undo me sometime. Please, Mopsa.'

As I spoke I wondered at her twisted-about appearance. She gave the impression of posing for the portrait of one of those men in the fields you see in old paintings. As if following my thoughts, she let out a kick. She was wearing clumpy, heavy steel-capped Doc Marten boots and the vicious cut, just under my left armpit, paralysed my ribcage.

'You dare to ask? You know all right. How you think I got off that friggin' roof?' She put on her "posh Limey" voice, her eyeballs rolling up. 'Eaow, hoy did hai get orf the woof? Eckcherlie hai took wather a toss orf that woof, doncha know, an wather buggered up my jolly old arse, old fwuit.' She gave another savage kick, this time on the outside of my left leg's thigh muscle, and resumed in her normal voice, '....which you know perfectly well, you dishonest dick.'

'......that you damaged yourself? Is that what you're saying? Of course I didn't know that. I told you, I couldn't find out anything about you before I left the 'States.....'

'......to live with Miall-Bitch.'

'......to live with Holly Miall, yes, as was my right. You

and I were not bound forever to each other, Mopsa. We were breaking up – we had broken up long before I met Holly.'

'HOLLy,' she repeated. 'Holl-EEEEEEE. Yes, your pathetic little slut of a mistress, your goo-ey dollybird prostitute. She's all you think of now, but you wait, that's all.'

I rattled my bonds. Mopsa at her most melodramatic I could take. Mopsa acting out her fantasies I knew well. But we were back to what had subconsciously worried me ever since the attacks with the darts. *Why* Holly should have been got at. I realised there was no rational explanation. There was nothing behind that except jealousy, mad hatred and fear.

'No point in hating Holly,' I said. 'She barely knows you exist. Someone she's heard about from Blundell. I'm the culprit, surely?'

'Yes, oh yes, yes siree, you danged well are. How long is it since YOU fell off a roof, Mikey? I mean, hell, do you know what's involved when you follow the guttering down to a – whaddya call it? – a buttress? Lucky for me Frank Lloyd Wright didn't know how to make a proper building or I'd've been a piece of red crap on the sidewalk. But Mike, baby, d'you KNOW what happens to your ass when you're in the altogether an' you're outa control on a roof?'

Mopsa began ripping at the baggy trousers she was wearing – trousers which I recognised as belonging to the peculiar young man of Glebe Place – and lowered them until her buttocks were bare. Horrified, I gazed at the puckered, raw slashes. They had healed, but not fully and not prettily. I took in that she was not wearing undergarments; I think now that she had had this unveiling scene prepared all along. 'Have I got as pretty an ass as Holly-Whore?' she snarled.

'Pull your trousers up,' I snapped. 'I can see you've suffered. But admit that it was *you* who decided to come after me in your birthday suit, *you* who pinched the hog, *you* who drove uptown, *you* who dived into the Gugg.'

'Hey! You hinting that these – these wounds are somehow MY fault?'

She straightened, her lips compressed. Fearing another kick, I hastened to say,

'Well, perhaps they are partly my fault, but not Holly's.'

No reply.

'Who did sort you out, then? How did you get off the roof? Where did you go?'

She pulled her lips down in an immense sneer, coming fully into my line of vision.

'Oooooh, suddenly we're all interested, now we've seen a few scars. Are we feeling a teeny bit sowwy that we were howwid to our poor Mopsa whose ass has lost its looks, on account of half of it still being on Frank Lloyd Wright's back porch? I got off the roof through a fire-escape. I found a coat thing. I got back in a cab to – to….never you mind.'

'Mopsa, will you please release one leg? I can't stand much more of this position.'

'Gee-whiz, a lil' cramp is upsetting the soft Brit while his lovely ex-girlfriend is exhibiting that she's down to half an ass.'

'I get the point. Pull your trousers up.'

'Eeow, hai don' laike looking up at such a lacewated wectum, doncha kneeow?'

'Will you just TELL me who got you to New York?'

Mopsa looked coy for a fleeting instant.

'Who do you think? It was through Georgie.'

'What? I thought you and Georgie had fallen out because she'd got into the habit of biting things off you.'

'I realised that was love.'

'Some love. Ten one-night stands and you've got no fingers left.'

Mopsa adjusted her attire and moved towards the door.

'So loooo-ng, traitor.'

'Hey! *Who* helped you to find me? Who did you get back to from the Gugg in that cab? Was it a guy called Adrian Booker?'

'Wouldn't you like to know, Mr Snoopy?'

'It was Booker, wasn't it?'

Silence.

'Who is Bruno?'

Silence.

'How long am I going to be here? Where am I?'

Silence.

'I want something to eat.'

'Lick your honey then, like a brave lil' teddy bear.'

'Oh, PLEASE unlock one leg at least, Mopsa.'

Silence.

'Just one leg!'

Silence.

'You bloody bitch, can't you answer?'

I realised she had left the room.

So began a night of hideous pain. Stretched painfully, my thigh muscles locked into a permanent rictus of cramp. My bashed head thudded as my blood sugar fell away to zero and pangs of hunger were added to the agonies of immobility. Unable to drift into sleep for more than a few seconds, my brain trod a maddened rut in which I went over and over again my reasons for thinking that my predicament lay at the door of Booker – a meticulous search for reason behind what had happened. Naturally, awakened to them at last, I saw the connections between my recent life and the art/culture series. Was Mopsa one of the "experts" Booker had assembled for advice on the kinetic concept art episodes?

Was I seeing connections where none existed?

The endless night wandered into grey dawn. Since early afternoon the previous day, I assumed, I had being lying on that floor. It was only then, at the approach of morning, that I realised how ODD the windows were in my prison. By full daylight I seemed to have got new energy and rattled furiously at the shackles. It was then, just as I watched a fiery squirrel of sunlight creep about the room, that I had my greatest fright.

I had been muttering, 'Rubber floor, rubber floor,' in delirium when I was energised by shock. Rubber? Rubber!

An operating theatre!

A savage animal fastened its teeth in my chest as I saw myself in the dark room out at Glendale with the young man with the pig-tail, watching a lunatic from the fringe of the kinetic art movement mutilating himself – or rather BEING mutilated by a disciple busily supervising cutters and blood drains.

In my misery I watched the squirrel flame over the windows and, as I say, for the first time I saw how STRANGE they were. I added to this observation the pronounced slope of the rubber floor.

It *can't* be an operating theatre! The relief of this certainty was enormous. For a while I felt almost free and I became aware of a release of a pain which had troubled me more than the cramp of neck and hips. With the ridiculous reserve of civilisation I had been praying that Mopsa would return to let me urinate. As she had not appeared, and as the hours had worn away, I had gritted my teeth, holding on. Now, in my rictus of fear, the all-absorbing pain of retention vanished. I realised my bladder had emptied of itself. Warm wetness spread under me, soaking into crumpled clothes, and then cooled.

There was a crash from below, as if a heavy door had swung back against a wall. The windows were glowing with light. It came to me that, astonishingly, and probably since urinating, I had slept.

'Gee-oh-dee. You've pissed yourself,' shrilled Mopsa's voice. 'Ugh!'

She came round to face me.

'Where have you BEEN?' I cried. 'Mopsa! This torture! You can't treat me like this. Think what I meant to you. You loved me.'

'Moral blackmail, is it?' she sneered. 'It's because I can't stop thinking of what you meant to me, you traitor, that I'm hardening my heart, and.….,' she bent down, her nose wrinkling, nodded and grimaced. I stared up at her strained face. The lines of drugs and monomania were clawed across it. Holly's bookish, innocent eyes seemed to superimpose themselves over hers for a second, so that behind them Mopsa dimmed into the loony, early-middle-aged, lonely psychotic she had become.

There was a silence between us which she broke. 'Well I guess I'm gonna release a bit of you, Mikey. Perhaps you've had a lesson. Besides, you've gotta be freer when my friend comes to measure you.'

'Measure me?'

'Measure you.'

'What do you mean by that?' I gasped.

'You'll see.'

She undid the padlock holding my right foot to its staple. At last the strain of having my feet apart was ended. I shouted out as I found that I couldn't move my right leg at all. It took ages for feeling to come back as I kneaded the cramped muscles. I struggled into a kneeling position, the dried trousers wrinkling about my bottom. The left foot remained pinioned to its fixing-point by a swivelling collet.

Mopsa watched, unsmiling.

'I suppose you like seeing me humiliated like this?' I muttered.

'Sure I do,' she replied. 'It's what I've bin living off for weeks.'

I staggered upright, my back to the glowing windows. Mopsa was bathed in their light, just out of reach.

'I'm hungry,' I said. 'And I'm dirty. Can't you get me something to eat?'

'Yeah, I've got somethin' for you.'

'What about washing?'

'I don' know. Washing is untrue to the idea of living naturally. I mean, snakes and geckoes don't wash; they jus' get wet in the rain.'

'Mopsa, if I'm a snake, I'm a snake that wants a wash.'

'No, you can eat, but you can't leave this room 'til the man has come to measure you.'

She went to the door. 'I'll get you some eats, I guess. We don' want you dying on us – yet.'

It seemed as if I was having to get used to my coating of honey and piss. Shackled, but standing, I looked around me. The room was fully lit by the sun. The rubber flooring, actually a sort of ancient composite, sloped towards three square holes in the far wall. As I couldn't make my way down there, I could only speculate about what lay beyond them. The bizarre windows were much nearer. I was glad that stupid Mopsa had released my right leg; I was able to step across the left staple to within a few inches of the window frames. Had she freed the left, I would have been too far away.

The design of the casements was Egyptian, the glass was coloured and the effect like a 1930s London tube station. The strong light came through the outline of huge letters which were fixed, I presumed, on struts on the outside wall, standing proud of the building by a foot or more. I spun round to see if their shadows were cast down the room over the three square holes. They were, and I made out G-U M - - T.

G-U M - - T?

The filth on the glass made it impossible to see clearly to

the horizon, so I grabbed up the padlock which had secured my right foot and which Mopsa had left on the floor. I was about to crack a pane of glass with it, when the door opened.

'I got you a sandwich an' some water,' said Mopsa.

She placed a paper packet and a bottle on the floor. 'What are you doing?' she asked suspiciously.

'Nothing.' She didn't notice I was clutching the lock.

'I know you. Sneaky. Low-down. Well, you try ANYTHING, Mikey, and see how you'd get on without the odd finger here and there.'

I got back onto the floor, shoving the padlock under my thigh. Mopsa smiled sourly down at me; she was happiest looking down on other people. She had always perched on sofa arms at parties. I ate, she stared at me – then left.

I waited for several minutes, and, sure that I was alone, wrapped the padlock in the sock from my freed foot. I gave the pane of glass nearest to me a sharp tap. Nothing happened. I recalled reading that it is more difficult to break a small pane than a large one because the small one has more perimeter of support relative to its area, so I reached up to a bigger expanse opposite G-U M - - T and bashed this instead.

Crrrack!

The pane splintered and a crescent-shaped chunk fell out. I heard it crash onto the roadway far below.

Aha! – Discovery Number One: I was several floors up.

Pulling against the chain on my left foot, I got as close to the aperture as possible and peered out.

What I saw caused me to gasp with recognition.

Below me was the street of my dreams!

And, always, in the dream, a queer, humped vehicle was parked a little way up on the left-hand side. I was never sure whether it was an old English car, a Ford Pop or Austin A35, but now I knew. Not on the left, but practically beneath me, was a big motorbike with a sidecar attached. I could see the spars and joints of its chassis clearly. Instead of a passenger body, this combo had a truck platform.

I am absolutely unable to comprehend why I should have envisaged this street in American dreams. I had always assumed that my brain had been digging up a shot from an old film like *"The Lady Killers"*. I stared down from my prison – the only time in an impercipient life in which I have felt briefly that there was a purpose in intuition and reason in the unexplained. Anthony used to think I had a feel for the supernatural; we both believed that our grandfather's house, Glenturret, was haunted – but children's instinctive belief is, of course, less overlaid with the commonplace and prosaic than ours. Enough to say that I was staggered for quite a few minutes before I did the obvious and struggled into a position where I could look right out.

With the chain ripping into my ankle, I forced my head through the jagged opening. Beyond the wall was a wire fence, a glimpse of shiny rail, and, to the far left, a coloured light signal. Part of the underground system? A main line railway track? Craning further, I nearly swallowed my tongue at the image which, just for an instant, imprinted itself on the corner of my eye. Away to the right was the familiar outline of Canary Wharf. It is difficult to judge how far way such huge buildings are, but I didn't think it could have been more than a mile. I had not doubted it seriously up to now, but it was a relief to have it confirmed that I was still in London.

I peered down into the street again. The fact that the motorcycle combination was the only vehicle visible had not, at first sight, struck me as odd. But London is over-run with cars, vans and lorries, so it seemed strange that this cul-de-sac should be empty, as if we were in 1959. For a weird second I fancied I had time-travelled back forty years to the life of some other man who would become the newly-born me when he died. Then I perceived that each little house down there was derelict. The street was on the edge of demolition, as, probably, was the building in which I was fettered.

There was a fumbling at the door.

I darted back between the staples and sat down.

Mopsa came in. I took every care not to let my eyes turn to the broken window in the hope she wouldn't notice it.

'Get up,' she said. 'You're gonna be measured.'

'Measured for what?'

'You don' need to know.'

'Who is measuring me?'

'My little man. He makes glass-fibre things.'

'You're measuring me for a glass-fibre THING? What thing? A coffin?' I tried to sound jokey-pokey, but couldn't quite manage it. Mopsa was such an unknown quantity.

'You are to cooperate, Mikey. I guess I don' want problems with this. I've got to make this show a success.'

'Show!' I gasped. 'Did you say "show"?'

'Yeah. S-H-O-W, you slow prick. What do you think I'm over in London for?'

I had figured that the bitch was over in London to wreak revenge on me. Otherwise, what was I doing in the building marked G-U M - - T?

'I figured you were over here to wreak revenge on me,' said I, giving thoughts words.

'So I am, you bastard. But an artiste of my stature has responsibilities too, y'know. I've a big show coming up at a place called – oh shoot! What is it called? Something to do with snakes. AND it's gonna be filmed for a TV series.'

'Snakes? TV?'

'And I'm in touch with the New Art people here. I'm getting to be famous – which YOU never accepted, you sneering little nobody.'

'I wouldn't have thought you'd have time to fit a sneering little nobody like me into The Grand Plan. Why don't you let me go?'

'Hey, he likes being ironic. Funny boy. Now look, I've decided to take you to my man to be measured, because I can hardly bring him up here to see you lying chained to the floor. So I'm gonna unlock you. BUT you have gotta behave quiet and easy.'

'Oh, so you don't want your little man to know you've got a prisoner up here?'

There was a silence. I hoped Mopsa wouldn't notice that I'd said "up".

'What happens,' I went on, 'if I make a break for freedom? And where are we going anyway?'

'We ain't leaving this building, so don' get cocky. An' if you "make a break for freedom", as you quaintly put it, Hollywhore's going to lose a finger or two.'

Here we were on the severed finger motif again. The latest mania.

'What happens if I get to Holly first?'

'Too late. Bruno is already WITH Hollywhore, an' he's got a pair of metal cutters aaaawl ready to go snippy-snippy-poo, if you don' do what yo' Momma tells you.'

She fixed me with a steely gaze.

I didn't know then that it was bluff. I hadn't credited her with the sense to plot ahead, of course, so the picture of the mysterious Bruno (whoever he was) with his poised metal cutters hovering over Holly didn't quite ring true – but......
And the thought that, because of "*Henry V*", she wasn't safe in Scotland at Glenturret....

I had no choice but to cooperate.

'Who IS this Bruno?' I asked. I then recalled that Blue-Jaw had called the fair man by that name at the time of my car "accident".

Mopsa brought her face into mine. Her breath smelled of vinegar.

'He,' she hissed, 'is one of US.'

'Who is "us" then? Is one of the "us" a freak called Adrian Booker?'

She made no reply.

'Do you KNOW Booker?' I shouted.

'I know him now. An he *knew* someone close to Georgie – an' I'm talking biblical here, Mikey.'

This information had to be pigeon-holed for puzzling out

later.

'Did he pay for you to come to London?' I asked.

'His company paid, I suppose. Why shouldn't they? I'm gonna be working on his film, his new project.'

'The – the new series? The TV series?' I stuttered.

'Yeah. The thing that stupid Brit boyhood crony of yours is tryin' to get together. But it's Adrian's film. Oh, Christ, how many times have I....? Oh frig! Now you've made me say His name. I've tol' you I've gotta show coming up at the....the....'

'Place like a snake. Yes – how exciting.'

Something impelled her to try to enthuse me. Poor cow.

'But I really *have* got a show there. Well, I'm part of the show. It's such a break for me. It's the latest thing, Mikey. There's Sarah Lucas there, an' whatshisname Angus Fairhurst, an' Tracey Emin. These are Top Names, Mike. They're at the edge. Then there's me. An' we're all goin' to be in Adrian's film.....'

'I've never heard of any of them, except the girl with the unmade bed,' I drawled. 'So where do I come in?'

'You're goin' to be measured. And you're coming now. Remember what I said about Holly-Bitch.'

My left foot was unlocked at last. I could move about the room. I could walk to the end wall to examine the three square apertures midway between floor and ceiling. I peered through them into a great void.

'Come back here,' commanded Mopsa. She looked as if she were up a slight hill as she stood crookedly at the far end of the sloped floor.

A slope!

Apertures halfway up the wall!

A void beyond!

My brain exploded into gear. Why had I been so slow?

I was in the projection room of a disused cinema.

The sun was moving along the derelict road outside. G - U M - - T followed on the grubby paintwork, thrown by the light on the big letters.

I tried to keep my face expressionless. "Look like the flower, but be the serpent under it", as Anthony is fond of saying. It was hard to stop my face becoming "a book where men may read strange matters" for I had, with a deeply satisfying surge of mental power, worked out what G - U M - - T stood for.

As children, Anthony and I were taken all over London by Ma (and sometimes Dad, before he died) looking for Space, Sinbad and Disney films. Before the '80s trend towards multiplexes, there used to be dozens of old big-screen survivors round London. We went to ABCs, Odeons, Essoldos, Rialtos and GAUMONTS. This empty cinema at the top of a street scheduled for demolition had been a *Gaumont*.

With very little spadework, I had found out that I was being held in an old cinema near a railway line within sight of Canary Wharf. Eat your heart out, Sherlock. It goes to show that kidnappers can't be too careful – especially if they're a bit thick, and crazy druggies on top, like Mopsa the Dummy.

This discovery had an immensely cheering effect on me, of course. I could now think of the next step: letting someone know where I was. In the meantime, my cue was to keep Bitch-face from guessing that I knew what I knew. Later, I would apply the mind that had made a lot of dollars on the property market to getting out of this idiotic nightmare.

'Weird room,' I said lightly. 'Okay, let's measure me.'

The door was opened. A dark stairway led downwards and we picked our way by the dim yellow slits of art-deco windows. I then made the discovery that the old cinema was not as deserted as I had thought. The ground floor, the erstwhile stalls, had been divided into workshops. In the corridor leading to the first of them was a lavatory.

'Get in an' sort yourself out,' said Mopsa. 'You'll find an old denim suit on the rail. I borrowed it from Reggie. I didn't tell him you needed it because you pee'd in your panties, so you don't have to feel embarrassed when you meet him.'

Reggie? Another Mystery Man to go along with Bruno and Blue-Jaw.

The finishing touch to my soaring morale was given by the change of clothes and the removal of honey and urine from my person. I stood on the lavatory bowl and tried shaking the bars at the window, but Mopsa hadn't been as stupid as all that.

When I emerged, dressed in a denim outfit and needing only a flat cap to complete my costume as an early-'60s odd-job man, Mopsa led me down the central passage to the last door on the right. A workshop in this position must debauch directly into the cul-de-sac.

Mopsa barged open the door. A clean, long working area met my eyes. In a corner were vast steel drums; in another a lathe and power tools. In the centre were presses with air-driven rams. There was a distinctive stink of glue and burnt plastic. By large double-doors, one of which was open, were five shapely bodies like little zeppelin airships. I recognised them at once as motorcycle sidecars, of a design not seen on the roads for forty years.

A man was wheeling a sidecar chassis on its one wheel out into the sunshine. It must have been heavy, and it certainly looked awkward, for, careful as he was, I heard a clunk as he dropped its struts onto concrete. Back he came into the workshop, wiping his hands on the bottom of a denim outfit exactly like mine.

'Hello there, Reggie!' trilled Mopsa.

'Ow, 'ello dear. Oi didn't see you'd coom in,' replied Reggie. He shuffled forward, grinning. 'An this is yow gentleman friend, Oi presume.' He gave me a wink. 'Sorry to 'ear you've mooked oop your close, Mister. But them dungarees is all yours for the toime being.'

I found I couldn't smile at him. There I was, a few feet from an open door with a friendly English bloke with a Birmingham accent you couldn't cut with a meat-axe, making sidecars, for God's sake – and I dared not walk past him into the sun for fear that the threat of Bruno standing over Holly with cutters was no bluff. 'Sow, you've coom for measurements, I suppowse,' continued Reggie. 'It's a foony old do, isn't it?' he asked me, 'this art world thing. But I down't moind. It's all mooney, isn't it?' He gestured to a table near the lathe. 'Lie down there, goov'nor, an' Oi'll get a pattern over you.'

I looked at Mopsa. She frowned and nodded at the table.

I lay down.

'Hm, it'll be toight,' said Reggie, making some passes with a flexible tape-measure, 'but Oi got a little sprung-wheel Watsonian that'll do a grand job to get yow there, after we've bolted it on. You've got to leave room between the body and the suspension movement, see? Good thing yow aren't fatter,' he said to me, 'ootherwoise yow wouldn't be able to squeeze the thing onto the frame. You see, it'ld taike a lot more mooney to start the metalwork from scratch.'

He measured my width, length, height, weight and – most sinister of all – where my eyes were in relation to the other variables. 'It's a matter of an exact fit, yow see,' he muttered. 'Fat lot of good it'ld be if yow was peeping awoy an inch below where the slits are.' He chuckled. Mopsa chuckled. Reggie laid some foil strips over me, humming as he did so. 'We'll maike sure later that the fixings are roight, when Oi've made the shell.' He chuckled again. 'It's a good idea, reely, Oi suppowse.' He chuckled once more. Mopsa chuckled once more.

This chuckling bonhomie was a bit one-sided. I didn't chuckle. From Reggie's arcane utterances I had gathered only that I had to fit inside something with eye-slits. Yet I couldn't feel truly menaced; Reggie's Brummie chuckles were hardly the trumpet-blast of doom. As I watched him laying strips of alloy by my sides, as I saw his mild, innocent eyes engaged in craftsmanlike measurement, I couldn't believe him to be a villain – certainly not an unhinged scion of the Excremental-Kineticists – and definitely not involved in my kidnapping.

I nearly said to him: 'Look, Reggie. I've been chained to the floor upstairs all night by a woman who wants to murder me, and her associate is with a friend of mine who will snip her fingers off with a pair of chain-cutters if he gets word of what I'm telling you.' But I knew I would just get an amused shake of the head and that indulgent chuckle. 'Well, booger me, yow artist folk'll be the death of me yet,' he would probably have murmured, true to his 1960s character.

So I said nothing.

The fact is, Mopsa had chosen well. A man who makes a sidecar body and its chassis for a "heritage" motorcycle fancier must be used to eccentricity among his customers. He regarded Mopsa as he regarded his normal punters: well-off original thinkers whose whims gave him his living. I imagined him at home saying: 'Fooney owld day today – I 'ad to maike a fibre-glass coat for a friend of that Yank woman Oi was telling you about. Foony ideas she's got, but she's a modern artist, of course.'

The session ended. Reggie folded up a steel rule.

'How long will it take?' asked Mopsa.

'Lets see. I'll hand lay it tomorrow morning. Yow know we're not open on Saturday afternoon or Sunday, but I'll get the coating on when it's dry, so yow'll be looking at Tuesday morning for the shell, so, because we're using an existing Watsonian chassis, Tuesday closing toime at the latest for the rig complete with fitments, Oi'd say.'

'We open on Wednesday, so it's gotta be Tuesday, I guess. You will definitely have it ready by then?'

'Yow can lay to that. Don't worry. Are yow in owver the

weekend?'

'Oh yeah, I guess I'm in this building for the duration,' smiled Mopsa, with a significant glance at me. Once again I had the overpowering desire to make a bolt for the street. 'We're going back to the studio now, C'mon, Mikey.'

The moment for the dash passed.

But do you know what my main obstacle was in speaking directly to Reggie? It was not only my fear of Bruno assaulting Holly over in Chelsea, but sheer embarrassment at the idiocy of uttering melodramatic phrases to the prosaic manufacturer of sidecars and receiving bemused, even amused, incomprehension in return. *That's* why the moment passed. It was the curse of being English in England.

So, with a continuing sense of dislocated unease, I ascended the staircase once more to Mopsa's "studio". I formulated a shadowy plan of grabbing her, throwing her into the projection room and turning the key. It seemed so tame, following her around like Mary's little lamb.

I stepped behind her and reached for her waist in order to chuck her off balance. As I braced myself to keep her down and yank the key from her pocket, a shape uncoiled itself from the only chair in the room. Mopsa staggered. She gasped, 'Hey, Mike! What....?' The shape came up swiftly. I saw in one blink the face of the man I called Blue-jaw. There was a crash, my legs gave way and I dropped to the rubber. A boot clumped into my face.

A little later I was nursing a cut mouth. Mopsa and Blue-jaw had gone and my left foot was once again padlocked to its staple.

Chapter 15: **The Mummy**

It was on the Monday that I could feel that intelligence was, at last, coming to my aid.   Over the weekend I stayed on the rubber floor. Mopsa had appeared alone with tins of sardines and bread rolls periodically. When I was taken down to the lavatory, Blue-jaw was with her. I was no longer trusted to behave without a sidekick.

During the long nights and longer days when I could sleep no more, I concentrated on plans for getting out. It wasn't until Monday's dawn, when pale grey began to flesh out the familiar G-UM - - T on the far wall, that I had my inspiration.

That game which Anthony played with us in Scotland, and I introduced to Holly's parents in Ventura – that maddening "telepathic" party game with which my brother annoys his guests at Glenturret and at which Holly distinguished herself by catching on so swiftly – flicked back into my head. If I could speak to her on the phone, I was sure I could tell her in code where I was being held.

I had spent so long hobbling to the cracked window and gazing out over the empty street that I had orientated myself with near absolute certainty. It wasn't the just-glimpsed shapes of Canary Wharf that had helped me, but the sudden gleam of water between buildings when the sun came out from behind clouds on the Sunday. At first, I idly appreciated the beauty of the sheen, my eyes following its evanescence in a broken crescent along my horizon. It amazes me now to think that I did not appreciate that this shining snake was the Thames. The window of my ruined prison was high enough to enable me to follow the curve of water from far left to far right. The just-visible towers on the Isle of Dogs lay within the curve. This meant I was north of the river. I had thought I might be looking south, anyway, because the low hills had a different shape from those at Hampstead, but I felt sure I was somewhere in Poplar or Bow. I knew Canary Wharf's post-code to be E14, so I could be in E14 too, or further north in E15.

On Monday, I banked all on Holly's intelligence. I thought that if I could spell out GAUMONT, BOW, using Anthony's methods, she'd have a chance of finding me.

A long shot.

I had no chance of putting the plan into action on the day I conceived it. Then Tuesday was a day of fussing by Mopsa, of dashing up and down to Reggie to see if the Project was finished, of the sound of hammering and the revving of a motorcycle engine and of the total ignoring of my needs and existence. Pleas to be allowed to go to the lavatory were met with avoided eyes. Pleas for food led to hoots of, 'For CHRIST'S sake, you whining bastard, can't you see I'm busy? I've gotta show to put on! AND you've made me use His name! Why I've gotta go to Hell because of you whining an' begging , I just don' know!'

I wondered if she had been drinking, although that had never been her vice. Her speech was wild and slurred. Then I thought she was on one of her trips, but she didn't seem lethargic enough for that. The truth came out when she was hysterically berating me for wetting myself again. What did she expect when she forbade me any visits to the john?

'Can't you stop shrieking, you ridiculous bitch?' I

shouted during a pause in her tirade. 'If you can't organise whatever stupid load of pretentious crap you're going to bore the London public with, at least you needn't take it out on me. I didn't ask to be tied up here. Cow.'

Her expression changed into her baby-about-to-cry pout and she puckered up her face like a crumpled paper bag.

'Oh, Mikey. You wouldn't be so horrid if you knew what news I've had.'

'Yes, I would,' I replied.

'It's Georgie. Georgie.'

'Don't tell me she's dead. Good.'

'Mike, Adrian's told me. She's got it.'

'Got what?'

'Whaddya think? She's HIV, of course.'

'So? Isn't everyone you know?'

'She's very ill. She had a sort of 'flu, then pneumonia, an' last week – last week she went into hospital. An' she's in one of those beds they have for poor people an' she's dying, an' I'm over here…..an'……'

She sat by me on the floor, awkwardly because her scarred buttock muscles seemed to have slowed her down, and blubbed theatrically.

Trying to ignore this, I said coldly,

'"*Adrian* told me". So you have been in contact with Booker again, have you? The missing link, eh?'

'Why shouldn't I?'

'What beats me is why Booker is bothering with all this. What does he gain from helping you in your stupid kidnap?'

'He doesn't know about you being chained up here.'

'What!'

'He doesn't. An' he probably wouldn't like it. He's soft on you, you know.'

'Of course he knows. It was thanks to his mysterious phone message that I was snatched by your yobs.'

'Oh – well – he knew I wanted to get hold of you…..'

'Get HOLD of….!'

'…..but he doesn't know I've had to – to discipline you, you bastard. He doesn't know that.'

'Holly will be in touch with the police, Mopsa.'

A sneer appeared on Mopsa's tear-stained face.

'Oh, WILL she?' she said. 'You'll never know about Hollywhore, you know. That's awwwwl over, mister.'

'What are you going to do with me?'

'You'll see today.'

'And you really think you and Booker are going to get away with it?' I cried, having visions of a thorough British police investigation initiated by Sherbert, in which every person I had been associated with would be arrested.

'Mikey, Adrian doesn't care any more. The series is all that matters to him.'

'In his position, I'd be worried. If anything happens to me, he'll be the first to be questioned.'

'He doesn't care, Mikey, 'cos, like Georgie, he'll be dead.'

'Oh, for God's sake, you don't mean he's….?'

'Yeah, he's a sick guy. An'you have frigged around with his great idea…'

'I just made a few suggestions. Besides, that project wasn't his idea, it was…'

'DON'T interrupt!' bellowed Mopsa. 'I haven't finished. You have frigged around with his idea. You needn't deny it, because he's told me about it. You've whinged an' snivelled about his scripts, you've threatened to back out of investment, and your old school chum had begun to listen to you. You've sniped an' criticised, but you haven't realised this is probably gonna be his TV epitaph. Your Brit pal with the silly name is gonna direct, but it'll be Adrian who gets the scripting awards. It's his ideas that matter – not yours. Anyway, you are leaving today. Apart from tomorrow night, you're gonna be in a lovely new home.' She scrambled to her feet and went to the door. 'Witold!' she called.

Immediately, Blue-jaw pushed into the room.

'We're ready,' went on Mopsa.

Blue-jaw had a thick roll of gaffer tape in his hand. Without warning, he wrenched off a length, came towards me and sealed my mouth, dragging the tape cruelly behind my head, tearing at hair. I felt my eyes bulge in silence.

'Ooooh!' cried Mopsa, lapsing into her fake Brit accent, 'Bugger-a-me! Ay hevn't hinterdooced mai fwiend Witold Koscynski. Witold, ay believe you've met this cad Greville. 'E's a bleedin' millionaire, doncha know. And, Mister Greville, let me in mai turn hinterdooce someone oo's visage should be familiar to you becawse you kneow 'is loverly sister. Yes, it's Georgie's little brother – the avenger. He is resident in London and, mai dee-ar, you could take 'im for an Englishman.'

'He's gone home, but he's left everything ready,' said Witold, ignoring me.

'Tape him up then,' said Mopsa.

Witold dragged more tape round my legs after kicking them painfully together. Mopsa jerked my arms behind me. I resisted, but Witold gave me such a box round the ear that I was nearly toppled. One leg was still padlocked and I feared that if I fell over when shackled I would damage my ankle. I put my arms obediently behind me. Tape was wound round them. When Witold had finished, I found that I couldn't move at all.

And what was amazing me more than anything else was *why* Witold should have been doing this. I had never met him; hardly heard about him, except once back in L A when I'd first seen the freak, Georgie. And why had Bitch-face referred to him as "the avenger"?

They bundled me downstairs, not gently. I had to hop from step to step.

In Reggie's workshop I was draped over a bench.

Witold went to the corner and pulled a large shape out on a trolley.

That's when I first saw the mummy.

So this was what Reggie had been commissioned to make. It was massy, black (except where some chromed fitments twinkled) and sinister. The eye slits seemed to hold my gaze masterfully.

Mopsa clicked at the fitments and the device opened in half.

'We want you to meet your mummy, Mike. You arrived in a mummy. Now you're going out in another one.'

Cryptic – but not that cryptic. And now I was leaving GAUMONT BOW with no chance of contacting Holly and putting Anthony's game to the test.

They took hold of me and tipped me over the edge, just like dropping a corpse into a coffin. Horrified, I gazed up mutely as they refitted the other half and closed it like a lid. I could see through the eye-holes. Reggie, with craftsmanlike care, had positioned them just right.

The trolley was wheeled out into the yard. I caught a glimpse of chromed exhaust pipes as I was wheeled past the motorcycle combination. There was a heave and I felt the mummy slide from the trolley onto the sidecar platform. There were four clicks. I seemed to be bolted in place next to the bike.

Witold said to Mopsa, 'Watch it at traffic lights. Reggie says it still has a tendency to stall. Blip the throttle.' From this I deduced that a works hack of Reggie's had been lent to Mopsa and Co to get me to – to wherever I was going.

Mopsa hopped aboard, fired up and crunched into gear.

'This is jus' absolutely unique,' she squealed to Witold above the thudding motor. 'Can you think of another art exhibit rolling up to the gallery on something like this? I hope we make the papers!' Exhaust puffed across my slits. I was positioned looking at the sky, my head at the back of the platform. The combo swung from the kerb and sharply turned a corner. Immediately there was a roar of traffic. I hoped Mopsa could cope with driving on the left. She was a good motorcyclist, but I knew that a sidecar outfit is very different from a solo. Anthony had one in the '70s and, although its quirkiness appealed to him, I felt ill at ease on the one occasion I drove it.

However, we had gone at least a mile without a crash, so

I stopped preparing for death and tried to make out in which direction we were heading. It was hopeless. The monstrous shapes of red London buses and big trucks came alongside, the rooflines of endless roads swept unrecognised along the edges of my slit-vision and I lost all sense of orientation. I choked, gagging on my tape, as diesel fumes belched over me. The motion of the outfit banged me up and down sickeningly in my black prison. I was deafened by the grinding of gears and the relentless banging of the engine by my ear. All I could see of Mopsa was a shoulder encased in a leather jacket.

At last, at the end of my endurance, we bumped over a kerb, turned violently and stopped. The engine died. Voices babbled: "Hey, this way, please!" "Look in this direction, Miss Greene!" "Stay in the saddle, Miss Greene; I want a shot of you driving!" "Can you lean over the mummy, Miss Greene?" "Mopsa, Mopsa, do you take sculptures to shows on a motorbike in Los Angeles?" "Hold still, can you, for a sec!"

Transient two-second fame for the stupid moo, I thought, as the babble died away, photographers moved on to another gimmick, and the contrived impact of our arrival (so much more Mopsa-ish than if the mummy had simply been in a plain Transit van) lessened. Mopsa had gone off to talk and posture, I presumed, for there was quiet for about quarter of an hour round the sidecar outfit. Then I caught her grating voice coming nearer.

'Guys,' I heard her say. 'I guess I need a little help here.'

'Terry has just delivered the Wing,' I heard cultured, whistling tones saying, 'The boys will help you in a few minutes.'

I lay, gazing at a sky fringed with branches from which the leaves were dropping. Were we in a park? Busy shouts came from within a nearby building and birds twittered. The sound of traffic seemed muted, as though from a little distance away. Eventually I heard Mopsa's voice, nasal and rasping, addressing someone crossly.

'I've done telling you I want it put in there NOW. I've gotta lot of things to sort out. I haven't unwrapped any of my other exhibits, so c'mon, for mercy's sake.'

Footsteps came up to the motorcycle combo. Fitments were snapped back and I felt myself lifted.

'Phew!' came a London voice, 'wotcha got in 'ere? It weighs a bleedin' ton.'

The mummy was dropped onto a trolley.

''Ere, that's clever, innit, Cled?' said the voice again. 'I dunno 'ow they do it. It's gotta be electric with batteries.'

The trolley paused in its bumpy motion.

'Wot?'

'Them eyes. Look.'

Two heads peered down above me. I rolled my optics like a couple of dice in a shaker. There was a gasp.

'Jest like real ones. I jus' dunno what they do it with.'

'P'raps it's digital.'

'No. I think it's glass ones with weights fixed so they roll when it moves.'

Mopsa snapped out from within the doorway of whatever building the mummy was being heaved into. 'Cut the crap, you guys. I gotta lot of positioning to do.'

Was it my imagination, or had there been a trace of

alarm in those grating tones?

I was being pulled down a long, bright room, with the odd bizarre exhibit already in place. I recalled Mopsa's escalating mania that summer for wrapping objects back in L A. I shuddered when I reflected that many of the "Living Art" parcels she made had contained poor creatures which, entombed forever, had withered and died. I forced myself to remember that the mummy had been made open-able, so I was, presumably, to be let out eventually, that I was clearly in an art gallery which would, I supposed, be visited by the Great British public – or the bollocks-art loving slice of it, at any rate - and that I was unlikely to come to real harm. Surely, during the course of the show, I would be able to persuade a member of that coterie to let out the Man in the Mummy? But then I went over Cled's and friend's conversation and hope sagged again.

The trolley stopped. I was heaved upright. Straining left and right I could see that I was in a corner. As such I had a superb view of most of the gallery. The exhibits were not, as yet, cluttered together. Bright sunshine came through tall windows on the left hand wall. Mopsa's mug swung into view, like a piranha homing in for a snack.

'This is where you stay, prick-features,' she hissed in a sibilant snarl. 'I guess I'm goin' to get a cawfeee. The "Exhibit" is getting nothing because he was awl hoity-toity about his Mopsa's serious art projects. The "Exhibit" is gonna have no foodie-woodie either for a bit while he looks round the gallery. And don't think the "Exhibit" can expect help from Witold. In case the "Exhibit" is wondering why Witold's bin a lil' rough on him – well, it's 'cause I've told him that you *raped* Georgie. The "Exhibit" has got to learn that he was reeeeal insulting to his Mopsa's intelligence back in L A – back before he ran off with a Hollybitch who doesn't know wheeeeere he is.'

She stuck her tongue out as far as the roots would allow and then went out with her ridiculous knock-kneed walk. In the sunshine of the door she lit up for a second then vanished. The men who had carried me into place had already left, so I was alone.

I had my answer to the puzzle: why Witold had been called " the avenger". This sobered me and it was some time before I felt able to take in what surrounded me.

To my left was a giant mouldering mattress with two melons, a bucket, a cucumber and two oranges on it. These were arranged in vaguely suggestive positions. Beyond was a black, rusty pram with what looked like goat skins draped on top. Between this and the door was a bust in clear acrylic with a sort of squidgy-looking filling. I couldn't see clearly what this was, but it made me feel inexplicably queasy. A plastic block near it proclaimed: "You Are What You Eat". To my right was a gorilla skin lying on a pile of crumpled newspapers. Whether these were discarded wrappings or part of the show, I couldn't tell. Near at hand was a jumble of things wrapped in foil and cellophane. I assumed these were Mopsa's. With a rumble of wheels, a further exhibit was bumped up the ramp from out in the sunshine. I could see the angular shape of a man-figure fashioned in Perspex. When it was stood firmly in front of a window, the head was taken off and two plastic sackfuls of stuff emptied into its hollow interior. One of the blokes gasped, 'Gawd! Makes yer want to puke, dunnit?' and I realised from their comments that the shell had been filled with compost and live worms. From my knowledge of Mopsa's interests in L A and from what I had skimmed in the papers, I could now comprehend that the piles of junk lying round the gallery were priceless *"objets d'art",* not the meaningless crap most sane people would take them for. It was very depressing to see London becoming as ready to swallow this *schlock* rubbish as the U S of A.

However, more pressing than maunderings about modern tastes in sculpture was my own plight. The black pod in which I stood, trussed with gaffer tape, hungry, panicky with claustrophobia and bursting to urinate, had not been approached by anyone since my arrival. What was clearly the last exhibit to be set up – a cross between a grandfather clock and a dying rosebush – had some chromed posts and braided ropes arranged round it, and then activity ceased.

Mopsa had seemed to be in a rush, yet had not reappeared. Had she gone back to the Gaumont? When was the show due to open? How long would I be left here? Would I be taken out at night?

In my agony I squeezed my legs together in their bonds. I tried to make a sound; a tiny gurgle came out. If I did not relieve myself I felt I should burst and perish. I had not had to overcome taboo consciously when I had urinated in my clothes at the Gaumont – it had just happened. Now I let myself go with a deliberate feeling of satisfaction. How silly our conditioning is, I remember thinking. A stream of hot liquid was soon coursing down my legs and forming a puddle in the mummy's base. The warmth turned chill, the stink wafted up and still Mopsa did not return.

Hours passed. The pain of standing grew maddening.

The man who had set up the chromed posts drifted out, slamming the outer doors. I could see that the sun was casting long shadows on the lawns outside.

Twice I tried rocking to and fro in an agony of cramp, but the mummy didn't move an inch. I had some idea of toppling over and drawing attention to myself, but I realised that the fitments on the mummy's casing must be tethered to wall or floor.

Then came the long night.

The gallery had closed and I was left with the disquieting exhibits and the susurration of distant traffic.

I sagged in my tomb, fainter and fainter. I suppose that some part of myself could not believe that I would not be noticed, rescued, freed, but this hopeful part withered as darkness closed around the mummy, black and bulky in the night, with only the glitter of desperate eyes in slits to tell of its living occupant.

I dreamed – mainly of blood gushing from veins that had swollen and the little valves of which had given up. My legs filled up with blood. My armpits had lumps that fought against the arms pinioned tight against them. I dreamed, standing, of swelling with blood and lymph until the shell of the mummy cracked and my liquid spurted first through the hair-cracks, then through splintered tears in the fibre-glass. I flowed, in liquid lymph and fire, along the gallery floor. I splashed, splashed in a rivulet against the acrylic block. My blood ran up and stained it. Then my blood ran off and it was still clear and pure, crystal and hard – hard against my – soft blood….and lymph……

Voices!

And the sudden brightness!

A long sunbeam fractured by walking legs!

I thought my dreams had spangled the world with light. I looked for spilt blood. I saw only legs, strutting in the blinding glare.

I could hear comments, snatches of praise, snatches of derision. My throat had closed with thirst. I forced my gaze out beyond my prison. If only I could have connected! Uninterested eyes passed over me. "Hm," they seemed to be saying, "a fibre-glass mummy. Well we've all seen one of those." There was a shouting, a growling. The gorilla skin no longer lay on its newspapers. An "artist" was inside it, prancing and snarling in a tight circle. People looked at other as if to say: "Sad guy".

I forced my gaze to the right. Yes, there was a familiar sight: a devotee of Excremental Kinetics sitting up to his neck in vile grey organic mess. I could not smell offal, so I assumed that the gallery authorities had insisted upon nothing stronger than porridge for this exhibit.

See what I mean? Mopsa, fundamentally unwise, had a developed streak of artful cunning largely unacknowledged by her, so busy was she in believing herself to be sharp. She may not have arranged it this way, but had taken almost instinctive advantage of it. Who was going to find anything weird or alarming about a guy standing in a fibre-glass mummy when hey! – there's another in a tub of slime, and another capering in a monkey suit?

As if to confirm that the Great Brit Public was not going to come to my aide, a boy of about twelve, dressed in a snazzy assemblage of designer gear and clutching a pair of roller blades, came and stood right in front of me. He was tall enough for me to see his face. He caught the mute glitter of my eyes and started. Then he grinned and winked.

Winked!

'Hey, Mum,' he called. 'There's a man IN this one!'

His mother – fair, smart, rich-looking – drifted up.

'What, Barnaby?' she asked, half reading her guide.

'There's a man actually IN this one,' said the kid again.

I frantically willed his mother to scream with horror and call the police.

'Oh, I expect it's – er – diodes or something, darling,' she said, hardly bothering to glance at me.

'It's NOT!' snorted the kid scornfully. 'It's a real guy. He's inside the plastic.'

Mother and child gave me the once-over. I flashed my eyes at them as violently as I could. They gazed into my furious stare. The mother nodded.

'So there is,' she said. 'How amusing.' She glanced at the catalogue '"The Walling-In. Not for Sale. In private collection",' she read out. 'Well, well.' She put her mouth close to the mummy. 'I fancy you more than the gorilla,' she said solemnly. She turned away. The child was already slipping his roller blades from under his arm. They drifted towards the exit. I shook myself in a rictus of frustration. The mummy stood rock solid.

A phantasmagoria of faces, eyes, legs and waving

catalogues wove its fevered pattern across the hours. The preview of the exhibition seemed a success – there were crowds, so there must have been interest. As my consciousness flickered in and out, like a faulty light bulb, I was aware that the smirking Mopsa was once again present. Sometimes I heard her platitudes: 'Gee-whiz, it jest came to me, like, in a dream.' 'I guess I want to make Plastic Art more tangible.' 'I wanna bring kinetic, LIVING Art to the people of this great city.' Sometimes a finger tapped my prison and my drooping, varicosed body received an impression from the outside world more solid and tantalising than the muffled voices.

During what I imagined was the latter half of the afternoon, the crowds grew thicker. The drinks set had arrived, probably by invitation. A different sort of person from the ordinary previewer was present. Shrill media yowls and camp, mincing intellectualities vied with each other. My brain spun, but, before my starved, urine-soaked frame lapsed again into coma, I had a dreadful shock.

Swimming up before me was Holly's dear little face.

For an instant I thought I was fabricating an illusion.

She was flanked by Sherbert and Adrian Booker. She clutched an invitation card to her chest and her glance was haggard. Signs of the acid attack still showed in some red welts. She looked everywhere but into the eyes of the mummy, so I, tearing my nails into my thighs to keep the thunder of insensibility at bay, could never catch her gaze.

Sherbert seemed bored and worried, but Booker had an air of triumph and hysteria. His hands fluttered constantly in front of his teeth and his voice, never lower than a squeal, grated like a jamming cycle brake. Mopsa had vanished.

The three didn't stay for long, but Booker came back to the mummy from the door. He peered into the gloom within, kissed his fingers and blew a kiss into the eye slits.

When Holly had gone, I was tossed into a greater despair than any I have ever felt. The pain in my legs had shifted to my back. I imagined that my back was wet. My head was bouncing up and down, a clattering roar was in my ears and a chilling draught flayed my newly-opened eyes.

I gave myself up to this strangely tangible new dream. I knew my mouth was open and that spit was running from it, but I didn't mind. My teeth chattered in time to the thudding sounds near to me. I think I believed I was on a raft breasting the rapids, for I heard my throat calling, 'Hold on! Hold on!'

Orange lamps succeeded each other in the eye slits. In a second of clarity, induced by the chilly air, I knew where I was – bolted to the bike's sidecar frame again and on the way home.

I then realised that I thought of my staple and rubber floor in the derelict cinema as "home" and I began crying, partly with relief, partly out of weakness and fear.

The combination thudded into the cul-de-sac after an eternity of traffic lights, exhaust fumes and swiftly-taken corners. As we had gone along I had heard shouted voices; when we arrived I realised they had come from Blue-jaw and Mopsa, conversing above the boom of the bike. Mopsa was hardly ever on her own with me anymore. My single bid for freedom had unsettled her.

The chrome fitments clicked and the top was pulled off the mummy. The houses above me twisted round and peered down malignantly. The wall of the Gaumont took a stab from the yellow sky.

'Get him out. God, how he stinks!' cried Mopsa. I was man-handled from the mummy and rolled over on the ground. 'Rip that tape off his legs, Witold. I guess he's gotta walk upstairs.' My ankles were freed at last, but my legs had stuck together and were locked in cramp. 'Oh, get up, you shamming bastard!' hooted Mopsa as I lay helplessly.

'Oh, I'll take one arm,' said Blue-jaw grimly. 'Bruno, take his other fin.'

So Bruno was with them!

Was Holly now out of danger?

Shakily, I stumbled upstairs into the projection room and flopped onto the rubber floor.

Mopsa's screech came up the stairs behind us. 'Get the lock on him, for Godawlmighteee's sake, guys!' The padlock was hardly needed. After a day and a half in the mummy I couldn't have beaten a poached egg in a straight fight. But Bruno leaned across and there was a click.

'Sorry about this,' he murmured.

The two young men stood looking down at me. I could not quite fathom the differing meanings in their gazes.

'What are you going to DO with me? Why did you bring me back?'

'Can't have our prize exhibit, our Living Sculpture, dying on us. Not yet, at any rate,' said Blue-jaw.

Mopsa came into the room carrying a plate and a mug.

'I got some eats for the bastard,' she said.

'Yeah, I was just saying we can't have our piece of Living Sculpture becoming as dead as a piece of marble crap by Rodin.'

'Oh, Mikey, Mikeeeee,' said Mopsa. 'Don' think this is a quick little job we've got on here.'

'We've got another ten days at the Serp....,' began Bruno.

Mopsa hit him on the arm as he stopped suddenly. Blue-jaw raised his eyes to the ceiling.

'SERP!' I gasped. 'Is THAT where I've been all day and night? Of course – you've already told me – a place to do with snakes! The Serpentine Gallery in Kensington Gardens! My God, that's why the traffic was quieter. That's why it was so silent at night!'

I was cheered. I had known the gallery fairly well when I'd lived in London. Who hadn't? Trust it to have an autumnal loonies' exhibition – it was that sort of place. I'd always believed it to be one of London's homes for creeps who can't paint, can't sculpt and can't draw, who win Turner prizes and have crap in the Saatchi collection; where it was more important to surprise than to educate.

'Okay, so you know. So what?' Mopsa snapped, making the best of a bad job. 'It's Thursday tomorrow, and for the next ten days in you go, out you come, in you go, out you come, until you go mad in the mummy for all I care. An' if it isn't convenient to git you home at the end of the day, why you just friggin' spend the night standing up.'

'What was Holly doing there?' I asked.

'She had an invite, of course,' said Mopsa, grinning

evilly. 'After all, she is Adrian's production assistant. She and your stupid friend went to the show with *your* lover-boy,' she spat in the direction of fair-haired Bruno (and that made more connections). 'I watched your little whore from the room at the back, Mikey. I thought she looked quite upset. He, he, he, he, he, he!'

'All right, Mopsa. Don't bother with the Cruella deVil impersonation. So Booker had a good gloat?' I looked round at Bruno. 'So Adrian Booker's a special CHUM, is he? That's where YOU fit in. God, what a collection.'

Bruno gave me a look of quiet dignity.

'Adrian is dying. Mopsa has already told me that you have tried to ruin his last project with your carping and unkindness. Stress isn't good for him, you know.'

'*His* last project!' I cried. 'I'm the one who's paying for the bloody project, not your precious Adrian.'

'His artistry and talent are….'

'DON'T GIVE ME ANY MORE CRAP ABOUT ART!' I suddenly screamed. 'Is the way you're treating me worthy of real artists? You're not artists, you're insane! You – you – uh – should all – guh – be locked up…..'

I had meant to preserve dignity in spite of hunger, in spite of pissing myself, in spite of everything. But this solemn puritan justification of acts of madness as part of a greater Art was the last straw. As my enraged words tumbled out – mingled, I must say, with a certain amount of the cheese sandwich I had started to wolf – I found myself shaking with sobs.

Yet, as I cried, part of me noticed the pain and embarrassment this was causing to Bruno. I instinctively knew that here was their weak link: Bruno's decency. Georgie's brother I could not reach, Mopsa would never relent, the craftsmanlike Reggie was unaware of anything amiss, but Bruno......

I wiped my eyes clumsily.

'I'm sorry,' I said. 'And you know it's all so ironic, Bruno, given that I meant no one any harm. Adrian and I were very friendly in New York. I was the angel that he and David needed to get their project off the ground. I and a chap called Dan Bright.'

'I've heard Adrian speak of Dan Bright. He was once a famous film producer, wasn't he?'

'A bit before your time, Bruno – if I may call you Bruno?' said I, trying to smile charmingly up at him through the drying tears, as it were. Bruno, I thought, was one of those gays who are drawn to older men. 'His great days were in the 'seventies.'

'I've had enough for tonight,' said Blue-jaw, steam-rollering over me. 'I'll be back at nine tomorrow morning.'

With a nod to Bruno, he let himself out of the projection room. His bike boots thudded off down the stairs.

I caught Bruno's eye again.

'I meant Adrian no harm. We are all artists in our own way,' I said.

'Oh Jeez!' scoffed Mopsa. 'Just listen when he gets awl sentimental. Misunderstood Mikey, the little boy who always tries to spread sweetness and light and is aaawlways being criticised. You're no Pollyanna.'

I took a deep breath.

'Can I just ring Holly?' I asked.

'No,' snapped Mopsa.

'Oh, why not?' murmured the uncomfortable Bruno.

There was a silence.

'Where's the harm?' I said. 'I can't tell her anything. I don't know where I am here. She looked so miserable today at the exhibition. If she just knew I hadn't had an accident, or.... Look, if you don't like what I'm saying on the phone, you can just snatch it back. You hold it. I won't touch it. You'll be listening to every word I say. Come on Bruno, it's just the sound of my voice she'll want to hear. She hasn't heard from me for days. Can't you imagine her anxiety? Just let me put her out of her misery.'

'Oh, for heaven's sake,' said Bruno, the big softie. 'Where's the harm?'

Mopsa's eyes darted from side to side. I could read her mind as if the contents were on a plate in front of her. She didn't want to oblige me, but she didn't want trouble with Bruno. Then again, I could see her thinking: it would distress Holly more if she had a tantalising call which told her nothing. It was like watching the second hand on a clock ticking round.

'It'll – it'll be a laugh, I suppose,' she said finally. 'Hollybitch might start crying.'

Bruno nodded and jerked a mobile phone from his back pocket. Mopsa grabbed it.

'Before you get this, Mikey, you understand three things: first – I hold the phone, second – I let you speak as long as I want, third – if you say one syllable about who you are with, the call stops, an' finally – something real nasty happens to Miss Hollyslut. You get me?'

Resisting the impulse to tell her that there were four things actually, I muttered,

'I get you.'

I was astonished that she was giving me this opportunity at all. Mopsa was never intelligent in the rational sense of the term – a classic case of managing to be, at times, clever, without ever being wise – but she had a shrewdness honed by flashes of lateral thinking. I immediately dropped my idea of trying to spell out the name of the Gaumont. The weakness, anyway, of that plan was that I only had the sketchiest notion of the area of London where the cinema was, I didn't know I could economically spell out the numbers of the zip code, and I might have been wrong. As the phone was held in front of me I had a much better idea.

I gave Bruno the phone number of the house in Glebe Place. After a long ring, during which my spirits sank to my padlock because I knew I would not be given this chance again, Holly's clear voice answered tentatively. Mopsa leaned in to listen.

So began the most important telephone conversation of my life.

'Holly. It's me, Mike.'

'MIKE! Where ARE you?'

'I can't tell you straight out.'

'How do mean "straight out"?'

'I can't say.'

'Are you all right? I've been terribly worried.'

'I miss you…'

Mopsa interrupted with a snarl. 'Oh, anagram of dog! Spare us the sob stuff. You got another few seconds.'

At the other end Holly gasped,

'Who was that? Is what we are saying being listened to?'

'Yes.'

'Are you in trouble?'

'Yes. I do so miss the times we had together. I miss the games we played at Anthony's and in Ventura.'

'The – the games?'

There was a vital pause at her end. I raised a silent voice to heaven. I needn't have worried. She had got it. There was a faint whisper that I only just caught. '*Say it.*' I knew Mopsa hadn't heard because I was permitted to go on. I drew another deep breath. The second gamble had begun.

'My, I miss seeing you and Sherbert.'

'Do you?'

'Undoubtedly.'

'Yes.'

'Mostly I miss being out and about.'

'I'm sure.'

'Maddening.'

'Yes.'

'Yes.'

'Incidentally, how is Sherbert?'

'Fine.'

'Nice.'

'And....?'

'So, that's about it – except for my emotional state.'

'Aha.'

'Emotionally, I'm worn out.'

'You would be.'

'Really, I hope this isn't going to last.'

'No.'

'Perhaps I'll see you soon.'

'Yes.'

The phone was snatched away from my mouth. Mopsa put her hand over the mouthpiece.

'The call's over, Mikey. You got nothing to tell anyway, lover-boy. You can say goodbye an' that's it.'

'Mike?' came Holly's voice. 'I heard that. Have you got to say goodbye? Make it a few brief sentences.'

'Entirely agree. Nothing more to say. Ta-ta. In a bit I'll ring you again. Nice speaking. Enjoyable. Goodbye then. And love to Sherbert. Love from me, Love to him. Enough now. Ringing off. You know I love you.'

This last sentence burst from me in the heat of composition – but as I said it I knew it to be true. Mopsa thrust the phone back into Bruno's hands.

'Weird call,' she sneered. 'All talk an' no meaning. Is that what you and she do in bed?'

I lay back on the rubber floor. I tried to keep the flashing gleams of satisfaction out of my eyes. I KNEW she was scribbling, with dawning comprehension, the message on the phone pad. Thank God for Anthony's bonkers game. My spirits soared at what I had managed to do.

They quickly ebbed, though, when Mopsa squatted down at my side after Bruno had left and, rocking to and fro while running her hands up and down my chest and legs, started hissing,

'In a day or two – a day or two, Mikey, I gotta do what you'll think is a nasty thing to you. I gotta make a little alteration to your beautiful body, baby of mine. Do you remember that interesting trip we took out to Glendale with Jonathan and Georgie? We saw how Spiro cut off little bits of himself and stuck things on the stubs? Hmmmmm? Hmmmmmm? I – I wanna try doing that, Mikey. I got Reggie to make teeny models of the mummy, Mike, an' – an' I'm gonna move the edges, edges, Mikey, of what *Art* is all about. Because.....' She rocked back and forth, inserting her fingers into my flesh and under my clothing, '.....you are going to be IN the mummy, but I'm gonna have windows in it, so people can see, like, tiny mummies glued right snap on to where you had your little fingers. See? But, privately, there's gonna be a mummy glued on to where your traitorous little wang used to be....'

She rocked back and forth over me like a deranged pendulum, detaching her and my clothing.

After what happened next in my degradation on the rubber floor of the disused projection room, I could only pray that Holly would act immediately on what I hoped she had worked out.

Chapter 16: **The Posse of Old Guys**

The stars rushed out in one high window. The gallery was silent. Ahead of me the cross between a cabinet clock and untidy bush obscured the doorway slightly. The gorilla skin lay crumpled. The curvy polystyrene wing framed my view to the right where the Perspex block gleamed like a sarcophagus.

I believed I was coming to the end of my period as an exhibit. Mopsa and Blue-jaw had left me overnight in the quiet room – starving, sagging, close to coma from exhaustion and despair. Of rescue there was no sign. I was forced to believe that Holly hadn't, after all, understood my torturous ref. to Anthony's game, and had not worked out: MUMMY IN SERPENTINE GALLERY.

I was not allowed to use a phone again, so I had no means of learning whether she remained unmolested or not. My thoughts sometimes took a sinister turn and I grew convinced that she had been killed. In my tortured brain, Mopsa's ridiculous insanities grew monstrous, omnipotent, beyond sense or law.

That night I could see a little of the floor through a transparent panel on the left-hand side of the mummy. The previous day, while I'd been shackled to my ring, Reggie had adapted the mummy's casing in his workshop by inserting a piece of cobex near where my hand would be. I knew what this meant. The art-loving public were to be able to see objects glued to the stumps of my fingers. Dismally, it occurred to me that I was being weakened for the final onslaught.

Meanwhile, I had become something of a celebrity. Bruno had brought in an article written by *The Evening Standard* art critic deploring the rubbishy, sensationalist, gimmicky, perverse nature of the current show at The Serpentine. He had reserved his greatest criticism for the bloke in the monkey-suit, but the mummy had been given a roasting too. Bruno had leaned on the window-sill in the projection-room while Mopsa had brought me another of her interminable tins of sardines and half a baguette.

'Hey, listen to this, kiddies,' he had said. 'Fame at last. *"Today I had the hard job of selecting, not the few poor pieces in a generally worthwhile show of modern art, but the one or good pieces in a barn-full of hopeless mediocrity and trash."* Sounds as if he didn't like it, eh?'

'Toffy-nosed, snobbish bastard,' had snarled Mopsa, tearing off the lid of the sardines as if ripping off *The Evening Standard* art critic's nose. 'I know the type – thinks yew can honly laike Hart if you hev a Hoxford or Boston haccent and paint lendscapes in hoils. Stuck-up little pimp.'

'And listen to this bit,' had gone on Bruno, reading a bit more, ' *"The silliest object of the lot – because its power to surprise is over the moment the onlooker has taken in the surprise – is a huge mummy-like shape, more reminiscent of an old-fashioned sidecar body than anything else. Granted, it is dominating, even sinister, but what is it trying to say? Inside it stands a man, his eyes alone visible through holes. Who this absurd man is, what he is paid for doing this and how long he is going to go on doing it, none can guess. It is all too sadly like the cheap sensationalism*

Iaposed toapos:

290

of the American West Coast Pop Art kinetic movement. Acclaimed all too frequently in a country devoted to novelty, I had hoped that the greater sophistication of the European gallery-goer would have laughed this sort of childish insult into the wilderness. Alas, it has not: attendance rates at The Serpentine are at an all-time high." Well, what do you think of that?'

'I've told you,' Mopsa had snorted. 'Don't give me any more of that piss.'

Ever since the sneering critic's article had appeared, the gallery had been packed. Hundreds of curious faces had stared into my prison. Surprisingly, few people had thought to address me through the slits; that's the instinctively reticent Brit public for you. I had actually heard one woman say to a young girl: 'Don't stare IN at him, Katie. It seems so rude.'

As the quiet of that horrible night in the gallery, only a few days from the end of the show, moved on, I was filled with ever-greater despair and with that lost sense that accompanies solitariness in a crowd. No one was going to rescue me because *The Evening Standard* had said I was being PAID for standing inside the mummy. It had become a breach of taste even to look too closely at the bloody thing because, after all, it was *occupied*.

With these thoughts battling waves of unconsciousness, it was some time before I became aware of light squibs twinkling on the ceiling.

There was another!

Above my eye-slits the ceiling seemed to have become a pond upon which moonbeams danced. I dreamed for a moment and in my ears was the familiar rush of faintness. I saw l-o-n-g ripples under the m-o-o-n.......

Then, in the utter quiet, I heard a crack – a loud crack. Inside my prison the hairs pricked on my neck. What was happening?

Oh! Another crack!

There was a whizzing sound. A drill, perhaps?

More lights!

I peered until my neck twisted into a rictus, but the thickness of the fibre-glass prevented my seeing anything more than the familiar quadrant. The sounds, I was sure, were round to the left, from a part of the gallery I had never seen. The little squibs of light shone up onto the ceiling from the back of the mummy and to its left-hand side.

Hyde Park is shut at night and, given the proximity of Kensington Palace and Knightsbridge Barracks, is policed. Surely this couldn't be a break-in?

The closeness of the alarming sounds drove exhaustion and cramp away and I felt alert with mingled hope and fear. I couldn't quite believe that given the nature of the bollocks on show – myself included – a robbery of *objets d'art* by night was in progress. Who was likely to risk arrest in order to acquire a gorilla skin? Could it be protest? Vandalism? I remembered the Chinese students who had jumped up and down on Tracy Emin's unmade bed at the Tate.

There was a change in the quality of the air. The cool autumn mist which lay along the lake and under the trees, seemed to have crept into the gallery. Whispered voices came to my ears. The flickering pools of light resolved themselves as torch beams.

'Cut out the lights, fellas,' said someone at normal conversational volume. 'Some recce patrol *you* would make. It don't matter how loud you talk 'cos there's no one around to hear, so you whisper like hissin' geese, but a light can be seen for a mile across the park, so you keep flickin' your torches on and off. Jeez!'

'Sorry, old bean,' whispered someone.

'Well, snap it off!' came the first voice. Then it called, quite loudly, 'Mike Greville? Where are you, baby?'

During this conversation I found myself a mass of wild emotions. Joy, wild joy, struggled with astonishment. With these came almost concrete relief – that relief the dreamer feels when dawn brings the nightmare to an end. Astonishment predominated. The first voice I heard was that of Blundell Capitanchik, commanding his platoon, as in the days of the war against the Viet Cong; the second was my brother's.

'A thing like a mummy, she said,' came Blundell's gurgle again. 'Jeez, there's a lot of crap in this shebang. Here, hold your hand over the end of the torch like this.'

A dim glow trembled on the floor between me and the grandfather clock. I was always taped across the face and my arms were pinioned. The only noise I could make was a wriggling, brushing sound against the inside of the mummy. In the daytime it passed unheeded, of course, but at night it went over loud and clear. There a gasp.

'Did you hear that?' said Anthony. 'Mike?'

'Here it is.'

A blinding glow flickered over my eye slits.

'Gee friggin' whiz, he's inside. Just like Holly said.'

A hand fumbled at the outside of the mummy. 'Here, grab the torch – but keep it dim. Shine it on these fixings. Hold on, Mike baby. Not long now.'

The chrome devices securing the lid-like frontage gave a series of metallic clicks. I felt the outside of my prison open at last. The mummy's front was dragged clear. In the torch's glow I made out the vast shambling form of Blundell and the figure of my brother.

'Mike,' said Anthony, his voice as calm as if we'd just bumped into each in Harrods. 'Holly told us your message and how you were stuck in this thing. So here we are.'

'Here, gimme a hand to lever him outa here,' grunted Blundell. 'I guess he's trussed up and can't walk.'

They tilted me forward, Blundell taking my torso, Anthony gripping my legs. A moment later I was lying on the floor and the gaffer tape was being ripped stickily from my limbs and from my mouth. I gagged as I took the first draughts of air through my dry throat and aching jaws. I lay, unable to move as the shootings of cramp and the maddening tingle of blood through the newly-freed extremities began. I found, however, the strength to croak,

'What – what ARE you doing here? How did you get in? How did you know?' Then a spasm of coughing took me and I spluttered between them, massaging the life back into one numbed arm then the other with stiff fingers. They stood, on each side of the mummy, staring down at me. Blundell, in the glow of the propped torch, looked amused. I didn't need telling that he was enjoying the adventure. Anthony's face was grim. The way I had been treated shocked him badly.

'Vamoose first, questions later,' wheezed Blundell, bending to grasp my arms. 'Can you walk, Mike?'

Anthony took my other arm. I found that I could heave myself to my feet. Then I discovered that I could take a step or two. I had been through this process many times back at the Gaumont.

'I'm okay,' I muttered. 'I'm just stunned seeing your hideous faces, that's all. How do we get out?'

'First we close this mother,' said Blundell. 'Your lady friend needn't discover you've gone yet, need she?'

So the frontage was put back on the mummy and the clips fastened. By the light of the torch pieces of tape were cleared from the floor. Blundell took my elbow. 'Boom, boom, man. Follow your leader to the servants' entrance.'

To the left, off the lobby, although I had not seen them, of course, there was a washroom for gallery staff, a kitchenette and a small store-room. We glided – or rather Blundell and Anthony glided and I staggered – through the connecting door to these regions.

'Isn't this kept locked?' I whispered. 'Pretty poor security.'

'Listen to him!' gasped Anthony. 'So you want the place much more secure so we couldn't have got in, do you?'

'No, you twit, what I meant was....'

'It WAS locked,' interrupted Blundell, 'but then again it wasn't. You see, Mike, your bro's friend was here at the show a coupla afternoons ago....'

'Peter Buchan?' I asked, amazed. 'Is he in on this too?'

'Peter Buchan, yes. He moseyed along in workman's

gear. First, he got into the kitchen when no one was looking, though he was ready with an excuse about seeing to the plumbing, and partly unscrewed the lil'part of the lock which is, like, fixed to the doorpost. So when the staff pulled it shut it stayed loose. We jus'jerked it open. Then he went to the john with this.' Blundell held up a thin tool. 'It's a glass cutter. He jus' picked a coupla panes and cut round the edges four or five times.'

'I see,' I said. 'So when you came back later, they were easy to cut through. Those were the cracks I heard.'

'Hm,' grinned Anthony, 'it wasn't quite as easy as we thought it might be; the glazing-bar had to be sawn out and the glass is thick and bits got stuck in the frames.'

We were now in the washroom. Through a gap in a window set above a narrow shelf the night air rolled. At a distance came the swish of cars near the Albert Hall.

'After you, son of a gun,' said Blundell.

'Can you manage?' asked Anthony anxiously. 'There's a drop into the place where they keep the dustbins.'

'I could climb Kilimanjaro,' I said, confidently hoisting a leg up to the shelf. The cramp in my muscles immediately bit and I gave an involuntary sharp howl.

'Sssssh!' hissed my companions, peering round in the darkness.

Eventually, I was out and standing by a high gate. Actually, I think I made a better job of getting out than Blundell who got stuck amidships. Two fat legs waved helplessly, two podgy arms clawed at the air. He grinned as our combined pull freed him.

'I know, I know. Peter Buchan said I'd never get in, but

I've got in AND out, ain't I?' Again there was that unmistakable note of enjoyment.

Anthony bent down to a large canvas bag which was hidden under the wall. 'Right,' he said, taking squares of Perspex from it. 'Blundell, undo the glue.'

Those two! Bookish Anthony, and Blundell, a wheezing greybeard – they had it figured like James Bond.

'I'm impressed,' said I. 'You were really well prepared.'

Glue was squirted round the edges of the Perspex sheets. A piece of white-painted, shaped wood with channels along its length and an eyelet screwed into it was held up, measured, given a final trim with a Stanley knife and also glued. Anthony turned to me.

'Bruv, take the first sheet and fit it in the frame, then push it tight against the glue. Blundell, you take the eyelet and hold the glazing-bar while Mike and I jiggle the Perspex into the channels. Then you can unscrew it.'

The window, from outside, was much easier to reach because there was no shelf in the way. In five minutes it looked as though it had never been broken.

'Might as well keep them guessing,' smiled my brother. 'I've tightened the door lock and by morning the window glue will have set. They'll have no idea how you got out.'

'I'd like to see Mopsa's face,' I said. 'But how did you manage.....about all this....?'

'What? The window and glazing-bar sizes? Peter measured them the first time he came. We had to know if we could get through. Then we got the Perspex cut and painted a strip of wood. Piece of gateau, really.'

'Well, I don't know,' I gasped, gazing at them both in

astonishment. 'Fancy you knowing all that sort of thing.'

'Oh yeah, we're Tin Terrors on Ten Wheels when we get going,' gurgled Blundell. 'But, as I said earlier, let's quit before we start gassing.'

'Yes, yes, you're right. We've got to take this bag....' Anthony held up another canvas bag which clinked, 'to the nearest dustbin. It's the cut window glass,' he explained to me. 'And, Mike, I'm sorry. We've got to hike across to the Bayswater Road. The police are all over the Ken Gardens bit by the embassies. I hope you can manage it. Now, use those folding steps to get to the top of the gate. We'll then hoick another lot up for you to drop them for getting down the other side.' He reached for a pair of compact aluminium steps, hidden behind a row of bins when they first arrived. I had wondered how we were going to get over the high gate and, later, the railings round the park's perimeter. After Blundell and I had landed, Anthony fished up the inner pair of steps on a cord. What planning!

'How on earth did you know I'd be in the mummy *tonight*? Sometimes I'm not.'

'We didn't. This was only ever Plan B,' said my brother. 'Plan A was to snaffle you from the sidecar outfit after closing-time just before you left the park. We had a box of barbed-wire twists to puncture the bike's wheels. But we knew you'd been left over-night a day or two ago. We've been keeping watch since tea-time and when the lady and that unshaven yob left on the bike alone: Plan B it became.'

Fifteen minutes later – and that walk was terribly testing to my cramped muscles – we were over the metal railings somewhere between Speakers' Corner and Lancaster Gate.

We crossed the Bayswater Road. Anthony stared round and an old-fashioned dark-green Vauxhall car, of a type I remembered from the early '70s, drew up from out of a side street. Buchan was at the wheel. We bundled into it.

A further quarter of an hour after that I stood in the little hall at Glebe Place.

It was a long night. The hot bath, the swigs of red wine, the celebratory steak and salad, the chunks of lemon cake and mug after mug of coffee renewed me. Only Blundell ate more than I did that happy night. Holly perched on one kitchen stool and Anthony on another. Blundell overflowed one chair, I sprawled in the second. Of course there were also a lot of questions fired at me which I had to leave unanswered: How had Mopsa made contact with Reggie? Who was paying him? Who was Bruno? Where did Witold fit in? Who found the Gaumont for her?

I too had questions.

'Right, Bruv. First, what *are* you doing in London?'

'There was that alarming-sounding request to put Holly up at Glenturret because of the danger of attacks on her; and then cancelling again. We thought *something* must be wrong. And then....well....'

'Holly cancelled, not me.'

'Um, yes. Just as well in the circumstances, because, to keep it brief, Peter and I have got nowhere to live at the moment.'

'What do you mean?'

'We're based at Meriel's for the present, see? Glenturret's a bit of a problem.'

'Meriel?' interjected Blundell. 'Who's Meriel?'

'Buchan's sister, over from New Zealand. Kids nearly grown up. Staying with her uncle in Fulham. Five bed house,' explained Anthony.

'Hang on! What do you mean: problem?'

'I'll explain another time. Let's say it's not practical to be there.'

'You're being ridiculously cryptic, Bruv. Why?'

'About a week ago, er, six nights precisely, actually, we made a decision.'

'What decision, damn it?'

'Don't tell a soul, will you?'

'Who exactly am I – are we – going to tell, Anthony?'

'It's made going on with Glenturret as a museum very difficult.'

'But – but why?'

'It got a bit hot for us,' said my unfathomable brother. Then, with a sidelong squint at the kitchen door, as if he fancied that sleuths might be behind it, he whispered, 'Also there is a matter of money – of compensation.'

'Compensation for what?' I asked, getting more and more puzzled.

'We were – are – absolutely broke,' said Anthony, avoiding the question.

'But – Grandpa's money?'

'Mike, the recording studio lost most of it, and it's not cheap keeping a narrow-gauge railway and a huge museum going with falling attendance figures.'

'Why didn't you tell me what you needed?'

'Oh, it's not easy to ask. Besides, Peter thought.......'

'And so you've come to London – to rescue me – and

left the problem up there unsolved?'

'We drove away in the old Vauxhall Cresta.' said Anthony. What with the drama of my own rescue filling my thoughts, I didn't get to the bottom of my brother's puzzling vagueness about Glenturret that night – but I was very shocked to discover, much later, what he had done. He and Buchan, in financial *extremis,* had commited an extraordinary crime! And I was used to thinking of myself as the sharp practitioner in the family!

He hurried on, 'We had no up-to-date number to call Glebe Place - it's changed since my time – so we thought we'd better get over there and find out what was going on.'

'So, you drove….'

'…..to Glebe Place and found Holly with her burn marks, you vanished and mystery all around. But we coincided with your coded phone message. Very brainy, that, by the way. Your Mopsa must be pretty thick. Holly had got the message down and we were able to tell her where the Serpentine was. In fact, you may not know it, but the exhibition was all over the papers anyway.'

'I did know that. Bruno read a review from "*The Standard*".'

'And SO clever of you, Holly,' said Anthony. 'Fancy remembering that jolly game we played at Glenturret. Fancy putting two and two together like that – and over the phone too.' He smiled fondly at her.

While this conversation was going on, Blundell was sloshing and gulping his way through the last slices of lemon cake. He leant back in his creaking chair with a sigh of repletion, a fat python after its kill.

'Right, that's you and Buchan explained,' said I to my brother. 'And, Anthony, I am so very sorry about Glenturret's problem – whatever it is. We have got to sit and talk about that.'

'There's more to tell you – but at another time. In fact I've written a sort of memoir about the house and all that biz. You can read it when your own mess is cleared up.' His mouth gave a wry movement – and I recall how Holly reached out and put a hand on his arm. She saw that he was strangely upset, but, as I say, I was still selfishly wrapped up in my escape, so I let the Glenturret story slip past and turned to Holly's vast honorary uncle.

'Now, Blundell, your turn. What on EARTH are you doing in London? Shouldn't you be starting a new term banging knowledge into the skulls of New York's delinquents?'

'Nope. Not this term, Siree-bob. I'm still ridin' the cusp of Number Seven.'

'Number Seven?' asked Anthony, on cue.

'Nervous breakdown,' said Blundell, with the very same satisfaction he had evinced when making the same statement to me in New York.

'But why LONDON? I couldn't believe my ears when I heard your voice at the gallery.'

'An' who else is Holly goin' to ring for help when her boyfriend is off playin' at bondage with his old squeeze?'

'Oh, Blun! What a way to put it!' she smiled, gazing fondly at him, like a slim mermaid at a walrus.

'Well, that's what it amounted to. My ole pal Miall – that's Holly's paw,' he said in parenthesis to Anthony, 'he is just not up to travellin' from Ventura, Cee-Ay, at the moment. And Twinkle says to me, "Blundell Capitanchik, you've talked about seein' England, an' you've talked about missin' Holly, an' you've talked about what a swell guy Mike is, so why don' you haul ass an' git over an' help where help's needed?" Besides,' continued Blundell, 'I feel that there's unfinished business between me an' that arty minx. You ain't forgotten she screwed my hog, have you? So, here I am. Came on Virgin the day before last.'

'Thank de Lawd for all of you – although I'm not sure that revenge is the most virtuous of motives, Blundell.'

Holly looked radiantly happy for a moment, although disapproving, no doubt, in different ways, of all three men round the kitchen table.

When, at last, we were all in bed, I confided to Holly that all I now wanted was to get away somewhere out of England. I had an idea that we would, after all, follow Sherbert to Rome and together explore the treasures of Italy. But Holly scoffed.

'You think I want to spend more time wondering if one of us is going to get kidnapped or injured by that wretched woman? What about what she's just done? You think it's a kid's game that she chucks acid over me and then locks you up in a plastic coffin for a week? I know you're used to her, but I've never heard anyone doing that outside a movie. It's entertaining in movies like *"Play Misty for me"* or *"Misery"*, but not in real life. People don't *do* the sort of things she's done and get away with it.'

'Okay. Point taken. I agree what she did was outrageous, but I'm out of it now. What else can she do? I'm on my guard. So are you.'

'Do? We can prosecute her; or *you* can, here in Britain. We should report her to the police and have her deported. We simply can't do absolutely nothing at all, just as if absolutely nothing had happened!'

'You decide what to do then, 'I yawned. 'I'm just too bloody exhausted.'

'Your brother thinks we should go to the gallery tomorrow – today, that is - for a start.'

'Yes, I remember he said he'd like to see her face when she finds the mummy empty.'

'Well then. Blundell thinks we ought to take matters into our own hands, at the very least. He's still sore about what happened to his bike. He thinks she needs a lesson.'

'Mopsa can't benefit from "lessons"!' I cried. 'She is insane, not just naughty. Hers isn't the sort of case that's cured by a darned good whopping. Blundell ought to know that. He must have taught the obdurate and unreachable.'

'We ARE going over to the gallery, anyway, aren't we?'

'Have you been in contact with Sherbert?'

'Don't change the subject, Mike.'

'No, but has he been contacted?'

'There hasn't been time. And I thought it best not to alarm Adrian if Sherbert started making enquiries; just in case Adrian *is* mixed up in it.' That was when I was able to put Holly completely in the picture. She had sat up in bed, leaning over on one elbow towards me. The light was out, but her eyes twinkled in the glow from Glebe Place's street lamps.

'I haven't had a chance to explain yet, but Booker IS

mixed up in it, as I said he was.'

When I had finished, she cuddled into me, and breathed,

'Sorry, Mike. So – you weren't being paranoid in seeing Adrian's hand behind everything?'

'No. And Sherbert having gone to Rome before I was snatched is further proof, isn't it? Booker gave me the message that Sherbert wanted to see me, over at Maida Vale – when he knew Sherbert had left. He gambled that I wouldn't think of contacting Sherbert to find that he hadn't sent for me at all.'

'I get it. So....?'

'So......?'

'So.....the *gallery*! We ARE going over today, aren't we?'

It seemed weeks since I had stood there in the mummy. It was peculiarly interesting seeing The Serpentine's interior from the punters' point of view. Everything was the same, but reversed. There was the rose bush, the mattress, the bust, the outline full of earth and worms, the gorilla suit, the plastic wing (which I had never been able to see fully), a group of paintings on the walls which hung to extreme right and left of my position, and – slap-bang centre in front of us at the far end, massive, black, frightening, still and menacing – the Mummy.

As I shudderingly drank in its big, shiny proportions, I realised that *The Evening Standard* critic had been wrong. It WAS a work of art. Empty, it teased the senses; with a living occupant, it was indeed the cryptic, bizarre, challenging force that Mopsa believed it to be. At that moment I came closer than I had ever been to accepting the tenets of the Conceptual Art movement. Art should shock, puzzle and appal; it should jolt the perceptions and destroy preconception. Few Gainsboroughs, Turners or Raphaels had such a definite, brooding presence as that carapace fashioned by Reggie to Mopsa's design – fashioned to become the coffin of a dying, chopped-up mute.

Holly felt the same, I thought, for she drew my arm close. Anthony broke the moment of awe.

'God, what a load of pretentious shit,' said he. 'It looks even worse in daylight.'

'See there,' I muttered.

Behind us, nearer the door, gazing at the plastic wing with a certain (and irritating) admiration, was the barrage-balloon shape of Blundell. Remarkable for his flowing hair and beard and circumference, he was the covert cynosure of many eyes. But what had taken my attention was the stare he was getting from the bulging-eyed Mopsa, who had just emerged from one of the side galleries.

'Is THAT Mopsa Greene?' Holly asked. I nodded, bracing myself.

Mopsa had not noticed us yet, but had taken rapid steps across the floor. She came to a halt in front of Blundell.

'Don' I know you?' she said, looking him up and down.

'You should,' was Blundell's laconic answer.

'What is this?' she snapped. 'What are you doing here?'

I moved to get a few steps behind her. Her head was quivering on its stalk and her peaky shoulders were going up and down.

'Thought I'd drop into this show, seein' as I'm in

London,' drawled Blundell. 'I see you ain't got no sad crumpled sickle on display this time.'

'Don't give me that horse-shit. You're not here by chance.' She gave a quick look round at the mummy. 'What exactly are you up to?'

Blundell regarded her calmly.

'I'm flattered you ain't forgotten me,' said he.

'Who'd forget a fat pile of dog sick who chased me practically to DEATH!' Mopsa suddenly shrieked. She grabbed convulsively at her thighs. 'Do you know what you've done to me, you freak?'

This was no way to speak to Blundell. His face hardened grimly into the expression it presumably wore when he was starting to put the boot into his delinquent pupil at the onset of Number Five, or whichever one it was. I took a step forward. Mopsa gathered her saliva, jerked her head back so that she nearly bashed it on my teeth and sent a splosh of spit into Blundell's face. Several punters, seeing this, gasped. In New York a crowd would have formed, but this was England. Everyone looked away and pretended interest in the *objets d'art*. Blundell slowly ran his hand through his spattered beard and wiped it on his jeans.

'GAWD ALMIGHTY!' he roared.

He reached out with a ham-like hand; Mopsa took a leap back and landed on one of my feet, but didn't look round. With Anthony, Holly and me in her way, she had no choice but to be collared. A few seconds later the sound of heavy smacks rang through The Serpentine.

History was repeating itself.

'Aaaaaa-eeeeeow! Yoooowp!' bawled Mopsa.

'Blun!' Holly gasped. 'Blun, really!'

With grim, jutting-out beard, Blundell carried on, warming to his work.

Smack! Smack! Smack!

'Aaaaargh!'

Smack!

'Yoooow!'

Smack! Smack! SMACK!

'Uuuuuurgh, you fat bastard!'

The gallery rang with the uproar. Eventually, with a superhuman twist, Mopsa got into a position to kick at Blundell's shin. She was wearing motorcycle boots and the hack she gave him would have felled a rhino.

'FAAAAARCK!' roared the unfortunate Blundell in his agony. His podgy hands let Mopsa go as he bent to massage his plump shin. She leapt back, bumped into me again, and spun round to face us. Her eyes sought mine.

She began to shake her head from side to side wildly.

She dragged me aside to shove by – convinced for a second, I'm sure, that what she saw wasn't me – and ran up to the mummy. She peered on tiptoe into its empty interior, then turned.

'How – how…..?' she stuttered.

Her expression amply repaid the efforts that Anthony & Co had put into securing my release.

Around us the gallery-goers had frozen into the positions they had adopted at the moment of Blundell's stupendous bellow. Mopsa broke the spell by dashing back to our group, punching me as hard in the face as she could manage, smacking Holly's cheek, administering a shove to the hopping Blundell that sent him tumbling over like some great felled tree of the forest, and darting through the gaping mob towards the sunlit square of the door. She was held for a moment in the beams and then was gone.

Uncertainly, one or two people broke into applause. I could almost see "*The Evening Standard*" critic's curling lip. "*Cheap Trick Of Slapstick Violence Fails To Convince Artgoers Of Worth Of New Exhibition*" would no doubt have been the next day's headline had he been there.

Blundell limped to the door. I followed, rubbing my jaw. Holly ran up behind us with Anthony.

'Well, Mike? What now? What are we going to do?' they all screamed at me.

'I don't see that we can do anything,' I replied. 'She's gone. I'm out. It's over.'

'Like hell it is,' gurgled Blundell. 'That girl needs sortin' out, an' I'll say that again. She's a Tin Terror....'

'.....on Ten Wheels,' Holly finished. 'Yes, we know. We all realise that by now. And we can't just lie down. I told you last night, Mike, I'm not going to spend the next x years of the twenty-first century waiting for her to bob up again and cause this sort of mayhem.'

'We should start legal proceedings,' said my brother.

'Where's she gone now?' asked Blundell.

'I don't kn....,' I started. And then I realised that of *course* I knew where she had gone. 'The Gaumont!' I cried at three blank faces. 'It's an idea I worked on during my spell on a rubber floor.'

I explained my certainty that I had been a prisoner in an abandoned Gaumont cinema in the postal district of E14.

'Sounds very plausible. Talk about Hercule Poirot,' said Anthony.

'It may not be as easy to find as all that. I'm not precisely sure where the little street is. I've not even seen it from the other end – only from the cinema itself.'

'Yes, but if the name overlooks the street,' reasoned Anthony, 'then the street looks onto the name. Isn't that right? The cinema must be a sort of wall at the end of the road. That should make it easier to find.'

'The far part of the street, beyond the way you get out of it, does have a brick wall at the end – like the wall next to the old woman's place in "*The Lady Killers*".

'There's got to be a way into the wretched street. How did you get out of it when you were being brought here?'

'How could I see? – lying on my back in the mummy?'

'Gentlemen and lady,' interrupted Blundell. 'Can't we have our chin-wag in a cab? She has a head start.'

'"Whiles I speak, he – or she – lives. Words to the heat of deeds too cold breath gives!",' cried Anthony. Holly and Blundell nodded. I must have looked utterly blank.

Despairingly the three Eng Lit types moaned at me in chorus, '*Macbeth*!'

Chapter 17: **Together Forever?**

The taxi rattled to the kerb. There was £57 on the clock. The driver's window slid back. We craned forward to hear.

'Not up this way, squire. It's all noo housing.'

We had been cruising E14 and district for some time. Blundell had been a gushing fount of information about the East End – extraordinary as he'd never been to London before.

'Hey, Mike. This is jus' SO exciting! Every corner I see a name I bin teaching about all these years. Whitechapel! I mean – jus' to SEE it! And there's a sign to Limehouse!'

'Well, guv,' said the driver, twisting his head round.

'Wild goose chase?' I asked Anthony.

'What twits we are,' he said slowly. 'You know what we should have done? We should have got hold of an old phone book and looked up this bloody cinema – or at least all the cinemas called Gaumont in this part of London.'

The driver's ears waggled.

'Never thought of that meself either,' he said. 'But it's the biz. Then we just eliminate.'

'Can we get hold of an old phone book?' I asked. 'I mean without having to write to some civil service department and having to wait three months?'

'Public Library'll help, won't it?' asked the driver.

The idea proved a winner. Except that it wasn't in a phone book that we found the information. An archive wodge of yellowed local papers yielded what we wanted. Among the adverts for Essoldo, Regent, ABC, Odeon and Rialto cinemas which seemed to have peppered the area north of the docks and the City in the mid-century was just one for a Gaumont. It had been showing "*2001: A Space Odyssey*" in a winter month in the late '60s. Our taxi driver, who was taking this investigation personally, as though his integrity and authority were at stake in the presence of two Americans, gave a yelp.

'Garrard Street! I know that one. It's just this side of Limehouse Basin. Just orf the Commercial Road. Backs onto the Regent's Canal. I'll 'ave you there in ten minutes.'

His estimation was out by half. Only five minutes later we had turned off White Horse Road into Salmon Lane and the bulk of a big cinema rose above a street of huddled Victorian houses.

'It's beyind that school, see?'

'Can you stop here for a second?' I asked. 'I just want to get out and make sure.'

'Drive yer rahnd if yer want.'

'No, no. Just hang on. I'm going to have a scout round in case I've got it all wrong.'

But I hadn't got it wrong. By the side of the cinema was a narrow cut which led into Garrard Street. The little road, its derelict houses looking like a film lot, ran down to the high brick wall which I now knew bordered the Regent's Canal as it angled down into Limehouse Reach.

How satisfying it was, how expressive of the innate mysteriousness of existence, to glance up and see on the side of the building a few flowing letters attached to a stub balcony. Had they been complete they would have spelt GAUMONT. I felt a greater sense of victory than any of my financial dealings had ever given me to know that my simple deductions about G-U M - - T had been bang on.

It was also a shock being there. I realised then how much I had been shaken up by the time I had spent shackled to the projection room floor. Satisfaction was replaced by a violent shivering.

As I was gazing at the crumbling bricks and art deco, I heard the creaking of a door. I made a jump backwards. I feared seeing Mopsa before I – we – had worked out some plan of action. As it happened, it was only Reggie. I saw him roll out a drum and push it against the wall. He did not see me. I whisked back to the taxi.

'Well?' cried you three.

'It's the place.'

'Oh, fantastic!' said Anthony. 'Bull's-eye!'

'Yes,' I said, 'but now we're here, what are we going to do?'

'Do we barge in, do you mean?' asked Anthony. 'Oh, I think so, after coming so far.'

'To say what?'

'To tell her that we are going to the police about what she has done,' Holly chipped in. 'I think that only some kind of order imposed by a court of law will stop her trying to start up all over again.'

'I think that little lady needs another spanking,' gurgled Blundell.

'But - *WHAT* - has - she - done?' I articulated. It seemed to me that they were all being very dense about this.

'What has she DONE?' Holly gasped. 'Need you ask?'

'Kidnapped you. Ill-treated you….,' said Anthony.

'Proof?'

'She put you in a mummy against your will!'

'Witnesses? So far I've got an *"Evening Standard"* article questioning how much I was being PAID for standing in the mummy. That implies I did it deliberately. Her pals aren't going to back me up – if I could find them. Oh, and there's Reggie – who made the mummy – and he thinks we're all having jolly good fun in the art world.'

'Oh, heavens, Mike!' Holly cried. 'What about her attacks on me at Glebe Place?'

'What? When she was done up as a young man? What real proof have we got that it was Mopsa? What witnesses are there apart from us?'

Everyone was silent.

'Then,' Holly said slowly, 'there's no point in going to the law?'

'Nope,' I replied.

'Nix,' added Blundell.

I glanced at the taxi's meter. £102.50 was on it. The driver's eyes followed my gaze.

'Sorry, mate. Waiting time at the library.'

'No, that's fine. Can you wait a bit longer?'

'It's all work, squire, and more of an interest than beltin' down to 'Eathrow.'

'Blundell, you and Holly wait here in the cab. Anthony, will you come in with me to see if Mopsa is still there?'

Blundell looked doubtful. 'I guess I wanna be in on….,' he began.

'I don't want Holly to go in. You don't mind, do you, Holly?'

'Have I a choice? What don't you want me to see? Her

screaming obscenities when Blun puts her over his knee again for a spanking?'

'Exactly what I mean,' I retorted. It wasn't what I meant; I just felt strongly that Mopsa might drop a heavy weight on her head or lunge at her with a knife – anything sudden, unexpected, illogical. 'Look, she knows you and Blundell. She hardly knows Anthony. That could be useful. I might be able to palm him off as someone he isn't if driven to it.'

'Mike, I'm sure I can play at being Inspector Wotherspoon of the Yard, or whatever occurs to you,' smiled Anthony.

'I don't know who else is in there,' I said. 'We'll just have to see.'

Holly gave me a serious, open-eyed look.

'I really don't want you out of my sight again,' she said.

'I'm ashamed she got me the first time. It seems so pathetic. All I can say is that I did believe she, or rather Bruno, could do you harm if I didn't cooperate. With Blundell to look after you, I can go ahead with a clear mind. Do you see what I'm driving at?'

'I do. But no Superman stunts. Anthony, you will see that he's sensible?'

'That's what a more intelligent older brother is for,' he grinned.

'See ya in a minute, Mike. Longer than ten an' I'm comin' in after you,' called Blundell, as the taxi backed out into Salmon Lane and parked on the main road.

Anthony and I went through the narrow entry into Garrard Street and came up to the steel door from which Reggie had trundled his drum. It was ajar. We pushed and went in. Here was the familiar workshop. Several fibre-glass sidecar bodies lay on the floor on wooden trestles. Chassis members and spoked wheels were stacked against the walls. In the distance a radio twittered.

'That door leads into the cinema and up to the projection-room,' I whispered.

The radio grew louder and a frosted partition opened. Reggie appeared.

'Thought there was soomone out here,' he said. 'How can I help, gents?' He gave me a familiar nod. 'Hello again. You're the artist chap. She's out, I'm afraid, if you've coom looking for her.'

'Oh,' I said blankly. 'Haven't you seen her today?'

'Ow, yes. Earlier. But I expect she's down at the Dome by now.'

'Dome? What Dome?'

'The Millennium Dome, of course. They'll all be there. I'm not ready to gow yet, but I'll be gowing down later.'

'Reggie,' I said. 'I'm sorry I don't know you by any other name. Have you got a moment or two to talk? This is my brother, by the way.'

With a nod of acknowledgement to Anthony, Reggie ushered us behind the partition into his office. It was the busy, crowded workspace of the one-man business proprietor. Trays of invoices were piled up. Boxes of parts lurked under his desk. We sat on battered chairs. A calendar from The Federation of Sidecar Clubs was over Anthony's shoulder.

'I really do need to get hold of Mopsa urgently, Reggie, 'I said. 'What do you mean about her being at the Dome?'

Reggie gave us a puzzled stare.

'I don't know where to start,' said he. 'You know, I suppose, that I'm involved in the acrylics.'

'Acrylics?'

'For my zone.'

'Zone?'

'The Millennium Dome's got zones. Yow must have seen about them on the telly. The one I'm working for is called "The Way We Live Now", or some such name, and in it they're gowing to bury, like, typical artefacts of British life embedded in acrylic blocks. That's where I coom in. I've been a subcontractor for the acrylic work for the last four weeks. That's how your friend got howld of me in the first place.'

'But how did Mopsa know about you? She's only just come over from the States.' I turned to Anthony. 'She came over when I did – after I did.'

'She was introduced to me by her friend. Oi remember when he brought her owver and told me. I had to make an adjoostment to my original order....'

'Hang on. What friend?'

'Well, Bruno Toidy, of course,' said Reggie.

'Why "of course"?' I asked. 'Who IS this Bruno?'

'His ooncle is Junior Heritage Minister....'

'Oh, Frank Tidy,' interrupted Anthony. 'Yes?'

'And his ooncle is, like, noomber two to Lord Wotsits – the Dome man.'

'Sorry, Reggie. I didn't know Bruno had another name – or, rather, what it was. I don't know him at all. I just got the impression he was a friend of someone I know in the

TV biz.'

'Ow, yes, there is a film side of it all,' said Reggie. 'That's where Mopsa's stuff comes in. There is gowing to be some TV filming of what we're doing at the Dome with the acrylics – for some future documentary, I think.'

'Of course!' I cried, nodding at Anthony. 'Booker wants to get the Dome into his project – the extra episodes. I might have guessed.'

Reggie grinned at us. 'Yow don't seem to know what's gowing on. I thought you were all in it together. I hope I haven't put a foot in it. But it's all been on the telly and everything – all this burying things for later generations to find. I think "*Blue Peter*" is involved.'

'My God! Is that still going?'

'My brother had been out of the country for quite a few years,' explained Anthony, as Reggie was looking at me as if I were Spock beamed from Star Date 8763.

'Look,' said the practical Reggie after a pause, 'I'm joost on moi way to the site now. Have you got a car?' We shook our heads. 'Well, I'll take yow in the van if yow don't moind that. I'm leaving after I've loaded these boxes. I don't know if I can get you in because of terrorism and security, like, boot we can find out if Mopsa's down there.'

'And what's she doing at the site?'

'Apart from giving artistic advice, she's working on a scoolpture to go into the ground. You'll have to speak to Mr Tidy about that. I wouldn't know. I,' said Reggie with a huge wink, 'am what my dad used to call the poor bloody infantry. I make the boxes. I don't say what gows into them.'

'We've got some – er – some associates waiting outside in a taxi,' I said. 'I just need to have a word with them to let them know where we're going. We'll be ready to leave when you are.'

Outside, in Garrard Street, Anthony grabbed my elbow.

He had an amusing mixture of determination and anxiety on his face.

'What do you want to do? Do you want us to go on to the Dome without Holly and Blundell?'

I thought quickly.

'Well, look, I'm definitely going to the Dome. I wasn't keen on getting involved, but now, once again, this damned Booker, whose bloody salary I'm partly paying, remember, seems to be at the centre of things. I want to find out what they're all up to. I'm sure Sherbert hasn't the faintest idea. I think perhaps Holly is right about putting a stopper on Mopsa running amok. She's an American citizen and I'd like to know how much immunity she has. The police'll never do more than caution her on the evidence we've got. But I do need to find out how to get rid of her, somehow. The Home Office would have the answers, surely?''

'Ah. And so you want me to talk to Jamie?'

'Well, he is your tame MP, isn't he? He's had enough meals at Glenturret in the past, hasn't he?'

A shadow of distress flitted over Anthony's face. He fumbled in his pocket for his packet of untipped cigarettes, pulled one out, shoved it between his lips and lit up. The mention of Glenturret had brought him back to his mysterious problems. I felt awful. In the quick rush of events in my own life, I had paid so little attention so far to his story and had still not got to the bottom of what his and Peter's troubles were.

'Jamie does sod all to help us when we really need him,' muttered Anthony. 'But I can ask him. He's in London treading water until the opening of Parliament. I suppose he might know something.'

'And I don't want Holly to get involved again. Could you look after her?'

'I'll try.'

Anthony and I went back to the taxi where we found Blundell in conversation with the driver about London and Holly's little face peeking out from a side-window with anxious shadows on it. The meter had advanced further. My brother's eyes dwelt on it with horror and fascination.

'I've met up with a man who has been working with Mopsa,' I said. 'She's not here, but he's going to take me to the building where she has gone. I'll see you later at Glebe Place.' I reached out to take Holly's hand as it lay in the open car window, but I don't think I actually did so. There was an immediate cacophony from within the taxi.

'Mike! You are *not* going near her again!'

'Hey, you nutty dude!'

'If you're going, I'm coming too!'

'I jes' gotta see that bimbo again….'

'Mike, *please!*'

'…..Man, she owes me!'

'Hang on!' I hooted. 'I'm going with a respectable Brummie plastics manufacturer in his van to a huge, busy construction site. I am now forewarned about Mopsa's little games…..'

'But, Mike….!'

'Hey, Mike, man! See sense!'

'Where's the danger?'

But Blundell had grabbed at the door of the taxi and heaved himself out. Relieved of his thirty stones it bounced back up, as if suddenly freed of gravity.

'Bullshit! Bull and shit, man. You need me. You can't go alone and you are just not, repeat no way and not, leaving me out. Shoot, these doors sure are small.'

I wished I could have been alone with Holly. I took her dear little face in my hands. I felt an overwhelming tenderness and love. Ignoring my brother, Blundell and Gawping Gilbert, our interested taxi driver, I tilted up her face and kissed her soft mouth. Out of focus, her eyes melted into seriousness. I took in every line of her cheeks, the ardent richness of her blood, infusing a gentle tan with life. I felt such sadness about the livid scars along the jaw.

And it has remained my image of Holly until this day, for I never saw her again.

'Please do as I wish, just for now,' I whispered.

I was partly amazed, mainly so relieved, when she gave one nod.

'Anthony, keep her with you until we meet up in Chelsea. In fact, why not take her with you to the Commons to meet Jamie? Here, take this for the fare.'

Clutching the £200 I had given him, he pressed Holly's arm. The taxi ground off, leaving me with Blundell.

As we came back into the cul-de-sac, I said to Reggie,

'This gentleman is coming with us to the Dome instead of my brother. I hope that's all right.'

Reggie gave a quick blink as he took in Blundell's uncommon circumference.

'Joost as yow say,' he replied. 'Give me a hand with this droom, will you?'

Blundell helped him heave a canister onto the van.

'My God, what you got in here, friend?' gasped Blundell, using his huge tummy to help barge the drum into the loading area.

'It's a powder. That's why it's a heavy booger. I've got two types, Acryron embedment acrylic and polymethyl methacrylate powder,' explained Reggie, fixing Blundell with a bright-eyed stare. 'I've also got drums of Lucite cold cast resin; that's a two-part polymer. They've got different properties. Lucite produces a lot less heat during its reaction prowcess than oother types.'

'Ah, hum,' muttered Blundell. He shot a look at me. Reggie assumed, clearly, that we knew under what conditions he used these powders for.

'For making your acrylic boxes?' said I. 'For burying things from now for future generations and all that?'

'That's roight. And they're not really boxes, like. They're solid and the objects yow want to poot in them are embedded. Acrylic's a non-organic polymer and takes thousands of years to break down – so it's joost the ticket. Yow moost have seen the sort of thing.'

He motioned us round to the front of his van. Blundell, grunting, took up most of the three-seat bench provided by Leyland DAF for passengers. I was squeezed between him and Reggie. I hoped the trip would not be a long one.

'Which way?' I asked.

322

'Blackwall Toonel, down to Woolwich Road and then back oop Bugsby's Way to the construction site.'

'This is some sorta millennium celebration building, is it?' asked Blundell.

'It's got to be ready for the New Year,' replied Reggie. 'The Queen and Tony Blair and all will be opening it. I don't know why they're bothering. Seems like a waste of mooney. Yow know what would be better?' He took his attention off the road to fix us with a watery glare. 'I'll tell yow. Bridges. Bridges owver the Thames. Imagine how useful four big new traffic bridges would be between Hammersmith and Waterloo. Londoners would've thanked Tony Blair for generations to coom. That's how I'd have spent the oompteen million it's going to cost – but then I suppose I'm a dull booger.'

We came out of the tunnel and, turning back on ourselves, headed up to the vast, squat, white mushroom. I recall feeling a slight sense of disappointment that, after all the hype, it didn't look higher from the outside. In a long fence of blue railing, at Gate 3A, a man slouched out and stopped the van. Reggie jerked a thumb over his shoulder to the drums of acrylic powder. The laconic man peered at a card Reggie held up, scanned our faces without interest, and nodded us through. I had thought that we might have had trouble, what with terrorism and all that, but then I'd been living so long in paranoid America that I was often being brought up with a shock at the casualness which pervaded such things in the UK. Reggie, however, seemed to feel we had been through a Soviet-style interrogation.

'Sorry about all that,' he said. 'Got to be careful.'

Once inside it, I was absolutely unprepared for the strange immensity of the Dome. Having only seen pics on TV, I had imagined it to be a glorified circus tent, all flapping and flimsy. The vast legs dwarfed the heavy machinery around them and the works seemed to stretch forever into an ocean of red concrete, cables, scaffolding and big trucks. As I've said before, about Blundell's temple, it was "like a Popeye tent".

'Gee-HO-sephat!' whooped Blundell. 'I'll say that's something else! I'm glad I came on this leetle passear.'

There was room for Reggie's van to tool round to a segment opposite the famous "human body", which lay in the ochreous leprosy of its tiled coverings like a titanic Cyclops, with head split open, caught in the act of expiring.

'We're working in the "How We Live Now" zone,' said Reggie. 'I've got my moulds and heaters there and the different mould sizes I'm using. We never know what we're going to have to embed in the resin until we get here. It's brought owver from soom design centre, or what not. A lot of it's a lowd of joonk.'

'Do you make the shafts for it all to go in as well?'

'No, no. They've been dug owt ages ago. But after we'd put a few cubes down we discovered that were all scratched by the concrete. So I line the shafts with MDF to protect everything now, and that means a saw-bed and circular saw and bloody miles of cutting oop to do. The last I heard, we were two moonths behind schedule, but apparently that's bang on time compared with soom of the zones. I can only do one's man's work per day – and Oi've got oother business, as yow know.'

'And where does – does Mopsa fit into all this?' I said. I couldn't see the connection between this celebratory embalming of the Best of British and an obscure nutcase from L A.

'I didn't ask, reely. I think it's all got to do with her pal Bruno Tidy, and he's a friend of that expert who's making the art film, and he's related to soom high-oop and they're both chummy with that fellow Witold, and he's the brother of some famous arty type in the States that Mopsa knows. So,' said Reggie, with the air of one making an original discovery, 'it's always WHO yow know.'

'It's the same back home, I guess,' observed Blundell.

The van stopped a little distance from the entry points.

'Here we are,' grunted Reggie. 'Can you gents help me with the drooms of powder again?'

We rolled the materials out and trundled them over to a three-sided shed. Above us, the canopy soared away between the legs. The circle of supports was huge. The Dome was an immense gravity-defying mushroom-cap covering acres of ground. The legs angled with a frightening thrust. While I was craning my head upwards, following the enormous, elegant, yellow-painted steel, I heard Reggie gasp, 'Soomone's been here!'

I gave my attention to the shed. Blundell and I followed each other inside.

'What do you do in here?' asked Blundell.

'I make the acrylic blocks in moulds. I use glass-sided moulds, held by aluminium cages. The block has to be kept crystal clear, yow see. Liquid acrylic resins can be cast in simple moulds and yow can use UV light to fix the resin and hardener – that's why yow need glass sides. For small things I use methyl methacrylate and it can bubble. But use of heat prevents bubbling during hardening. That's why I've brought two low temp ovens in here. But soomone's used a mould cage. And where's the trolley?'

We gazed vaguely. Not knowing what we were supposed to be looking for, we weren't much help. Reggie poked round the shed. 'The noomber two oven is warm. What the hell has been going on?'

'Has the day's work begun?' I asked.

'Shouldn't have done. I've got a programme to follow. Acrylic work isn't tricky, loike, but yow've got to get the mixture of resin and hardener and heat bang on or yow end oop with crazing or opaqueness or it not setting at all. Soom of the blocks are big and need a long, careful period of curing. No one should be fiddling around with my stoof.' He checked a timer on the side of the oven and shook his head. 'Where's today's delivery? It should be here. I'd better see if it's coom.'

I felt superfluous. Reggie didn't need Blundell or me. Obviously something had gone wrong, but I had no idea what. An unseen person had begun work which Reggie regarded as reserved for himself. He was clearly extremely put out. Blundell and I exchanged glances. He jerked a podgy thumb towards the van. We slipped back behind it.

'I reckon this is nothing' to do with us,' he muttered. 'There's nothin' we can do to help this little guy. We should look for our lady friend. That's what we came for.'

There was a sudden yelp from Reggie.

We hastened back and found him cutting tape from stout

boxes with a Stanley knife. He pulled the lid off the biggest of the packing-cases.

'Booger me!' he said. 'Look.'

We peered over his shoulder. Wrapped in bubble-film was a teapot. Next to it was a cafetiere and an egg-timer. Beneath them could be discerned other domestic items.

'You building a kitchen?' asked Blundell.

'Looks loike it, doosn't it?' Reggie grinned ruefully. 'This is the stoof we're supposed to be encapsulating into blocks today. Typical items of late twentieth-century everyday life, yow might say, and it hasn't been unpacked. Whoever had the oven on wasn't at this job. And yet,' went on Reggie, pointing out a small carton which was lying empty on its side, 'this has been taken out.'

'What is it?' I asked.

'A toaster. I would use the bigger mould for that.'

We gazed at the empty box. *"Dualit Four Slot Toaster"* was inscribed on it.

'A bit of British breakfast, eh?'

'Suppose so,' said Reggie. 'I joost have Shreddies.'

'So what's happened here, then?' enquired Blundell.

'Looks like soomone has embedded the toaster in a mould. God knows why they couldn't wait 'til I got here. It's my job.' Reggie spoke resentfully; he hated seeing his equipment used without permission.

'You had better check whether it has been buried where it was supposed to be,' I said, 'or whether someone has just made it and walked off with it.'

'Not very likely. It takes some time to set – although it's possible if they got on to it early. Let's gow and look. Each block fits a shaft, there's twelve blocks to a shaft and twelve shafts. We use suction pads to lower the blocks, then the shaft is sealed and no one sees any of it again until World War Three or the next millennium.'

'A modern Avebury,' I said.

'Coom again?'

'Like Stonehenge,' I tried again, pointing at the disturbing and huge circle of angled legs.

'Joost as yow say.'

We set off for the other side of the zone. 'Hang on,' Reggie said. 'I'll joost get the suction cup in case we need it. Yow can't get the blocks oop without it. I'll meet yow owver there.'

And so it was that Reggie was not with us when Blundell grabbed my arm and yelped,

'What's THAT, Mike?'

'What? Where?'

'Over there! Look! At the base of that leg! On the ground by that hole! Oh, Jesus! What IS it?'

Blundell began a lumbering run towards the base of the gigantic support. Sharper of eye than I was, he had spotted something lying near the mouth of a shaft at the edge of the zone. For the first time I saw in the shadow of the zone's outer wall my old acquaintance: the motorbike and sidecar platform. Either Witold or Mopsa, or both, were here.

As soon as my eye had found what Blundell had seen, I came to a halt. I jerked my head back sharply as I focused.

It was a body. Blundell's wobbling shape, running ahead of me, kept eclipsing the exact spot at which I was trying to look. In spite of this I did think there was something very odd about this body. For a moment I was sure it was Mopsa's, but no – it was taller.

No, it wasn't. It was THINNER – longer – and its HEAD was so big!

Blundell bobbed in front of me. He was crying, 'JEEsus! JEEsus!' over and over again.

He halted over the corpse – the half-corpse.

I dreaded seeing round his untidy circumference.

Then I saw.

My throat constricted. I thought, with a distant surprise, that I ought to be doing what Blundell was doing. He had dropped to his knees and was retching. The sunlight caught a running spindle of spit and gleamed him to earth for a second, like Gulliver caught in tiny ropes.

I had been on the left-hand side of the body. Now I moved round and it reminded me of one of those sectioned engines I used to like in the Science Museum – where you see all the working parts inside. And what a square head!

The half-torso and leg lay, carefully arranged. The naked flesh, pale and hairy, was indecently exposed to the daylight. The cutting had been astonishingly precise – from the frilled windpipe all the way down, the blade had been kept steady. At the groin the cutting had stopped – the left leg was whole. Of the right-hand side of the corpse there was no sign. A drying pool of glutinous arterial blood fanned in a delta from the bruised frills of the severed neck tubes. On this small delta, pressed to the neck bone and collapsed windpipe, was a shiny new toaster. The effect was that of a reposing, newly-caught hammer-head shark.

Blundell knelt up, his face green.

'Urrrgh!' he gurgled, wiping bile with his sleeve. 'Sorry, Mike. It puts me back in mind of Vietnam. I guess I've seen Cong beheadings in my time.' He straightened up, taking my hand. I heaved and he resumed the perpendicular. 'Shit, it looks like some sorta robot alien. That's what did it, Mike….'

With shaking finger he pointed to a machine saw-bench. This piece of equipment was what, I supposed, Reggie used to cut MDF sheets to clothe the shaft sides. I forced my gaze away from the body and went over to the bright saw. The blade had tendons of flesh between its teeth. There was a long smear of liquid along the metal bench, but no sign of the quarts of blood, nor of the missing half.

'Blundell, come and look,' I said.

'Why is there no blood?' he whispered.

'The corpse has been bled, like in an abattoir.'

'But why?'

'Sssh!' I felt my back prickle and my eyes start. I had heard a scrabble behind the zone wall.

Blundell cocked his ears under his long hair. I motioned him to go one way round the wall while I went round the other. There was a rattle of link fencing. We dashed behind the walling (it was only made of fibre-board on battens, like a stage set) and came face to face with Mopsa.

'You! What have you been *doing*, you mad cow?'

She pressed herself against the wall, her fingers clawing at the battening.

'Did you do that?' I asked her, jerking my head over the wall towards the corpse.

She nodded twice very rapidly, her tongue darting across

her lips.

But I knew my Mopsa – something about her expression made me sure she was lying.

'No, you didn't, you liar,' I sneered. 'You couldn't do that by yourself.'

'Yes, I did.'

'What did you do with all that blood?'

'We – that is, I – put it down one of those shafts.'

'How did you do that then?'

'The body was held upside down before it was sliced in half, so the blood could run out of its throat, like....'

'....like a pig.'

'Yes.'

Blundell drew closer to her, his chest heaving. I also got closer. I could see the flutter of her rib-cage.

'How did you hold the body upside down?'

'I – I – I ....'

'All right. You won't tell us who this "we" is. Whose is the body?'

Silence.

'Who helped you? It was Witold, I suppose. He looks mad enough. But what does he get to gain?'

'Uh, he – he gets to keep organs.....'

'What!'

'He sells human organs, you bullying shitbag. It's like a sorta spin-off of his art....You know what I mean....'

I stared at Mopsa, aware that my eyes were fixed on her slack, silly face.

'Okay, okay. But why in GOD'S name did YOU get involved, you murderous slut?'

This was a question Mopsa seemed able to answer; the words poured out of her in a tirade.

'You ask WHY? Why?' she screamed. 'You can stand there an' ask WHY? I'll tell you why! It's because I can't have YOU, can I? Oh, God, I'd got it all set up – yup, aaaawl set up so you get altered in the mummy, then you die an' then we – I – cut your body in half, an' I cut mine in half an' they are put together, by Witold, in an acrylic block. Even *you* must've heard of Gunther von Hagens.' (I hadn't.) 'He's developed plastinization, Mike, an' he takes the water an' lipids out of the body with vacuum an' then replaces them with epoxy resin an' silicone. He can move his dead bodies into poses. Jeez!' she shrieked, 'You've gotta have heard of *"Body Worlds"*. He was in the US before you left. But I'm going beyond that, Mike. It's you and me fused, embalmed in solid resin. See?' She gaped at me. I did see. 'I was gonna have it called *"Together Forever"*. Mike, it would have been the greatest art work of this century – or the next. You an' me together in acrylic – buried in the HEART of London, an' no one knowing about it for maybe hundreds of years!'

Suddenly she flopped awkwardly down onto her knees as if someone had filleted the bones of her legs.

'Oh get up, you silly little bitch!'

'Ooooooooaaaaaaauuuuuuurgh!' came a long shuddering howl – half gurgle, half cry.

I felt a wave of pity – almost of tenderness – for the hopeless, deluded freak. Just then, with dried blood on her clothes, a sectioned corpse a few yards away and a plan of monstrous insanity foiled purely by good luck, I felt nothing but a desire to protect her and get her out of this snare. What she had said reminded me that she and I had once thought we loved each other. I recognised that she was still raw with her loss of me.

I took her thin frame in my arms.

'Uuuuuh, uuuugh, aaaauuuurgh,' she sobbed.

'You and me together forever, eh?' I said gently. She nodded – again with that swift, mad jerkiness I had noticed a few moments earlier – and articulated, in a voice lowered and changed from her penetrating shriek,

'My mummy was the *womb*, Mike. After you had died in my black womb, you would have been reborn in the clear, pure acrylic. You died in ignorance and treachery; you would be reborn, Mike, naked and pure and ONE with me. We would have been together and the FUTURE would have known it.'

I looked into her mad eyes.

I admit I saw her vision in that instant. Like her black mummy, sinister and brooding, her great plan *was* a work of art. Known about now, or in the future, her block of acrylic with a welded half-man, half-woman embedded forever inside it – incorruptible and unashamed in nakedness – would have caused the stir of the age. I shook my head slowly, partly in admiration of the boldness of the conception, partly at the understanding of the fierceness of her obsessive love.

Then came a shout.

'Bull S-H-I-T!'

Blundell had spoken. Blundell was unmoved by admiration or tenderness. His roar snapped the spell.

Mopsa tried to wriggle quickly between us.

'Get a hold of her, Mike! Reggie'll have to call the cops.'

Mopsa tore at us wildly, but Blundell's squidgy embrace seemed to enfold her from sight, like a duvet thrown over a wriggling cat.

'Okay,' I snapped, gripping the only part of her I could see. 'You couldn't have me, so why did you kill someone else? A bit extreme even for Witold to get a few bits and pieces to sell.'

'Uh, groooch! I wasn't gonna waste the BEST idea for a sculpture since the beginning of time.'

'WHOSE body is it?' I snarled, shaking her.

'Uuurgh, it's – it's Bruno's. Shit, why shouldn't I tell you? It's Bruno's.'

'Where's the rest of it? Where's a mould big enough to take a whole body?'

'I – we – brought the mould over from Reggie's. On the motorcycle outfit. It's the one Reggie uses for his Mosquito sidecar. We saw it was long enough. We brought the casing over. It's in two halves. We left behind the former that goes inside because we don' – didn't - want it hollow.'

'Does Reggie know?'

'Let me go!'

Blundell twisted her arm. She shrieked wildly.

'Does he know?' I repeated.

'No, no. he doesn't! Shit! He doesn't!'

Blundell lowered her arm again.

'All right,' I continued. 'How were you going to get the block down one of the shafts?'

'Witold's digging a new one, but not down, just along, a few feet deep, like a grave; it's over by the bike.'

Blundell straightened up, holding the wriggling Mopsa.

'Do you know this Witold guy, Mike?' he asked.

'I think I do. He's a tough looking biscuit with a lot of dark stubble.'

I suddenly became aware of a gleam flaming in Mopsa's eyes. I began to turn, my grip on her arm tightening. A quiet, deep voice spoke behind us.

'I helped her, yes.'

Blundell also turned to face the calm features of the man I had called Blue-jaw: Georgie's brother.

'You helped her to murder this Bruno guy?' gulped Blundell. 'Are you mad?'

'Don't be …. impertinent, fat man,' said Witold. 'And as for you,' and he jabbed a finger at me, 'you should be dead. It was you we wanted.'

I heard another gurgle from Blundell and caught sight of the meat cleaver in the same instant. Witold had been holding it behind his back in his left hand; now he swung it to his right fist, jerked it up and aimed at my neck.

I winced away towards the ground and the heavy cleaver, missing me, slashed poor Blundell on the shoulder. With a screech he fell to his plump knees. I saw that his coat was sliced open. His eyes popped. I broke away from Mopsa and ran round the wall back towards the saw-bench and the shafts. Blue-jaw, smiling grimly, pursued me, Mopsa gibbering in the rear.

'Do it! Do it!' she kept crying.

'You presumably have guessed my motives,' hissed

Witold, heaving the meat-axe from one hand to the other.

'What? That nonsense about my raping your sister? How can you believe such crap. Mopsa made it up. Have you any idea how manipulative she is, you stupid man?'

'I have – and I didn't believe her.'

'Then why are you doing this?'

'Do you know what my – my trade is?'

I had backed as far as I could up against the shed wall.

'Trade? Selling organs on the black market?

'No. I didn't mean that.'

'What did you mean then?'

'I am an ARTIST. It is a *wonderful* concept.'

I caught my foot in one of the cables which snaked away from Reggie's ovens and power-tools and stumbled heavily, my back to the saw-bench. My hand fumbled at the edge of the bench as I struggled to stay upright. It met resistance from a round knob which, as I pushed onto it, clonked into its casing. There was an immediate squeal of electric motors and a rushing sound. Witold quickly came up to me. I could see he was selecting the spot where the meat cleaver would fall. I thought I saw a shape behind him. Blundell, his hand pressed to his ripped jacket, came barging on. Mopsa tried to stop him, but he punched her in the face, dropping her to the concrete. As Witold was aiming, Blundell toppled into him, knocking him onto the humming saw-bench. Witold shot past me as his feet were enwrapped, as mine had been, in cables. There was a shriek from the motors. The shiny, round blade, which I realised I had started into motion, was throwing dried flesh from its spurs. Witold, on his back, wriggled hopelessly. Blundell, his eyes shut, shoved hard and Witold disappeared from my sight, cut in two.

The great blade had only momentarily slackened as it severed his spine. The bench had its feed rollers working; probably Witold himself had needed them to assist in the passing of Bruno longitudinally through the same blade. It has been the most terrible thing I have ever witnessed, but part of me was irresistibly reminded of a Tom and Jerry cartoon, and I don't think I felt more than a pang of horrified wonder at the time.

So, due to no intentional deed of mine or Blundell's, Blue-jaw left this life. His top half dropped onto a pile of neatly-stacked MDF and his legs, still thrashing, though separated from his torso by the width of the bench, clattered down onto Reggie's tools.

Blundell opened his eyes, his face sheet-white. Mopsa bent to take the cleaver from Witold's dead grip. In a second she was whirling it round her head. I looked down for an instant because I had the sensation of standing in liquid mud: a certain instability under my footsoles. Witold's torso, the offal inside him bulging in gleaming whirls from its sacs, was pouring blood onto the concrete floor. In that moment of inattention, Mopsa leapt at me. Blundell gave a croak. I backed behind the bench. The meat cleaver whistled in the air. Mopsa crept towards me, her teeth bared. I backed further, reaching the warmed oven. A strong smell of resins and fixative came up from a sluggish square of clear liquid in a mould. Looking round quickly, I divined that it was acrylic gently warming. There were two lights on a panel, one winking.

'Mopsa, give me that meat-axe,' I said.

'Ah. Ah. Aaaah!'

Mopsa waved it vaguely and slashingly.

'Enough harm's been done. GIVE IT TO ME!'

'Mike! Watch it!' came a cry from Blundell.

Mopsa had thrown the meat-axe. Reggie had handed each of us a protective yellow hat when we had arrived. Thank God for mine. The cleaver crashed dizzyingly onto my skull and fell by my feet. I was about to grab at it, but Blundell ran forward and seized it. He thrust it into my hand. He had seen, while I was fighting for consciousness, that Mopsa, robbed of her weapon, had snatched a big plastics trimming knife from the work surface. She dashed at me, jabbing the knife with strangely elegant gestures, like a fencer stylishly parrying and thrusting. The pointed blade stuck into my stomach. The pain, which belonged to someone else who was telling me about it, had no reality. I found that I couldn't move my legs. I stood, statue-like, puzzling out this distant pain and Mopsa thrust again. I warded off the knife with my right hand – the hand gripping the meat-cleaver – and, unable to gauge how much force I had put into this sudden movement, was rewarded by seeing the trimming knife clatter away out of her reach. I recall that I had the sensation of a stop or impediment to the swing of my arm. Oddly, I couldn't bring it back to my side again. This was because I had imbedded the meat-axe in Mopsa's neck and the blade wouldn't come out.

She looked surprised and was making crab-like clawing gestures, vaguely near the axe's direction, but failing to get a hold on the handle. Some vital nerves had been severed.

All this was so swift that I hadn't time to react sensibly. In less than a minute I had – unwittingly – helped to kill Witold and had butchered Mopsa's neck. I think a realisation of the awful agony of that blow flooded my brain. The blade was bedded in, but a torrent of blood was spewing around the wound.

'Oh, oh, oh,' I kept gasping.

She turned on me a look which later I understood. Agony and frustration were there, but pre-eminent was a flash of triumph. She turned – amazingly keeping upright – towards the gently swimming, slowly setting, warm acrylic. She fell to her knees, then – in a graceful, prayerful movement – plunged her head into the liquid.

Blundell had his hands clasped, echoing the prayer of her immolation. Round, hunkered down on podgy knees, he looked like Winnie-the-Pooh in church.

The muscles of Mopsa's back writhed. Sluggish waves of setting resin flowed out of the mound, displaced by her head. Her will-power kept her there, I believe, drowning in warm acrylic. Those muscles were still twitching and her feet still tapping when I bent over, squinting, and dragged out the cleaver. It had gone a long way in between two vertebrae. It wasn't such a great effort to bring it back down again: its weight did the job for me. The tendons parted and at once her body slumped to the ground. Her head sank to the bottom of the acrylic block, attached to her body only by a long skein of stubborn skin. This snapped and the resinous surf closed over the raw neck stump. I could see that, as the compound cooled, the hardener was having its effect and the block was solidifying fully.

In the distance – surreal touch – men moved unconcerned about their work on the other zones. We were as alone as if in space: Blundell and I, with our three dismembered corpses to explain.

There was a long silence.

'What are we going to do?' I asked, in a whisper.

An aircraft passed overhead.

Under its sound I thought I heard the cachinnation of an alarm clock going off.

It was Blundell giggling.

'He, he, he, he, he, he, he, he, he, he,' went he, rocking on his knees.

I saw he was not going to be much help for a while. He was certainly in the grip of Number Eight. Poor Blundell – not what he had expected from his trip with me to the Dome.

Chapter 18: **A Secret from the last Century.**

'Where is Bruno's head?'

That was the question I heard myself asking.

'Where CAN the head be?' I said again.

I glanced across the red desert of concrete towards the van. With a start I recognised Reggie making his way back to us; so much seemed to have happened recently, that I had forgotten all about him, although he had been out of my sight for less than five minutes. He was only a few yards away, carrying a length of chain with weighted suction caps on the end of it. I ran over to him.

'Have you got your mobile?' I asked.

He raised his eyebrows in surprise and his gaze travelled over my clothes. They were splashed with blood, although I didn't know it, especially where the knife wound in my stomach was weeping.

'Er...what? The phone? It's in the van, but.....'

'Go back and call the police,' I said. 'Please.'

'But what the foock....?'

'There's no time to lose. People are dead here. There's been......been an accident.'

'Accident?'

'Yes, yes, yes. Look, give me the suction cups.'

'Dead? Why, how....?'

Reggie's jaw hung open. He had gone ashen. I saw that he was not as young a man as I had taken him for. His hair was dyed, I realised. The last of the old craftsmen, and all that. I didn't want him to see Bruno's half-body with its four-slot toaster head by the shaft, nor the two halves of

Witold on each side of his saw-bench, nor Mopsa's headless corpse at his oven.

'*Please*, Reggie. This is an emergency.'

'Roight. Roight. Roightee-oh.' He tottered off, repeating this mantra. I turned my attention to Blundell. The worst of 'Nam, the worst of New York's school corridors had been capped by the bloodbath at the Dome. He was shaky, he giggled. He had difficulty in standing; his rotund bravado had oozed away and even his great belly had shrunk, but he pulled himself together to help me, a virtual stranger.

'Urrgh. Sorry about the hysterics, Mike. Groooch....'

Saliva hung from his mouth. His beard was bloody.

'Are you badly hurt?' I asked, as gently as I knew how.

Loss of blood and shock had robbed him of his rubicund glow, but his gash had stopped bleeding. He carried the lacerated shoulder awkwardly.

'Naw. I guess I'm okay. It's deep, but a clean cut.'

'Look,' I said, 'can you help me find Bruno's missing bits? The police'll be here soon – but I want to clear things up. For Mopsa's sake. See?'

'Sure. But whaddya....? I mean.... I'm looking for this guy's head, right?'

'Yes. I want to figure out how these suction cups work.'

'Mike, I'm sorry, but I guess I don' know what Bruno looks like. I never met him, you know.'

I stared at him. He stared at me.

Then we caught each others' eyes and "*The Way We Live Now*" zone echoed to insensate laughter.

'Ha, ha, ha, ha! Don't know what he – oh, ha, ha, ha, ha!..... What he LOOKS like!' I screamed.

'Oh God, oh, ha, ha, ha, ha, haw, haw! – 'cos I never MET him!' hooted Blundell.

'You'll recognise him! Ha, ha, ha, ha, ha! He's – he's the guy without a BODY!'

'Without a…..! Oh, Jeezus, haw, haw, haw – oh! Oooh!'

We rocked to and fro, until our guffaws subsided into sniggers and then silence.

I cast a guilty look away to where a circle of men had been pouring over their designs, but they had moved off. We had a vast area of concrete to ourselves.

'Right,' gasped Blundell, heaving himself up. He waddled off towards Reggie's little shed.

I laid out the suction-cup stuff on the ground by the shaft which Reggie was working on. I peered over the edge. Nothing visible. I found a metal bolt and dropped it. A clunk came up from below. The shaft clearly had a few of its twelve boxes in it, but there was plenty of space left.

With a peculiar inner clarity, my mind, freed by shock from disgust or moral outrage, planned ahead to do the right thing. I was at my closest to an understanding of Conceptual Art. With the artist's freedom from the constraints of conventional parameters of action, I saw how Mopsa's wishes must be protected, her triumph assured. No, it was not just for Mopsa that I began to make plans – it was for ART itself. There is a moment (I could see that then) when only one course of action is correct, given that all other structures are in place. Mopsa was going to have her apotheosis.

Another segment of my brain – the cautious property-dealer's part, no doubt – was thinking about establishing the innocence of M. Greville and B. Capitanchik. Blundell hadn't meant to saw Witold in half. I hadn't really killed Mopsa – not in the truest sense of the term; she was not saveable by the time I had severed her neck-bone. Drowning in acrylic had come before de-capitation. So I laboured to get the suction-cups down the shaft, gobbing on the rubber pads to make them stick. The trick was to drop the wetted metal cups down smartly – their castings were very heavy – and then to tighten the slender wire which ran alongside the big hauling chain. This pulled up the centres of the cups, creating a vacuum, after which the block could be lifted to the surface. This was the theory, but I think the device was primarily for lowering blocks; it took ages to drag the first one into the light because I kept releasing the vacuum by mistake just as the hoist was beginning. I hadn't twigged that the thin wire had to be kept tight all the time. At last a sparkling, clear cube appeared with a BT telephone inside it. The second contained a little *"Roberts"* portable radio set. The third had five *"Caithness"* paperweights arranged in it. It was very beautiful. Then the chain rattled down again and met only MDF lining. The shaft was now empty.

Meanwhile Blundell had found the head.

'Ah! Jeez, Mikey! Mike!' came his shout.

I straightened up and went over to a pile of crates beyond the acrylic moulds. Blundell bent over one of them, greeny-white.

'I feel such a goofball, Mike, but I can't bear to touch the motha….'

'It's there, is it?'

'It's here.'

I peered into the crate. In partial shadow lay Bruno Tidy's severed head. It had an odd coating which had rendered the hair one solid piece, like a Dick Tracey drawing. The jaw and left cheekbone had been smashed by cleaver blows. The windpipe ran out of the frilled neck. One eye was open – with a surprised, outraged stare, the other was lost in a dark puff of bruised, blood-gorged flesh.

'This was a first try,' I heard myself saying. 'Mopsa made a right mess of hacking it off. She was always bad at aiming *and* impatient with it. She must have tried to encapsulate it in resin, got it wrong and withdrawn it. See the hair? That must have been why there was a mould of resin and hardener waiting in the warming oven. She knew it was all ready. I suppose she was about to try embedding Bruno's head again just before we blew in.'

Not sure if I could do it without vomiting, I made the discovery that I was able to lift the head from the crate. It felt heavy, but compact and easy to hold, like a portable TV. I carried it over to the long, thin, sectioned body, kicked the toaster to one side and placed the head where it belonged. Blundell had vanished into Reggie's shed and now came out again on tottery legs. He lay back against some slabs of concrete breathing heavily.

'Do you want the rest?' he wheezed. He, who had strutted conqueror-like around Glebe Place after engineering my freedom from the mummy, now seemed to look, with a pathetic eagerness to please, to me for the lead in everything.

'Why – have you found it?' I cried.

'It's in the corner of the shed,' he gurgled, gesturing.

I nerved myself to explore where the shadows waited, and yes! There it was, laid against the wall, almost like a huge draught excluder: Bruno's other half, bled dry and minus its head. I wasn't sure how to manoeuvre the surprisingly heavy slab of flesh. I knew I would not be able to heave it over my shoulder, so I compromised by pulling it by its ankle. I dragged it beneath Blundell's popping gaze to join its mirror-image. In a moment Bruno looked better. One could see the joins, of course, but the kit was assembled, as it were.

'Urrrgh,' grunted Blundell. 'Poor guy. Mike, just look….. Look at what's missing…..'

'What?' I said. Head, left half, right half: all in place, if a bit disjointed, like the giant millennial model of the human body that postured itself at us from an acre away.

'His pecker,' hissed Blundell.

'What?'

'His dick. It's not there.'

We peered at Bruno's tattered groin.

'I expect the saw ripped it off,' I ventured.

'Oh,' gasped Blundell.

'Now for Mopsa's head,' I went on. 'The plastic should be solid by now. I may need help getting the mould off the acrylic. Do you feel up to it?'

Blundell gave a long, husky-like shudder.

'Brrrrrrrr……I think I see what you're getting at.'

'Do you?' I didn't quite believe that Blundell could have spotted how eager I was a) to give Mopsa her artistic due, b) to rob Booker of a high point in his stupid modern art series and c) to save us both from inculpation.

'Sure, Mike. Let's get it over with.'

Mopsa's corpse lay in an enormous pool of drying arterial blood. No one was going to touch that. It didn't matter any more. But the head.....the head was ART.

I fumbled at the screw connectors on the mould. The aluminium straps parted and the hard, rubbery side plates and lubed sealed glass fell away. In a clear cube, Mopsa's head was revealed upside down.

'Mike, I'll be honest with you, man. I don't know that I can examine this so calmly. For Chrissake, Mike, a woman we know has just died.....and how she died was so – so horrible that I guess – I mean....' Poor Blundell tailed off, his gooseberry eyes bulging at the block of clear resin. I tapped the block. It was still warmish and, I realised, needed longer to harden fully, but, using a piece of sheeted material to hand, I lifted it out to get it the right way up. It was remarkably heavy. I had already had a chance to compare severed head weights that day; clearly the acrylic made a big difference.

How Mopsa would have appreciated that moment! How eagerly she and Georgie would have discussed this if one of the EK apostles had managed such a feat in some fringe West Coast gallery! What a shame that her audience was only two middle-aged men, one so forcibly reminded of atrocities seen in the theatre of real war that he could barely keep from fainting.

'I was only going to say, Blundell, if it helps, that she did it voluntarily. Her head was in the resin for at least half a minute before I acted. Look how far it sank down – and see this long piece of skin, like a worm? When her head was severed the block was already setting.'

'Oh heck, Mike! This gets worse an' worse. You're saying that you didn't kill her when you got her head off?'

'Of *course* I didn't kill her, Blundell. She had already committed suicide.' I turned the block the right way up. 'Look! There's a bubble pushing her lips open. I bet she found it warmer than she thought when she dived in.'

Blundell forced his gaze back to the work of art. The head seemed to be shouting rudely at him – as Mopsa would have done in life – and the eyes had just that look of vague malice which Mopsa had always worn, and also that strong air of triumph, of resolution with which, I am sure, she had plunged her face into the squirming surface of the pool of acrylic. Her hair lay flat to her scalp, making her head totemic, elemental and ancient.

'Ugh. Her eyes are like glazed. Is that the warmth of the plastic, do you think?' murmured Blundell, venturing to peer more closely into the block.

'Mm. And her skin seems a little puckered, almost cooked, doesn't it? There's no air in there to redden it like a scald, but it has a tanned, loin of pork sort of colour.'

'An' there's no blood round her face.'

'Quite. That's because her neck was severed AFTER most of her head went in; otherwise there would be wisps of gravy captured as they were swirling about.'

'So, you *do* say you didn't kill her? Not that I'd blame you, but....' Blundell seemed almost feverishly anxious to establish this point.

'I've TOLD you, Blundell. Besides you SAW what

happened.'

'No, I didn't. That's just it. I couldn't bear to look. So you are saying you *definitely* didn't kill her?'

'Did you kill Witold?'

'Hell, no. That was a terrible accident, man. It was an accident. You saw….'

'I couldn't *bear* to look.'

'Oh.'

'So, just to get it right, I didn't kill Mopsa, and you didn't kill Witold.'

Blundell wiped the back of his hand across his mouth.

'Jeez, you're a real hard guy, Mike. All that jokey-pokey stuff…but underneath…'

'They wanted this – or something like this – to happen.'

'It doesn't bear thinking of. Christ, what are we gonna tell that little guy?'

As those words popped out, I thought: God, Reggie will have called the police! They'll be on their way.

With a strange clarity I pulled Blundell towards me. I absolutely knew that Mopsa's head would not be found if it were buried in the shaft beneath the items that Reggie had already put down there before we lifted them out. I don't know how I knew it – but time has proved me right.

'Hurry up! Hurry!' I gasped, grasping the weighty block to my chest. I stumbled back to the shaft, round which the radio, the telephone and the paperweights in their glossy squares waited stolidly. 'Spit on those cups!' I cried, shoving the lowering tackle under Blundell's nose. While he gobbed, I heaved Mopsa's baked head on to the lip of the shaft. "Thank you, Mike", the puckered lips in their clear prison seemed to be saying. 'Pass them to me!' I rapped over my shoulder. Blundell fumbled them at me and I stuck the wet rubber cups on to the top of the block. I held the block over the hole and Blundell stood over me, taking the pull on the chain. 'Okay! Lower away!' Mopsa's exclamatory mouth and triumphant glazed eyes sank silently out of sight. Something in me muttered: "Goodbye". I jerked the freeing wire a little too early, the suction was released, far below came a brief heavy slam, and the chain rattled up empty. 'Now for the others!' We repeated the operation three more times. Telephone, radio and the paper- weights disappeared on top of Mopsa in the same order that Reggie had sent them down the previous day. With a final jerk, I snatched the chains up and threw the whole apparatus into the back of the shed.

I looked at Blundell's face and found understanding in his expression as his shaggy head turned from the mouth of the shaft to the far-off exit area. Four policemen were coming quickly over the snaking cables. In the distance, outside the Dome, blue lights on a car were flashing.

I suddenly saw myself trying to explain everything in a neo-Gothic magistrate's court in East London. The magistrate was puckering his lips in distaste. "Art? What do you mean by Art?" he was saying......

Then, all of a sudden, overlapping my imagined picture of the courtroom, was the banging home of a great layer of happiness, like carpet laid on knotted, tortured planking.

SHE was dead!

It was terrible to roll in delight, as on a thickly planted lawn, away from the cave in which my soul had shrivelled, stretching now and grasping at the sunshine of her obliteration. And the neo-gothic courtroom and the fresh green lawn, with its tiny perfect flowers, one of which was Holly, came together and I began screaming with laughter. I howled and howled.

'Mike! Oh God, Mike!' shouted Blundell in alarm.

I shrieked – peal after peal and bellow upon bellow clanging up in sedate London air between the Dome's mighty legs – and Reggie stood behind the four police officers: a ring of puzzled men with distaste on their faces, mirroring the larger ring of steel around them, looking down at the ragged, spurting neck of one body, the four-slot toaster near three sections of another, the separated legs and torso of a third and the screeching hysteric who felt he had come home at last.

I am at the end now.

Only a few more things are left to say.

The police would have to cope with the three bits of Bruno, the two bits of Witold and the one bit of Mopsa – and I suppose they did. I could have done no more. Two of them, stepping stolidly through the wonky wonderland of the Dome, took Blundell and me off for questioning. Blundell was released by evening and Anthony collected him from Mile End police station. I remained held in custody for further questioning.

At the inquest, which took place long after Holly had left for the USA, I said nothing about Mopsa's head. Bruno's blood was on my clothing, my finger-prints all over the half of his corpse I had dragged out. Poor Reggie was questioned for a long time about the few days leading up to the deaths, but all he could tell them was that Bruno, Witold and Mopsa had been involved with me in a successful art exhibition at the Serpentine Gallery, were planning to appear in a future documentary series on TV and had no obvious enemies. I don't think I explained very well that Mopsa died voluntarily after assisting in cutting up one of her confederates. The coroner seemed not to have understood me when I stood there and told him that I knew she had done it all for Art. My hysterics, which marred my testimony, went on until the time of my first sedation.

I am no murderer (although, as I have written once before, in a sense I am); and English law knew it too. Blundell, Reggie and I discovered the atrocities – and I was ill-informed and thoughtless enough to have moved one of the bodies, for obscure reasons. We could not be held long – keen though the police were to find a culprit – and I was able to afford the best of legal representation.

As for Blundell, Anthony told me that he had not stopped crying before he was put on the plane. He seemed, Anthony informed me, to be weeping for Mopsa; somehow – what with the spanking and the chase on the Hog – an odd bond had formed. Her villainy, like that of the 'Cong, was not really her fault – just a difference in point of view.

London's Millennium Dome was opened on time by the Queen. It wasn't very successful or much praised. The popular New Labour government had inherited the idea from the previous Tory administration. By mid-'99, following the resignation of its first artistic director, and in spite of the energetic support of his successor, it became clear that the public didn't admire it. Almost every day the newspapers featured reports about its spiralling costs and tacky, unimaginative displays.

What no one will have read is that when three corpses (two male, one female) were found inside the building in the autumn of '99, the government took the decision to keep details of the police enquiry out of the news – even though one of the bodies was that of the nephew of Frank Tidy, then a Labour junior minister. It was with the greatest difficulty that the Home Secretary was persuaded that a disclosure of full details would not be in anyone's interest on the eve of 2000, given the Dome's pivotal role. Anthony learned from his tame SNP MP Jamie Flynn that those closest to the PM were adamant that further sensational bad news about the Dome was deemed totally unacceptable.

Anthony also heard that the police originally believed the dismembering to have been the work of suicidal Millennial freaks in a death pact. Class War had been mentioned. So too had Fetishism from extreme American-inspired New Art devotees. One inspector credited the disappearance of the female's head to practitioners of witchcraft. All that ever appeared in print or on the news – well into the new century – was a reference to three corpses found in "London's East End". Inexpert handling of heavy machinery used for an art project was to blame.

All the time I hug to myself the secret that will not be known until after all of us are dead. What a vindication for Mopsa and extreme *schlock* sculpture when some curious myrmidon of government – a 3000AD Millennial committee man, perhaps – brings that puzzling block of acrylic back into the light, sits it among its toasters and radio sets and ponders on the inscrutable motives of the English peoples at the end of the twentieth century!

One other nagging little detail was cleared up for me at the time of my own breakdown. I had never found out where Mopsa had been living during her time in London. But when Sherbert was clearing out Booker's apartment, he saw Mopsa's things, as she had left them. Among the papers were photographs, designs and drawings for the end of Booker's TV series on Art: the mummy, the acrylic blocks, the conjoined bodies were all there. I took them as proof that she and Booker had worked on ideas together.

Sherbert was most put out that the TV series came to nothing. He visits periodically, and we don't talk about it. I'm very glad that so little of my own money had been squandered; I'm going to need it as I get older. I'm also glad that Booker too is, at last, dead. He got a mention on Channel 4 news in the UK and a bit in "*The Times*".

I spent a long time in a rehab clinic in Forest Row, Sussex – a victim of post-traumatic stress syndrome, so I was told. After chronic fatigue and such long, deep dreams of exhaustion and loss everything has now fallen into place. The past is where it belongs: in the last century.

My brother and I now share an apartment in London. I have learnt that Holly lives with her parents in Ventura, looking after her Dad and working in a local publishing house. Sometimes, I toy with the idea of contacting her, but it has been so long.....

Anthony said I would eventually come to realise, as he

has done, that most of our lives are lived in the following absurd delusions: that suffering can be avoided, that happiness is a right, that property is desirable, that the past cannot reach out into the future, and that the unexpected happens to others. I have also learned that an untried person is a weak person, just as is un-tempered steel. Living, Anthony and I agree, strengthens us and breaks down only our dreams.

THE END

(Anthony's story of his obsessive fascination for Glenturret, his and Mike's grandfather's magnificent haunted Scottish house, their boyhood there and its later history, are told in the comic novel **"Losing it All"**, *available from Witley Press Bookshop and from Amazon as an illustrated paperback £4.99 and Kindle ebook £2.99*   ISBN: 978-1-9164295-2-9*

About the Author

Simon Potter's published work includes fiction, non-fiction, literary criticism, history, poetry and articles for magazines on- and off-line. He has taught English in London, England for over 50 years and has directed, written and adapted plays for young people. He is a member of the Society of Authors and received an MBE in the 2016 Queen's Birthday Honours.

oOo